The Embers of Hope

The Embers of Hope

Sally Laity
&
Dianna Crawford

Tyndale House Publishers, Inc.
Wheaton, Illinois

Library of Congress Cataloging-in-Publication Data

Laity, Sally.
  The embers of hope / Sally Laity and Dianna Crawford.
    p. cm.—(Freedom's holy light ; v. 5)
  ISBN 0-8423-1362-1 (sc : alk. paper)
  1. United States—History—Revolution, 1775-1783—Fiction. I. Crawford,
Dianna, date. II. Title. III. Series: Laity, Sally. Freedom's holy light ; v. 5.
PS3553.R27884E47   1996
813'.54—dc20   96-14241

Printed in the United States of America

02   01   00   99   98   97   96
8   7   6   5   4   3   2   1

August 1776

Summer reigned in proud glory, hot and seemingly endless in the rolling, wooded countryside of New York.

To Prudence Thomas, who had never been more than twenty miles from Boston in all her eighteen years, the foliage of Manhattan Island seemed particularly lush and verdant as she rode her newly purchased Narragansett mare along the post road. She tried her best to focus on the rich green beauty surrounding her . . . anything to keep her mind off the very real possibility that her husband would be furious when she arrived at his encampment. *Please, don't let Morgan be too angry,* she prayed silently. *He knows the patriot cause is as important to me as it is to him.*

It couldn't be much farther. Almost all the traffic she had passed since crossing on the ferry an hour ago had been military. Now, as one more band of Continental soldiers marched toward her, she fought the impulse to check and see that no telltale lock of black hair had escaped her tricorn. Instead, she guided her gentle mount into a bank of moss and ferns along the edge of the roadway to allow the platoon to pass.

Up ahead she could make out a sprinkling of tents and crude wooden shelters, and her heart began to race.

She tried to convince herself that her husband's handsome

face would light up when she rode into his supply camp out of the blue. Surely he would be so overcome with joy it wouldn't matter that she had come with neither his permission nor an escort. After all, there was no longer any reason for her to remain at home, and her brother's clothes had kept her from undue attention during the journey.

Soldiers seemed to be everywhere. The prevailing air of expectancy reminded her of Boston during those months when the patriots laid siege to the Crown forces that occupied the town. Here, royal warships had been anchored in the outer bay for weeks, with more arriving by the day. Thousands of enemy soldiers gathered on Staten Island, poised to attack the port of New York, a few miles away at Manhattan's southern tip.

Nearing the conglomeration of canvas shelters, Prudence could see that it wasn't a supply camp after all. She released a tense breath and pressed onward, careful not to make eye contact with any of the men lounging idly about. How much farther could it be? Morgan had written that he was stationed a mile or so this side of New York. As quartermaster, he would be positioned a sufficient distance from the English ships.

The road before her looked deserted as it curved into the woods. Without passersby to pay her any mind, she mulled over for the hundredth time the speech she had memorized. A convincing argument and very logical, she had no doubt. But when she emerged from the trees and found herself in a large clearing filled with acres of supplies and equipment, her noble sentiments rang hollow. Trying not to pass her own skittishness on to her mare, Prudence reined in near the center cluster of makeshift buildings.

A handful of soldiers were unloading a wagon, and another pair stacked barrels against the side of a wooden shack. Nary a woman was in sight—another gaping hole in her prepared argument. But Prudence could not give in to her cowardice and leave, not after having ridden so far. At the very least she had to see Morgan. It had been so long.

Gathering her courage, she nudged the horse's sides, and the weary animal moved forward.

Just then, a strikingly tall man exited one of the large tents on the far side of the camp. She recognized Morgan's stride immediately, and her heart skipped a beat as she took in the sight of her husband. An immaculate blue and cream uniform molded itself to his strong contours, the shining boots and crisp three-cornered military hat adding to his height. His face, with its compelling planes and angles, was averted from her, the deep-set eyes hidden in the shadow of his tricorn.

To her dismay, Prudence saw her husband move swiftly to a waiting horse and swing into the saddle. He then wheeled around and trotted the chestnut Thoroughbred down the road toward New York.

There was nothing to do but chase after him, regardless of the attention she might attract crossing the compound. Perhaps it was for the best that their reunion would be out of earshot of his men. If he happened to unleash a tirade, no one would know. She urged her tired mare into a gallop.

"Morgan!" she called as she drew near.

He glanced backward, then hauled his mount to a stop. "What on earth are you doing here?"

The instant she drew abreast of him, he reached over and plucked her right off her horse, settling her across his lap.

Prudence felt her body flood with warmth as she leaned into his kiss. Evidently he, too, had longed for her over the past five lonely months.

But all too soon, the kiss came to an abrupt end. Morgan's cobalt eyes darkened to a deep indigo as he searched hers.

"How did you get here?"

"I-I rode my new mare. Isn't she beautiful?"

His even brows met in a stern line. "From where?"

"Why, Boston, of course."

Morgan's gaze raked her from head to toe. "And look at you. Wearing men's clothes again!"

Prudence felt the heat of a flush and promptly forgot every

word of the logical speech she had spent miles and miles perfecting. Only one recourse remained. "I was expecting a far more affectionate greeting," she said in her sweetest tone.

Her words did not distract him. "Please do not tell me you rode all the way from Boston by yourself."

He had always been a little too clever. Still, a wife was not a slave. Prudence mustered what little dignity she could in her present awkward position. "I did. And without the slightest problem. Certainly you must know by now that I'm perfectly capable of taking care of myself."

He shook his head in frustration. "This entire island is on the brink of blowing up in all-out war, and you pick today to come for a little visit. And what did you do with the store? Leave it in the care of your stepmother and all her babies?"

"I did not," she spewed back, highly insulted that he would even think such a thing. "My brothers have returned. I wrote and told you weeks ago."

"It's been more than a month since I've gotten a letter."

"Oh. Well, I can hardly help that," Prudence said, beginning to soften. "Word of the patriot revolt reached all the way to the Indian Ocean, you see. When Nathaniel and Zachary heard about it, they immediately set sail for home. Of course, no more had they arrived, when Nat signed on with a privateer, leaving Zachary to run *my* store. He, in typical highhandedness, expected me to go on home and help Miriam with the little ones."

Prudence thought she detected the beginnings of a smile, but Morgan quickly squelched it.

She reared back. "Oh, you're as bad as every other man. Not one of you will take a woman seriously, no matter how much you promise to do just that."

He tightened his hold and eyed her. "I take very seriously the fact that you placed yourself in jeopardy *again* by spending days on the road all alone."

"Well," she huffed, "as you can see, I'm perfectly fine. Besides, are you the only one allowed to be concerned? We've received nothing but ominous news in Boston, and you're the only husband I've got. And—" Her voice became breathy. "I missed you far more than I ever dreamed possible."

Morgan exhaled and folded her within his arms again, holding her tight.

"Please, let me stay, won't you? I could keep the supply-camp ledgers. I know how you hate dealing with those. Surely General Washington would not object to your having help."

"Washington?" He shoved her to arm's length. "I'm supposed to be at headquarters this very instant. The general himself summoned me." He maneuvered his horse closer to hers and helped her remount.

"Does he request your presence often?" she asked, impressed that the commander in chief of the Continental army would meet with her very own husband personally.

"No, only rarely. It's quite possible the British are about to commence their invasion. I do wish you hadn't chosen this moment to arrive, Prudence. But then, you do have a knack for jumping into the middle of things."

She tossed him a flippant smile. "I thought that's what you loved most about me."

Morgan stared at her for a moment, his gaze smoldering as he reached to cup her cheek. "Trust me, my dear," he returned with a very familiar smile. "That is not what I love most about you. And as you know, I've vowed never to lie again."

In a straightback chair at Washington's headquarters, Morgan clicked open the cover of his pocket watch and grimaced at the lengthy wait. It had been more than two hours. But if the commander had expressly requested to see him, he must have discovered details regarding a British attack and wanted Morgan to organize the disbursement of specific supplies.

Back in his own spying days, Morgan realized with chagrin, he might have uncovered such prime information himself. Now he could only sit and wait . . . and worry about Prudence becoming impatient enough to wander from the room at the coaching inn. The streets of New York were crawling with uncouth soldiers and ne'er-do-wells. One close look at the refreshing beauty of her heart-shaped face and luminous silver eyes, and her ridiculous men's attire would be of little protection.

After all it had taken to win her love, he could not bear the thought of his fetching black-haired bride being in peril. Why could he not convince her that part of the reason for this struggle against British tyranny was to make the colonies a safe haven for his own priceless wife and the wives and children of the other colonists? And why couldn't he make her see that he would be a far better soldier if he had the peace of knowing his loved ones were out of danger?

Yet he couldn't forget how her soft words and comforting hands had eased so many in the aftermath of the Bunker Hill battle. He could still see the grateful eyes of those she had tended, men whose bodies had been ripped open by a musket ball or bayonet. Despite her usefulness, however, Morgan was not willing to have Prudence within a hundred miles of any conflict.

Expelling an impatient breath, Morgan observed the other equally anxious men pacing the anteroom as they waited for an audience with the commander in chief.

"Aye," he heard one of them remarking. "The hills of Staten Island are white from top to bottom with British tents. What are those English blackguards waiting for, more reinforcements?"

"It was bad enough to have General Howe's lobsterbacks breathing down our necks," another said. "Now that his brother, Admiral Lord Howe, sailed his fleet into our backyard with his high-priced mercenaries from Germany, I'd call that a few too many already."

Morgan couldn't resist joining in. "Don't forget General Clinton. He and his force are now out in the outer bay as well."

One of the men guffawed. "That shouldn't scare anyone. The bloke's attempt to take the southern colonies was a miserable failure. He came sailing in here still licking his wounds."

"Aye. With his tail tucked between his legs," snorted another.

"Morgan Thomas," a voice announced from an open doorway.

At last! He unfolded himself from the uncomfortable seat and strode into the large book-lined room where General Washington sat behind a desk. Struck, as always, by the commanding presence of the Continental army's leader, Morgan gave a sharp salute. "Reporting as ordered, sir."

Washington rose and returned the salute, then extended his big hand with a weary smile. "Lieutenant Thomas."

"At your service, sir."

The general nodded. "Have a seat, Lieutenant." Indicating a chair facing the large mahogany desk, he sank back down to his own. "I've a mission, a vital one, I'd like you to handle. I won't order it, but I do hope you'll volunteer. I can't think of anyone as suited for the job."

The last statement particularly piqued Morgan's interest, and he was more than flattered. "Of course you can count on me, sir. I'll do whatever you ask."

"It might be prudent to wait until you've heard me out," Washington said, his gaze unflinching. "Your name was put to me by some of your fellow officers. They report that your spying activities in Philadelphia and Boston remain to this day undetected—that you somehow managed to skirt the blame for all those Tory ships which were diverted to the cause."

"I believe that's true. From what I've been able to discern, no Loyalist other than my father has any knowledge of my subversive work, and he has promised to keep silent."

The general's pox-scarred countenance brightened considerably. He leaned forward, resting his forearms on the open maps spread across the desktop. "It's gratifying to hear that one of the staunchest Tory merchants in all of Philadelphia is wavering in his resolve to support the British. You're quite positive you can trust your father, Lieutenant?"

"Completely. He would not betray his son. As he once put it, 'Political differences come and go, but family is forever.'"

"I only hope that is true, lad," he said, eyeing him steadily, "because I need your services again."

Morgan raised his brows. Being dispatched on a secret mission would solve his problem with Prudence. He would be obliged to send her back to Boston, where she'd be much safer.

"I need someone I can trust in Philadelphia," Washington went on, scarcely stopping for breath. "Someone who'll attend all the parties, the theater, be included in all the gala events and gatherings. The British army has been close-mouthed with the New York Loyalists. My spies have gleaned nothing. Perhaps letters to their Philadelphia friends have been somewhat less discreet. I seriously doubt Crown secrets would be so closely guarded that far from the battlefield."

"Philadelphia," Morgan declared flatly, trying to cover his disappointment. Back to living the useless life of a Tory dandy among his family's friends. He sighed. "I'll do as you wish, sir."

"Splendid, Lieutenant! Splendid." The general rose. "Then I shall dispatch you immediately. It's imperative for us to ferret out information regarding when General Howe plans to launch his attack."

Morgan trudged wearily up the enclosed staircase of the coaching inn where he had deposited Prudence in a rented room. A part of him couldn't help worrying that she'd gotten bored and wandered out on the street. He had been gone a long time, and it was now late afternoon. With some trepidation, he inserted the brass key into the lock and opened the door.

Morgan smiled at the sight that greeted him. His new wife lay asleep on the bed, looking soft and angelic, her fine features outlined by the subdued window light. Awake, her feisty spirit came swiftly to the fore, but now . . . ah, now, he could revel in her fragile beauty. She was so much more than he had ever hoped for, so different from the raft of simpering, manipulative females his mother had constantly prodded in his direction, mirror images of his mother herself. Unable to resist, he bent down and brushed his lips across hers.

She stirred, and her lashes fluttered open. "You're back," she murmured in a sleepy voice, a tender smile on her lips. Then the smile vanished, and she sat up. "You left me for hours in this dreary place."

Not at all perturbed by how quickly she came to herself, Morgan sank down beside her and took her into his arms, bestowing a promising kiss on her upturned lips. "I know, my sweet. But I'm afraid it could not be helped. I had to wait my turn to see General Washington."

She melted against him. "What did he want?"

"That I go at once to Philadelphia to spy for him."

"Philadelphia!" Prudence drew away slightly and looked up at him. "Why, that's wonderful!"

"Won't you miss me even a little?" he asked, deflated by her response.

"How can I, when I'll be right there with you?"

"I think not. I'm going to arrange to have you escorted safely home."

Her loosened topknot shifted off-kilter as she shook her head. "Just listen to yourself, sweetheart. Wouldn't it look more than a little suspicious for you to return to your own family's home without bringing your new wife along with you?"

He breathed out slowly. "I'll simply tell them the truth. That you have a store to look after and aren't able at the moment to shirk those duties."

"I'm sure *that* will please your parents," she said with a frown. "They'll be thrilled to learn that their son has married a common shopkeeper."

Morgan tightened his embrace. "You are not common," he insisted fiercely. "Besides, all I care about is getting you home, where you'll be safe and out of trouble."

In one fluid motion, Prudence withdrew from his arms and sprang to her feet. "I know in my heart I was meant to be of great service to the cause. I've always known it. If God didn't want me to serve, then he wouldn't have instilled within me this compelling need to do so."

Morgan also rose and squared off, his nose a mere fraction from hers. "And if I had a burning desire to go downstairs and get myself roaring drunk, would that, too, be God's will for me right now? or simply my own wish to escape this endless argument?"

With a huff, Prudence crossed her arms and presented her back. "Very well. We shan't argue about it anymore."

"Then you agree not to go?"

"Certainly not."

Though she put up minor resistance, Morgan turned her around and grasped her upper arms. "What you're suggesting could get us both hanged. You know that, don't you?"

A spark of stubbornness flashed in her eyes. "You don't consider me clever enough to prevent that?"

"Cleverness has nothing to do with it," he said gently. "Spying is a very subtle art. One must be able to move about with undue notice, and you are incredibly lovely. Who wouldn't notice you? And you've never socialized in the circles I grew up in. You've no concept of the accepted mode of dress, the particular way city belles have of talking, flirting, conducting themselves. Not that I have any desire to have you putting on those kinds of airs in the first place. I love you the way you are. That's what drew me to you, what made me want you for my wife."

"But as your wife, I *need* to help you. I can learn whatever is required. You can teach me. I'm a very fast learner, you'll see. And, my dear husband, I am not averse to obtaining a fashionable wardrobe. In times like these, old standards must be put aside for the greater good."

He hugged her to his chest. "Prudence, Prudence. What am I going to do with you?"

"You're going to teach me how to become a proper wife. After all, I do happen to be married to a prominent member of the merchant class of Philadelphia. It's high time I acquired the necessary graces required to be an asset to you."

Gazing down into her shimmering eyes, Morgan felt his pulse gathering intensity. "You have no idea what you're asking. If you knew my mother, you'd turn around right now and run for your life. All through my youth she was determined to handpick the belle I wed. Even if your manner and mode of dress were absolutely perfect, she would never forget that you weren't her personal choice. I shudder to think of how abominably she'll treat you."

"And I," she whispered with an impish smile, "will be all sweetness and charm to her. I'm ever so clever, you know."

A muffled boom rattled the windowpane, followed by another.

Morgan grabbed her hand and rushed with her to the window, flinging open the sash. "What's happened?" he shouted down to the street.

"More British ships are sailing in," someone hollered back. "The tubs at anchor are giving them a cannon salute."

Exhaling, Morgan settled back onto his heels and drew Prudence close again—but not before he caught the glint of excitement in her eyes. Suddenly a heavy realization all but pressed the air from his lungs.

Left on her own, his beautiful bride would always get herself dangerously close to the fray. Like it or not, he would never have peace of mind unless he knew her whereabouts at all times.

But how much safer would she be as an accomplice to a spy?

2

Prudence adjusted to a more comfortable stance atop the stool in the dressmaker's shop. Elated at the thought of actually accompanying Morgan to Philadelphia rather than being sent back to live with her stepmother, she found herself more than enjoying the experience of having a gown expertly fitted to her by two nimble-fingered women.

"It's truly a pity," Mistress Jennings, the proprietor, remarked around the straight pins clenched between her thin lips. "Maddie and I could have sewn some new frocks for you if you could've waited a few days." Small and slight as a broomstick, she removed the remaining three pins and put them in place one by one along the seam she was adjusting. "Of course, these lovely secondhand gowns your husband purchased for you cannot be faulted. He has an excellent eye for fabric and fashion."

Prudence had to restrain a giggle as the plump fingers of the employee called Maddie gathered a fold of excess material at Prudence's waist, tickling her in the process. She tried not to breathe too hard, lest she hinder either woman's work.

"'Tis a wonder 'e managed to find three day gowns in such marvelous condition," Maddie said in her thick London accent.

"We did have to rummage through five used-clothing shops before anything caught his attention," Prudence admitted. "He seemed to know exactly what he was seeking."

"Ah, but this apricot lawn is exquisite," Mistress Jennings said, taking a few steps back, her blue eyes critically assessing her handiwork. "It must have belonged to a very rich merchant's lady."

Maddie wagged her braided head and clucked her tongue. "*Spoiled* merchant's lady'd be more like it, I'd say." She tied off a final stitch, then snipped the thread. "Couldn't 'ave been worn but once or twice."

"I'm really sorry you've both been put to such an unduly quick task," Prudence said. "But my husband and I are in extreme haste and must leave your fine city to go to Philadelphia. He wants to be sure his own merchant family will find no fault with my appearance. We New Englanders, I'm afraid, tend to be quite conservative in our dress."

Two pairs of sharp eyes swung to her plain, gray linen gown, draped over the back of a chair. The women exchanged a wordless glance, but at least they had the grace not to smile.

"I'm glad I set up shop here in New York," the owner said, reaching to check the shoulders and lace-edged sleeves on Prudence's frock. "I would find Boston somewhat . . . tiresome."

The comment, though said without rancor, might have incited Prudence to indignation. But as a spy she was convinced she must learn to adapt to new places and new situations—blend in, rather than draw attention. Still, she couldn't help but take stock of the excessively bright bolts of fabric lining the shelves behind the counter, the jars of colored beads and bouquets of dyed feathers. Several dress forms bore gaudy party gowns in various stages of progress. Obviously the women of this city had no qualms about arraying themselves like strutting peacocks. "From things my husband has told me, I assume the ladies of Philadelphia dress much the same as those here in New York."

"If not even more elegantly," Mistress Jennings said as Maddie fluffed out the sweeping skirt of Prudence's gown and checked to see that it draped evenly. "You'll find you'll need many more afternoon and evening gowns than these three."

Prudence felt a jolt of excitement. That also meant there would be an abundance of spying opportunities . . . beyond her imaginings.

The proprietor stepped away and joined Maddie, eyeing the finished product.

"And all three done before your husband came back for you," Maddie said with a nod. She brushed perspiration from her damp forehead. "Seemed he was in a bit of a lather to get on the road."

Mistress Jennings shrugged. "Perhaps, with General Howe's ship anchored off the Long Island coast, Lieutenant Thomas wants to escort his bride to safety before the British start bombarding us in earnest."

"Or worse," Maddie said, her faded brown eyes wide. "Unruly and uncouth as those former countrymen of mine were in Boston, with us at war now, no woman along the seaboard will be safe from bein' ravaged."

"I wouldn't be borrowing trouble, Maddie," the head seamstress remarked. "Our brave boys drove them out of Boston. They'll do no less here. Certainly are enough of them underfoot," she added, chuckling.

"Aye, they—" Maddie, on the verge of elaborating, caught Prudence staring. She flushed and cleared her throat. "Well, now. We've got you properly dressed—except for the hair. We'll see what Florence, next door, can do about that severe bun of yours." She snatched Prudence's hand, pulling her to a chair. "Sit."

❦ ❦

Robert Chandler watched his two closest friends strap a secondhand trunk to the packhorse Morgan had just obtained.

"What do you say, Robby?" he heard Morgan ask the younger Scotsman, whose wiry frame had acquired strong muscles from his former duties as a wheelwright. "Think it's secure?" He yanked at the straps, testing them.

Narrowing his clear blue eyes to appraise the load, Robby MacKinnon raked fingers through his thatch of black hair, then replaced his tricornered hat. "Aye, 'tis secure."

"Excellent." Morgan brushed off his hands. "Then it should hold all the extras I've had to purchase today. It wasn't my plan to take Prudence home to my family so suddenly, but if I don't, heaven only knows what folly she'll get herself into."

Chan shook his head in disapproval, amazed that his friend had not taken time to consider the daftness of such a hasty decision. "Do you think allowing her to be part of your spying venture is safe?"

"Not entirely." Morgan looked at him in frustration. "What I'm hoping is that by the time we arrive in Philadelphia, I will have convinced her that she'll be my greatest asset by becoming so enchantingly distracting that attention will be diverted from me."

Robby leaned against the horse's rump with a chuckle. "'Enchantingly distracting'? Our Prudence—the Puritan? the Yankee-thrift shopkeeper? That'll take a bit more than convincin'. I doubt she even dances."

Morgan pulled a wry grimace, then brightened. "Imagine how many people she'll be able to enlist to teach her the fine art. In fact, there's a jeweler yonder. Perhaps I'll find her some earbobs to wear with her new gowns. Come on."

"Say, Morgan," Chandler remarked as they headed toward the jewelry shop. "Prudence went out of her way to be kind to Robby and me when we were repairing the store. Would you be opposed to my picking up some little trinket in appreciation?"

"Not at all. And I'm sure she'd be pleased as well."

Chandler, drawn to a heart-shaped locket displayed in the window, lagged behind as the other two entered the shop. Habitually, he pulled the similar one of Julia's from his fob pocket and smoothed his fingers over it. It was the one keepsake of hers that he had kept near his own heart.

He looked again at the one in the window. On a simpler chain and not quite so intricately filigreed as Julia's, it was beautiful in its own quiet way. Perhaps Prudence would admire its simple elegance. With a last long look at Julia's locket, he tucked the treasure back into its haven and went inside.

In a surprisingly short time, Morgan found two pairs of earbobs and a fancy comb for Prudence's hair and gave them to the clerk to wrap.

Meanwhile, Robby decided against a cameo brooch he had been admiring and instead placed a bracelet of inlaid silver on the counter for his wife, Emily.

"Splendid choice." Chandler put the locket that would soon belong to Prudence near Emily's present. The simple locket would suit Prudence, he was certain—just as the more elaborate design had suited his wife.

Moments later, their gifts tucked away, the men arrived at Estelle Jennings's dress shop. The tiny bell above the door announced their entrance.

Three women near the back of the establishment glanced up. The one seated in the center, willowy and dark haired, rose gracefully. The small smile on her lips added astonishing beauty to an already perfect face as she glided toward them. "How wonderful, Morgan. You found them both!"

Chandler stared in wonder at the transformation before his eyes. When last he had seen Prudence, she had worn her typically austere dress beneath a crisp starched apron and house cap, with her waist-length hair tied at the nape of her neck. But now, wearing a lavish apricot gown cut surprisingly low and her glorious black hair piled in a swirl of curls and peach ribbons, she was a vision. An absolute vision. He swallowed.

"Robby!" she gushed, drawing him into a warm hug before turning to Chandler. "And Chan! So lovely to see my two Roberts again. Though you, Chan, appear to have lost weight again—and after those pains I took to fatten you up. What a shame."

Morgan closed his own gaping mouth. "You make him sound like a pig," he said teasingly. "One you were trying to ready for market." He paused momentarily and shook his head, lost in the sight of his bride. "Here, let me take a good look at you."

Blushing, Prudence smiled and tilted her head, her silver eyes dancing as she turned in a slow, fluid circle.

"I daresay," he remarked, letting out a whoosh of breath, "you've never looked more enchanting. I do believe even my mother will be forced to approve."

The shop owner tapped Morgan's arm. "Your wife said that you haven't purchased a powdered wig for evening as yet. I've a friend in Philadelphia who makes the most glamorous wigs in the entire city."

"If that is so," Morgan answered cheerfully, "without a doubt, my mother and sisters have already found her." He returned his gaze to Prudence as he took the package from his breast pocket. "These may complement that enticing gown, love."

"Why, thank you." Nibbling her lip, she untied the ribbon and removed the wrapping. A sparkle lit her eyes when she discovered the diamond earbobs. "Oh, how very lovely. They're just beautiful! I've never owned anything so exquisite." She raised on tiptoe and gave him a kiss, then held one of the bobs to her ear for him to admire.

Chandler couldn't have spoken then if his life had depended on it. He was caught in misty memories of gifts he had bestowed upon Julia during their short time together. Her responses had been much the same as Prudence's, and the recollection stabbed at his heart.

"No one will ever know I'm a fraud, sweetheart," Prudence said gaily, going to a looking glass to try on her new jewelry. "I'll try very hard to make you proud of me."

"You're no fraud, young lady," the seamstress assured her. "You're every inch a lady."

But Chandler caught Prudence's deeper meaning . . . that she, the staunch patriot, hoped to assume the role of a Loyalist in a city of Crown supporters. Yet as honest and forthright as she'd always been, and outspoken to a fault, he had to wonder if she would be able to pull off the deception for long. For her sake and Morgan's, he prayed she would.

Chandler retrieved the little package from his pocket and placed it in her hand. "I, too, saw something I hoped you might like."

"Why, I don't know what to say. How thoughtful." She tugged the ribbon free and spread the paper open, exposing the locket. She raised her eyes to his.

"It reminded me of the shape and beauty of your face. I hope it'll remind you of the pleasant times Robby and I spent with you."

Prudence lifted the fragile chain. "I'll think of you both whenever I wear it. Thank you." After clasping it around her neck, she touched it lightly, then turned to him and Robby. "And while Morgan and I are away, you both must be careful. Really careful. Chandler, I'd better not hear ever again about your being the last to leave a battle scene, as you were at Bunker Hill. I insist that both of you dig the deepest trenches for yourselves and don't take foolish risks. I don't wish to think of you as dead heroes—and Robby, neither does Emily, I'm sure."

Morgan stepped to her side and slid a proprietary arm around her slender waist. "That goes double for me. After all, I won't be around to look after you—"

"You have a job of your own to concentrate on now," Chandler interrupted sternly. "Looking after your wife. Nothing in this life is more important, believe me." He clamped a hand on Morgan's shoulder. "Promise me y'all won't get so caught up in the game that you lose sight of that. Promise."

The stout helper tittered in the background. "Truly, Lieutenant Thomas has nothin' to worry about concernin' his little wife. These gowns are all of the latest fashion. No one will fault them—*or* her."

Chan suddenly realized he had almost betrayed their confidence. He dropped his hand and stepped back, collecting himself. "Of-of course. There could be no fault to find in someone so . . . lovely." Then, before he uttered anything else that might place them under suspicion—or anything that might disclose the morose thoughts threatening to swamp him—he tipped his head. "Farewell, my friends. I'll be thinking about you night and day."

3

Prudence fanned herself with her hand, but the slight breeze did little to assuage the mugginess of the hot day as she and Morgan rode their horses over the cobbled streets of Philadelphia.

Compared to New York, she found the "Red Brick City" much more attractive, with its streets neatly laid out in a grid, its brick buildings symmetrical and elegant. Many of the fashionable homes were lavish, indeed. Even the trees and shrubbery appeared well tended. The townspeople they passed were attired in finely tailored clothing, and those who recognized Morgan seemed especially amiable.

But she did have definite qualms about meeting Morgan's well-to-do family. "How much farther is it to your parents' home?"

Oddly enough, her husband didn't look much more at ease himself. "Before I take you there, I plan to stop at my father's warehouses."

Prudence knew that Morgan was anxious to discover if his Loyalist father had experienced a change of heart since his last letter. The man's response to Morgan's written confession had been a surprise, to be sure. Mr. Thomas, after a considerable span of silence, corresponded by claiming he had forgiven Morgan for swindling him and his fellow businessmen by diverting their cargo to the patriot cause. He had decided to remain silent about the matter.

"I'm sure you realize that should Father have changed his mind about me and betrayed me to his business associates, we will have come here for naught," Morgan continued. "But now that I think about it, perhaps that would be best. I could take you back to Boston and return to my duties with the army."

Prudence arched her brows. "You'll not get rid of me quite so easily, Morgan Thomas."

"It's far more than that, sweetheart. If you'll recall, a few short months ago I made a vow to the Lord to stop lying. Now here I am, all too ready to lie and spy again. The two go hand in hand."

Reaching to give his arm a squeeze, Prudence offered him an encouraging smile. "We've already talked about this, haven't we? Don't forget how Moses sent spies into the land of Canaan. Joshua and others also sent out spies. It's part of the process of war—and I truly believe deep within my heart that we are in a holy war just like those in the Bible. If we remain faithful to the cause and do not become weary or faint of heart, God will be faithful to us."

"I know, I know. And afterward," he went on, parroting earlier statements she had made, "we'll have the freedom to worship almighty God as we see fit, to decide how our taxes are spent, to trade with any country we choose." His exasperation was far from comforting as he exhaled wearily, guiding his mount around a freight wagon directly ahead of them.

A sudden surge of guilt caught her off guard. *But am I right?* she wondered. *Or am I his Eve? his Delilah?* She immediately rejected such inane comparisons. Tapping her quirt, she caught up to Morgan. "Sweetheart, please don't be upset with me."

"You know you're not the problem, Prudence," he answered quietly. "It's the complexity of lying on a grand scale that worries me. Keeping all the stories straight, knowing what I've said to one person and what I've said to someone else. Floating on a sea of lies is very harrowing."

It did sound ominous, put that way. Prudence pondered his

comments for a few silent moments. "But *together* we'll help each other not to forget. We've rehearsed our story often enough. And this time you won't be alone. I'll be here with you. We can do this, Morgan. We can. You'll see. We'll be wonderful, working together, praying together, helping each other. We can do it."

With a thin smile, he tenderly brushed a lock of hair behind her ear. "You have the faith of a child, love. If only I could see with the same clarity."

Another stab of uneasiness made it harder to maintain her own reassuring smile. She *was* beginning to see . . . far more clearly than she was willing to admit.

As they approached the waterfront district, she could hear the noise and bustle, the increased traffic and shouting hawkers, the clatter of goods being loaded aboard ship or hefted down gangplanks. She saw the name *Thomas* emblazoned across several warehouses—huge, looming buildings that testified to the power of Morgan's family. They were more than merely affluent. They were very wealthy, indeed.

Morgan reined in at the largest of the warehouses and dismounted, then turned to her. "I probably should have given you an opportunity to change into one of your new gowns before reaching the city. But I've told my father a bit about your strict New England background. I think he'll rather appreciate your simplicity. Aside from his ruthless business dealings, you'll find he's quite a decent sort."

Prudence blanched and pushed his hands away the instant her feet touched the ground. "You think I'm a simpleton?"

With a laugh, Morgan grabbed her and hugged her. "You, my dearest? a simpleton? By no means. But when you meet the women in my family, you'll discover I've just paid you a sincere compliment." He released her and placed an arm around her waist. "Come along, we'll find Father."

The cool interior of the building provided welcome relief from the sticky heat outside. Prudence blinked as her eyes adjusted to the shade. She was taken aback by the vast amount of open space everywhere.

So, apparently, was Morgan. "I've never seen it so empty," he remarked, looking around with a frown.

Prudence surveyed the cavernous structure. Morgan had more than proven how inventive he was in procuring supplies for her own new mercantile, as well as for the patriots. Perhaps he now experienced guilt over having left his father's service. If the Loyalists of Boston ever discovered the ways in which he had diverted their shipments to the Continental army, his career as a spy—not to mention his life—would be in dire jeopardy.

"I can see how sorely my presence here was needed," Morgan admitted. "By now it has become all but impossible to get a Tory merchant shipment past the British navy—or the patriot privateers, for that matter."

"Do try not to feel bad about it," Prudence said in reassurance. "No matter how many shiploads of men and cannons the British send, with God on our side the patriots will win. I'm sure the war will not outlast the summer."

"I pray you're right."

Scraping and muffled thuds of crates being moved echoed from the opposite end of the warehouse. From above them, a man on a catwalk gave a sharp whistle, then shouted directions.

"Father!" Morgan called out with a wave. Grabbing Prudence's hand, he hastened toward an open staircase.

When they paused on the top landing, Prudence bit back her nervousness as the distinguished gentleman approached them.

Not quite as tall as Morgan, yet somehow almost as handsome, he made no effort to disguise his delight. Dark blue eyes crimped at the corners as a wide smile lifted his well-shaped lips. His neatly combed hair was somewhat less abundant than Morgan's, but it was the same rich shade of brown, with a sprinkling of gray at the temples. "Well, well," he said, spreading his arms open as he neared. "You've finally come." Wasting no time at all on proprieties, he embraced his son exuberantly.

"I was afraid you might have changed your mind," Morgan admitted, "considering my rather thoughtless betrayal of you and your friends."

"Well, be that as it may, Son, it's in the past. And best forgotten. I'm extremely glad to have you back where you belong." He released Morgan and took Prudence's arms. "And you, my dear, would have to be Prudence." His slow gaze took in her plain riding attire but revealed neither approval nor disapproval. It was a relief when he smiled warmly. "What a delightful surprise."

After a moment he turned back to Morgan. "Well, Son, left to your own devices, you've done admirably well. Admirably, indeed. She's quite flawless. With an added frill here and there, not even your mother will be able to find fault."

Instead of easing her tension, his complimentary words increased Prudence's disquiet. She had heard only curious, guarded remarks about the "Lady" Thomas.

"Have you told Mother about my marriage?" Morgan asked.

Embarrassment tilted the older man's awkward grin. "If I'd had word you were coming, I would have had the chance to prepare her. But no, I'm afraid not."

Morgan nodded, his expression obviously worried. He recovered quickly and flicked a casual glance at Prudence, but he was a few seconds too late. "Actually," he said to his father, "this trip was unexpected—and when I disclose the reason behind it, you may be less than happy I've come." He drew Prudence close. "I've been sent back here to spy again—*if* I've not already been exposed, of course. General Washington feels I can be of far more use here than with the army in New York."

Mr. Thomas's countenance, which had sagged noticeably within the last few seconds, darkened even more.

"Have I been found out?" Morgan asked.

The older man shook his head. "No. But—"

"I'm more than aware how difficult this whole thing is for

you, sir. I'll turn around and go back to New York at once if you ask me to."

Mr. Thomas searched his son's face for a moment, obviously mulling over the disturbing news he had just been given. Then he inhaled a deep breath and slowly released it. He placed a hand on Morgan's shoulder. "To be quite honest, I never once thought Pennsylvania would succumb to rebellion's call. We've always been the most reasonable, the most civilized of all the colonies. But since Ben Franklin returned from London, he's been chipping away little by little at the people's resolve. Of course, that dissertation of Thomas Paine's, *Common Sense,* has fueled the fervor. Then last month even William Penn signed that fool Declaration of Independence, so our colony has now aligned itself with all the other radicals intent upon shedding the motherland once and for all."

Prudence looked from one grim face to the other. There was a distinct resemblance, not only in the stance of the two men, but in the way they held their heads, in their stalwart features. When Mr. Thomas glowered, Prudence could see Morgan in his eyes.

"When I told your mother about it," he went on, "she became quite hysterical. She's convinced there'll be no stopping the rebels now, that they'll burn us out—or worse."

"I wouldn't expect that sort of thing here in Philadelphia," Morgan said. "At least, not for the time being. After all, the Congress meets here. They'll want to appear as legitimate as possible. Allowing mobs to run amok in the streets would be most detrimental."

"Yes. I hadn't thought about it in that light. I do pray you're right." The older man pulled a wry grimace. "As a Loyalist, maybe the best insurance I could have against fire is the presence of my rebel son in the house."

"It would be . . . but only if my true affiliation were discovered." Morgan paused significantly to let the words sink in.

"Ah, well . . ." Morgan's father cocked his head. "I'm becoming more and more a man with two faces myself. I once was dead certain exactly who was right and who was wrong in the world of politics. But I have serious doubts now." He exhaled in frustration. "I just don't want to lose all that I've worked for all these years. Most particularly, I don't want to lose you. I'll be no hindrance . . . but neither will I assist you. I hope you can understand that."

Morgan nodded, and Prudence saw him relax slightly. "I thank you for that, Father."

The older man stepped closer and hugged him hard. "I'm so delighted to have you back, Son. It's a comfort that you'll be away from New York when the British do finally decide to attack."

His sincerity touched Prudence deeply. Perhaps in business dealings he might be considered ruthless, as Morgan termed it, but he certainly had the utmost respect and love for his son. It made her feel closer to her distinguished father-in-law.

"Is there some private place where Prudence might change into something more elegant, sir?" Morgan asked with a grin. "I'm about to introduce her as my very wealthy, very loyal, *Tory* bride."

"You're not serious!"

Morgan chuckled and gestured graciously toward Prudence. "Yes, Father. My beautiful, hardheaded Yankee insists upon being my fellow conspirator."

"He's . . . *married?*" The woman's gasp carried remarkably well from upstairs. So did the ensuing silence.

Prudence stood like a statue, afraid to draw a breath.

Morgan, beside her in the mansion's marble foyer, chuckled as he squeezed her hand and gave an excessively nonchalant shrug.

Running footsteps echoed from the floor above. "What's happened, Mama?" a younger voice asked. Then a door clicked shut, leaving only muted voices . . . but the flustered tones and exclamations were surprisingly distinct.

Prudence chewed the inside corner of her lip. "Perhaps we should come back later. . . ."

"Oh, don't despair," Morgan said. "She'll recover from the shock quite quickly, you'll see. Mother's amazingly . . . *adaptable,* when she has to be. However, if you'd like, we might take a walk in the garden." He led her across the hall and through the magnificent ballroom to a bank of glass doors opening onto a flagstone veranda.

The fresh air, sweet with the perfume of roses and other late summer flowers, wafted over Prudence like a blessing. Despite the immensity of the huge home, she had begun to feel confined, strangled. Now she drew a strengthening breath and tried to shrug off her dread while Morgan strolled with her to an intricate fountain flanked by curved marble benches. For several minutes, she watched the slender arches of crystal water shooting from the mouths of a trio of dolphins.

"I would love to have seen Mother's face when Father broke the news," Morgan said, the rakish gleam in his eye adding to his devilish grin. "High drama is her dearest forte."

Prudence, trying unsuccessfully to lose herself in the grandeur of immaculate hedges and exquisite flowers, dragged her gaze from them and looked disapprovingly at her husband. "That sounds uncommonly callous of you."

"Quite right." He reddened. "I suppose over time I've become insensitive to Mother's theatrics and manipulations. But be alert, my love. She is a formidable adversary. Never let down your guard around her. As they say, forewarned is forearmed."

Unable to truly believe such alarming statements, Prudence turned to face him. "And you, my dear husband, are more than clever yourself. Methinks you're trying to scare me into returning to Massachusetts." Taking his hands in hers, she looked directly into his eyes. "But home for me is wherever you happen to be."

"Then this, dear child," a well-modulated female voice said, "is surely your home. We have no intention of allowing our son out of our sight again for a very, very long time."

Prudence turned with Morgan and saw a stately woman of medium build coming toward them on Mr. Thomas's arm. Her corseted figure matched perfectly the contours of the understated gold taffeta gown she wore. A lace cap hid some of the silvering strands amid the elaborately dressed, dark brown hair, and her eyes, nearly the same cobalt blue as Morgan's, stopped just short of smiling. Prudence was more than relieved to see a distinctly pleasant expression on the woman's oval face, especially when she reached out a tapered and manicured hand in welcome.

A younger girl, dark-haired and appealing, stood a few steps behind and off to one side, but she did not speak.

"Welcome, my dear," Morgan's mother said. "Welcome to the family."

Taking the proffered hand with its jeweled rings, Prudence dipped into a polite curtsy. "Thank you, Mistress Thomas. I've been so looking forward to meeting you." Surely Morgan, for some reason known only to him, must have exaggerated, she told herself. Mrs. Thomas couldn't have been more gracious.

"And, Morgan," she went on, sweeping a glance to him with arched brows, "such a lovely bride you've brought us. I do commend your choice—though you are, nonetheless, a most naughty boy. With all the trouble that brewed up in Boston, you might at least have sent us word regarding your well-being, especially when you were held in that city's siege by those unsavory outlaws. When the situation worsened to such a degree that all those loyal to the Crown had to retreat to Halifax with the British, you must have known we'd be concerned."

"I've no excuse for my thoughtless neglect," he admitted. Smiling sheepishly, he took her shoulders and kissed her on both cheeks.

She gave him no chance to elaborate further. "And now you've finally come home, just as handsome and unscathed as ever, *and* with a new bride. We do have considerable catching up to do, don't we?"

"That's a fact, Mother."

"Well, you must tell us everything. And what of Dan, Sophia Haynes's son, up in Boston? I assume he, too, was trapped in that city during the besiegement, along with that—wife—of his. You remember, don't you, Waldon," she went on, tilting her head toward her husband, "that bondservant he married to spite his poor, dear mother?"

Prudence felt a sudden chill.

4

Though every last word his mother uttered to Prudence had
been gracious, *excessively* so, Morgan could not escape the
conviction that the woman's actual feelings were anything but
accepting. After having endured her scheming and manipu-
lation throughout his entire life—her attempts at arranging
an advantageous marriage for him, in particular—he knew
she had to be in high dudgeon over his having taken matters
into his own hands. He could only wonder how long this farce
would last before her true emotions came to the surface.

As the family meandered back up the walkway to the house,
his mother gestured toward Morgan's sister. "Our Evelyn, I'm
delighted to say, has a young admirer taking supper with us
this eve—Clayborne Judson Raleigh. He's in the colonies with
his father, a tobacco buyer."

"Is that so?" Morgan asked, catching up to his youngest
sibling. He slid an arm around her narrow waist and hugged
her.

Evelyn smiled becomingly, adding striking beauty to her
fragile feminine features . . . but the guileless smile lost some
of its appeal when spoiled by a self-satisfied glimmer in her
pale blue eyes. "A very rich tobacco buyer with close royal
ties," she announced proudly.

Morgan thought he had detected a change in the winsome
fifteen-year-old when he first glimpsed her flying to Mother's
room a short while ago, and his suspicions were confirmed by

both her carriage and her reply. She had blossomed in the time since he went to Boston. During his absence, not only had she become a captivating young woman, but evidently she had been Mother's apt pupil as well—molded in her image.

His spirits sank. So far he hadn't found it necessary to speak less than truthfully, but how long would that last? On this, his very first night home, there would be some British pup to entertain. "What about Frances?" he asked, returning his attention to his parents.

His mother fluttered her hand. "Why, your sister has made a most fortuitous match *while you were incommunicado,*" she answered pointedly, "to Bradford Hendricks, that young man she had been seeing before you went away. He's from a good British family, you recall, and has now been made an officer of the king's army. Your sister returned with him to England. Southampton, to be precise. Of course we miss her terribly. Your father and I are already planning a trip there next summer—if this awful rebellion business doesn't prevent us from doing so."

"It was the *loveliest* spring wedding," Evelyn murmured dreamily. "Wasn't it, Mother?" She reached the back door ahead of the others, opened it, and went inside ahead of them.

"Absolutely," her mother gushed as they crossed the ball-room again. "Even though the worst troublemakers from all the colonies were stirring up a hornet's nest over at Carpenter's Hall. 'The Continental Congress,' they call themselves." She sighed and shook her head in distaste. "We do our best to ignore them. But sometimes . . ."

Morgan met Prudence's gaze and squeezed her hand as they returned to the foyer. "Speaking of married couples, you might be interested to hear that Dan and Susannah are now living in northeastern Pennsylvania's wilderness." He watched his mother's eyebrows arch. "By the time of the Boston siege, their church had been sacked by the British, and most of the city's Presbyterians had left. Dan has been sent to start a new flock in the Wyoming Valley."

"You don't say," his father remarked. "That's the place we've been disputing with Connecticut regarding ownership, is it not?"

"Quite right. But from what I understand, the settlers there have switched to fighting the British."

"It's enough to make one swoon," his mother said, fanning herself. "Sophia Haynes must be beside herself, knowing her oldest son is forever embroiling himself in one hotbed of revolt or another. Thank heaven you've kept a cool head on your shoulders. If those Continental delegates have their way, everything we've ever worked for will go to rack and ruin." She pursed her lips.

"I agree wholeheartedly," Prudence chimed in.

Morgan held his breath, waiting to hear what she would say next.

"Without the civilizing influence of the mother country," his wife went on smoothly, "these colonies will degenerate into an uncouth rabble, as did my own poor dear Boston."

Flabbergasted at the depth of Prudence's sincerity, Morgan could not believe someone who had always held the truth in highest reverence would now utter lies without a qualm—and after she had once found his own dishonor toward his parents so sinful.

A manservant hired in Morgan's absence walked into the foyer. "You needed me, madam?"

Mother considered the small trunk and valise Morgan and Prudence had left sitting in the marbled entry, and she frowned slightly. "Yes. See that their luggage is taken upstairs, Charles."

"It pains me to admit it," Prudence said as the uniformed man complied, "but I'm afraid your son married an impoverished woman. During the siege, my family's home and business were wantonly burned to the ground by the most despicable criminals."

At least that much was true, Morgan conceded. The Crown

forces did cannonade her family's house and store—and she did consider them despicable. Yet she seemed to possess amazing skill at twisting the truth, and that made him very uncomfortable.

"I've scarcely more than the clothes on my back, now," Prudence went on coyly. She shrugged a shoulder in helpless embarrassment.

"Why, my dear." Mother stepped near and took her hand. "How absolutely dreadful. What you must have suffered." She turned to her husband. "I'm telling you, Waldon, if something is not done soon, the same fate could be ours."

Prudence rushed to Morgan's side, her eyes enormous and frightened. "You told me we'd be safe here. You promised."

Even to him her charade appeared convincing. He put an arm about her as he caught the twinkle in his father's eye.

"Never you worry, dear," Mother cooed, patting Prudence's shoulder. "That won't actually happen in this city. Will it, Waldon?"

"Of course not," he answered. "This is, after all, the City of Brotherly Love."

Prudence pulled a kerchief from Morgan's pocket and dabbed elaborately at nonexistent tears, then swung back to his mother. "And merry, isn't it?" She sniffed. "I've always heard Philadelphia is very lively. Even with this bothersome trouble, there are still parties and plays and balls. Morgan has promised to take me to all of them—and in an entirely new wardrobe, too. Fashioned from the latest Paris fabrics and designs." She whirled around to him. "He's quite the dearest thing, isn't he?" Her back to the others, she winked as she raised on tiptoe to kiss his cheek.

Morgan realized, to his dismay, that she was having the time of her life!

His mother, coming near once more, placed an arm about her and turned her around, leading her toward the curved staircase. "Why, of course you shall. The wife of my only son does have a certain *standard* to maintain when we introduce her to our friends. But first, come upstairs, and I'll show you to your room. You must be exhausted from your long journey. You can rest awhile before supper. Afterward we can discuss which fabrics and colors will set you off to your best advantage. Your eyes, of course, are your greatest asset."

Evelyn wasted no time chasing after them. She grabbed Prudence's hand. "It'll be just like having a sister at home again. What grand times we shall have! Mother, may I have some new gowns made, also? All the girls have already seen everything I own."

Morgan was almost hesitant to look at his father. In his earlier spying ventures, he'd had no one but himself to worry about. Despite the success of these initial moments, heaven only knew what still lay ahead.

❧ ❧

Robert Chandler and Robby MacKinnon, crossing from Manhattan to Nassau Island with a wagonload of supplies, reached the top of the Guan Heights, west of Brooklyn village. The wooded hill overlooked the outer bay, where the afternoon sunshine glistened over the choppy water—and the vast array of British ships at anchor off Sandy Hook.

Robby halted the two-horse team. "Would ye look at that."

"An awesome sight, that's for sure."

"Every time we come up here, there's more of them. No wonder our ranks are beginning to thin. I overheard some captains just this morning talkin' about daily desertions in their camps. One of them sounded frightened himself. He said General Washington should've swallowed his pride and gone over to Staten Island when the British were wantin' to talk. I canna' help but agree."

Mildly amused, Chandler smiled. "Ah, my friend, you would have to be a southern gentleman to understand his reasoning. To have a letter addressed to *Mister* Washington, rather than *General,* was a low-down insult—one the good general would find impossible to swallow."

"But with so many inlets and beaches down there, we'll not be able to defend them all. Every night I pray for a miracle, yet I canna' shake me feelin' of doom. And with naught but a small portion of those men and their mighty armada, they could overrun Rhode Island in a day. I should've taken leave. Emily and the bairns are in grave danger so close to Narragansett Bay. I've no doubt General Howe will detach a force to take Providence. They won't ignore the rebellious Rhode Islanders much longer. Me family would be far safer in Princeton."

Chandler, having visited with Emily MacKinnon and their children on the march south from Boston, remembered her winsome beauty. She had a fragile quality about her, yet she seemed to possess the same steady strength Robby normally displayed. He knew the couple shared not only a deep love for one another but a strong and abiding faith in God as well. But if they ever were truly tested, as he himself had been, were ever to suffer a loss beyond belief, how would they fare then?

He shook off his morbid thoughts. "Better get the team moving again if we want to get unloaded and back to New York before dark."

Robby cast a last long look at the ships, then snapped the reins over the animals' backs.

Chandler promised himself that if he had anything to say in the matter, the Scot would never know a loss similar to his own crushing experience. "Tell you what," he suggested. "Nothing's stirring down there yet, no sign of the redcoats getting ready for an assault. Let's report sick tomorrow and get some men to cover for us. In less than three days we could be at the Hayneses' farm."

His friend's dark mustache quirked beneath doubtful blue eyes.

"I'm sure that in no more than nine or ten days at the most," Chan insisted, "we could have your family safely tucked away at Princeton and be back here. I'd stake my life that the English will still be sitting down there, with no more than an occasional growl coming from their cannons. Their mere presence is scaring so many into deserting. Soon all they'll have to do is just sail into New York and plant their flag."

"Ye know better than that. Going after me Emily is mighty tempting. But we canna' be sure they won't attack before we get back. I deserted once. No matter that I'd been unjustly impressed into service aboard an English ship, I don't want that dishonorable word attached to me name again. Ever." He paused. "But perhaps we could ask permission. . . ."

Chandler gave a dubious shake of the head. "We could try, but that new quartermaster doesn't know us from Adam. I wish Morgan hadn't been fool enough to traipse off to Philadelphia and drag our little Puritan along. Speaking of Prudence, can you even imagine her trying to spy? or even more unbelievable, lie? The two of us should have stopped them somehow."

Robby chuckled and nodded. "Aye, perhaps. But the lass is as stubborn as she is persuasive. Puts me in mind of me bonny Emily when we first met. But for her stubborn logic, I'd have been hanged as a deserter. She saved me life . . . her and the Lord, of course."

Chandler rubbed his thumb over the lump Julia's locket made in his pocket. He and Robby should have tried harder to stop Prudence from going into the lions' den . . . but by hook or crook, he'd see to it that Emily was taken to the safe haven of Princeton.

Princeton. The thought of setting foot in the place where he and Julia had known their brief time of happiness—and where he had experienced immeasurable sorrow—was almost unspeakable. But hard as it was, somehow he'd do it.

Hoofbeats sounded from behind them as a rider approached. Out of habit, Chan reached for his musket and checked its load.

"'Tis me brother-in-law!" Robby remarked. "Ye remember Ben, don't ye?"

"The courier? Of course."

"Could be he's got a letter from Emily."

Chandler felt deader than ever inside. There would never be such a letter for him, ever again.

5

"Will that be all, mum?" Lucy, a thin, pleasant maid of the Thomas household, asked Prudence.

"Yes, thank you so much."

"Very good." The servant quietly exited the guest chamber.

Prudence stared in awe at her own elegant reflection in the winged looking glass of the dressing table. Lucy had styled her hair into a braided coronet with a cluster of ringlets dangling behind one ear.

Her gaze lowered to the sprigged muslin gown. The color, a soft ivory trimmed with violet-edged lace, made her olive skin glow. But was it fashionable enough to fit in here? The word of a mere New York seamstress didn't seem sufficient for someone hoping to give the impression of being a spoiled belle—and soon she would be expected to select an entire wardrobe! Merciful heavens!

Thinking back on when she'd sought employment as a serving girl in order to spy on the Boston Tories and their British allies, she recalled how the women in attendance had spoken of little other than the frocks other attendees had worn. How would she ever carry off this charade?

The bedroom door opened, and Morgan strode in. His eyes met hers in the mirror.

Springing to her feet, she turned to face him. "Do you think I'm presentable?"

His admiring gaze meandered slowly downward from her

hair to her toes and back; then he shook his head in wonder as he came to her. "More than presentable, actually. You look ravishing. Far more beautiful than any one woman has the right to be." He drew her into his arms and kissed her.

"But am I wearing the latest style?" she asked, drawing away slightly when he attempted a second and more passionate kiss. Flattery might be fine for some, but her husband's biased view would not help her to learn the proper ways to act or dress. She twirled around, then sought his opinion once again.

"All I can say is that any man—wealthy or otherwise—would be proud to have you on his arm. Other than that, I'm afraid I've not paid that much attention to what is all the rage this season."

Prudence's enthusiasm withered.

"If you *should* happen to be lagging behind the others in some small way," Morgan went on, "I'm sure no one will hold it against you. Boston port has been blockaded for over two years, remember."

"Yes," she said with renewed hope. "I hadn't thought of that. So your mother shouldn't find it strange that I'll be putting myself wholly at her disposal, relying upon her good taste and guidance in choosing my wardrobe. I'll be so pliable and appreciative she won't be able to help liking me."

"Quite." Stripping off his shirt, Morgan crossed to the commode. He poured water from the pitcher into the basin and began to wash.

Prudence went to the ornately carved mahogany wardrobe and removed a fresh shirt for him. "I asked Lucy to have this pressed for you. I hope I made a good choice."

He gave it a perfunctory glance.

"Won't it do, Morgan?"

"Hm?" Grabbing a towel, he rubbed his face and arms briskly. "Oh. Of course. It's fine."

"Then what is it? Something's troubling you."

He draped the damp towel over the bar on the edge of the washstand. "It's this whole business."

"What business?"

Morgan turned. "We happen to have come here for the express purpose of deceiving my family. That's what is troubling me. Now, correct me if I'm wrong, but when I told my father a rather elaborate lie in the not too distant past, you were so upset with me that you were ready to shut me out of your life completely. Yet here we are, eager to tell my own mother all the things she wants to hear, simply so we can use her and her social connections to further our own *righteous* cause."

Aware of the warm flush flooding her cheeks, Prudence inhaled deeply. "But that was different."

"I fail to perceive how." Morgan turned away and began pulling on the clean shirt.

"The . . . lie . . . you told your father was done to trick him out of a large sum of money that would ensure your own pleasure and comfort, which was an outright sin. But this isn't the same thing, Morgan. Please know that I will never do anything to deliberately bring hurt to your family."

"Lying or tricking one's mother—no matter *what* the reason—is far from honoring a parent."

Someone rapped on the door.

Prudence caught her breath. Had this conversation carried beyond the room?

Fastening the last of his buttons, Morgan went to answer.

"Dinner will be served in five minutes," a voice said.

"Thank you." He closed the door and turned to Prudence. "One more reason I shouldn't have an accomplice in these circumstances. Sooner or later, we're bound to be overheard."

She fluttered one hand and sat down to put on her shoes. "That is simply rectified. We'll never speak of the matter again unless we're positive it is safe to do so."

Morgan drew on a dove gray dinner coat, and Prudence, having finished with her shoes, rose to adjust the ruffles on his cuffs and shirt front. It was the first time she had seen him dressed like a dandy since their first meeting. "Now I recognize you for certain," she said teasingly. "That flirty, bossy upstart from the Clarkes' Christmas ball."

"Ah, yes," he said wryly. "Back in those sweet carefree days before you became the worry of my life."

Raising up on tiptoe, Prudence caressed the lines from his brow and brushed his lips with hers. "I do hope I've become more to you than that."

The tension left his expression, and a spark of desire darkened his eyes. He pulled her near and kissed her neck.

Prudence laughed lightly and pushed him gently away. "Forgive me, sweetheart, but you mustn't muss my hair just now." She took his arm and looped hers through it. "Afterward," she whispered, "you may tangle it to your heart's content."

With neither the answering grin she'd anticipated nor a glint of mischievous fun, Morgan filled his lungs and gestured toward the hall.

Prudence drew a strengthening breath, also. How would she ever convince him they were doing the right thing? Surely her reasoning was sound, logical. Their motives were pure, the cause righteous.

Nevertheless . . .

❧ ❧

As Morgan escorted Prudence downstairs, he could hear his father conversing in the library.

"But to have that happen in New York!" the guest was saying as they drew near. "From what I understand, that city had no fewer Loyalists than your fair city. I fear it does not bode well for Philadelphia."

Father gave a noncommittal shrug, then brightened as he caught sight of Morgan and Prudence entering the book-lined study. "It's my son and his bride." He set down his glass of sherry and came to meet them, kissing Prudence on both cheeks. "You look lovely, my dear."

"Thank you," she said softly.

"Morgan," he went on, "I'd like you to meet Clayborne

Raleigh. He's become so fond of our gracious town, he chose not to accompany his father to the tobacco warehouses of the South. Clay, this is my son, Morgan."

"Your servant," the visitor said, extending his hand.

So this is my baby sister's admirer? Morgan took immediate stock of the well-dressed man. Light brown hair, hooded hazel eyes sloping downward at the corners, snobbish lips, impudent chin. Of medium height, he had to be nearly thirty if he were a day. *Surely of sufficient age to be buying tobacco in his father's stead, not languishing here while his elderly sire labors. Nor dallying with the affections of impressionable young girls. With Evelyn.* But Morgan shook hands and forced out a polite greeting. "How do you do?"

"So you're the brother who found himself trapped in Boston during the bombardment," Raleigh said, the nasal tone of his British accent indicating his distaste. "How utterly tiresome it must have been. I hear that society is devoid of all grace and culture." His interested gaze fastened on Prudence. "And dare I say, even our own soldiers can be quite common, indeed. Circumstances must have been very trying in Boston for one of such beauty." He bent elaborately and kissed her hand.

Morgan's mind was still coming up with labels for the useless bounder. "It's unwise to prejudge a city," he said, pulling Prudence close with a proprietary arm. "After all, I plucked this rare flower from those very gardens."

The newcomer appeared flustered.

Prudence tapped Morgan's chest with the tip of her closed lace fan and smiled. "I fear my husband is jesting at your expense. 'Tis true I'm a daughter of Boston. But its reputation as a city with no sense of humor, no imagination, is more than deserved. And alas, now that it is teeming with rebellious upstarts, it is suffering an even worse fate. Soon, I fear, it will be nothing but rubble."

Clayborne Raleigh sniffed. "Speaking of rubble, I was just relating to Mr. Thomas what I heard at the Barkleys' last night. It seems there is—or perhaps I should say *was*—a marvelous statue of King George astride a steed in New York. The very moment the outlaw army squatting there found out about their *Declaration of Independence*, they dared to pull the figure off its very foundation. Then, from what Barkley said, they melted it down for bullets to shoot at the king's own men."

"Yes," Father remarked. "Appalling conduct, to say the least."

Morgan fought to subdue a smile. His own efforts had been lent to accomplish the deed. He could still feel the tug of the rope in his hand.

"'Tis shocking, I know, Mr. Raleigh," Prudence mused. "But I have faith that this disgusting violence will soon come to an end. Too late, perhaps, for the loyal citizens in Boston, but not for the rest of our beleaguered colonies."

"I say," Morgan cut in. "You seem privy to the latest gossip, sir. Perhaps you've heard something definite regarding the attack General Howe is planning. I'd hoped this dreary business would be over before the first leaves of autumn fell."

His father cleared his throat. "I do believe I hear the ladies coming down." At the hint of discomfort in his tone, Morgan concluded it would be best to refrain from gleaning information while in his father's presence. The man was compromising himself enough as it was.

"And for my own lovely wife's comfort," Morgan announced, his fingertips pressing on her waist, "let us refrain from war talk for the remainder of the evening. It was a long and tiresome ride down from Halifax, and we've heard little conversation along the way save that."

"You poor dear." Raleigh sidled alongside Prudence as they started toward the foyer. "Obliged to evacuate Boston with the army, then forced to endure the ramblings of backwoods Yankee-Doodles all the way here. Well, don't despair. We'll see that you are thoroughly entertained this eve—and each and every one for the next fortnight, as well." Reaching the staircase, he switched his gaze to Evelyn. "Won't we, my pet?"

Morgan was struck by how grown up his sister appeared,

with her shining hair in a cascade of ringlets and her lips sporting a faint touch of lip rouge. Then he caught the way Clay Raleigh's eyes lingered on her budding bosom as she smilingly took the rake's arm. The effort to throw the lecher out on his ear was almost too strong to resist. Morgan was amazed his father didn't appear to have noticed the cur's disgusting conduct . . . and was more than thankful that Evelyn still sparkled with innocence as she tipped her head at her older brother and Prudence.

"I see you two have already met our charming guest," Mother announced, gifting the man with a warm look. "He's the son of one of England's most prominent merchant families. As well as his father's expertise in tobacco, he has an uncle who imports great quantities of spices and another who's deeply involved with the Chinese silk. Isn't that so, Mr. Raleigh?"

"We do try our utmost to keep abreast of the needs of England," he returned.

We? Morgan thought with a smirk. The man appeared worse than useless—unless there was more to him than met the eye, which he seriously doubted. But one never knew. Clayborne Raleigh might bear watching for reasons other than the safeguarding of Evelyn's virtue. Under no circumstances would Morgan leave the cad unchaperoned with his sister. Suddenly he was very glad to be home. It would appear he and Prudence had arrived just in time.

Prudence crimped her lips in disgust. Morgan had dismissed her to their bedchamber almost immediately after supper on the pretense that she was exhausted from their trip! Why, she had hardly risen from her chair before he began questioning Clay Raleigh regarding the Crown's commitment to loyal merchants. Obviously Morgan intended to exclude her from his activities at every opportunity. Well, he would hear about it when he returned. She had been waiting more than three hours in the unlit room for him to join her!

Emitting an angry breath, she pushed the partially open windows out as far as they would go, then leaned to catch the slight breeze. Her night dress was much too heavy for these sultry climes.

Had it not been for Mistress Thomas, who unwittingly aided Morgan in his ploy by deciding that the men needed to become better acquainted, Prudence might have objected to leaving the supper table. But the older woman had announced that dreary business talk was too dull and uninspiring to endure. She had taken Evelyn upstairs and retired.

The thought of young, dark-haired Evie brought a smile. The girl did possess an abundance of youthful charm. It was not hard to understand why she was already being courted at such a tender age. But not yet sixteen, she was much too naive to be left unattended with a man of the world.

Clay Raleigh epitomized everything Prudence disliked and distrusted . . . and everything the colonies now rebelled against. He didn't bother trying to conceal his own lustful arrogance, his vain intent to devour youthful purity. Advantageous match aside, how could anyone's own mother willingly cast her trusting daughter to such a wolf? Hopefully Morgan would find a way to utilize Raleigh's excessive ego—and perhaps even cajole out of him some detail of major importance.

The grounds below were bathed in silvery glow as the moon emerged from behind a lone cloud and painted the hedges and fountain spray with magical splendor. The lavish gardens attested to the Thomas wealth, as did the elegance of the interior of the mansion. Truly, she and Morgan came from very different worlds. Would she find the same acceptance from Mrs. Thomas as Morgan had found from Pa? But Papa had been in dire need of Morgan's talent and experience. Would Morgan's mother ever have need of her?

Well, no matter. She and Morgan were, in fact, married. His mother would *need* her to be an asset to her son. Prudence smiled. The poor woman had her work cut out for her. Mistress Thomas had been stunned to discover that Prudence had no musical accomplishments whatsoever, and had adamantly declared that the matter would be rectified. Prudence had been unable to resist playing that up for all it was worth, divulging that her father had considered dallying in the arts to be frivolous and had insisted upon instructing her in how to keep ledgers instead. *My father,* she had added without batting an eye, *wanted me to fully understand that money does not simply fall from the sky, as so many young women of my station believe.*

What priceless indignation had flooded Mistress Thomas's patrician features. Prudence savored the memory of it and could still hear the woman's remarks echoing in her mind. *Women,* she had said, *have enough of their own concerns to contend with without being burdened with those of men. Which, my dear,* she had added with an almost sincere smile, *you will soon learn, when you are blessed with children of your own.*

A bittersweet twinge caught at Prudence's heart. She and Morgan had been married for more than five months now, and her time still arrived as surely as the new moon. Of course, he'd been away from her a good portion of those months. Now, at least, they'd be together for a while. But with the uncertainties of war, perhaps it was best they not be blessed just yet.

Returning to the big empty bed, Prudence flopped impatiently across it. What was taking Morgan so long?

Within moments, footsteps and murmured good-nights drifted from outside the chamber door.

Prudence jumped up as Morgan came in, and she rushed to him. "Well?" she whispered, propping her hands on his chest as he wrapped his arms about her.

He pulled her some distance away from the door. "Nothing definite, I'm afraid. With my father present, I was hesitant to pry."

"Oh, you," she groused in disappointment. "Then why did you banish me to my room as if I were no more than a mere child?"

He rubbed her nose in the darkness. "Actually, love, I was far more interested in seeing that Evelyn was taken upstairs.

And it worked, didn't it? There is no way on earth I will allow that philanderer to have his way with my little sister."

Prudence nodded in agreement.

"One thing, though," Morgan continued softly. "The bloke does have a loose tongue. He said the British will initiate an attack before the month is out. That, of course, would be no surprise to anyone." Drawing away, he crossed to a chair and sat down to remove his shoes. "A pity he did not know the exact date. He did confirm what our generals suspect, however. The attack will be massive and—they hope—decisive. They are counting on total victory before winter."

"Oh, my."

He raised a palm. "The windows are open, and Mother's sitting room is next to this one."

"We haven't spoken above a whisper." Nonetheless, she went to close the windows.

Movement below caught her attention. Stepping back slightly, she motioned for Morgan to join her.

A figure stepped from the shadow of a tree. The blue-white light of the moon illuminated a billowy night shift. Evelyn!

Then from the hedges near the back, a man came forth.

Morgan went rigid. "That sneaky—," he hissed under his breath. He thrust the upper half of his body out the window.

Grabbing his shirttail, Prudence yanked him back inside.

"What in blazes has been going on here while I've been away?" He wheeled around and charged out of the room in his bare feet.

"Oh, dear," Prudence whispered, heading for the window again. She had never seen Morgan in such a rage. If only there were some way to warn her new sister-in-law . . . but that much noise would surely also be heard by the girl's parents.

Then she saw Evelyn melt into the man's embrace.

Prudence tucked her chin. And she and Morgan had actually believed the girl was an innocent!

6

His hand on the latch of the back door, Morgan paused just long enough to gain control of his rage. He was more than merely angry with his sister. He was deeply disappointed in her. Evelyn, always his pet, had claimed to have hated the vapid way their mother and older sisters acted. How could she have changed so much in such a short time? Apparently the two years he had been away had been very crucial ones for her, and all that time he had been such a careless dolt he'd scarcely given her a thought.

Well, that was about to change. He was home now . . . and perhaps this reason for returning was far more important than taking up his role as a spy again. After all, the answer to that dilemma had eluded him thus far.

Inhaling a calming breath, Morgan slipped quietly outside. It would be best to catch the slimy snake in the act. Even as he pictured the despicable spoiler, Morgan's fingers balled into fists. He wouldn't mind giving that aquiline nose a new shape.

He moved toward the steps to the garden and from there could already hear whispering. The trunk of a massive oak provided an effective shield as he eased on silent feet toward the pair.

Peering ever so gradually around the base of the tree, Morgan saw the bounder boldly kissing Evelyn full on the mouth. Livid, he tapped the cad's shoulder.

The man started in surprise and turned. A sharp jab to the chin sent him sprawling onto the grass.

Evie gasped in shock.

Jamie Dodd! Morgan recognized the gangly, copper-haired younger brother of Micah Dodd, one of Philadelphia's Sons of Liberty. The lad sat up, dazed, rubbing his jaw, his eyes narrowed in pain.

Evelyn, too horrified even to look guilty, sent Morgan a withering glare as she reached down to help Jamie up. Then she stared at her brother, hands on her hips.

Morgan looked from one to the other in total confusion as he rubbed absently at his sore knuckles. He cleared his throat. "What were you and my sister doing?" he demanded quietly with as much authority as he could muster.

"Certainly not what you imagined," Evelyn hissed. She glanced at the flustered Jamie with a frown and brushed some grass from his shoulder. "I've never been more humiliated in my entire life."

"I only came to tell Evie good-bye," Jamie said, his voice cracking on the last word. "I'm off to New York tomorrow to join the Continental army."

Morgan was not ready to let go of his doubts yet. "And I suppose you just happened by at the very time my sister decided to take a moonlight stroll in her nightclothes. Surely you don't think I'm such a dunce I'd fall prey to that!"

"Will you be quiet?" Evelyn pleaded under her breath. "You'll wake the entire household." She grabbed Morgan's arm and tugged him into the shaded seclusion while the young man followed. She stopped and turned. "If you must know, dear brother, I've been meeting with Jamie these past two years since you so blithely shirked your duties here without so much as informing the Dodds or any other of your fellow Sons of Liberty that you were leaving Philadelphia. The very night after you left, poor Jamie waited half the night for you. When he didn't give up and go away, I came out to explain."

"You?"

"Yes, me. And since I happened to have heard an interesting tidbit of my own, I passed that along. Otherwise, poor Jamie would have stayed out here all night for nothing."

"You were aware of my affiliation with the Sons of Liberty?" Morgan asked in alarm.

"Of course. Though you didn't have enough confidence in your own favorite sister to tell her yourself."

"Who else knew about me? Frances?"

"That ninny?" Evie scoffed. "She can't see anything beyond her looking glass—unless it's red as a lobster coat."

"Then earlier tonight, with Clay Raleigh . . . You really aren't—"

Evelyn rolled her eyes and shook her head. "I simply allow the useless fop to think anything is possible. It makes him most willing to attend me at parties where talk is as loose and free as he'd like to be with me."

In a surge of brotherly pride, Morgan seized her and hugged her hard. "Oh, bless you. I needn't tell you what I'd been thinking up till now." But then another realization dawned on him. He eased her away. "Wait a minute. You're far too young to be playing such dangerous games. All manner of evil could befall you." He swung to Jamie, seizing him by both arms. "How dare you enlist the aid of my little sister to spy?"

The lad straightened to his full height, which was several inches shorter than Morgan. "I did no such thing. I tried my best to talk her out of it. But she said she would use your signal, then wait until I came—even if it meant days or the risk of being caught. She gave me no choice. So whenever I saw just the one curtain fastened back, I came as soon as it was safe."

"Some excuse that is." Morgan had to fight a strong impulse to throttle them both as he digested the discomforting news.

Evie stepped forward, her eyes aglow in the subdued light of a half-moon. "Well, it's the truth. He tried to get me to quit every time he saw me."

"That's right," the lad said, nodding. "And I did get her to promise not to deliberately spy. Only to pass on information she heard naturally."

"So you might as well let go of him, Morgan. This has all been my idea. Jamie never once used the signal asking me to meet him. Not once."

At the quiet fervor in her voice, Morgan eased his grip and released him.

"So today," Evelyn went on, "when I saw his string tied to the lamp post, I knew he must have something terribly important to tell me. It was the longest, most unbearable evening of my life, with you men downstairs droning on about how the patriots can't possibly hold off the British. I thought you'd never bid Clay good night and go upstairs to bed. And now, to learn Jamie is going away . . . to take part in a hopeless battle . . ." She threw her arms around the lad. "Oh, please don't do it, Jamie. Please, don't go."

He held her tight, his own expression strained. "I must, kitten. Our boys need all the help they can get, or it *will* all be for nothing. We've worked too hard and too long to give up now. You've always wanted to do your part, Evie. Well, your part is to stay here and wait for me. Will you?" As she nodded, he looked over her head to Morgan. "I'll inform my brother you're back—that is, if you are."

Morgan winced at the accusation conveyed in the young man's tone. "I am. But this time I'm here on Washington's orders. Tell Micah that anything of importance must be taken directly to him. Can that be arranged?"

"Of course." A slow grin widened Jamie's cheeks. "So you haven't deserted the cause after all. My brother and the others will be glad to hear that—*and* glad to have you back. You were the best man we had. Now, if you don't mind, I'd like to have a few moments alone with Evie before I depart."

Hesitating, Morgan eyed the two of them.

Evelyn stretched up on her toes to whisper in his ear. "Yes, do go away. Please. He was just confessing his love for me. *Finally.*"

"But—"

She gave him a gentle push. "Go. Now."

With a last stern look at the young couple, Morgan relented and returned to the house. He was getting old. His own baby sister was blossoming into womanhood, and she had been spying for the patriots for two whole years already! Wait till Prudence heard about it!

This was certainly going to muddy things up, though. Now, not only would he spend untold hours worrying over what his wife might be doing, but he'd have to keep track of his sister's actions as well. To say nothing of the new risk posed by the possibility that someone might inadvertently overhear yet a third member of the household discussing matters of extreme importance. Returning inside, Morgan started up the stairs.

And Robby thought he had worries merely because his wife and children were in Rhode Island! At least they were with her parents and a good hundred miles from the nearest enemy . . . *not supping with them!*

"The children are finally down for their naps," Emily MacKinnon announced cheerily. "Peace and quiet. Even their doting grandma should appreciate it today." Removing the pins from her bedraggled hair, she twirled the length of it and deftly swirled it into a bun again as she sank down beside her brother Ben's wife.

Abigail smiled and set the big bowl of fresh beans between them on the porch step. "It's nothing like it was when all the other grandchildren were here. Then, a quiet moment was completely unheard of." She snapped the ends off the beans in her hand and took another bunch.

Emily took a handful and began helping with the chore. Having heard quite a bit about timid little Abigail before she met her, Emily had taken to her right away, glad to have another sister around again. Abby still tended to be quiet in large family gatherings, but no remnants of apprehension remained in her turquoise eyes now. Her children and Emily's seemed to get along surprisingly well, too.

"I truly love this wonderful farm," Abby said in her airy voice. "There's always so much happening here. Cassandra and Corbin are fascinated by the horses, especially the foals and colts. And if someone mentions that some of the other cousins are coming for a visit, they can hardly sleep for the excitement."

Emily nodded, gazing off toward the pastures. The animals were mostly clustered in the shade beneath the trees, motionless in the lazy afternoon except for the swishing of their long tails as they kept pesky flies at bay.

"I've even started looking forward to the family visits, if you can believe that. I wondered, at first, if I'd ever truly fit in . . . but everyone has been so kind and caring. They've all gone out of their way to make us feel at home. Now I really enjoy being around the other women . . . especially since we've all been left behind to wait for our husbands."

"You know, of course," Emily teased, "that the lot of us are all quite jealous of you."

"Of me?" Abby said, amazed.

Emily nodded. "Unlike the rest of us, your husband manages to come home every week or so."

"Oh." A flush pinkened Abigail's fair cheeks beneath her wheat gold hair. "Well, I suppose being a courier does have its advantages," she said gently. "But Ben complains that his saddle sores are turning into calluses. Speaking of traveling, I do hope your sister Jane and her husband made it back safely to Vermont."

"I'm sure they did. There's been no word of the British moving down from Canada." She paused, looking off into the distance again. Some of the deep green leaves of summer were just beginning to fade. "From what Papa heard this morning in Providence, every last redcoat in the Americas is camped on an island just offshore from New York. Along with some regiments of mercenaries."

"Mercenaries?" Abby echoed.

"Soldiers King George hired from Europe. Germany, I believe. They're called Hessians."

"How awful." Abigail reached over to squeeze Emily's hand. "That must be very upsetting for you, what with your Robby encamped right there in New York."

"I try not to think about it," Emily confessed. "I pray for him a lot, and I rest in the fact that our heavenly Father loves Robby and all our other men very much, even more than we do. No matter how grim things might seem at the moment, that thought does help a little."

Abby didn't answer for several seconds. "I hope one day I will think that way as naturally as you do. It still takes someone to remind me."

"Don't feel bad about it," Emily said with a chuckle. "I'm still learning, along with many other things, to look to God first and trust that he knows best."

"I'm sure your brother Dan always does. He seems so wise."

Emily laughed aloud. "Considering he's a minister, he was rather a mess when he was separated from Susannah those many months. But, yes, most of the time they're both God's faithful servants. And they know the importance of being examples to their congregation."

Finished with the beans she had been snapping into her apron, Emily spilled them into the bowl, then took more. "I suppose I've always admired their love for God and their devotion to one another despite severe trials.

"But it does amaze me that he and his wife would choose to go to some faraway settlement. With Susannah being an English lady and all, I do pray they fare well in the wilds of Pennsylvania."

"Jonathan Bradford, a good friend from Dan and Susannah's Princeton days, said the troubled Wyoming Valley was in much need of an impartial man of God. His plea was quite convincing. And Felicia will be with them, too. After spending time of her own in the Virginia mountains, she should be a big help."

"I don't understand why Felicia went, really. With her husband being a sailor, she'll never get to see him."

"Yancy needed to know she was safe. Since he's off at sea so much, he didn't want to be worrying about her welfare."

Abby shrugged. "I guess it's not too different with you and Robby. He wanted you to go back to Princeton. But you're still here."

"You mean you don't enjoy my company?" Emily asked with a droll smile.

"Oh, I do. Truly. It's just . . ."

Emily gave a comforting squeeze to her sister-in-law's shoulder, then snapped the last bean. "With all the men away, and old Elijah barely able to work anymore, I don't want to leave Papa with the entire farm to run by himself. When he finds help, then I'll go." Tipping the slender vegetables into the bowl with the rest, she stood. "In fact, it's nigh unto feeding time. I'd best go to the well and start drawing water. If Katie and Rusty wake up before I'm through in the barn, would you mind keeping an eye on them?"

Returning from the water trough a short time later, Emily heard Abigail squeal. She gazed toward the porch of the sprawling two-story house and saw her sister-in-law spring to her feet and run down the lane.

Ben came into view. Emily heard her brother's delighted laugh, then watched him leap down from his mount and gather his wife into his arms, his tricorn tumbling from his tawny head. Abby's feet didn't touch the ground as he swung her in exuberant circles. They smothered each other with kisses.

Emily's heart constricted with loneliness. No wonder all Abby's sisters-in-law envied her. Watching the passionate reunions of the recently married pair intensified their own solitary existences.

Oh, Robby, where are you? How are you? Do you feel as empty as I do?

Emily recalled her own former days with a sad smile. She had been slightly younger than Abigail when Yancy Curtis came to hide Robby MacKinnon in one of the outbuildings of the farm. Ruthlessly impressed into service as a cabin boy aboard the ill-fated *Gaspee*, Robby had jumped ship mere moments before Rhode Islanders torched the vessel, which had run aground on a sandbar. When two British officers came to supper later that afternoon—one of whom was Susannah's own brother, Ted—Emily had whisked the charming Scot to safety right from under their noses. What an adventure! Even yet she smiled at the memory of how Dan had insisted Robby marry her to salvage her name. Her older brother's solicitation hadn't been necessary. Their love had grown so quickly they never wanted to be apart again.

Closing her eyes against the pain of her longing, Emily swallowed hard. Four long months, and only once in all that time had she seen her husband's handsome face. It seemed a year.

Before she started to cry, Emily turned away from the sight of the lovebirds and concentrated on her task.

"Emmy!" Ben called, coming toward her with Abby. "I saw Robby last week. He sent a letter for you. And a little present."

"How is he?" she asked breathlessly. "Does he still look fit? Has he lost weight?"

"You've nothing to fear concerning him. He's in the rear of the army, sitting on all the food and supplies. Trust me, he'll be the last to go hungry. That is, unless he gets transferred to a different company."

"Why?" she asked, suddenly concerned. "What do you mean?"

"Morgan is gone." Ben glanced around. "This information must not leave this farm. Morgan has been relieved of his duties as quartermaster and sent to Philadelphia again to spy."

"I see."

"That's only the half of it," he continued. "The day he received his order to go, who showed up out of the blue but Prudence, and she convinced him to take her along."

"I don't blame her." Emily folded her arms. "If it weren't for the children, I'd have been in New York ages ago!"

A frown connected Ben's straight brows. "As you well know, that is not where Robby wants you. While I was with him and Chandler, he tried to get leave to fetch you back to Princeton. But since the British are poised to attack any day, it was denied."

Denied! Emily had to fight tears. Only once in all this time had Robby been given leave. It wasn't fair.

"He asked me to try to find someone going to New Jersey who would be willing to escort you."

"And what about the horse farm, Ben? Papa's all but alone here, you know. I can't leave him with all the work."

"Where is Pa?" Ben asked, scanning the grounds.

"He left a while ago for Boston with a string of horses. He's had a number of orders since folks up there lost so many during the siege."

"Right." Ben rubbed the bridge of his nose. "Mostly eaten." Stepping away from Abigail, he withdrew a letter and a small package from his inside vest pocket and handed them to Emily. "From your dearly beloved. He told me to kiss you for him, but I declined." He grabbed Abby close. "I'd rather kiss this pretty lass. But you can imagine this is Robby kissing you, if you like." With a teasing smile in his light brown eyes, he claimed Abby's lips.

It was more than Emily could bear to watch. She snatched the water bucket and walked away, Robby's letter and gift clutched tightly in her other hand.

Once she was out of sight, she stopped alongside the barn and set down the pail. She lowered herself to the ground and removed the ribbon and wrapping paper from the present. Her eyes misted at the sight of the lovely silver bracelet Robby had sent her. She could envision him standing at the jeweler's, eyeing every item in stock as he selected just the perfect extravagance. Having come to America with limited funds, he had never been one to waste money on frivolities, but he would sometimes surprise her with a little bauble for no particular reason. She cherished each one. Now he had spent money he could ill afford, just to send his love.

She pressed his unopened letter to her heart. She would save it until she'd finished with the horses and had some time alone without fear of interruption. And for those few precious minutes, she would pretend Robby was there with her, saying all the sweet words he had written . . . and more. So much more.

Chandler gradually opened his eyes and stretched his sore muscles. The bed of the tarp-covered wagon hadn't seemed quite so hard when he and Robby first sought shelter there last night. Now, with the arrival of morning, his whole body protested in discomfort.

Beside him, Robby stirred.

"Did you hear the shots?" Chan asked sleepily.

"More thunder, no doubt." The Scot sat up and began untying one of the ropes securing the canvas covering. As he raised the edge of a flap, the brilliant glare of the rising sun reflecting over the bay struck their weary eyes. "On second thought, it couldna' be that. The sky is crystal clear."

Chandler squinted and tugged at another knot pulled tight by the force of last night's wind. Oftentimes throughout the gale he wondered if the meager covering would hold. The storm had prevented their prompt return to New York after delivering supplies to Colonel Hand's outpost.

Three more measured shots ripped the air. Almost instantly movement could be heard outside.

Eyeing one another, they put on their boots and crawled out of the opening Robby had managed to make.

The grass around them was slick and wet. Members of the First Pennsylvania Rifle Battalion were emerging from the various canvas shelters, some still yanking on boots and buckling belts.

Something was amiss. Chandler ran into the open and gazed beyond the planted fields. The Narrows between Staten Island and the shoreline, less than a mile away, glistened white with sails. Landing craft of every shape and size were reaching shore, discharging Crown regiments. Already there were hundreds of redcoats on the beach, while many more longboats ran aground to debark additional soldiers. It had been rumored that the enemy numbered more than twenty-five thousand, and it appeared that at least half that number were on their way. Chan felt a twinge of fear even as adrenaline coursed through him.

"May the Almighty have mercy on us," Robby said beside him. "We should've gone back to New York last night, storm or no."

The rat-a-tat of a drum called the men to arms. Colonel Hand, a levelheaded Irishman who had served most effectively as an officer in the British army before settling in Pennsylvania, raised the flap of a large tent and came out. He pulled on his gloves, then took a spyglass from a young soldier at his side.

To a man, everyone stopped what he was doing and waited while their leader surveyed the distant scene. A few untried men whimpered among themselves. After today, they would be less likely to bawl like babies, Chandler assured himself. If they survived this day, they would be hardened veterans.

"We should get going," Robby whispered. "The ferries crossin' to New York will be clogged soon, and it's a good ten miles from here."

Feeling guilty at the thought of leaving this lonely battalion of sharpshooters here at the forefront, Chan hesitated, but he and Robby did have their own duties to consider. Besides, the Scot had never yet faced a British volley, and Chan would just as soon keep it that way. He joined his friend on the wagon they'd left hitched through the night.

"Atten-tion!" one of the sergeants hollered, mustering the men.

Robby snapped the reins over the team's backs, and the wagon lurched into motion.

"Halt that thing at once!" the colonel yelled.

A sergeant strode quickly toward them. "Where in blazes do you two think you're going?"

"Back to the main storehouses," Robby replied. "We're assigned to a quartermaster on Manhattan Island."

"Not today, you're not," the colonel said, joining them. "Today you will help us move our own stores and be available for any other detail."

Robby's chest puffed out as he saluted. "Yes, sir!"

"Report to the supply sergeant."

"Yes, sir!"

As they obeyed the new order, Chandler couldn't help feeling more than a little apprehensive about this development. He noted the small force of perhaps five hundred around them. Last night he had considered that a substantial number . . . but now, compared with the opposing army, it seemed pitifully small. Certainly no match for what would be coming at them across the open farmlands. On this neck of Nassau Island, barns and other outbuildings were few and far between.

The colonel raised his hand to silence the mumblings in the ranks. "Men, nothing usable is to fall into the hands of the enemy. No field crop, no grain in the barns, no hayricks. Burn the lot of them. Sergeants! Collect torches and disperse half the men. I want to see a wall of fire from the Narrows to the creek."

Wise plan, Chan decided as Robby guided the wagon toward the supply tents. Colonel Hand was covering their backsides, while never actually telling the men they were retreating. They would be kept far too busy to panic . . . and at the same time, a fire of that magnitude would signal the rest of Washington's army.

"We'll be loadin' up again," Robby muttered, "everything we unloaded last eve."

Chandler chuckled grimly. "Or burning it. Just keep your

musket close at hand, and do exactly what I tell you. Emily would never forgive me if I don't get you out of this in one piece."

❦ ❦

A knock sounded on the bedchamber door. Prudence, busy composing a letter to her stepmother in Massachusetts, quickly slipped the missive into a desk drawer. The unfamiliar weight of her lavender silk gown and petticoats felt cumbersome as she started to rise.

Evelyn stuck her head into the room before Prudence managed to untangle her feet. "The music instructor is downstairs waiting for you."

"Your mother certainly isn't one to waste time, is she?" With a light laugh, Prudence crossed the room to her new friend. "First you helped me select patterns and fabrics, then went shopping all day yesterday for accessories with me. You've been such a blessing, Evie. I had no idea there could be such a thing as an unfashionable style of wig. You've guided me wondrously through what seems a maze of social dos and don'ts."

Evelyn grinned and tossed her unbound brunette hair. "I've never had so much fun outwitting everyone. All this la-di-da folderol is just so much nonsense anyway."

"Nevertheless, you've been a godsend to me. Most of all, though, I'm so pleased Morgan and I don't have to fear being honest with you. I've already begun to think of you as my little sister . . . which reminds me." Turning to gaze at her reflection, Prudence repositioned a loose hairpin, then turned back. "Morgan asked me to speak to you regarding your—spying." She mouthed the last word. "He told me to convince you to leave that business to him, now that he's come home. He wants you and me to do nothing but continue to be the *lovely distractions* he considers us."

"Lovely distractions!" Evie's expression became sulky. "Surely you don't agree with my stuffy brother, do you? Just last night you told me how much you resented the intrusion

❦ 64 ❦

of your two brothers into the affairs of your own store after you'd worked so hard to get it running smoothly. Well, Morgan merely walked away from all his responsibilities here. I *had* to take over. And I know for a fact that I've been so good at it no one—not anyone at all—has even begun to suspect this *child* of anything." She batted her lashes most innocently.

Prudence stifled a giggle as she snatched Evie's hand and squeezed it. "That must have been so exciting for you."

"Oh, yes," Evie said with a huge smile. "Ever so."

"Well, you and I, we'll do as Morgan asks. We won't *deliberately* eavesdrop. We'll simply go on as you have in the past, being gracious minglers. *And very attentive listeners.* But we must agree to stay together. Morgan is beside himself with worry as it is, and I've promised to look after you."

"As *I* will look after *you.*" She tugged Prudence toward the door. "As a matter of fact, I've already solved your musical accomplishment dilemma."

Prudence slanted her a curious glance. "I can't imagine how. I've never so much as held a musical instrument in my entire life."

Evelyn fluttered her hand. "Before I came upstairs, I told the music teacher you have the sweetest, however untrained, voice!"

Prudence's mouth fell open. *"You didn't.* Surely I would be expected to get up before company and sing. I'd die of embarrassment."

Evie just grinned. "With the talent you have for playacting, all you need to do is pretend you can sing, and trust me, you'll have no problem whatsoever outdoing Millicent Sears. The silly music teacher once told her she had perfect pitch, and now we can't silence her. Why, I've heard cats yowling on the back wall at night that sound better than she does!"

"I'm sure you're exaggerating to make me feel better."

"I wish I were." Evelyn opened the door and swept out, the ruffled hem of her red polka-dot dimity brushing the jamb. She curled her index finger in a gesture to follow. "Come along, let me introduce you to the insipid Master Stanton.

He's such a namby-pamby; you're sure to hate him as much as I do. Always scraping and bowing to any influential Tory in sight. Just watch . . . no matter what Mother says, he'll agree. Remember, I've already praised you, so he'll rave about your singing and soon have Mother believing you're an enchanting songbird."

Prudence pulled the younger girl back into the bedchamber and closed the door. "Evelyn, please don't lose sight of the fact that mothers are to be treated with respect, even when we don't always agree with them. And as for your Master Stanton—surely you don't really hate the gentleman. You may hate what he stands for, but—"

Evie tipped her head and laughed. "What my brother said about you *is* true. When you're not playacting, you truly are a very proper New England Puritan!"

"Please don't consider that a bad thing. Even though we must perpetrate a charade to aid the cause, I would never want you to lose your sweet spirit. Morgan and I want you to always be as lovely inside as you are on the outside."

The younger girl's confident expression faded noticeably. "Do you think Jamie Dodd would still love me if he knew I was only fifteen and three-quarters? He thinks I'm eighteen, you see. He would never have allowed me to take over when Morgan left two Decembers ago if he'd known I had just turned fourteen that month."

"I see." Prudence knew better than to make light of it. Morgan had already informed her that the Son of Liberty was barely old enough to shave himself. His only expertise as Morgan's contact had been his ability to scale the back wall—though his boyish appearance didn't hurt, either. No one would suspect someone so young. "Well, if he truly does love you, your age won't matter."

"*If* I ever get another chance to see him alive again!" She became even more woeful. "In the last two whole months, I haven't heard a single person express belief that Washington's army has a chance against King George's forces. Our men will all be slaughtered—everyone is saying so. Even Jamie."

Prudence wrapped an arm around her and opened the door, and they stepped into the hall. "Don't you believe it for a minute. God is on our side. Now, come along. Let's go down and make your Master Stanton work for his money. I do believe a duet is in order, don't you? Yes, you and I shall become accomplished harmonizers."

"The . . . two of us?" Evelyn stopped.

Prudence nudged her gently onward. "Yes. You and I."

"But—"

It was almost impossible for Prudence to contain her growing merriment. "And won't we create the very distraction our Morgan desires? The oh-so-talented singing Thomas sisters."

❦ ❦

Distant booms from the British cannons had rarely ceased since the Crown force started their landing some hours ago. Chandler, at the front of the team, hauled on the lead gelding's halter, trying to urge the horses forward. On the seat of the wagon, Robby cracked a whip above their backs. With the trees around them and billowing smoke from the fires to cover their retreat, any view of the scene below was completely obscured.

"Up, you two! Giddap!" he urged.

The animals strained in their traces, hauling the loaded wagon through a dip so it could continue up the steep incline. With a great lunging leap, they finally managed to roll out of the hole and gain the top.

Chan released his hold on the halter and patted both geldings' necks. "Good boys. Good boys." He glanced at Robby. "Let's give them a few minutes' rest."

"Aye. They've earned it." He hopped off the high freight wagon. "'Tis a pity to have to resort to misusing the poor beasts like this."

"I know." Chan blotted his forehead on his sleeve. "But we

couldn't take a chance going up the road." He drew some water from the barrel in back and gave the horses a drink.

"Got any to spare?" someone called from a group of riflemen jogging up the hill.

"Sure do." He filled his and Robby's cups again and again and passed them to the thirsty soldiers.

"Happen to know the way to Green's entrenchments?" an unshaven regular inquired. "We're to regroup there."

"To the north," Robby answered, pointing. "See over yon? The banked dirt on the top of that hill. 'Tis his redoubt."

The fellow nodded and gulped down the cool liquid.

"Have you engaged the enemy yet?" Chan asked.

Wiping his mouth on the back of his hand, the man shook his head. "Hasn't been time. Been burning up and down the neck. Can't believe these local farmers refused to move their grain and livestock when Washington asked 'em to."

"The stupid New Yorkers never would believe there was gonna be an attack," another said. "By the time I had to shoot several fat cows and leave 'em to rot, I'd have gladly done the same to their owners."

A rawboned man came from behind the wagon. "Got me off a clear shot once, thanks to the breeze. Fired at a column of redcoats moving up the road toward Gravesend. Dropped one, too." He grinned, revealing a gap between his front teeth. "Did a little jig while the devils took potshots at me. Always did love that look they get when they discover I'm outta range of their puny Brown Besses. I reloaded to get another shot, but the wind shifted, and I couldn't see them no more through the smoke."

"'Twas one of God's creatures ye killed, me good man," Robby said quietly. "May the Lord rest his soul."

"Lobsterbacks ain't got souls," a low voice grated.

"We don't need to hear any more of your talk, Scotty," a gruff sergeant said. "We got enough on our plate without you trying to heap guilt on it besides. We're at war."

Chandler had to wonder if Robby would be able to hold his own if they found themselves in a heated battle. At Bunker

Hill, there had been no time for philosophizing, only time to load and fire at the redcoats. Load and fire until they ran out of powder. And the British kept right on coming. Climbing over their own dead comrades didn't even slow them down. Nothing stopped them.

"Look!" someone shouted.

Chan turned. For the first time since early morning, a wide panorama slowly became visible. A line of red stretched along the shoreline for five or six miles. Another red line moved inland on the road leading to the redoubt on the hill, exactly as the rifleman had reported . . . the very road Chandler and Robby would have preferred rather than taking the wagon up this rugged terrain. And worse, there wasn't a single soldier down there trying to stop them!

The colonial army had only two defensive positions between Brooklyn Heights and New York—a pair of redoubts, two mud-banked square holes. One was at the top of a ridge on the Heights of Guan, flanked by a few trenches, and the other on the plain between the two heights. They were in dire need of more. Many more.

Chandler wasn't the only one stunned. No one around him uttered a word.

"Stop lollygagging," the sergeant finally ordered. "Get moving again—and step lively."

Robby, ashen-faced, climbed aboard the wagon and snapped the whip.

Chan hopped on as it sprang into motion. He tried to distinguish the redoubt, about half a mile to the north along the ridge, but its size was so insignificant and the trees so many, there was rarely a clear view of it. How could General Washington put all his efforts into protecting only the port city and the Hudson? Surely in the past four months this area could have been fortified much better than this!

But as he mulled over the thought, he knew the answer. Washington wasn't to blame. The general's efforts to build a cohesive army had been blocked at every turn. Congress rarely sent supplies, and they neglected to pay in a timely fashion as well. Most of the volunteers, who hadn't seen the action Massachusetts men had, were not taking the war any more seriously than Congress. By the hundreds they invented ailments to relieve them of duty. Some just plain deserted. It had been reported that last week an entire New Jersey company got tired of digging ditches and went home, saying they'd be back if anything ever happened.

Some army, this Continental force. Well, now they would have to become one . . . or be crushed.

8

Morgan saw his mother glance at the mantel clock and sigh. Evelyn, studying her nails while their father paced the study, met Morgan's glance and raised her eyebrows. Out in the parlor, the grandfather clock bonged seven times.

He cleared his throat. "I'll see what's keeping Prudence. We'll be down directly." Taking the steps two at a time, he made short work of the staircase, then went straight to their bedchamber.

He entered, only to find a glorious profusion of saffron ruffles and white lace sticking up from beside the four-poster. His wife was on her hands and knees, feeling around beneath the bed. "Where *is* it?" she muttered to herself in exasperation.

Unable to resist such an inviting sight, Morgan smiled and crept noiselessly behind her. In one fluid motion he dropped down beside Prudence and rolled her atop himself, her wig sliding askew in the process.

"Morgan!" she gasped, making a futile attempt to right the elaborate powdered creation.

He grinned and pulled her back down, sprinkling her with kisses.

"So, you want to play games, do you?" With a smile, she flung her arm in a wild arc and sent his wig toppling to the floor.

"Ah, now see what you've done," he said, manufacturing a

scowl. "I shall, of course, have to retaliate." He reached to yank one of her white curls.

She dodged, and her skirts billowed about them as she grabbed his wrists. "Do be serious," she pleaded. "You'll spoil my entry into Philadelphia society."

"Now there's a thought," he returned, drawing her face to within inches of his. He took the briefest second to drink in beauty not at all diminished by such trifles as a lopsided wig or a somewhat inglorious pose. "If your attire were to meet with some mishap or other, I shouldn't have to worry about your giving us away this eve."

"Me?" she asked. "You're the one who ran out into the night chasing after your sister, who, incidentally, happened to be spying herself. You might have given her away."

"Is that right?"

"Yes." She brushed her nose playfully across his.

He knew he had but one recourse. Breaking her grip, he grabbed her on either side of her slender waist and squeezed.

"Oh, please, stop!" she giggled. "You know I'm ticklish."

"You are?" he asked in mock innocence as he intensified the assault.

Prudence could only shriek and writhe in helpless laughter.

"Whatever are you doing?" Evelyn cried, looming suddenly over them, the cornflower blue of her gown intensifying the color of her eyes.

"He-he's trying to muss me so I have to stay home," Prudence confessed between giggles. "He knows I'll show him up if I go."

"You don't say. We must see about that." She leaned down and tried to pry his fingers loose. "Let her go, you brute!"

Prudence took a deep breath and seized his other hand.

With a mighty roar, he tossed the girls off but grabbed both of their waists, pulling them close to sit beside him. "Now hear me. I am the lord and master here. Therefore, you must both obey what I say without question."

Prudence rolled her eyes, while Evelyn stuck out her tongue.

"Besides," he went on, relaxing his grip a little, "*I* happen to have orders from the commanding general, and I'm the one who's been ordered forth. You two shall be decoys, and that is all. Delightful, frilly, silly distractions. Evie—" he kissed her nose— "you are to stay close to us. Particularly to Prudence. Help her with the subtle details of etiquette—and nothing else."

"But what about Mr. Raleigh?" she asked. "He does so yearn to take me out into the night air to whisper sweet Tory nothings in my ear."

Morgan turned to Prudence, kissing her upturned nose also. "If I'm occupied, don't you let this *child* out of your sight, even for an instant. It's bad enough I caught her trying to—"

"Caught whom?" Mother demanded from the doorway. "Doing what?" She planted her knuckles on either side of her swagged brocade skirts, her face drawn.

Morgan felt a jolt of panic, wondering how long she had been standing there and exactly what she had overheard.

"And for heaven's sake," she went on in her customary tone, "get off the floor, the lot of you. Here it is, past the time we should have left for the Somerwells', and you're down there crushing everything it took the servants hours to iron."

"It's his fault," Evie said, pointing to Morgan. "He's being a bully. As usual."

"Then, child," Mother retaliated, "since you are so ready to accuse, you won't mind telling the rest of the misdeeds in question. Whom did Morgan catch doing what?"

Evelyn clambered to her feet. "The bully thinks I flirt with Mr. Raleigh." She smiled at Morgan in triumph as she straightened her skirts, fluffing out the ruffles. "He feels that because I occasionally smile at an admirer, I'm acting unladylike."

Mother tightened her lips and shifted her glare to Morgan still on the floor. "Your sister has become quite the accomplished young miss while you were away. It is most acceptable for her to flirt a bit with her young man. And, might I add, most advantageous. The mere thought that he might take more than a passing interest in our dear Evie makes my head light. Do you have any idea what an exceptional catch he would be for her? Not to mention the marvelous business connection for us all." She swung back to her daughter. "Go over to the mirror and center your wig, dear. It's crooked."

While their mother was preoccupied, Morgan stood up, then reached down to assist Prudence.

"Not just yet," she whispered. She lifted the hem of the bedcoverings and resumed her search.

"What are you looking for?"

She turned her eyes up at him. "You'll think I'm careless. I dropped one of those enchanting earbobs you bought me, and it bounced under here."

He knelt to help her.

"Mercy, Prudence," Mother chided. "Get off that floor. Let your husband find it for you. And from now on, if he's not available, ring for a servant. That's what they've been hired for." She whirled around. "And if all of you are not downstairs within the next two minutes, we'll leave without you. I'll not be conspicuously late for you or anyone else." She stomped away.

"Yes, Prudence," Evie said with a giggle. "Don't ever forget. Husbands and servants. Servants and husbands. They're all at your beck and call. So don't let that brute make you think otherwise."

"Oh, I won't, I assure you."

"Ha! I found it." Morgan scooted out from under the bed, the sparkling diamond bauble in his hand. He switched his attention to his sister. "And now, I'm coming to set *you* to rights, brat. 'Tis high time you had a good tanning."

Evelyn squealed and ran from the room as he lunged to his feet.

As Prudence reached for the ornament he held in the palm of his hand, Morgan clamped his fingers tightly over it. "Not so fast, my love. Even a bully deserves some reward."

"Oh. How utterly thoughtless of me." With a beguiling smile, Prudence wrapped her arms about his neck. "Will this do, my handsome and ever so chivalrous brute?" The light kiss turned swiftly to one quite passionate.

Morgan pulled her close, inhaling the enticing perfume she wore as he responded to her with fervor of his own.

"Morgan! Prudence!" came the screech from below.

Releasing a ragged breath, he reluctantly loosened his embrace. "Don't forget where we left off," he breathed against her temple. "When we return, we'll pick up from this point."

Her silver-gray eyes shimmered with unconcealed anticipation as she took the earbob from his hand.

❧ ❧

Chandler lost count of the thousands of British campfires glowing far below the earthen wall of the redoubt. He and Robby wolfed down their biscuits and beans after a long and tiring day, their legs dangling over the enclosed defensive fortification. Occasional rifle shots, undoubtedly from their sniping Pennsylvania riflemen, split the quiet.

With a low chuckle, Chan stretched his sore muscles. "Colonel Hand isn't planning to let them sleep in peace tonight."

"Aye," Robby said, "just like at the Boston and Charlestown barricades. Those awesome long-range rifles will shoot at anything that moves throughout the night."

"Well, we sure don't want those puppets getting it into their heads to take a stroll up here just yet." He took another mouthful. "Hey, there's something odd. I'm surprised I didn't notice it before."

"Notice what?"

"Except for the colonel's riflemen, there aren't any of our regulars in this assembly. Just a couple local militias with virtually no training."

Robby nodded slowly. "When I was fetching our food, I heard somethin' else just as disturbing. General Green, the officer in charge of the defense of this whole island, is down with a fever."

"Someone better send reinforcements soon, or there's no

sense in staying here on Nassau. Funny, isn't it? If the redcoats knew that, they'd be having supper with us right now."

"Ye see humor in that?" Robby asked with a scowl.

Chan averted his eyes and straightened. "Don't look up, but here comes that sergeant we talked to earlier. Landers, I believe someone said his name was."

When the man was too close to ignore, the two put down their plates, then stood and saluted him.

He returned the salute. "One of my men told me you two saw action on the Concord road and at Bunker Hill."

"Only me friend, here, sir," Robby admitted. "He was one of the last to leave Bunker Hill."

Chandler glanced disparagingly at his loose-tongued buddy. What was he trying to do to him? "Nothing to brag about, sir. It just so happened I came upon a full horn of powder as I was in retreat, so I used it up before I left."

"Aye, that he did," Robby added, nodding. "Covered the retreat of scores of others. His friend, Lieutenant Thomas, told me all about his heroism."

Already Chan was composing in his mind the little speech he would soon cram down the Scotsman's throat—just before he throttled him.

"Here. Take this." Ruddy-faced Sergeant Landers thrust his Pennsylvania rifle to Chandler, then followed it with a haversack containing the required fixings for it.

Chan suppressed an inward groan. So much for being assigned to safe duty with a quartermaster.

"I don't have enough seasoned men," Landers continued. "I want you to go down there for a couple hours and keep the lobstercoats entertained. Just remember to stay out of range, and keep moving."

"Yes, sir."

"I volunteer to go, too," Robby announced, his expression as wary as it was determined.

"Sure. I'm not fool enough to turn down a volunteer."

"But—sir," Chan cut in. "I'll not be responsible for him out there."

"I'm not askin' ye to be responsible for me," Robby said, hiking his chin. "I can take care of myself."

Chandler shook his head and offered the firearm back to the sergeant. "I'll not go if you send him, sir. He's got a wife and two babies back home."

"So have half the men here, lad."

"But he's never faced a volley of fire. We don't know yet how he'll react under that pressure. He could get the two of us killed." Hating himself for intimating that Robby might be cowardly, Chandler reaffirmed his decision that the young Scot would remain out of harm's way.

"What's your name, Corporal?" the sergeant asked, his tone menacing.

"Chandler, sir. Robert Chandler."

"Well, Corporal, get yourself off this hill—and don't come back until you're out of powder."

"Yes, sir!" Slinging the haversack over his shoulder, Chan picked up his mug and drained the last of his coffee as the older man strode off.

Robby, obviously fuming, reclaimed his plate and stabbed at the food remaining on it.

"Sorry about what I said," Chandler began. "I know you're no coward. That's precisely the problem."

The wiry Scot leveled his gaze at him, his blue eyes unwavering. "You're not responsible for me . . . no matter what Morgan told ye."

"Well, we are responsible for that team and wagon," Chan said pointedly. "One of us should stay alive long enough to return it to our supply camp, right?" With a grim nod, he turned toward the nearest sally port.

"I'll pray for your safety all the while you're down there," Robby said quietly, no lingering trace of anger in his voice.

Chan saluted with his rifle. "Find a deep hole to sleep in. If I know General Howe, he'll have the big guns brought up before morning."

9

As Morgan helped her down from the family carriage, Prudence assessed the brick mansion owned by the wealthy friends of the Thomas family. The setting sun cast a rosy hue over the generous dormers and large Palladian window above the columned portico, lending a lovely contrast to the candle glow pouring from every window of the two-story home. But even in a grand city like Philadelphia, it seemed excessive. With her hands on Morgan's arm, she started up the walk, smiling with as much confidence as she could summon.

The ornate white front door opened, and a uniformed butler admitted them up the hall to an open doorway beyond, where a stately middle-aged couple waited. Both had amazingly similar squarish faces and high foreheads, though the woman's features were noticeably more defined and elegant, and her coloring was fair in contrast to his. "Waldon," the man said with a welcoming smile. "And Mildred. Splendid of you to come."

"Good evening, Landon, Rose." Morgan's father and their host exchanged warm handshakes, while the others entered amid a flurry of greetings.

"And how wonderful to see Morgan," the host went on. "I'm sure the young ladies in attendance will be quite thrilled."

"Landon, dear," his wife said with well-modulated politeness. "I must have forgotten to mention that Morgan has wed.

I was quite taken aback when Mildred told me a few days ago."
Switching her attention to Prudence, she offered her hand.
"Am I to assume, my dear, that you are the one who somehow
managed the impossible?"

Morgan stepped forward. "She is, I am most delighted to
confess. I should like to introduce my wife, Prudence." He
turned to her. "These are old friends of our family, sweetheart. Mr. and Mrs. Somerwell. We've known them for as far
back as I can remember." Smiling graciously, he nodded to
them. "This happens to be my darling wife's introduction to
Philadelphia society."

Prudence, touched by the love and manly pride in his
voice, felt a blush rise on her cheeks as the couple appraised
her. "I'm very pleased to meet you both."

"We are most happy all of you were able to come this eve,"
Rose Somerwell said pleasantly. "Some friends of ours have
written a new play, which they will enact for the first time just
for us. Later, there will be games, music, and, of course,
dancing. It is my fond hope, Prudence, that afterward you'll
think kindly of our fair city . . . the true Philadelphia, as it
once was before all the uproar. May it soon regain that glory."
She closed her blue eyes for a brief second and shook her
head.

"And in the meanwhile," her husband announced, "we
shall take our seats. Alas, there's not time to offer you refreshments just now. The production is about to begin."

"We must offer you our most sincere apologies," Mother
Thomas said, "for being so tardy."

Knowing that it was due in large part to herself, Prudence
vowed silently not to repeat this blunder. She certainly didn't
intend to earn a bad mark in the eyes of her mother-in-law or
any of the family's influential friends.

"Now, Mother," Morgan said smoothly, "you mustn't accept
blame that is mine. Cad that I am, 'twas I who made us late. I
was holding my beautiful wife captive in our chamber."

At Landon Somerwell's chuckle, Prudence felt her flush

return in force. She didn't have to wonder what he was thinking.

"And but for your age, Son," Mother chided, "I would reprimand you for teasing the poor girl. She lost one of the earbobs Morgan gave her, you see," she explained to the Somerwells, "and wouldn't leave until it was found."

"That was when the bully took her captive," Evelyn blurted in delight.

Her mother branded her with a stern look, then stepped closer to the sequined-gowned hostess. "I simply don't know where I erred with these two. Our other children were so wonderfully pliable." The two women glided toward the rows of chairs in the room as the lighting was subdued in preparation for the performance.

"Evie," Mr. Thomas said, sidling up to her, "knowing the sort of memory your mother has, I would suggest you find a way to make amends before the evening is over."

"You're right, Papa." She gave him a dutiful peck on the cheek, then hooked her arm through his.

Morgan's attempt to follow was interrupted by their host.

"I heard something to the effect that you had left our fine city with Ben Haynes. Have you, perchance, seen Cousin Sophia and the rest of Ben's family while in your travels?"

"Actually, I spent a most delightful time at the Hayneses' farm with the entire family two Christmases past. Due to the blockade and the siege of Boston, however, I've seen them but once since then. They were all in good health—and remarkably good spirits, considering."

Watching the man assimilate this information, Prudence thought of Robby MacKinnon, Sophia Haynes's son-in-law. Not knowing what kind of peril he and Robert Chandler might be in at the moment, she sent a swift prayer heavenward for the safety of both young men.

"A plight which now is affecting all of us," Mr. Somerwell replied sadly. "Well, come along. We wouldn't want to miss the play. It's a farce featuring Saint George and the Dragon." But before they had taken a few steps, the door knocker tapped.

"Excuse me," he said. "We were expecting one more couple. I must go and greet them."

"What a pity the play isn't about King George meeting up with a few fire-breathing, monarch-eating dragons," Prudence whispered to Morgan after the host strode away.

He patted her hand where it rested in the crook of his elbow. "Let's hope, my darling, that Parliament has some of those very animals just waiting for the opportunity to devour him. The force he's assembled in New York harbor is costing a king's ransom, if you'll pardon my pun."

Prudence was amazed to see at least a hundred people gathered to watch the production. When the stage curtains parted to the applause of the audience, she didn't have to feign interest. She looked expectantly toward the set.

The scenes bordered on hilarious, with the man inside the silly dragon costume clumsily and haphazardly trying to manipulate the various parts of the ungainly beast. When he managed to blow red silk streamers from its mouth to simulate fire, it was comical enough to set everyone to laughing. And the hero, "George of the Willow Sword," was equally amusing. The entertainment ended with roaring applause.

Watching the small cast taking their bows, Prudence was convinced that Philadelphia truly was the liveliest city in all the colonies. Such free and easy laughter would have been unheard of in staid Boston.

Of course, there was no denying that in her former days she would have condemned such frivolity herself. Up until quite recently, she would easily have scorned anything or anyone who wasn't as starched and proper as she. But thankfully, the Good Lord had softened those judgmental feelings considerably, and now her only condemnation this eve lay in the fact that the charming, happy people around her were Tories.

As the clapping died down, the servants relit the candle sconces along the walls, illuminating the grand room with its satiny, pale green and ivory wallpaper and the garlands of fresh flowers that draped the tall windows. Musicians mounted the stage.

Mrs. Somerwell rang a small crystal handbell. "Your attention, please," she called above the noise and buzz of voices. "We must ask everyone to help clear the floor for games and dancing. If you would all please carry your chairs to the outer walls, it would help greatly. Thank you."

Evelyn, who had been sitting with friends a few rows ahead, lifted her chair and joined Morgan. "Honestly. That Clay Raleigh is such a dullard," she whispered. "All through the play he kept trying to attract my attention, but I pretended I couldn't hear or see him. You'd think he would take the hint. But," she added, with a mischievous smile reminiscent of her dashing brother's, "innocent-child-with-a-huge-dowry that I am, I'm incapable of deliberately toying with him, aren't I?"

Even as she spoke, the single-minded Englishman threaded his way toward her through the milling crowd. A split second before his arrival she set her chair down and coyly began fanning herself, then whirled around and collided with him—a move which appeared accidental. Her shell fan clattered to the floor.

"Oh, I must beg your pardon," he blustered, bowing to retrieve the fan. "Do forgive my clumsiness."

Prudence looked askance at Morgan, hoping her expression conveyed her amazement that the two of them had been worried about their poor little Evie, so innocent regarding the ways of the world.

"I believe you promised me the first dance," Raleigh said, offering her his arm.

Evelyn batted her lashes. "Why, how gallant of you to remember. But first, I have a dreadful thirst. We arrived too late for refreshments, I'm afraid."

"I noticed," he said, his voice rife with meaning.

"Then, if you'd be so kind." She gifted him with a charming smile, then turned to Prudence. "Oh, I am being rude. Pru, you and Morgan must be equally thirsty. Would you, Mr. Raleigh?"

His eager smile faded a shade. "But of course."

Once the man was out of earshot on his way to the crowded

beverage table, Evelyn rolled her eyes. "Now, isn't he just the handiest sort to have around?"

Morgan frowned. "Just remember, even pets have been known to turn on their masters. Your obedient bear could just as easily do the same to you. Don't let him get you alone, or you might find out exactly how handy he really is."

"I shan't worry about that overmuch," she said brightly. "You've vowed to shadow me this entire evening." Quickly she swung to Prudence. "Of course, I welcome *your* company, so I suppose I shall have to endure the bully's as well."

"Morgan!" a voice called from across the room. "Morgan Thomas!"

Looking toward the source, Prudence observed a young man waving. Within seconds, others converged on Morgan, all smiles, everyone talking at once.

Prudence knew her handsome husband had been rediscovered.

"Don't fret," he whispered with a quick hug. With his other arm he caught hold of Evie and tugged her close, too. "Ah, what a pity," he said with chagrin. "After having been so carefree all my life, now to suddenly be burdened with not one, but two damsels to look after."

Clumps of recently scythed grass felt prickly and rough through his shirt as Chandler crawled on his belly across an open field. The moon, rising higher, lent a pale blue glow to the world around him. What he would have given for some of the fog that now shrouded the ships anchored in the Narrows. He wasn't completely certain he was beyond the range of the British Brown Besses.

The silhouette of a redcoated sentry passed before a distant campfire. In his tall military hat he presented an excellent target, if only Chan had taken aim quickly enough. He'd wait for another chance.

From far away, a rifle report sounded. At once the guard and three other shadowy figures bolted from the vast encampment and into the field, heading toward the telltale flash from the rifle's pan. Professional soldiers all, each knew precisely what action to take without so much as a whispered order.

Chan could only hope the sniper had possessed sense enough to remove himself immediately from the spot, since the main fault with the long-range Pennsylvania rifle was the extra time needed to reload after firing. The redcoats could easily be upon the man before he managed that feat.

Another flash and crack shattered the air. One of the charging soldiers fell to the ground.

His cohorts halted and fired their muskets at the new flash, one of the balls digging up the ground dangerously close to Chandler. He froze and held his breath, knowing that they, too, would require time to reload.

Within seconds, crunching footsteps revealed the fact that the two king's men had managed to reload and were now running across the field toward the second sniper. A third stopped and brought up his musket but didn't fire.

Chan raised his head enough to scan the dim area.

When another crunch came from a new location, the sentry took aim and fired toward it.

A brief silence followed.

Knowing that the redcoat's musket was now empty, Chandler eyed him. The man was a good fifty yards from the others. A perfect time to take a bead on the fellow.

The sentry became aware of his vulnerability when moonlight glinted off the steel blade of his bayonet. He began backing toward the camp.

With the enemy framed in his sight, Chandler couldn't bring himself to pull the trigger. There seemed something cowardly about lying in wait for an unsuspecting man. Besides, his orders had been to keep the British awake and nervous, nothing more. He relaxed his hold and watched the soldier hesitate cautiously, then return to his post. His two comrades also returned to camp carrying the fallen man. Snatches of angry oaths carried easily to Chan's ears.

More flashes and shots rang out—this time from the British

side. Musket balls fell several yards short of the positions occupied earlier by the snipers. Chandler couldn't help wishing he could trade the cover of darkness for a few sturdy trees to hide behind.

He lay motionless for several minutes. Would they order a column out to send volleys into the night? He waited, tense with the uncertainty of it all. But the camp gradually settled down again. Wood was added to the fire, and several soldiers milled about, pouring coffee and talking.

Still, he couldn't simply lie there all night without doing something. Chan tried to choose a man to fire at . . . pick the one to send a shot ripping through. But the most tempting target hung a few inches above the fire. Steadying his rifle against his shoulder, he took deliberate aim, then squeezed the first trigger. He held his breath and moved his finger to the second, a hair trigger, and tapped it.

The flash blinded him momentarily, but with the explosion he heard a loud ring. Men yelped. The spots before his eyes cleared, and he saw soldiers leaping clear of the scalding coffee sputtering from the flames. He had hit his target.

"Get the blasted coward!" one of them yelled. They scrambled and ran for their weapons.

Chandler sprang to a crouch and beat a swift retreat.

A shot rang out somewhere nearby.

Within seconds another explosion roared, this one much louder, closer. The concussion all but knocked Chan off his feet as he sprinted through the night.

The British had brought up some artillery. The game was about to get rougher.

10

Morgan managed to smile at the merchant sea captains from England who were attending the gala. It was difficult to focus on trying to gain their trust, what with Evelyn flitting about from one man to another on the dance floor and Prudence, too, surrounded by eager swains. Though dancing was an entirely new venture for his wife, she had spent hours under his and Evie's tutelage and managed to learn fairly quickly the intricacies of the various minuets and reels. Now as he watched her glide gracefully over the floor on the arm of their host, he felt a strong surge of pride and struggled against cutting in.

Granted, when a horde of old friends converged on him and Prudence, he figured he was in for a merciless round of teasing—or worse, would have to endure their tattling to Prudence about his wilder days. But to a man, from the moment they gazed upon that incredible heart-shaped face of hers with its wide-set gray eyes, eyes just now perfecting the art of flirting, his so-called friends had stumbled over one another's feet vying for a turn on the dance floor with her. Loathe to be termed a jealous husband, he now had to stand by and watch, however hard that was to do.

"I, too, am becoming most impatient these days," one of the captains remarked to the others, his glance settling on each of them to ensure that they were in complete agreement. Nodding, they lifted their drinks. "Hear! Hear!"

Aren't we all, Morgan mused silently. He expended great effort to turn his attention away from his wife and make some headway toward what he was sent here to do.

"I'll tell you one thing," another ship's master said. "Unless something substantial is done posthaste to resolve this frightful mess, I shall set sail for Canada. I understand our friends in Boston suffered severe privation during the lawless siege, then had to leave most of their belongings behind when they fled to Halifax. That is true, is it not, Mr. Thomas?"

Morgan met the stout captain's concerned gaze. "Quite. Personally, I believe Parliament should see to it that they are reimbursed for all their losses."

A lantern-jawed sea master on the edge of the group scowled. "I hardly see how Britain should be expected to recompense colonists for what other colonists do to them, do you, gentlemen?" He circulated a scathing grimace.

"I daresay," Morgan interjected, "they were dwelling on one tiny peninsula supposedly under the protection of thousands of your military—who, I might add, promised to do just that. Protect them. But alas, the army quite shamefully neglected to fulfill its obligation. Not only did these poor loyal folk have their harbor blockaded by their very own protectors, depriving them of their livelihood, they were then starved, then forced to leave all their worldly goods behind. Do you not consider that appalling?"

One man gestured with his glass. "You know very well, lad, that Parliament's punitive action was directed at the outlaws."

"Ah, yes," Morgan responded. "But whom did it hurt? Not your outlaws, certainly. For the most part they had already left the city and reestablished themselves. But, on the other hand, my own wife's family home and business were burned to the ground. And now my dear mother is in terrible fear for her life as well, and for everything we've worked generations to build. All of this in a city where these Continental Congress rebels are meeting openly, recruiting armies and raising money to finance them. All to wage war against their own motherland."

"Armies?" one man asked in alarm. "Did you say *armies?*"

"I did." Morgan gave a decisive nod. Despite the fact that it was only wishful thinking at the moment, there was something quite appealing about the sound of it. "Why ever else would my mother be so fearful? And speaking of protection, I do believe it is time that I rescue my lovely wife from the wilds of Pennsylvania." Chuckling for effect, he gave them an opportunity to do the same. "If you'll excuse me, gentlemen." He bowed his head graciously and took his leave.

In mere seconds he spotted Prudence on the opposite side of the room, dancing with Dirk Martingale, a chum from his bachelor days. Morgan paused, admiring the beautiful vision she made in her saffron silk and fashionable wig as she dipped and swayed to the patterned steps. While he watched, his thoughts shifted back to the captains. He relished the impression he was certain he had made on them. It had been jolly fun putting the stuffy merchant seamen on the defensive about their government's inability to maintain order. Henceforth, they could only think of him as one more pompous, demanding Loyalist. Or so he hoped.

With the most beautiful wife here, he added, smiling to himself. He observed the way the candlelight sparkled over her necklace and earbobs and radiated from her luminous eyes. She made such an enchanting picture, it was hard to wait for the final strands of the minuet so he could reclaim her.

When the piece at last ended, he strode purposefully to the couple. "Sorry, old man," he told his friend as he snagged Prudence around the waist. "My wife has promised this next dance to me."

"Then I shall, with some reluctance, relinquish the enchanting damsel to you," Dirk said. Always a bit of a rake, he bowed over her hand as she curtsied, the gleam in his eyes more wolfish than anything else. Then he walked away.

Prudence lifted her gaze and smiled at Morgan with relief. "I am utterly parched. Do take me to the nearest cup of punch, or I shall swoon."

"As you wish." But as they started for the refreshment table,

Morgan suddenly remembered Evelyn and made a quick search among the guests. He spied her standing nearby with Clay Raleigh in the midst of a cluster of young people. The Englishman appeared even more feral than Dirk Martingale had, if that were possible. "I rather think we should cool our little Evie down, too," he told Prudence, steering her in that direction.

"That might be wise."

Morgan tapped his sister on the shoulder. "We're stepping across the hall for something cool. Care to join us?"

Evelyn looked from him to Prudence. "Why, that sounds lovely."

"I heartily agree," Raleigh added, without releasing her arm. He fell into step with them. "Afterward, perhaps a nice stroll in the garden might be appropriate." His intent gaze centered on Evie.

More than certain that the cad had some very inappropriate things on his mind, Morgan had to force a grin. "I say, that is an excellent idea. Don't you think, love?"

"Oh, yes," Prudence murmured. "A stroll in the garden would be divine. The late roses smell so wonderful."

The Englishman's own smile stiffened around the edges, while Evie's curved upward in wicked delight.

As they exited the grand ballroom and started across the entry hall to the dining room, a man burst through the front door. Panting and out of breath, he rushed to the wide entrance of the room, which was teeming with guests. "Hear, hear, everyone! Listen! The British landed a force on Nassau Island this morning. And they promise to deliver New York by the end of the week!"

A great commotion broke out. A man raised his arms for silence. "Who told you this?" he asked.

"An express rider by the name of Joseph Galloway just rode in from Staten Island. Said General Howe landed over fifteen thousand infantry and marines. His brother, Black Dick, moved his fleet into the Narrows. The rebels haven't a chance! They'll be nothing but bloody corpses when we're through with them."

With a broad smile, Landon Somerwell stepped onto the stage and raised his glass high. "This calls for a toast!"

"No! A cheer!" someone else yelled, leaping beside the host. "Hip hip hooray!"

"Hip hip hooray!" came the excited echo from all present. "Hip hip hooray!"

Morgan nudged Prudence, and together they made a valiant show of enthusiasm. But he could feel the tense grip of her hand on his arm.

Just as suddenly, she released her hand and took Evelyn by the shoulders, leaning close so Evelyn could hear above the uproar. Then she said something into the younger girl's ear. Morgan noted that Evelyn looked pale as death.

Prudence was up to something, of that he was certain. But what?

"Sweetheart," she said, swinging back to him. "I'm afraid your sister's upset stomach has returned. All this excitement, I'm sure. She needs to leave at once."

Evelyn hadn't been ill earlier. Nonetheless, Morgan picked up his cue. "You mean, she's about to . . ." He clutched at his throat.

Evelyn cupped her hand over her mouth with a frantic nod.

Clay Raleigh, having overheard the exchange, slanted a glance at her. "I must sadly bid you Godspeed, Miss Thomas. I pray you feel better soon." He distanced himself from her with such haste, Morgan might have laughed . . . if only his heart weren't so heavy.

He and Prudence each took one of the younger girl's elbows and led her outside. And none too soon. She all but crumpled the second they closed the door after themselves, her face already awash with tears. Trembling, she flung herself at her older brother. "Oh, Morgan," she sobbed. "Jamie's there. And all that awfulness is about to happen—or has happened. He could be shot. Bayoneted. He might even be

. . . dead." Burrowing her face into the front of his satin frock coat, she cried uncontrollably.

"I know, little one," he crooned, wrapping a comforting arm about her and the other around Prudence. His own fearful thoughts were of the other two patriots he knew personally . . . the two Roberts.

Prudence, understanding his pain, reached up and placed a palm against his cheek, her eyes searching his. "They'll be fine. After all, they're safely tucked away behind the port of New York, aren't they? That's miles from Nassau Island. Miles."

But Morgan knew her assurances were as much for herself as for him. He sent a fervent prayer to heaven for his two good friends and for Jamie. But an unexplainable feeling of dread made it hard to breathe. He tugged the girls close and escorted them to the waiting carriage.

11

Trudging through the incessant drizzle, Robert Chandler made a futile attempt to brush some of the grime and splattered blood from his clothes as he marched along the muddy Gowanus Road paralleling the shoreline of the Narrows. It had been a very long four days since the British landed on Nassau Island. After nights of scant sleep, two of which had been in the pouring rain, the other men in his squad scouting the British advance moved as wearily as Robert.

They stayed at the redoubt on the Heights of Guan only one night after they had been chased back up the hill by the enemy's artillery. The riflemen, with their long-range firearms and excellent marksmanship, had been ordered by Colonel Hand to rout approaching Hessians from advantageous positions on the Bedford Road. But the Germans' muskets could be reloaded twice as quickly and were fitted with bayonets. Despite their losses, the relentless mercenaries had closed the gap, and Chandler's battalion had been forced into a bloody retreat. Now the enemy held possession of all the orchards and fields on the east side of the hills.

Thankfully, Robby MacKinnon had been spared having to face the enemy. He had been given the detail of driving casualties back to the village of Brooklyn. Not having the Scot near the line of fire was a relief to Chandler. One less worry.

Chan hoped that since General Washington had ferried six regiments to the island and had come personally to direct the battles, he would turn their failures into triumph. But rumor had it that all the American positions were under heavy artillery fire. General Stirling, Colonel Hand's superior, now led a force no more than half a mile from the First Pennsylvania's own encampment.

Approaching their makeshift camp on high ground, Chan wondered if Robby had managed to keep their blankets dry. Three or four hours of undisturbed sleep would be pure heaven.

When he saw the wagon parked beneath a tree, its canvas cover dripping from the rain, Chandler's spirits lifted. Perched at the rear of the bed, unharmed, was the gentle-hearted Scot. He veered toward his friend. "Robby!"

"Thank the Good Lord ye survived another day," the younger man said, his dark mustache spreading with his welcoming smile. He patted the space beside him in invitation.

Chan hopped aboard and leaned his tired bones against the side for support as he watched Robby gnawing on a rock-hard biscuit. "Didn't run into anything but one of their scouting parties. We sent them packing. These backwoods Pennsylvanians sure do know how to shoot." He grabbed the biscuit his friend tossed to him and bit into it. "Too bad we don't have more of those sharpshooters."

"I could hear a battle ragin' down near the water," Robby said.

"The redcoats have been trying all afternoon to find a weak spot in General Stirling's line."

"Isn't he guardin' everything from the other side of the road down to the marsh?"

Chan nodded. "So I wouldn't recommend getting too cozy."

"Aye." Robby chewed thoughtfully. "Washington should've sent more than six regiments. We're still outnumbered two to one, and our losses are mountin' all the time. It's been reported that the Brits are movin' into position against General Sullivan and General Woodhull. And the First Pennsylvania has suffered many more casualties than it appears. Our own reinforcements just make it less noticeable."

"You're not telling me anything I don't already know. I've seen it myself."

"Aye, but I'm tellin' ye we've been cut down by half."

"Half?" Chan sat up straighter at the dire news.

Robby gave a grave nod. "The First is down to about two hundred men."

Chan mulled over the numbing fact in his mind. "Well, we were the first line of defense. I suppose seeing action every day since the British landed, we have to expect a large number of casualties."

"Ye wouldna' be thinking of 'em as mere numbers if ye'd been transporting 'em as I've done these last days. Me heart has been nigh onto burstin' at the endless suffering. And, Robert, 'tis even sadder how many of the lads had yet to make peace with the Lord. I'm thankful I was here to help, to answer their questioning spirits." He paused. "Odd, is it not, how often one must sink to the lowest point before he thinks of lookin' to the Lord, before a man will reach up and take the hand that's been waitin' all along to lift him up."

As his friend talked, Chandler found himself even more grateful Robby MacKinnon had been ordered to stay with the wagon. The wounded must have appreciated having someone as sympathetic as this sensitive young man to comfort them. Still, it was a struggle for Chandler to justify the fact that a God whom some called loving would allow the death of youth dedicated to fighting for liberty. Or, for that matter, that God could have taken someone so unselfish and giving as his own Julia for no reason at all.

"I do have a bit of good news, though," Robby said with a grin.

Chan stared incredulously. "Short of the Crown forces magically disappearing from Nassau Island, what news could be good?"

"We're to be sent back to the village near Brooklyn Heights

to rest up, soon as Major Burd's battalion is ferried over to relieve us."

"You mean," Chan said, brightening, "a whole night's sleep?"

"From what I hear. But according to the sergeant, it'll be a few hours before they arrive."

"Is this Landers you're talking about? our favorite sergeant?"

"Aye."

"Did you think to remind the man that we don't even belong here? We should've been permitted to go back to New York days ago."

Robby's mouth curved upward in a smile. "Landers said that Colonel Hand has been so pleased with our efforts, he's requestin' we be transferred to his unit. Busy as he is, he actually noticed us. He's even talkin' about a commendation for ye."

Chan groaned. "Just me, or the whole battalion? I'm not the only one shooting at the enemy."

"Maybe. But you're the one who carried that wounded lad across open ground the first night and back up to the redoubt. Carryin' him under cannon fire all the way up the hill, at that."

"He was just a skinny kid," Chandler protested. "Anyone would've done the same. How's he doing, by the way?"

"That *skinny* kid," Robby chuckled, "owes his very life to ye. He's on the mend."

"Well, that's good to know. But I sure didn't do anything out of the ordinary." Embarrassed that someone was making a big to-do out of nothing, Chan pulled out his blanket roll and curled up in it. "Wake me when the relief column gets here."

❦ ❦

"Chandler?"

The whisper came from far away. Chan huddled deeper into his blanket.

Someone shook his shoulder. "Chan? Wake up. The sergeant wants ye."

"What?" he asked, still groggy. "Are we leaving? Has our relief arrived?"

"Nay, lad," Robby said.

Chandler sat upright and rubbed his gritty eyes. The dim glow from the dying embers of the campfires did little to dispel the darkness under the layer of clouds. "What does our beloved sergeant want this time?" he asked with more than a little sarcasm.

"Didna' say. But he wants ye to go to Colonel Hand's tent."

Sliding down off the wagon, Chan couldn't decide which ached the most, his feet or the rest of his body. He did his best to stretch out a few kinks while taking note that most of the other soldiers within the circles of light remained close to the warmth of their fires. It was not a general order to fall in. "I'd say the sarge has taken a definite liking to me, Robby. Could it be he wants to adopt me?" He laughed at the ridiculous notion.

"For a lad as scruffy looking as yourself at the moment," the Scot chuckled, "ye'd best not get your hopes up too high about that."

"What do you mean? I'm in fine fettle." Running his fingers through his tangled hair to restore some semblance of order, he plunked on his tricorn, then grabbed his rifle and haversack. "See you later."

"Aye. Just be sure ye stay alive. And Godspeed."

All but Colonel Hand's tent had been taken down in anticipation of their imminent departure, so Chandler had to step over a number of slumbering forms to reach the one canvas shelter. Outside it, enough men to form a company were gathering.

The Irish colonel faced the group, looking no more rested than any of the rest of them. "I know you lads expected we'd be behind the lines by now, getting a good night's sleep. But one of the sentries has spotted what he thinks are a couple

British platoons sneaking into the apple orchard to the south."

Groaned rumblings spread through the group as the colonel continued.

"The lobsterbacks are most likely probing, hoping to find a vulnerable spot to breach between us and General Stirling. Divide and conquer, so to speak. Well, we're going to do some sneaking of our own. You men have been handpicked by your sergeants because of your proven ability under fire. You are to crawl down through the watermelon field below us and wait till the redcoats emerge from the trees. I need not tell you to wait until they're in the open," he added with emphasis. "Sergeants, move out your men. And God be with you."

"All right, men," Sergeant Landers added quietly. "Listen up. We're to take the far flank. Spread out. Keep a good rod between each of you. Chandler," he motioned, "take the far outside edge of the patch. Take Trudell, Carter, and Reynolds with you. The rest of you men come with me."

Chan didn't need the knotting of his insides to remind him how he loathed being responsible for the lives of others. Hadn't he left his North Carolina plantation for that very reason? He rued the day he had allowed Morgan to make him a corporal. He started to protest, but Landers had already crouched low and taken off.

Chandler felt three pairs of wary eyes trained on him. He lifted a shoulder in an uneasy shrug. "Never should've given the man my name," he mumbled to the others. He turned and crouched to follow the sergeant, letting his men be responsible for their own fates.

A wide field yawned before them in the gloomy night. Beneath a tangle of watermelon vines, the mud was ankle deep. Chan's rifle, slung high, bounced against his back as he led the way. Knowing that the assigned men were following him added to his tension as he kept an eye out for movement in the deeper darkness of the orchard.

Already they were passing others from the company who had taken up positions on their bellies out of range of the enemy muskets. Nearing the end of the vines, Chandler stopped and motioned for one of his men to drop down. The redcoats would most likely come from the center, so he cut at an angle toward the outer edge, placing his other two men as he went. "Remember to wait for fifteen seconds after the first volley before firing," he told the one in the middle, "so the others will have cover while they reload. We don't want to give the British time to rush into range." The lesson learned on Bedford Road had been invaluable.

At the farthest, most vulnerable, position, Chan sank down to the cold ground, more willing to expose himself to the flank than to place someone else in peril.

Several minutes passed. No sign of lobster red. Another wild-goose chase? Had the sentries been seeing things? Surely if redcoats were coming they would have reached this side of the orchard by now. It was no more than ten acres across. On the other hand, he would rather lie in the mud than fight in it.

He eased up enough to check as far as he could see through the darkness. Barely able to make out his own motionless men to the side, he strained harder to peer into the orchard.

A flash of white—no, two—moved forward. White-clad legs. Another pair followed. Then more. They stopped at the edge of the field. Waited.

Chan held his breath, his pulse racing. At least the melon patch provided cover for his men. It would be hard to make out their heads among the rounded shapes on the vines.

More white legs emerged from the trees. Again they were all down near his end. Chandler caught the faint glint of a large steel barrel. Artillery was being rolled out into the open. *They're planning to set up a battery to fire on our encampment!*

Despite the cold, sweat beaded on his forehead.

A minute passed. Then he saw more cannons being rolled into position, yet no one down his line had ordered a volley. Obviously no one else was aware of what was being planned. It was up to him.

He cocked his rifle and sighted on the nearest pair of legs.

He mopped sweat from his face, pulled the first trigger. Eyes closed against the blinding flash, he tripped the second.

An instant after his shot, his comrades fired a volley. Cries of pain split the night as several British crumpled to the ground.

Patriots at the other end of the line lunged madly across the vines until they sighted the British and got off more shots. No one wanted the redcoats to take cover behind their cannons and discharge them.

Reloading in frenzied haste, Chandler heard an order from down the line. "Fire!"

A second volley downed more redcoats.

"Retreat!" a Crown officer yelled, and those left standing ran back into the trees.

A man to Chan's left leaped up to give chase. Others followed, firing wildly into the deep darkness.

After reloading again, Chandler ran toward the grove. The enemy would soon regroup in the inky blackness of the orchard and get off a volley of their own at the charging Americans.

At the brink of the trees, he stopped and crouched behind the wheel of an abandoned cannon. Not a single telltale click of a hammer could be heard. Only the thudding of feet and the groans of the casualties lying in their own blood mere yards away.

"Disarm the wounded," Chandler shouted to the men who ran up to join him. "Carter, you and Reynolds scout down the west side. Make sure the lobsters don't double back on us."

As the pair took off, Chan recalled Robby's wagon. "Trudell, go back to camp and have MacKinnon come to transport the wounded." Then he swung his attention to the line of fieldpieces. Had the sentry not spotted these redcoats, he and the rest of Hand's men would have had a very lively wake-up call. But now the cannons were theirs, and he had no doubt the Irish colonel would make quite good use of the windfall.

Colonel Hand appeared out of the darkness while Chan

searched for the best route to roll the cannons out of the field and up to the encampment. The leader's face was grim, and so was Sergeant Landers's. "Over here," the sergeant ordered.

Aware that he had been usurping their authority, Chandler traipsed out into the vines to them. He saluted. "Begging your pardon, sir. I don't know what came over me."

Landers shook his head. "You've been so levelheaded up till now. I can't believe you didn't wait to fire until they were farther out in the open where we could all get them in our sights."

"From my vantage point, sir, I could see that the enemy wasn't planning to come any closer. They were lining up their fieldpieces."

"Fieldpieces?" Colonel Hand pushed past Chandler, leaving him and Landers to follow.

The colonel took stock of the cannons and the crates of balls beside each. He turned around. "It would appear we owe you an apology, Corporal—Chandler, isn't it?"

"Yes, sir. Another minute or two and they could've answered our volleys." As Chan spoke, he became aware of a new look of respect from his superiors. He felt all the more awkward. "If you have no other need of me, sir, I'll go help with the prisoners. Oh, I sent Carter and Reynolds down the side of the orchard to make sure the redcoats don't double back."

"Very good, Chandler," Hand said, his expression all the more approving. "I won't forget the initiative you showed here this night. You're dismissed to aid the prisoners."

As he strode away, he heard the colonel speak to Landers. "Yes, sir," the sergeant answered. "That's the same Carolina man who distinguished himself at Bunker Hill."

Chan wasted no time blending in with the other men, trying his best to become anonymous as the wounded were moved away from the dead. Administering whatever help he could while awaiting Robby and the wagon, he hoped against hope that his friend would come bearing news that the relief column had arrived.

None too soon, the slosh of the wagon wheels carried to his

ears. The Scotsman pulled up alongside. "Grand to see ye've not been wounded," he called down.

"We were lucky this time."

Robby wrapped the reins around the brake and climbed over the seat. "Luck, or God?"

Chan shook his head. The Scot never gave up!

Then he turned to a man at his elbow. "Give me a hand, will you?" Together they lifted a grimacing redcoat into the bed, with Robby helping from above. "The relief show up yet?"

Robby grinned down at him. "Aye. Came while you lads were down here shootin' up the place. A green bunch, they are. Ye should've seen their eyes when they heard all the ruckus."

"Sleep." The other soldier thumped Chan's back. "Now we'll get some blessed sleep."

"In a dry place," Chan returned.

"Well, move aside, then, so we can get the rest loaded," Robby said.

Chandler turned to see a line of others waiting with bleeding, gasping men.

From somewhere in the orchard a shot rang out.

Reminded of the two men he had sent to track the enemy, Chan swung toward the trees.

Nearby, someone grunted and fell.

Chandler whirled back to the wagon.

Robby lay crumpled beside the wounded soldier, Scottish blood mingling with English.

12

"No! Robby!" Chandler hurled himself onto the wagon and grabbed his friend, hugging him to his chest. "Please, please," he begged, his eyes seeking the heavens, "don't do this. Not to Robby. Not to Emily." Everything blurred before his face as he looked down again at the limp Scot. As if from a great distance he heard the order given to turn the cannons, and the men nearby began shooting their rifles into the orchard. Chan's only concern was the lad's labored and raspy breathing. A crushing heaviness compressed his lungs. "Oh, Robby, Robby."

He felt his friend stir.

Snatching at even the slimmest hope, Chan held him still. "Robby?"

He moaned.

"Where are you hit?"

"Chest." The word came out on a gasp.

Chandler touched the mushy, bleeding crater in the younger man's torso. *No! It can't be, it can't be.* Desperately he tried to stem the flow, but blood surged through his fingers.

"'Tis . . . bad," the lad whispered.

Chan gathered the remnants of his shredded hope. "Oh, not so bad." But even as he spoke, he knew the truth.

Robby grasped the front of Chandler's shirt. "Take . . . Emmy . . . bairns . . . to . . . Princeton." He coughed.

"Y-you don't know what you're saying," Chan said.

"Please," Robby grunted. "No one . . . else." His grip on Chandler's shirt tightened.

Chan rocked him in his arms. "We'll both take them. You and me. Together."

Robby shuddered, and another coughing spasm racked his wiry frame. In the faint light, Chandler saw his eyes open wide and fill with a wondrous glow. "Mother?" he murmured, a tiny smile lifting the corners of his mouth. "Father? Ye've . . . come."

"No," Chan pleaded softly. "No." But in his heart he knew it was for naught.

And then a peace transformed Robby's face as he looked up at him. "Take care . . . of me . . . sweet . . ." He emitted a long, slow breath. His hand slid down Chan's chest.

Chandler bent over his friend's bloody form and wept.

"Robby!" Waking from a deep sleep, Emily sat up with a start. Her heart pounded with panic, beating almost audibly in the silence. Instinctively, she reached to touch him in the darkened room. Of course. He wasn't there. He was in New York, helping Morgan.

But with the oppressive emptiness, she knew the truth.

Clutching his cold pillow to her breast, Emily buried her face into its softness, trying to capture some tangible remembrance of him there. A very slight, almost imagined trace of him lingered. It stabbed at her heart.

Oh, Lord God in heaven. Why? I need him so. She slid off the bed and onto her knees. Tears coursed down her cheeks and neck and into her nightdress as she crumpled against the wall and looked heavenward. "Please, heavenly Father. Please, let it not be so. Not my Robby."

But the only answer in the depths of her soul was her husband's own whispered words the night he left. *'Twould never be my own choice to have somethin' keep me from coming back to ye. But if it should come to pass, ye must be brave for me, for our wee bairns. 'Tis what drew me to ye those few short years past, sweet*

Emmy. You've been so bonny and brave. If it should happen, be brave again. I'll wait for ye over yonder. Me love will guide ye Home.

Be brave? A cold draft washed over her, raising gooseflesh. "Oh, Robby," she murmured, "I was only brave for you. I don't know if I could be that way again, without you. I love you." Her breath caught on a sob, and she sank to the floor.

❦ ❦

Someone tugged at the leg of Chandler's trousers. "Move aside, man."

Chan looked up to see a pair of soldiers carrying a wounded redcoat.

"Reach down and give us a hand," one of them said. "Help us get him into the wagon."

He just stared. "My friend . . ."

"Sorry, I didn't know the lad." The touch of sympathy in the voice made Chan feel worse as the pain of his loss settled around him like a fog.

"Dreadful shame," the other said. "A lone sniper, from the way it looked. Just when he was about to be relieved, too."

"He-he wasn't even in the fighting," Chan said, his gaze drawn once more to the lad lying so peacefully in death. "All he ever did was try to help people. Took care of our wounded boys—*and* theirs." He shot a scathing glare at the wounded British soldiers whose cohorts were responsible for the senseless waste. "Gave them comforting words. There wasn't a violent bone in his body. He was purely a good man, a godly man."

"The two of us are both plumb sorry, Corporal, but our arms are about to give out. You wouldn't want us to drop this here man, would you now?"

Chandler didn't care one way or the other about the redcoat suspended between them, but he realized he wouldn't be able to take Robby out of here until all casualties were loaded. Before stepping down to lend a hand, he carefully laid the young Scotsman out, closing his eyes, folding his hands, straightening his legs. His dear friend deserved respect.

❦ 105 ❦

There was no time for grieving when Chan drove the wagon back to camp. He was ordered to take the prisoners on to the village up on Brooklyn Heights, where a makeshift hospital had been set up. But the drive provided time to think. To decide.

Chan wouldn't bother asking for permission this time. He would simply leave. He would let no one stop him from taking Robby back to Emily and his dear children—not even General Washington himself.

Once the wounded were unloaded, Chan climbed back onto the wagon seat for Robby's journey home and threaded his way through the arriving soldiers clogging his path. Often he was forced to wait while a column of marching men commandeered the roadway. Despite his churning emotions, he forced himself to relax, fearful of attracting attention as he traveled the last mile to the ferry.

Nearing the landing, he gazed out over the half-mile expanse of water. Small boats of every description, heavy with men and supplies, came out of the night, heading toward the dock to be unloaded. With the arrival of so many more troops adding confusion and bustle, he doubted he would be missed.

Torches burned brightly across the wharf. As Chandler unfolded a tarp and gently covered Robby's body, he paused. It had been much too dark before to really see, but now the gaping wound in his chest was shockingly visible, and he looked so young. How would Chan ever find words to explain this to Robby's Emily . . . his widow. The ache in Chan's throat brought back full force his own tragedy. He knew all too well the devastation of Emily's loss.

With a shuddering sigh, he covered the purest friend he'd ever known, then gathered the reins again, flicking them over the horses' backs.

"Halt!" a beefy boatman shouted. "By whose authority are you boarding?

Chan straightened. "We need more powder. I've been dispatched by General Stirling."

"Then you must have a written order."

"No."

"Then you ain't leavin' this dock."

"What's your name?" Chandler challenged.

The muscular man took on a stubborn expression. "What's it to you?"

"If I have to go back for a paper," Chan said evenly, "I want to be sure to tell the general what idiot is responsible for this holdup. I'm fairly certain he'll not forget you. What did you say your name was?"

He moistened his lips. "I got my orders, same as you."

"Then you have no reason not to give your name."

The man rubbed his mouth, then grinned at the other boatmen. "Arnold Pell," he announced defiantly.

"Arnold Pell," Chandler repeated, as if committing it to memory. But he was more than aware his bluff hadn't worked. In despair he pulled on the reins. "Back! Back!" More than likely, every available craft was already in use, leaving none for the ferry dock even as far up as Kip's Bay. Well, if he had to, he'd find some narrow spot and swim across with Robby's body and the horses.

"Wait!"

"Whoa." Chandler pulled up on the reins and stared wordlessly at the boatman.

"Just where's the general sendin' you?"

"The arsenal near the port battery," he lied wearily.

"Oh, all right. Come aboard, then. But next time you make sure you get your orders in writing, hear?"

"Next time. Sure, I'll do that." It was going to be a long night.

With longer days to come.

13

A rhythmic duel between crickets and tree toads kept tempo with the creaking of Emily's rocking chair as she stared pensively into the fading twilight. How could there still be such quietness, such peace in the world, when the dearest dreams of her life had turned to ashes? How could the sky beyond the western rim of trees cast that breathtaking rose and lavender glow over the pastures of her girlhood home, when deep within her all was colorless and bleak?

Moths fluttered against the globes of the lanterns on the porch railing. Their futile struggle to touch the flickering candle flames reminded her how desperately she wished she would wake up and find that the past two days had been nothing but a nightmare, a horrid dream. She had prayed so hard that it was untrue. But the dull ache refused to diminish, a constant testimony that nothing would ever be the same again as long as she lived.

On her lap, two-year-old Rusty stirred in his sleep, and Emily looked down as a tiny smile touched his lips and then vanished as quickly. An angel kiss, Mama had always called sleep-smiles. Could it have been something even more dear . . . a kiss from the daddy who'd been taken from him? The bittersweet thought brought the sting of tears, and she blinked them away.

She should have put her little son up to bed an hour ago with his big sister, but he had been fussing over a new tooth.

And, in truth, Emily needed to hold him. Except for the auburn hair he had inherited from his grandma, he was the very image of Robby. The same smiling blue eyes, the way he walked and carried his head, made him a duplicate in miniature. Somehow it made her feel as though Robby was not so far away. She inhaled the delicate scent of her son's silky reddish hair, loving the smell and feel of him.

Her gaze gravitated to her mother and father, keeping her company on the porch. Her parents' marriage had always been so solid, particularly over the last few years since Mama's spiritual commitment. Emily had planned to follow their splendid example in her own marriage . . . back when she envisioned it lasting forever. Almost from the moment she had told them that she knew Robby was gone, they had been hovering over her in their quiet way, not wanting to intrude, but unable to accept her certainty of his death. "Papa, how long has it been since Ben came through?"

Her father looked up from the leather rope he'd been braiding, his deep brown eyes revealing his love and concern. His calloused hand stilled.

In the chair beside him, Mama paused in her knitting, uncharacteristic worry lines marring her regal features. "It was when your father took that string of horses up to Boston. When was that, dear?"

"I've been back almost two weeks now."

Emily nodded. "Then surely he'll come again soon. He rarely stays away from Abby more than a fortnight."

Mama smiled, but the deep sadness in the depths of her green eyes did not abate. "I never expected Ben would turn out to be such a considerate husband after his reckless and thoughtless boyhood. He was downright rude to your sister Jane."

"And she to him," Papa said with a low chuckle. "But then, of all our children they were the closest in age." He switched his attention to Emily. "Why are you concerned about your brother?"

With a small shrug, she tipped her head. "I . . . need to hear it from him. To have him say the words. So you'll believe me. And . . . it might help me to—" Her voice cracked, and threatening tears made it impossible to finish the thought. She took a firmer hold of Rusty and stood. "I guess it's time to put him to bed."

"I'll do it," Papa said, rising. Gently he took the sleeping tot and went inside, his faint footfalls quickly receding as he carried the child up the stairs.

Arms empty now of her one small comfort, Emily lowered herself once more to the rocker. In a way, she was relieved not to have to go into the bedchamber herself, at least for a while. During the daylight hours, she could keep busy and avoid it. But the endless empty dark of night was another matter. It was then that she would relinquish her brave front and the last shred of hope and surrender to the agony of her loss. Weeping into her pillow at night made putting on her cheerful front a little easier when the morning finally dawned. She had not informed the children of their father's passing.

She shook off her morose thoughts and turned to her mother. "Mama?"

"What is it?"

Emily struggled to formulate the nagging question, then decided just to let the words tumble out in whatever fashion they might. "I've been trying to work something out in my mind. About . . . about God. If he's so very interested in us and in our lives, then why would . . . how could he—" Her words drifted off helplessly.

Mama didn't answer right away. "You must remember, darling, none of us is completely certain Robby . . . is gone."

"But I am, Mama. I can tell you the exact moment he was taken. We were so close. Soul mates. If he were still on this earth, I wouldn't have such an emptiness in my heart. Or such an ache. What I need to know is—*why*? What possible purpose could the Lord have for taking such a good husband, such a wonderful father?"

Her mother glanced down at her hands in wordless silence. Then her eyes met Emily's. "I'm very sure God loves you now

FREEDOM'S HOLY LIGHT

as much as he ever did," she answered with quiet conviction. "Having to part from someone dear is truly the hardest thing any of us must face. It's been the curse of humanity since the fall of Adam and Eve. When we lost two of our own dear babes in infancy, I wondered how I could go on. But the Lord's promises are true, and I was never more aware of God's presence than I was then."

She paused, as if caught in the poignant memory, then went on, her voice steady, comforting. "Should the day ever come when your father must depart and leave me behind, I don't know how I'll get through the rest of my life without him. But I know someday God will call one of us to be with him. And should I be the one left here, I know God will be there with me at that moment, providing all that I need."

Emily, in her sorrow, had already experienced moments of indescribable peace. She had not spoken of it as yet, but in the solitary hours, after the tears, the certainty that the Lord was holding her up wrapped itself around her like a comforting blanket. But it was still too new to express in words, and it did little to lessen the deep ache inside.

"And do not forget," Mama continued. "God's very own precious Son was not spared from pain—or from death. So the Father knows and understands how deeply we grieve."

Yes, but we had so many dreams, Emily thought sadly. *Such grand plans. Now they'll never come to pass.*

"Remember how bitter I was when Dan defied me by marrying a lowly bondservant?" Mama asked with a little smile. "My, what a fool I was, and what a hard lesson the Lord had to teach me. But now I thank God every single night for Susannah and *for the things I suffered, as well.* Once I let go of my selfish pride, God enriched my life beyond measure. You tried to tell me this once, as I recall."

Emily almost smiled at the memory. "Me and just about everybody else in the family!" She rose, crossed to her mother's side, and kissed her cheek. "I'll try to trust God for tomorrow. I'll really try."

Her mother caught her hand and squeezed it. "Ask him to

give you his peace, sweetheart." She sadly shook her head. "This awful war has been very hard on all my girls. The waiting, the uncertainty. But please, don't bury your dear Robby prematurely in your mind. For all you know, tomorrow he could quite possibly walk through that door."

"I wish he could," Emily whispered. "You'll never know how deeply I pray that I'm wrong. But think back, Mama, to Christmas two years ago. You knew with utmost certainty that all of us would be here, remember? Even Dan, who was imprisoned in Boston without hope of release. Yet you never wavered in your belief. Well, that's the kind of knowing I have inside *me* now. My Robby will never come back to me alive. He's . . . gone to the Lord."

Mama stood, tears shimmering in her eyes, and wrapped her arms about Emily. "If that were to be so, my darling daughter, I can only tell you how very, very sad I would be. He's been so special to us all."

Emily could not keep her own tears back. She swayed against her mother, desperately needing the reassurance and serenity that were such a part of her. "But I feel so lost, Mama," she said, weeping softly now. "So very lost."

"I know, sweetheart. But I'm here for you now. We all are."

"Faster, Mommy! Faster!" Katie bounced along on a sedate mare the next day as Emily guided the horse around the field. Behind Katie, Rusty giggled so hard he could barely keep hold of his sister's waist.

Cassandra and Corbin, Abby's children, squealed in delight on a second quiet-tempered mare led by Ben's wife. "Us, too! We wanna go faster, too!"

Emily exchanged a sidelong glance with Abigail and smiled. The children's laughter was like a tonic. She wondered if Robby were looking down on the sweet scene and grinning. It was a nice thought, one to cling to—for a little while.

"Hold on real tight," Abby told her two offspring, then

jogged ahead, trailing the trotting pacer behind her as she navigated a huge circle. Her long wheat-gold tresses ruffled with her movements, shining in the sun.

Emily, more hesitant since her children were a bit younger than Abby's, kept her animal at a more tranquil walk as she turned and headed past her mother, who watched from the fence.

The sun was high in the azure sky and so far had not been obscured by any of the small fluffy clouds blowing in from the coast. Emily found the beauty of the day consoling. It fit with the solace she had derived from her morning Scripture reading in Philippians. She, like Paul, was *in a strait betwixt two, having a desire to depart, and to be with Christ* . . . and her Robby, but knowing all the while that *to abide in the flesh is more needful* for the sake of the children. The unexplainable sense of peace that surrounded her since her husband's passing was even more evident in the perfection of this afternoon, as if the Lord were assuring her that he would always be there, holding her up.

"Faster, Mommy. Please!" Katie begged.

"Well," Emily hedged, "if you promise to hold tight. You, too, Rusty." At their eager nods, she began a near jog in a slightly smaller circle than the one Abby had run. She needed the children to be as lighthearted as possible. Once she told them about their father, they wouldn't have the Psalms to turn to for comfort, or the hymns that had helped keep her own spirits up. She would be all they had. *Oh, precious Lord, help me to find the right words to make them understand. Don't let me fail them or break down. I must be brave for their sakes. For Robby.*

Mother's throaty laugh joined in with the children's, her first cheerful display that day.

Turning the far bend, Emily met up with Abigail on her way back, and the two girls slowed to a walk again, panting side by side. "Somehow I don't feel as young as I used to be," Emily admitted. "All this running has worn me out."

"More! More!" Cassie pleaded, bouncing up and down excitedly on the horse's back.

"Not just now, angel," Abby groaned.

"Your poor beasts of burden are tuckered," Emily told the little girl.

"At least the two-legged ones," Abby added with a giggle.

"Let's do something else," Emily suggested. "Let's sing." Veering the pacer in the direction of her mother, she started the hymn she had been humming most of the morning, one of Robby's very favorites. "Rejoice, the Lord is King! . . ."

"Your Lord and King adore!" Abby chimed in exuberantly.

A baritone voice joined them from the direction of the barn. "Rejoice, give thanks, and sing, and triumph evermore."

Emily smiled at her father, and he doffed his work hat with a flourish as he approached her mother and draped an arm around her shoulders.

The sight of their easy companionship almost made Emily's throat close up. It took all her effort to go on to the chorus with the seemingly personal words. "Lift up your heart, lift up your voice! Rejoice, again I say, rejoice!" She couldn't finish.

Her father, holding her gaze steadily as if to impart his own strength to her, took over. "Jesus, the Saviour, reigns, the God of truth and love; when he had purged our stains, he took his seat above."

Emily let the rest sing the last two verses. The familiar refrains soothed her heart with the sweet assurance that with the Lord and her loving family supporting her faith, she would make it through this hard, sad time. If not for herself, for Katie and Rusty, who needed her so very much. And—she gazed upward into the sky—for Robby.

"Mama! Mama!" Katie exclaimed. "Somebody's coming!"

Down the lane, a wagon rumbled into view . . . and following behind it, a Narragansett pacer tied by a rope.

Emily's heart stopped, then throbbed in ominous thuds. Moving mechanically, she swung the children from the mare and handed them to her parents. "Mama, why don't you give them some of those gingerbread cookies you and Tillie baked this morning?" Then she crawled through the fence boards and smiled at Katie. "You and Rusty go up to the house with Grandma now, and help her fix a treat for our company, will you? We'll make it a nice surprise."

"That sounds splendid," her mother said, her sad gaze offering her understanding. "Come along, Abby. Bring Cassie and Corbin, too." Together they moved quietly off.

Her father stayed behind and gave her an encouraging hug. "It may not be what you think."

Recognizing Robert Chandler now, Emily looked her father squarely in the eye. "Yes, it is, Papa. Pray for me. Help me to be brave."

He inhaled a deep breath and gave her a harder hug as he stood by her side.

On the wagon seat, Chan looked thinner than Emily remembered, and his face was drawn, with dark circles beneath his eyes. He couldn't possibly have eaten or slept on the way. For him to have expended himself so was an indication of the deep friendship he and Robby had formed since her husband had first gone to Boston Bay to join the Continental army. He reined to a stop.

Careful not to allow her eyes to drift to the wagon bed just yet . . . or the canvas-covered form at the edge of her vision, Emily focused on him.

Robert's fingers shook as he wrapped the reins around the brake. He climbed down and took both her hands, and his red-rimmed eyes searched hers. "Emily."

"You've come a very long way," she told him. "Please let Papa take you inside for something to eat and a quiet place to lie down."

"B-but you don't understand. I—"

"I know," she whispered, unable to trust her voice. "I know."

His gaze flicked to her father and returned to her as he released a ragged breath. "I'm so very, very sorry. I tried to keep him from . . ."

Emily tried to see through a haze of tears. She nodded and squeezed his hand, placing it to her cheek. "Please, I-I'd like to have a few moments alone with him."

Papa stepped near and took Chandler's arm. "Come on, lad," he said, gently drawing him away.

For the first time, Emily allowed her gaze to drift fully to the back of the wagon, and her knees grew weak. She inhaled deeply, gathered herself together, then, trembling, climbed aboard.

Kneeling down, she slowly pulled the canvas covering away. Her tears ran freely now, and a sob caught in her throat. Robby lay so still, so peaceful. He appeared merely to be asleep, and he looked so very young. "My love," she whispered on a sob, lightly combing her fingertips through his hair. There wasn't even a hint of silver among the ebony strands yet, barely a line on his face. The clean clothes he wore were evidence that Robert wanted to spare her from whatever wound had taken her husband's life. She wasn't sure she really wanted to know anyway, and a surge of appreciation coursed through her at his thoughtfulness. He had been a faithful and true friend.

But as she continued to gaze at her dear, young, dead husband, anger sliced at her heart. It wasn't really Robby lying there, not now. It was just an empty shell. Robby had gone on ahead, to be with Christ for all eternity. He would never come home to her again. "Why, Robby?" she cried softly. "What possible reason could there be for you to leave us? How am I to go on without you? And the children—" No. She mustn't give in to even a hint of anger. She had to be brave. *Brave.* But right now, she had not the slightest idea how she would accomplish that feat.

She memorized each feature for the last time, the broad forehead, the unruly shock of black hair, his square chin. She tried to imagine life without his lilting laugh, the trill of his *r*s as they rolled from his tongue in the Scottish brogue she loved so dearly. The plans and dreams they had shared would be laid to rest now, too. Forever.

Raising her eyes to heaven, she swallowed hard. "I do thank you, dear God, for hearing my plea, for bringing my Robby back to me so quickly . . . but how will I tell our babies? Please,

please give me your strength. How can they understand something like death? You must give me the right words to say, Father. Please, do this for me."

Looking once more at her gentle husband, she tried to smile. "I will always love you, Robby MacKinnon." She leaned down and brushed a last kiss to the lips so still and cold. New tears speckled the tarp as she gently placed it over his face.

It was time to go and thank a dear friend for his kind thoughtfulness . . . and after that, to have a sad talk with her children.

14

Evelyn's melodious laugh, near the other end of the long table of guests at the Neville Heath mansion, sounded unusually false to Morgan. He knew his sister had to find this gathering of merchant friends of his father's very wearisome. Besides himself and Prudence, Evelyn and Clay Raleigh were the only other young people present. As usual, Father, Mr. Heath, and another distinguished merchant, Jude Rossiter, allowed the topic to drift time and again to the subject uppermost in their minds—the countless affairs concerning importing and exporting, and how they were affected by the war.

To Evie's credit, no one had seen through her inane chatter or the engaging smile she had lavished upon the others during the hour since the Thomas coach had brought the family to supper. Especially fetching in cranberry taffeta and powdered ringlets, she was the very epitome of charm. Even Raleigh had to be basking in his exalted opinion of himself as she laughed at his silly jokes. But Morgan knew that Evelyn's determination to do whatever was necessary to help her sweetheart, Jamie Dodd, and the other patriots was paramount in her mind.

Switching his attention to his parents across the table, Morgan marveled that neither of them seemed to note his sibling's playacting but appeared to be bursting with pride as they beamed at her throughout the meal.

Now, as slices of rich butter cake with plum sauce were

brought in by the servants, Evelyn took a dainty sip of punch and set down the silver goblet. "I feel so much safer, Mr. Heath," she gushed to their host, "knowing we're being so well protected. How many man-of-war ships did you say were plying the colonial waters just now?" Her long lashes fluttered in feminine innocence.

Having already probed the uninformed gentleman along that same line himself, Morgan didn't even bother to wait for the reply as the portly man blotted his trim mustache on his napkin and turned to her.

Morgan's greater concern was the false smile fastened to Prudence's mouth since the moment of arrival here. His mother had magnanimously offered his wife's talents for the entertainment following the meal, and he could see that Prudence was suffering from an acute case of stage fright. She appeared nearly as colorless as her ivory gown, and her fingers trembled as she pushed uneaten cake around her plate with a fork.

He barely managed to stifle a grin. His little Puritan wouldn't be more petrified if she were about to become a sacrificial lamb. Her campaign to win Mother over had a greater price than even she had bargained for. Mother had insisted that Evie merely accompany her on the harpsichord. His mouth twitched into a grin as he swallowed the last morsel of dessert.

"Ahem." Mr. Heath rose to his feet and gave a polite bow to his wife at the foot of the table. "I believe the gentlemen and I will retire to the study. Mr. Raleigh has generously provided us with a rare selection of cigars from several of our Caribbean islands. And—" he turned to Clay, "a new experimental leaf from North Carolina, is it not?"

"That is correct." Raleigh gave a smug nod and stood. The other men, except for Morgan, followed suit.

With Prudence's death grip on his knee, Morgan's attention swung to her face, which was white with panic.

Her eyes widened in desperation. "You must take me home," she whispered. "Now."

He peeled her fingers away and kissed her open palm. "Something must be in the air," he murmured softly, "or we would not have been included on the guest list. Be brave." He got up, elevating his voice to a level others could easily hear. "I shan't desert you for long, my sweet."

"Oh, don't hurry on my account," she said with forced acquiescence. "Take all the time you want."

"Absolutely not," his mother intervened, placing a jeweled hand on the sleeve of his indigo frock coat. "Twenty minutes should be quite sufficient. Any more than that, and we women will join you, won't we, ladies?" She smiled at the three older women who were part of her social circle.

"Only if we may smoke as well," an amply bosomed matron in a royal blue gown announced, chuckling at her own jest.

Mrs. Heath made a distasteful grimace. "What? Those smelly things? Only out of extreme generosity do I permit the disgusting weeds to be lighted, even in that one room. We shall adjourn, ladies, to the music room, where we'll await our husbands."

Morgan cast a backward glance at Prudence, who remained stiffly in place as the others rose. Hoping to allay her fears, he winked at her. Still, Prudence resembled a frightened doe on the verge of darting away. How amazing to recall that she was the same woman who had risked her life to join the army at Bunker Hill.

He expelled a breath and entered his host's private domain and was immediately caught by Mr. Heath's collection of rare Greek and Latin books. Scanning some of the titles, he paused to study a display of ancient coins enclosed in a glass case. The man lived well.

"I urge you to choose the cigar you would most enjoy," Mr. Heath said invitingly as he circulated an embellished wooden humidor.

From the corner of his eye Morgan saw each gentleman sniff two or three before selecting. The host clipped the tips of the cigars with a silver cutter.

"And now you, Morgan," Heath said, extending the bounty toward him.

Withdrawing his gaze from an exquisite Roman coin, he raised a hand of refusal even as the heavy aromas blended in a gray-blue haze. "Thank you, but I'm afraid I shall have to decline. My stomach is unsettled this eve." *And it never hurts to lay the foundation for a hasty exit, just in case.*

Mr. Heath frowned. "What a pity. Perhaps next time, then." He took his seat in an upholstered leather chair behind the desk.

Clayborne Raleigh expertly puffed a smoke ring and smiled as he propped a foot on his opposite knee. "Gentlemen, my father would be most glad to take orders for any of these fine cigars, I'm sure."

Morgan slid him a glance. The stuffy Englishman was no less a pretender than he. It would be difficult to picture him dirtying his hands on something so plebeian as merchandising. Yet with so few aristocrats for the snob to keep company with, why had he even deigned to come to the colonies in the first place?

Comments Evelyn had made about Raleigh's being in love with her dowry rather than herself began to take on deeper meaning. Without a title of his own, Raleigh would need a great deal of money to find acceptance among the upper class. Morgan's respect for his sister's intuition took a sudden rise.

"When do you expect your father to return to our fair city, Mr. Raleigh?" Mr. Rossiter asked.

"I'd say within a week or so, sir." One side of his thin mouth curled upward. "He'd not miss the opportunity to be the first to offer the victorious soldiers and the restored New Yorkers a celebratory cigar."

"Can't fault a businessman for his good sense," Heath remarked.

Morgan restrained himself from voicing his own derisive thoughts. No matter how confident the Loyalists were since word came that the Crown now controlled Nassau Island,

Jamie Dodd's brother, Micah, had discovered that most of Washington's army had evacuated safely. Under cover of night, they had sneaked across the East River to New York, right beneath the noses of the redcoats and the guns of their warships. The patriots termed the feat a miracle, and Morgan was all the more convinced that God was with their cause.

"Speaking of New York," Mr. Heath said, "Mr. Rossiter and I have a proposal to set forth." He turned to Morgan. "We should like to offer you the opportunity to represent our interests in New York. If, that is—" He looked at Morgan's father. "If Waldon can spare you for a time. We believe you are the best choice, since you spent more than a year with General Howe's officers in Boston while it was under siege."

Morgan tried not to show his alarm. He left Boston long before it was barricaded and had spent no more than two weeks in the company of Boston Loyalist merchants and the British army. And, to his dismay, he had managed during that short time to acquire a dangerous enemy. He had made the wise decision to leave the city before the vengeful Captain Long started checking into his business dealings . . . in particular, his unlawful diversions of Loyalist shipments to the patriots.

Nevertheless, he rationalized, New York *would* be an ideal spot for someone trying to ferret out information. Captain Long might not have come from Halifax with General Howe. It was a chance worth taking—one which might be wise to check out with General Washington first, however.

He glanced at his father but could not read his expression. "I say," he said, turning to the host. "It does sound rather interesting. Father and I will discuss it and have an answer within the next few days."

"Splendid." Mr. Heath fairly beamed as he puffed on his fat cigar.

"You do realize, Waldon," Rossiter began, "that unlike Philadelphia, New York will now be open to English trade without fear of rebel reprisals. We could even purchase wharf-front property and build warehouses."

"Yes," Heath agreed, stroking his mustache. "We should not sit idly by while the New York merchants keep all the profits for themselves."

As the men's voices escalated, the door opened, and Mrs. Heath leaned in, waving aside the smoke. "Neville, it's time you and the others joined the ladies, don't you think?"

❦ ❧

Only with utmost effort could Prudence make her rubbery legs carry her toward Morgan as the men filed into the music room. It was imperative she get to him. He simply had to take her home. At once! She was becoming more nauseated by the second. In desperation she mopped the cold perspiration beading her brow. Never in her entire life had she so much as hummed a tune in public. Properly raised Boston Bay women did not make a practice of putting themselves on exhibition. It was simply not done.

Finally reaching her husband, she latched onto his arm.

"Evelyn, my pet," Clay Raleigh piped in from beside Morgan. "I've splendid news. Your brother and I shall be departing for New York very soon."

Prudence sought Morgan's eyes.

"Wouldn't it be marvelous," Clay continued, "if you might accompany him and his wife? A victorious army throws magnificent parties, to be sure."

Mother Thomas moved quietly to their side. "Morgan, you only recently arrived home. I do hope you aren't thinking of leaving again so soon. Tell me you're not."

"Oh, Mother," Evelyn cajoled. "It's only two days by carriage. Just think of the advantages!"

As the older woman pondered her daughter's words, Prudence could see that the possibility of a truly splendid marriage for Evie was not lost on her. But she couldn't know her daughter's secret goal—going north to find Jamie Dodd.

As for herself, Prudence was willing to say or do anything at all to avoid becoming a singing fool. Now *or* later. "Why, darling," she said, turning to Morgan. "This is so sudden.

Surely we women should be included in a discussion of matters that pertain to all of us. I'm in complete agreement with Evelyn. I'd simply love to go to New York. I would leave this eve. This very minute, in fact."

An amused grin revealed that Morgan saw through her ploy. But it vanished as quickly. "Father and I have yet to decide if I'm to go. But regardless, you and my sister will be staying here in Philadelphia. My mission would involve stimulating more business opportunities, not being a constant chaperon—which even you would agree would be necessary in a city overrun with hordes of loose-living soldiers."

"Oh, please," Evie cajoled. "Please!" She grabbed onto Morgan.

Clay Raleigh appeared similarly disappointed. He had likely already counted on this chance to have the elusive young heiress more frequently to himself. "I would be only too glad to see to Evelyn's welfare."

"Why, how very kind of you, Mr. Raleigh," Mother said. "Now, there's been quite enough talk of war and business for one evening." She nodded emphatically toward the other ladies, then at Evelyn. "Evie, dear, go to the harpsichord. We've kept our friends waiting long enough. My new daughter-in-law's tutor, Mr. Stanton, says she is a pure find. He's quite elated with her progress."

Prudence felt her knees begin to fold. Why, oh, *why* hadn't she been more insistent when she tried to coerce Evie into singing a duet?

Morgan's steadying grip kept her from dissolving to the floor. But Prudence knew better than anyone that even if she made it to Evie's side, nothing but a pitiful croak could possibly emerge from her paralyzed throat.

"Actually, Mother," Morgan said smoothly, "Prudence and I have a bit of a surprise for you ourselves."

Prudence clung to this startling announcement with all the fervor she possessed as she gazed up at him. *Oh, please, dear Lord, let him have a plan to save me. Let it be that.*

He appeared somewhat flustered momentarily.

She was doomed.

Morgan cleared his throat. "After much pleading on my part, my dear wife has agreed to allow me to harmonize with her. Isn't that so, sweetheart?" His slightly cornered expression met hers. "We do, after all, like to think of our marriage as a duet in every way."

Speechless with shock, Prudence almost forgot to close her eyes as he lowered his lips to hers amid a chorus of *ooh*s and *aah*s from the assemblage.

Could he even carry a tune? What on earth would the two of them sing? Raising her lashes again, she pressed closer to the strong beat of his stalwart heart . . . this man who would willingly make a public spectacle of himself just for her.

Who knows, maybe they could pull it off. Together they could do anything, couldn't they? Even sing.

Morgan nodded to Evelyn, and she took a seat at the harpsichord, fingers poised above the keys. She looked expectantly to him.

"We'll do 'Barbara Allen,'" he said bravely, and donned a magnanimous smile as Evie played a few measures of introduction. "Just come in when I squeeze your hand," he whispered to Prudence, then broke out in a strong baritone:

> " 'Twas in the merry month of May
> When all gay flow'rs were blooming,
> Sweet William on his deathbed lay
> For the love of Barbara Allen. "

Prudence was hard put not to laugh at the lovesick expression he wore, and some of her fears began to evaporate as he continued:

> "He sent a servant to the town
> Where Barbara, she was dwellin',
> 'My master's sick and sends for you
> If your name be Barb'ra Allen.'"

But when she felt pressure from his hand, her terror rose to the fore. If he hadn't winked in devilment, she might not have gathered her wits so quickly. She moistened her lips and began, timidly at first, then buoyed by his delighted smile, in a clear soprano that surprised even her:

> *"So slowly, slowly she got up,*
> *And slowly went unto him.*
> *And all she said when she got there:*
> *'Young man, I think you're dyin.'"*

Morgan took up with the next verse, and Prudence the one after, as they alternated verses of the sad ballad. Incredibly, Prudence even saw one of the matrons dab at her eyes with a lacy kerchief. The last two stanzas seemed upon them all too quickly as they blended their voices in harmony:

> *"Sweet William was buried in the high churchyard,*
> *And Barbara buried by him.*
> *And out of his grave grew a bloodred rose*
> *And out of hers a brier.*

> *"They grew and grew to the steeple top*
> *Till they could grow no higher;*
> *They lapped and tied in a true love knot—*
> *The rose around the brier."*

As the last notes died away, there was a long silent moment, then a burst of exuberant applause.

Prudence felt herself crushed in Morgan's embrace. "To think you've hidden that talent from me all this time!" she murmured.

He chuckled against her ear. "Just hope they don't plead for an encore. It's the only tune I know, except for a rather humorous version I heard recently of 'Yankee-Doodle.'"

15

"Thank you, Mistress Harnell, for coming," Emily said, escorting the older woman to the door. The neighbor was one of the last of the many who had come to extend condolences. "It would have meant so much to my Robby to know so many people cared."

Mrs. Harnell patted Emily's hand with her own slightly rougher one. "If there is anything we can do for you, dear, anything at all, please do let us know. I fear Robert will not be the last brave young man we'll lay to rest before these dark days are past."

"I pray that isn't so," Emily returned softly.

With a gracious nod and a last kind look, the woman adjusted her lace shawl and joined her husband waiting at the edge of the porch.

Emily sighed and stepped out after them to check on her children. Abigail was supervising Katie and Rusty and several other youngsters under the shade of the big maple in the side yard. For a few seconds, listening to their sweet voices, Emily could almost forget the sadness of this day.

"Ashes, ashes, all fall down!" they chorused. Katie's and Rusty's bright smiles and laughter were as carefree as the rest of the children's as they all tumbled to the ground.

In a way, it seemed a blessing to Emily that the children were too young to grasp the finality of their father's passing. When she had tried to explain that he had gone to heaven to be with God and that they wouldn't see him again for a long, long time, Katie had scrunched up her face in confusion. "Is it more days than this, Mama?" she asked, holding up her fingers. Perhaps it was best. They would understand too soon what death was all about.

Mother and Tillie had a lot of cleaning up to do after the company, Emily remembered. She closed the front door and headed toward the kitchen. But as she passed the parlor, she saw Papa and two friends hovering around Robert Chandler. Chan, seated with his back to the doorway, had scarcely spoken last night when he arrived and had slept long into the morning. If she hadn't felt compelled to awaken him for the funeral service, there was little doubt his exhaustion would have kept him sleeping still.

She paused momentarily, wishing the rest of the mourners would depart. Emily desperately wanted to speak to Robert alone, to find out how Robby had died. She needed to know for her own peace of mind. But that would have to wait.

"If the battle for Nassau Island was going so badly," one of the neighbors remarked, "I'm surprised you were given leave to bring young MacKinnon home."

Curious, Emily pressed closer to the doorway.

"The morning the British landed," Robert drawled in his slow way, his voice flat and without emotion, "he and I were out on the long island, delivering supplies to the battalion stationed there."

"We've heard all manner of wild talk," the other man said. "How many redcoats did the British really send against you?"

"Judging from the number of their landing craft, I'd say somewhere between fifteen and twenty thousand. Their artillery created too much smoke to allow an accurate count. The two of us found ourselves having to stay with the First Riflemen, from Pennsylvania. Their sergeant ordered us to move supplies away from the enemy's advance and do whatever we could to cause delays until Washington was able to send reinforcements from New York. In the end, Robby used the wagon to evacuate the wounded. He was . . ."

Emily strained to hear.

"Speak up, lad," the man told him.

"I said," Robert announced, his voice weary but stronger, "Robby had a way of giving hope to the wounded when they needed it most." He exhaled an uneven breath. "On the fifth night, fresh troops relieved the rifle battalion, and we were sent to the rear to rest. That's when I brought him home."

"With him assigned to a quartermaster," Papa mused, "I figured he'd be out of danger."

"So did I." Chan lurched to his feet. "If y'all will excuse me, I need to check on my horses." He charged out of the room, giving not the slightest indication of whether he noticed Emily.

She felt her heart constrict. If it pained him so to speak of it, then surely Robby's death must have been horrible. But something inside her needed to know the details . . . whatever they might be. She would give Chandler a bit longer, then go to him and find out what she could.

For several hours Emily threw herself into a cleaning frenzy. She washed every last pot and then, on her hands and knees, put every ounce of energy she possessed into scrubbing the plank floor. By the time she finished, the neighbors had all gone, and Abby had settled the children down for the night. Now was the opportune time to seek out Robert. She dried her hands on her apron, then untied the strings and draped it over the back of a chair.

He wasn't in any of the downstairs rooms, she discovered, but voices carried from the front porch. Perhaps he was with her parents.

She saw him as soon as she opened the door. Propped on the railing, he stared pensively into space, seemingly oblivious to her or her parents' conversation. Emily moved quietly to one of the empty chairs and sank into it. The soft breeze felt refreshing on her overheated face. She had been working harder than she realized. She gazed at Robert, wondering how to begin.

He turned then, and his sad blue eyes met hers, reflecting

the depth of her own pain. He had always been a melancholy man, but now . . .

Not expecting him to speak just yet, Emily was startled by his voice. "I know this is probably too soon. Nevertheless, it must be said."

Aware that her mother and father had stopped talking, Emily gave him her full attention.

"I . . . made Robby a promise, just before . . ." He swallowed. "It was something very important to him. He asked me to take you and the children to Princeton."

"New Jersey?" Mother gasped, springing to her feet.

"Now?" Emily asked, astounded. "Leave here?" She had not for an instant considered taking such action, especially since she depended so upon the strength and comfort of her family's presence. She still needed Papa's counsel to get her through periods of anger, jealousy, and sometimes even hopelessness. He had a way of putting things into the proper perspective, which did much to undergird her own faith.

"Robert," Papa began, "this is not a matter that must be decided tonight, is it?" His tone seemed to request Mother's patience as he switched his gaze to her.

She retook her seat.

Emily noted that Chandler's attention had not veered to her parents but remained fixed on her so intently she had the impression he hadn't even heard them speak. "Emily, your husband was certain the British would attack Rhode Island very soon."

"I know," she whispered.

"With his last breath he made me promise to take you and your children where it's safe." He paused. "I . . . could not keep him from dying. Please, don't make me fail him in this, too."

"But our daughter needs her father and me around her now," Mother said.

Emily couldn't imagine leaving the people most dear to her just yet . . . not so soon after laying her beloved mate to his final rest. She felt caught between Robby's last wish and her own needs. She pushed aside the suffocating prospect of leaving the farm. "You must give me time. I . . . I can't make that decision just now. I'm sorry." She paused, gathering her frayed emotions. "What I would like, Robert, is for you to walk with me a bit. If you will excuse us, Mama and Papa," she added, turning to them, "I'd like a few moments alone with this very good friend."

Chan's guarded expression was tinged with panic. After a moment's hesitation, he stood and accompanied her down the steps.

As they passed beneath the trellis at the end of the walkway, the heady fragrance of the last summer roses wafted over them. No more would bloom this season, and the realization almost brought tears to Emily's eyes. She would miss their perfume. Many of them now adorned the fresh mound of earth on the rise. Forevermore, the fragrance of roses would carry a measure of sadness. She struggled to dismiss the memory of fading, wilting blooms scattered on the rich dark soil.

A horse stirred in the nearest paddock, and Emily moved to the fence. Chan, in silence, followed as a leggy year-old colt stretched its head across the top of the rail with a companionable whinny.

Emily smoothed a hand across the soft velvety muzzle, aware that Chandler was staring at her. "I'd like you to tell me," she murmured, turning to him. "I must know everything."

He glanced away.

"Please, Robert," she said, forcing herself to keep using the name she loved above all. She placed a hand on his forearm. "I will never quite be able to lay Robby's memory to rest unless I know all there is to know about his final moments."

Chan didn't look at her as he shifted his weight to his other leg. He let out a shuddering breath and slowly shook his head. "It was me. . . . I issued the order that brought him onto the field. I sent for him to come fetch the wounded." He flicked his gaze directly to hers, then, as if he couldn't bear to witness her sorrow, he averted it once more to stare into the darkness. "I should have waited until we were absolutely certain there were no more redcoats in that orchard, but I didn't. I placed Robby in peril . . . and after vowing I'd do my utmost to keep him from it!" Sagging against the wooden fence, he averted his face.

Emily didn't respond at first. She now understood what had compelled him to bring Robby home to her instead of allowing him to be interred in some lonely place with others who lost their lives that night. He had been driven by guilt. Robby had explained about Julia's untimely death, and now another unbearable weight had been added to that loss.

The more she thought about that, however, the less fair it seemed. Robby had been *her* husband. This loss was *hers*.

It took a few moments, but inhaling deeply, Emily managed to control the anger that surged through her. "You said you sent for him. You and the others were already on the battlefield, then?"

He nodded. "A company of us had just sent an enemy artillery detachment hightailing it back into the orchard without their fieldpieces."

"So you chased them away, and then you needed to see to your wounded."

He uttered a groan. "That's the worst of it. We had no casualties! Not a single scratch in the lot. Robby died as he helped a wounded redcoat aboard. I risked his life for a blasted lobsterback! I'll never forgive myself."

Emily considered that information for a moment, then crossed her arms. "If you had not been there, given the order, would those redcoats have been left out there to suffer? I think not. I know my Robby. He wouldn't have left anyone— friend *or* foe—lying on some field bleeding to death. You know that as well as I do."

Chandler stared at her in mute shock.

"Anyway," Emily said, having relinquished a fraction of the rage inside and now able to quell the remainder, "I need to know—did he suffer? I don't care overmuch about the rest of it."

"No. He did not suffer. The end came quickly, I can assure you of that."

"Is that the absolute truth?"

"Yes, I swear." His hand went to his heart as if in solemn oath. "And you were on his mind to the very last."

Not allowing herself to visualize the unbearable, unthinkable scene, Emily latched onto the facts with a measure of relief. "I never would have been able to bear knowing he had endured endless hours of pain."

Robert gave an empathetic nod.

"I . . . never truly allowed myself to dwell on the possibility that when Robby left to join the army, he . . . he wouldn't . . ." Her voice wavered as a quivering began inside. Emily had to turn away to gather herself, and Chan graciously remained silent until she could go on. "The Bible says that all things work together for our good. I confess, I have my doubts in this instance, but I do not doubt that God dearly loves his children. I have to rely on his promise and his love to get me past all this sadness and emptiness. Katie and Rusty need me more than ever now."

Chandler shook his head in amazement. "You sound exactly like Robby. That's the sort of thing I'd expect him to say. To him, the chance to aid the wounded was but one more opportunity to save someone's soul."

"I'm not the least surprised." Emily resumed stroking the horse. "Robby had great faith in God. It was the most important thing in his life. He was forever poring over the Holy Scriptures and passing on to me the various gems he found there. It would have been his dearest wish to assist others in finding the same peace he had."

"Then knowing he had some success in doing just that should comfort you. He spoke of more than one dying man who came to know the Lord before the end."

She paused and looked at him with a small smile. "Thank

you. That means more to me than you'll ever know. And . . . I shall always be grateful that you brought him home to us."

Another silent moment passed. Then Emily's eyes met his once more. "How soon must you report back? I'm surprised you were given leave at all, considering the great battle you must have left behind."

"I wasn't given leave, actually."

"You . . . deserted?"

"Not exactly. I'll return once I have you and the children safely tucked away with Jasper and Esther Lyons in Princeton."

Emily wasn't quite ready to discuss that subject yet, and she started to turn.

Robert caught her arm. "Don't look away, Emily. It was his dying wish. I can't forget it, and neither can you. Try to think of your children, if not yourself."

His relentless stare touched her deeply. She felt as if it burned straight through to her soul. "In my heart, I know you're right. Everyone around here is certain that should New York fall, the British will come here next."

"Or sooner. With that immense force at their disposal, they could easily spare enough ships and troops to take Rhode Island at any moment. Robby said a number of times that as rebellious and arrogant as the Rhode Islanders have been, the Crown must attack—if for no other reason than pride."

Emily could only agree. She nodded slowly. "Part of me would prefer to stay here with my parents and accept along with them whatever happens. But it would not be fair to Robby to risk the legacy he left me . . . our children. *If* I must go, then I want it to be swift. Tomorrow morning, as soon as I've packed our things. I'm not up to dragging out my farewells." Before any second thoughts assailed her, she turned away. "Good night, Robert. I'd appreciate it if you would have your wagon hitched and at the side door first thing tomorrow."

16

A cool, salty breeze off the Atlantic ruffled across the wagon as Chandler skirted the Narragansett Bay before heading south along the Boston Post Road. It was near sundown, and Emily, on the seat beside him, silently blotted the tears that appeared from time to time. She had been amazingly brave bidding good-bye to her parents earlier this morning, but he shouldn't be surprised. From what he knew of her, she would be strong—would do her best to alleviate her parents' anxieties. He admired her staunch acceptance of life's sad turn as well as the peace that seemed to be with her most of the time. He had to admit, her example put him to shame.

He glanced over his shoulder at the children, sitting on their knees on the pallet their grandmother had fixed for them behind the seat. They gripped the side of the rail in speechless wonder at the passing scenery. Katie, her green eyes wide, clung to a worn rag doll, and Rusty's carved wooden colt was right beside him.

The meager stack of belongings piled beyond them had come as a shock. Even with the incredible amount of foodstuffs Emily's mother had insisted be brought along, there was still quite a lot of space remaining. But then, he remembered, Robby and Emily had left their household goods behind in Princeton when they came north.

Ever watchful, Chan searched the ragged edge of the shore to his left. He needed no reminder of the dangers they could face along this route. A fleet of warships hiding in a sheltered cove or behind one of the islands speckling the bay could be unloading a thousand soldiers at any given moment.

At the clatter of rapid hoofbeats behind them, he quickly swung around to see a strapping young man suddenly slow his horse to a walk. The fellow's attention settled on Emily, who made a very comely picture without a bonnet covering her honey blonde hair.

Chandler glanced at his Pennsylvania rifle. Rammed into a scabbard spiked to the side of the bench, it was within easy reach.

The stranger caught Robert's stare and quickly nudged his gelding to a faster gait and went on.

And he is just one ordinary man, Chan thought grimly. If the enemy had reached the bay, the wagon could be swarmed unexpectedly by an entire regiment, and he had but a single shot to keep Emily safe from a horde of woman-hungry soldiers. All too rampant were stories of the scores of women who'd been ravaged on Staten Island.

"Mama, I didn't like that man," Katie whined.

"Hush, sweetheart," Emily crooned. "He's gone now. And you must remember that God is watching over us."

"See what I mean about taking this route?" Chandler groused. "The interior road would've been far safer."

"Yes, I'm sure it would," she returned evenly, her composed expression making her appear even more innocent. "But this one's faster and more direct. You'll be able to return to duty sooner."

She was only echoing the sentiment she had voiced earlier, when they had argued about which way to go. "I have enough on my conscience right now without having your absence last any longer than absolutely necessary," she had stated with finality. He would never have guessed that someone who appeared so feminine, so gentle and soft, could also be an immovable force at times. Robby had never once hinted at it. He had referred to her only as his "sweet Emily." Well, one thing was certain . . . tomorrow before leaving South Kingston, Chan would purchase more firepower. Two pistols, at the very least.

Sometime later, the darkening evening sky revealed a sprinkling of lamplights as South Kingston came into view. Despite the light load, the cumbersome wagon had not made very good time. Chandler knew he probably couldn't count on more than thirty miles each day on this well-traveled road, not with a woman and small children along. Part of him wished Robby had asked someone more worthy of such a responsibility.

He glanced down at Emily, now lying in back with the children. She looked so much more fragile and vulnerable since she'd curled up with them and drifted off an hour ago. Knowing how weary she must be, he was relieved to see signs of a travelers' inn twinkling in the dimness ahead.

Emily sat up as he pulled the horses to a stop in front of the stable. "Where are we?"

"South Kingston. I thought we'd get rooms for the night."

"The sun has gone down already?"

"Yes." The day might have seemed short to her, but for him it had been interminable. Now the possibility of stretching out on a soft mattress was appealing after so many hours on the wooden wagon seat.

"I didn't think I'd actually fall asleep," she mused.

Without anyone but himself to consider for the past several years now, Chandler at once felt remorse for his selfish thoughts. Of course she would be exhausted, having just buried her husband. He would make a greater effort to be considerate of her from now on.

"Day after tomorrow I'll spell you and take over half the driving. You shouldn't have to do it all," Emily offered.

"Take all the rest you need."

She climbed to the seat and settled her skirts about her. "Did you, perchance, see a Presbyterian church as we rode into town? If not, a Baptist will do nicely."

He stared at her. "I know tomorrow is Sunday, but if we

delay our departure until after services, we won't even make fifteen miles before sundown."

"Robert, surely you don't expect—"

"As I recall, you were the one so adamant about time being of the essence. It's dangerous enough taking this road in the first place. I don't intend to waste half the day singing psalms with total strangers."

She set her lips in determination and didn't immediately respond. "Well, fine. You go on, then. I certainly wouldn't think of stopping you. My children and I, however, will not break any part of the Sabbath . . . especially now, when it's paramount to keep faith."

"If you had no intention of traveling tomorrow, then why did we bother to leave this morning? We could easily have waited until Monday."

"No, that's where you're wrong," she said quietly, with a sad shake of her head. "I really couldn't face prolonged farewells just now. I just couldn't. I'm sorry."

"No, I am the one who must apologize. Of course, if it will comfort you to attend church, that's what you shall do."

She reached over and touched his arm. "Thank you. I appreciate that. My husband thought of you as his kindest, most faithful friend, and a very, very good man. I can see why. Forgive me for not expressing my appreciation once to you this whole long day. I'll try to do better tomorrow."

Emily's green eyes shone with guileless sincerity in the glow of the pair of lanterns hung on either side of the stable door. He could see why his best friend had adored this delicate, yet strong young woman.

Immediately dispelling the thought, he jumped down from the wagon. "Wake the youngsters while I go see about rooms."

The following morning found Chandler more refreshed than he had been since the day he left North Carolina to join the Continental army. Resigned to the fact that Emily did not want to travel on the Lord's Day, he had settled her and the children into a room, then paid to have a hot bath and to have his clothes pressed. As an added, almost forgotten, luxury, he had even slept late. Now as he came downstairs, a leisurely breakfast was all that was required to round out his respite to perfection.

As he stepped onto the landing, he caught sight of his dull boots, and he rubbed them across the backs of his trousers. Maybe after breakfast he would see about finding someone to polish them. A man coveted small pleasures when denied them for so long, he mused, striding through the foyer into the common room.

Emily waved to him from across the sea of tables. She and the children had not yet eaten, as he might have expected. He wove his way toward her, noticing as he neared the children that she had taken extra care in readying them for church.

Neither did it escape him that Emily herself looked particularly lovely. An abundance of white lace on the shawl collar of the austere widow's-black gown made her features all the softer. How perfect a match she'd been for Robby, he told himself, just as Julia had been for him, with her easy laughter, her nonsensical little pranks. It was the laughter he missed most.

"Good morning," he said, reaching Emily's table.

"Good morning to you. Won't you join us?"

She hadn't quite smiled, but then, Chan knew it would take some time before smiling would come easily again . . . if ever. He wondered if, as time went by, she would retain that quality of honest innocence she had shared with Robby. Or would it die the way his laughter had died with Julia?

"Morning, Mr. Chandler," Katie said, and beside her Rusty giggled.

A mobcapped serving girl appeared with a mug of hot coffee. "Will ye be havin' eggs and bacon with your wife and children? or somethin' else?"

He flicked a look to Emily, who quickly shook her head with a pleading expression. "I'll have the same," he said, and the server left.

"Thank you for not correcting her error," Emily breathed. "I didn't want to . . . hear the words. I hope you understand."

He more than understood. It was far easier to allow strangers the impression that these three were truly his family. After all, had fate not decided otherwise, he might have been papa to a couple of little ones by now. He had already fathered one—the child who died with his wife.

He glanced at the two youngsters at hand. Except for a stubborn cowlick, little Rusty's auburn hair was all slicked down. Katie, in a Sunday dress that was all flounces and lace, now appeared younger than her three and a half years.

It suddenly dawned on Chan that both pairs of wide eyes—one pair green like Emily's, the other blue as Robby's—were staring back. He cleared his throat. "My, don't you look pretty, Katie. All the other little girls at church will feel plain beside you this day."

She glowed. "Will they?" Then her happy smile collapsed. "How do you know? We never came here to church before."

Catching Emily's amusement, Chan knew he was on his own. "Oh, but who else would have such soft black hair or sparkling green eyes as you? I can't imagine a prettier princess anywhere."

The little girl frowned. "But my cousin Cassie said Uncle Ben told her *she's* the prettiest girl in the whole world."

"*Cassie* has *curls,*" Rusty announced emphatically.

Giving Emily's daughter a simple compliment was proving very difficult, Chandler realized, and he sought the mother's help. She, however, was looking away, sipping her coffee. And which child at the funeral had Cassie been, anyway? "Well, your cousin might have curly hair, but yours is as shiny as a polished boot."

"My hair looks like a smelly old boot?" Katie asked in horror. Rusty dissolved into giggles.

"I-I mean—" Chan scratched his head. "Like a thousand black satin ribbons."

Her face looked a bit more hopeful. "Is that more than a hundred?"

He sighed in relief. "Yes. Hundreds and hundreds."

"Oh, goody." She settled back in her chair.

"What about me?" Rusty asked.

The panic that seized Chandler abated as the serving girl returned, her tray piled high with food—a distraction sufficient to keep him from putting his foot in his mouth again.

Rusty was all set to pounce as soon as the plate was set before him, until he caught the stern stare from his mother.

"We will remember our manners, won't we?"

"Yes, Mama," both children chorused. They joined hands with each other and with her.

Emily looked with some hesitation at Chan. "Um, they're used to making a circle while we say grace. Would you mind?" Tentatively she offered her hand.

"Oh. Not at all." Closing his fingers around hers, he took Katie's and bowed his head. In the awkward silence that followed, he realized Emily expected him to do the honors. He felt heat rise from his collar, and he racked his mind trying to remember some snatch of a prayer after so many bitter, prayerless years. "Almighty God," he finally mumbled, "we thank you for this bounty. Amen."

"Amen," the others echoed.

Chan was absolutely certain the tips of his ears must glow, but no one seemed to notice as they began to eat.

"I'd be most grateful," Emily said after a few moments, "if you would escort us to service. I . . . don't quite feel up to talking with strangers, answering questions."

After his own deep and longstanding anger at God, church was the last place Chandler wanted to go. Even at military camp he had been successful in not complying with General Washington's order that all enlisted men attend services. Chan opted for guard duty instead. He fervently wanted to refuse now, too—to make some reasonable excuse why he couldn't do as Emily asked. "I'm afraid I haven't any decent Sunday clothes along," he blurted.

"Considering you're a soldier, you're exceptionally presentable," she replied. "No one would expect better."

"Anyway," Katie piped in, "we need to see if I'm the prettiest, remember?"

"Katherine Faith MacKinnon," Emily said scornfully. "We go to church to become pretty on the inside, not on the outside."

"You mean our bones?" the little girl asked in total confusion. "But nobody can see inside my skin."

Emily silenced Rusty's giggle with an arch of a fine brow. "Perhaps we can't, but our heavenly Father can."

Rusty dropped his spoon. "Is Daddy looking down at us, too?"

His mother's color fled.

Chandler saw Emily swallow, noticed the throb of her pulse in the hollow of her throat. "I'm fairly sure the church bell's about to ring, lad," he said. "We'd better eat up."

"Will you sit next to me, Mr. Chandler?" Katie asked.

"No! Me!" Rusty sprang to his knees.

"No need to fight over the poor man," Emily said, her color almost back to normal. "One of you may sit on his right, and the other on his left."

"Oh, goody." Katie slid her tiny hand into his.

How could a man refuse?

17

Chandler couldn't think of a thing to say on the way to church. With Katie skipping happily along and Rusty running circles around them all, he couldn't very well drag his feet. As the simple whitewashed church loomed before them, growing larger with each step, he assured himself that if he could put up with Robby MacKinnon's constant preaching, an actual sermon couldn't be that much harder to endure. Surely it couldn't last more than an hour or two.

Reaching the meetinghouse and going inside, Chan swiftly ushered everyone to an empty pew in the back, acknowledging nods and polite smiles afforded them as newcomers and strangers. He couldn't help but notice again how handsome his borrowed family was, sitting all prim and proper with their expectant expressions. The sight stirred buried longings deep within, and he realized how honored he felt showing them off.

With a smile, Katie slipped her hand into his, and Rusty snuggled close. Did the little pair even have a concept about death, or were they so used to Robby's being gone that to them heaven was merely somewhere on the other side of New York?

Emily glanced over with a slight smile of approval . . . one that tugged at Chan's heart.

The pump organ off to one side began to wheeze as a stout woman in Sunday finery worked the pedals, and the opening strains of music filled the modest sanctuary. Yet it took several bars before Chan recognized the familiar hymn as the congregation rose and began to sing. It had been so long.

> *"Come, thou Almighty King,*
> *Help us thy name to sing,*
> *Help us to praise:*
> *Father, all glorious,*
> *O'er all victorious,*
> *Come, and reign over us,*
> *Ancient of Days."*

Having tried his best to dismiss everything that reminded him of God, it amazed Robert how much of the piece he still remembered. The many times he had sung this hymn during his student days at the College of New Jersey must have taken deeper root than he realized. By the close of the second verse, and anticipating the moving words of the third, he found himself joining in:

> *"Come, Holy Comforter,*
> *Thy sacred witness bear*
> *In this glad hour:*
> *Thou who almighty art,*
> *Now rule in ev'ry heart,*
> *And ne'er from us depart,*
> *Spirit of pow'r."*

When a sheen of tears misted Emily's eyes, Chandler lost track of the last stanza and fell silent. Katie's gentle tug at the end reminded him to sit down.

The minister, a narrow-faced man in a flowing black robe, climbed the steps of the unadorned pulpit and raised his hand for silence.

Chandler felt the children snuggle against him, getting comfortable for the tedious dronings their young minds could not grasp.

"In these trying times," the man began in strong voice, "with so many of our fine men away from us, I'm pleased to see so many faithful coming together each week to bear one another up. Before I proceed, Mistress Barker requested that I pass along her most sincere thanks for the long hours of unselfish labor provided by so many of you dear brothers and sisters in the replacing of her barn roof after the fire. I'm certain her husband, Lawrence, will be equally grateful when he learns we replenished their grain and straw in his absence as he represents South Kingston in the Continental army."

That said, he drew a breath and continued. "At critical times such as these, I consider it my sacred duty, dear children, to pass along information important to our well-being. Therefore, in lieu of the reading of a sermon, I should like to take this opportunity to answer some of the rumors that have spread like wildfire around us. This, I trust, shall enable you to pray more effectively for the cause, and so I must ask that you pay close attention as I relate some information I've only recently been given myself."

He stopped as if to see if anyone objected, then went on. "The British, it is true, have taken the big island just offshore of New York port. With General Washington concerned more with New York and the passageway up the Hudson, very little had been done to fortify Nassau Island. But even in that loss our Lord has shown his mercy. On the twenty-seventh day of August, the British surrounded our troops on three sides, leaving nothing but the bay to our boys' backs. All the while, the Royal Navy attempted to move into position to bombard our army from the rear. Upon that dire day, both Generals Sullivan and Stirling were captured, along with their commands. . . ."

The news astounded Chandler. Stirling had been to the immediate right of the First Pennsylvania Rifle Battalion when the order came for his battalion to retire from the field. Even if Chan had stayed, he knew he would have been spared death or capture—he, who cared so little whether he lived or died. It was men like Robby MacKinnon who died—ones with so much to live for.

Where was justice in all of this? Couldn't these people see that life was little more than the toss of a coin? What true and loving God would have taken Robby and left someone so much less deserving behind?

"The situation could not have been more grim," the minister said, grabbing Chandler's attention once more. "A complete defeat was imminent . . . except for God's intervention. As the Lord did in biblical times and other periods throughout history, he provided a miracle. A great storm sent the British in search of shelter. The heavy rains fell for days, and the wind blew unceasingly. Complete and total victory at hand, General Howe allowed his army to stay under cover. As the elements raged, the Royal Navy could not maneuver its ships past the Narrows to bombard our army from the rear. However, accustomed to such ill weather as we New Englanders are prone to endure," he paused for effect, a broad smile widening his mouth, "we saw no reason to wait for perfect conditions. If we did, would we ever go to sea?"

"Amen," someone volunteered.

A low chuckle made the rounds.

The pastor nodded. "Men from Marblehead and Salem manned whatever flatboats they could find and ferried our boys across that night, with nary a second's thought to the storm our bountiful Father had provided. Whether or not they figured they could get the whole army across, they simply trusted the Lord. And to honor that faith, near midnight, our Lord changed the direction of the wind, making it possible to then press our sloops and other sailing craft into action. Praise be! They ferried *almost every man* across before the light of dawn!"

Several women drew in audible breaths.

"As the dawn brightened into morning, the rain stopped, and a blessed fog rose up from the water and wrapped itself around the last few boatfuls, just as if the Lord himself had cupped them in his mighty hand. And not a single man who had been rescued doubted that it was a miracle."

He spread his billowy sleeves wide. "Brothers and sisters, have no doubt in your hearts and minds. Because of unwavering faith, because of fervent prayers, God is standing with us in this righteous cause of ours."

Chandler couldn't help his own misgivings. Even at this very moment the Pennsylvania riflemen could be under heavy attack. After all, the English forces had not shown any regard for the Sabbath so far. He felt a surge of guilt for not being with the riflemen now, lending whatever support he could. But when he glanced at Emily, her vulnerability convinced him of the opposite. No matter what, he would have taken Robby home to her.

The booming voice of the minister cut across his wandering thoughts. "I urge every one of you to uphold in prayer all of our men who've been taken prisoner and all of the stalwart soldiers who remain steadfast. And," his voice softened as he lowered a glance to someone near the front, "let us remember, too, the families of those who gave their lives for freedom. It is my sad duty to pass along word that one of South Kingston's own brave Sons of Liberty, Sylvester Jones, has gone to his eternal reward."

Muffled sounds of weeping came from women wiping their eyes with kerchiefs.

Chandler heard Emily take in a ragged breath. He caught the wrenching sight of her, sitting rigid, her eyes closed, with tears seeping between her damp lashes. He shifted Rusty to his lap and tentatively reached a hand toward her.

To his surprise, she gripped his fingers and held on tight as silent sobs shook her slender frame.

It came to him with all certainty then. . . . Robby had been right to send him. No one else could have understood her grief as he did.

"Let us pray," the minister continued, "that the British will be given an unequivocal send-off to England, leaving us to bask in the light and glory of our God-given right to freedom in Christ."

"And in closing," the Anglican priest in Philadelphia pronounced, much to Prudence's relief, "let us pray that this unpleasant rebellion will soon be quashed. That we can all resume enjoying the benefits of our benevolent mother country." He spread his arms in a wide flourish of luxuriant velvet-trimmed black sleeves. "This mighty empire, lest we forget, has ever possessed the most sane voice of reason and civilized conduct in the entire world."

Prudence ground her teeth in disdain as she observed the pompous representative of the Church of England standing in the intricately carved pulpit. He hovered ten feet above the congregation—high above the mere commoners in the physical sense, she assured herself, as well as in the hierarchy of the Holy Anglican Church.

Sacrificing her own Congregational Church service for the very one her Puritan forefathers had come to the New World to escape had been the most difficult adjustment for her since coming to Philadelphia. How she missed worshiping with her own kind. She ventured a glance at Morgan next to her. He wore a bland expression, but then, he had been raised in this stuffy church with its self-serving clergy. And of course, he had been a successful spy long before her path crossed his.

"Let us pray," the priest went on, "that when next we meet on the Sabbath, we shall be rejoicing in the restoration of New York City and the end of this barbaric rebellion."

On Prudence's other side, Evelyn reached over unobtrusively and applied pressure to her hand. The younger girl was undoubtedly galled by the man's sanctimonious tone and victorious words, but she was also distressed about her Jamie. Prudence hoped with all her heart that someone would soon dispel the rumors of the heavy patriot losses.

When the Eucharist was finished, the final hymn sung, and

the benediction pronounced, Prudence breathed a sigh of relief. She and Evie sprang to their feet.

But Morgan's staying hand dampened his wife's enthusiasm. "We must be sure to relay to the good Father what an inspiring message he delivered today." His attention swung to Evie. "Very encouraging, wouldn't you say, Evelyn? Most uplifting."

Her demeanor became markedly solicitous. "Quite right, Brother, dear. Now that you've mentioned its finer points, I realize how truly wonderful it was."

He grinned. "Ah, look who's trying to get our attention. That fine figure of an heiress-seeking Englishman, Clayborne Raleigh." Morgan waved.

As they made their way up the aisle toward the entrance where Raleigh stood, Evelyn looked at Prudence. "Please don't leave me alone with him. He's getting more persistent by the day."

Prudence had to agree. True to form, he had a decidedly predatory gleam in his watery blue eyes as he reached them and took Evie's hand to kiss it.

Reflexively, she snatched it back, then recovered. "Not in the sanctuary, Clay. I say, did you ever see such boldness?" she asked Prudence in a coy tone, adding a sidelong look of pleading at her brother.

Morgan, obviously at his limit with the pompous oaf, no longer deemed it necessary to keep smiling. He began herding them toward the exit. "Fine sermon, was it not, Mr. Raleigh?" he inquired.

The Englishman gave him a look of tolerant impatience. "Quite. However, one can't help but surmise that with all of General Howe's mighty army, the man should have simply finished off the rebellious trash when he had the chance, instead of allowing them to escape back to New York. Oh, well," he said with a sniff. "Perhaps Lord Howe wants to toy with them a bit longer, like a cat with a mouse."

When he reached the priest, Morgan extended a polite hand. "Splendid sermon, Father, and thought provoking."

The rotund clergyman accepted the flattery with a satisfied tip of his wigged head. "I notice your parents are not present this morning. I do hope they've not fallen ill."

"Not at all, I assure you, Your Grace. They've simply gone to visit friends in Baltimore."

"Ah. Well, then I shall expect to see them next week." He dipped his head toward Clay Raleigh and offered a pudgy white hand.

But Prudence had caught the devilish glint in the Englishman's eye when he heard that Evie's parents were away. Now she watched Raleigh tuck Evie's hand within the crook of his elbow and whisk her down the steps of the grand church.

Evidently, Morgan noticed it, too. Drawing Prudence away slightly, he bent close to her ear. "That London wharf rat seems to think he's going to play with our little kitten while Mama and Papa are away."

She chuckled. "Lucky for us, this little kitten is too quick for the rat. And she does have claws."

"Still, a rat that big might just devour a little kitten when she's not looking. We'll need to keep our eyes on him at all times."

"I say, Thomas," a man behind them said. "Are you, perchance, having a rodent problem?"

Morgan and Prudence both turned to see his father's prissy haberdasher. "No, Mr. Beatty, nothing so serious as that."

"One must not let them get the best of us, you know," the gentleman went on, elevating his brows. "I recently came across a marvelous new poison at the feed store. Here, I'll write down the name of it." Pulling out the stub of a writing stick and a scrap of paper, he scribbled a few words.

"Actually, that won't be necessary," Morgan started to say as Prudence squeezed his arm with an amused smile.

"Don't be silly, my boy, of course it is." Beatty pressed the paper into Morgan's hand. "I'm sure this will help."

"Thank you." Prudence watched as he absently shoved it into his pocket.

"Pray, look at it first," the haberdasher insisted. "It's a Latin name, and my penmanship is not what it used to be."

Prudence suppressed a grin as her husband struggled to be patient with the intrusive man. She rose on tiptoe to read the paper as he opened it.

Your bread is done. A message from Micah Dodd! Micah needed to see Morgan now! Suddenly Mr. Beatty didn't seem quite so irritating.

"Why, thank you, sir," Morgan said with a smile. "I shall purchase some of this at once."

The perfectly tailored and powdered man touched his tricorn. "Good to have you home again, lad. Come by soon and sort through my latest fabrics. I've a royal blue satin that would go fabulously with your eyes." With a wink, he strolled off.

"A blue satin as fabulous as your eyes?" Prudence barely concealed her delight as they joined Evelyn and Raleigh. "Such a find is worthy of announcing to all your gentlemen friends, don't you agree?"

"Sweetheart," he said to Prudence. "Forgive me, but I'm afraid I must go down to the warehouse. I just remembered I neglected to hang the invoices, and the workmen won't know what to crate tomorrow."

"Ohh," she groaned in false disappointment. "Can't you do it in the morning before the men arrive?"

Morgan inched nearer to Clay Raleigh. "Can you imagine? My wife would have me rise before the sun!"

"A ghastly prospect, to say the least," Clay answered with a laugh.

"Well, my good man," Morgan told the Englishman, "if you will be so kind as to see my ladies home for me, I'll join you all within the hour."

Prudence shrugged in resignation. They needed an escort, after all, and as much as they all despised Clay Raleigh, he *was* the logical choice.

"And, of course," Morgan continued, "we shall expect you to join us for Sunday dinner."

Prudence glared at Morgan, but he was already beating a hasty retreat.

❦ ❧

The delicious aroma of freshly baked bread and biscuits permeated the whole area when Morgan arrived at the docks, and it grew even stronger as he entered the Dodd Baking Company. His stomach growled as the bell above the door jangled.

"Morgan!" Micah called out from across the workroom. "Good, you're here." He plucked the baking hat from atop his dark head and beckoned. "Had a special order that couldn't be put off," he added by way of explanation for working on the Sabbath.

With a nod of greeting, Morgan strode through the rows of flour-dusted tables to the back, then followed Jamie's older brother into a small office.

Micah's floury fingers left white impressions on the back of the dark wooden chair he grabbed and tugged to the high window. Climbing up, he peered outside, then pulled the window shut. "Glad you could come so quickly," he said, dusting his hands on his work apron before offering one in a warm handshake. "My good wife has the Sabbath dinner waiting at home. Now that you've fallen from bachelorhood yourself, you must know the pickle being late for Sunday dinner can get a body into."

Morgan grinned. "Actually, I've not had that pleasure as yet. Let's get down to business, shall we? But first, have you news of Jamie? My little sister is on tenterhooks."

"Nay. But he's a quick lad. I gave him my best Pennsylvania rifle and told him to report to Colonel Hand. The man was a professional soldier before he settled here, don't ya know. A no-nonsense man, if ever there was one. He'll keep the boy alive and in line, I'm sure of that."

"That will be welcome news to Evelyn. She's quite taken with the lad."

Micah gave a hearty laugh and nodded. "Puppy love. How well I remember."

"I take it you have a message for me?" Morgan asked.

"Aye. And I want to say, gettin' an audience with His Holiness, General Washington, is like goin' through the eye of a needle! But I managed." He hopped on the chair to take another look outside, then climbed down.

Morgan checked outside the office door.

"The general said that if the merchants of Philadelphia want you to represent their interests with the British army in New York, his answer is an enthusiastic *Godspeed*. Said he couldn't imagine a less suspicious entrance into the privy circles of the Royal High Command."

"That's about what I expected him to say," Morgan admitted. He was all the more glad he would be going, for the deceptions with his family were beginning to bother him as never before—especially since he'd had to withhold from his father his knowledge of Evie's spying activities.

"Speaking of Washington," Micah added, "I seen him comin' and goin' last year, along with the rest of the representatives to Congress. A body couldn't miss that giant. Seemed a bit unapproachable, he did . . . yet when we talked privately, I saw another side to the man. He expressed true concern about you. He wanted me to be sure and tell you not to take any undue chances. If you ever suspect you've been exposed, he said to leave immediately. Spies are not treated like other prisoners. They are executed."

Morgan snorted in derision. "That's exactly what I keep trying to tell my wife . . . *and* that reckless little sister of mine!"

18

"Big stick!" Rusty hollered. He gave a few hearty swings to the large twig he'd managed to find in the underbrush, then jabbed at some dead leaves.

"It sure is," Chandler agreed. He added another branch to the bundle of deadfall in his own arms. "I think we have enough now. We'd best get back to camp."

Katie turned to him, her eyes shining. "I see a real good one, there!" As she hopped over a fallen tree to retrieve it, her foot landed on a protruding twig. She went sprawling, and the tiny bunch of kindling she was carrying flew everywhere.

Chandler watched her jump up without a peep and brush off her dress, then gather in earnest the bounty she had been so proud of. This time she didn't drop any. Observing her movements, he couldn't help but recall that his own son would have been six years old by now, more than two years older than Katie, had Julia not suffered a miscarriage from the fall that claimed her life. Their child would have had neither Katie's dark black hair nor Rusty's auburn, of course, but inheriting some of Julia's fun-loving personality, he'd have been every inch as energetic and exuberant as these two, Chan surmised. "Find all your sticks?" he asked as the little girl started toward him.

"Yep. Every single one."

"Me, too," Rusty piped in, coming over with a swagger reminiscent of his father's.

"Then let's get back to your mommy." Chan couldn't believe how quickly he'd grown used to having the children around. He even enjoyed it.

At that thought, Chandler slowly exhaled. He had felt himself coming back to life during this past week and a half of travel. It was an incredible change for him, after so many dreary years with only himself to think about. Now he anticipated each new day in a way he'd almost forgotten, finding delight in so many little things.

He still chuckled over a remark Katie had made when it had been impossible to secure lodging at a roadside inn because of the hordes of people fleeing New York. The child had stood up in the back of the wagon and planted her hands on her hips. "No room at the inn. Just like Joseph and Mary," she had said in dismay, then brightened. "Oh, goody! Maybe we'll stay in the manger, with lots of cows and horses."

Alas, that night, and every night since, they'd had to resort to camping beside the road, along with so many other families. But even that was not without benefits, for Katie and Rusty could play with other children. Already they had traveled as far as the outskirts of Elizabeth, New Jersey. Tomorrow evening they would arrive at Princeton, and he could deliver Emily and her "wee bairns" into the capable hands of Jasper and Esther Lyons.

So far, Chandler hadn't permitted himself to dwell on returning to the town where he'd lost everything worth living for. Only the promise given to Robby MacKinnon could have made him consider going there. He would do no more than bid the MacKinnons farewell and then make a hasty departure. He could not tarry in the heart of his sorrow . . . nor could he ponder how much more solitary his life would become, once he left this little family behind.

He and the children emerged from the woods into a grassy field where they and several other families were setting up camp for the second night in a row in honor of the Sabbath. Were it not for her rigid beliefs, she and the children might be enjoying this very evening the congenial company of the old Lyons couple in Princeton.

Emily was kneeling in the back of the wagon bed, chatting with a gray-haired woman and a young girl as she put some things into a basket. When he was not beside her for comparison, it was easy to forget how tiny she truly was. Her slender form and long fluid strides seemed deceiving. As always, struck by the natural grace of her movements, he had to remind himself that both Robby and Morgan had told him she was a tomboy as a child, out working with her brothers on the horse farm more often than sitting on the porch with her sewing. It was hard to picture her in anything other than ruffles and lace.

His gaze lingered on her expression. Even as innately friendly as Emily was wont to be, it still wasn't any easier for her to speak of her widowhood to strangers.

Reaching the campfire, Chandler and the children dropped the wood beside it. The supper simmering in the iron kettle gave off a delicious aroma. After more than a year of army fare, this pungent smell was ambrosial.

"Rusty," Katie said, "there's Eddie. Let's go play." And the two started happily off.

"Hey! Wait one minute," Chan called out, stopping them in their tracks. "Supper's about ready."

Emily and the women looked up.

"Oh, it's good that you're back, Mr. MacKinnon," the older one said. "We need you to lift the pot off your fire and tote it over to the Hansons' camp. Being Sunday and all, we thought it would be nice to share our bounty this evening."

Mr. MacKinnon? Chandler cut a glance at Emily, who gave a helpless shrug. Knowing her, she would have been far too polite to refuse the eating arrangement. "Sounds like a mighty tasty idea."

Approaching him with two pot holders, Emily gave him a grateful look. "Thank you," she mouthed, then raised her voice to a normal tone. "I'll bring the basket with our plates and utensils."

"Can I carry something, Mama?" Katie asked as Chandler lifted the kettle off the tripod he had rigged above the coals.

"I suppose we could use a blanket to sit on, honey. Bring the one with the berry stains, all right?"

"Me, too," Rusty chimed in.

Noticing Emily's bewildered frown, Chan racked his brain. "A good strong lad like you might lend a hand with that heavy basket your mama's carrying. Can you do that?"

"Aye. See my muscles?" Shoving up his sleeve and bending his spindly arm, Rusty displayed a minuscule bulge.

Chandler widened his eyes in feigned awe. "I see what you mean." Chuckling, he turned to the women. "Well, ladies, which way to the Hansons'?"

When they arrived at their neighbor's camp, a long table made of boards propped on barrels had already been set up. Chan set the heavy pot on one end, then found himself being waved aside by bustling women readying the feast. His stomach growled in anticipation as he walked toward the men lounging against a fieldstone wall. All of them appeared past fifty, except for one who hobbled about with a decided limp.

"Wait and see," he heard one of the men say. "Washington will outfox those king's puppets yet."

Chandler was not surprised by the topic. Everywhere he went, men discussed little else.

A silver-haired gent eyed him with disdain. "How do. The wife tells me you just come down from Rhode Island on your way to Princeton. Some new trouble up that way?"

Chan shook his head. "Not yet, anyway." He could tell from the mild stares of disapproval that all of them must have been speculating about why a fit man such as himself wasn't with the army. But for Emily's sake he chose not to explain.

"My boys have all enlisted," another remarked pointedly. "So have Rayford's."

A nod came from the one named Rayford. "And I've a mind to enlist myself, just as soon as I get my daughter-in-law and her young'uns to her folks' in Trenton."

"I might just join up with you," a third said. "Maybe I'm not as fast as I used to be, but General Howe's movin' so slow against us that it shouldn't matter much."

"Davis," the crippled one said, "they aren't gonna want a couple of old coots like you two around, gettin' in the way."

Seeing how much the older pair wanted to lend a hand, Chandler shrugged. "I wouldn't say that. If you don't mind loading wagons and taking supplies out to regiments, you could report to Major Kendall. He'd probably be glad to have you. It would free up some younger men to be sent to a fighting unit."

"Think so?" one of them asked, perking up along with his crony. "You know this Major Kendall?"

"I've loaded a wagon or two for him."

"Then you were enlisted for a spell? served under this officer?" A slight note of respect colored his tone now.

"I'm still in, actually," Chan responded. "But I've been transferred to the First Pennsylvania Rifle Battalion. I'll be reporting for duty again in a few days."

Now all the men's expressions became markedly friendlier. "A rifleman, you say," one remarked. "Been in any skirmishes? I'd sure grab at a chance to get off a shot or two at them lobsterbacks."

Chandler didn't bother to elaborate. He didn't especially find the matter of killing or being killed appealing. He decided to change the subject. "Well, don't discount Howe's ability because he seems reluctant to take action. The huge losses he suffered at Bunker Hill would sober any general, make him not want to endure a slaughter like that ever again. I'd wager that from now on when he makes a move, he'll do it confident of a victory."

"Slaughter, eh? Were you at Bunker Hill, lad?" the man with the limp asked. "If I didn't have this cussed leg, I'd have been there, like as not. Must've been one glorious day."

"No one thought so at the time," Chandler assured him, disliking the way the battle on Charlestown Neck was being glorified with the passage of time. "It was a terrible day. A day of smoke. Blood. Broken bodies."

The man seemed no less enthusiastic. "Aye. A glorious victory for us."

"Time to eat," a woman called.

Chan felt a wave of relief. They couldn't truly understand the horrors of a massacre unless they had been part of it. And it was no less horrifying merely because the enemy got the worst of it.

Rejoining Emily, he noticed that her face appeared drawn. Already he was able to read every small change in her expression and demeanor, and obviously she was not coping well. Had there been too many probing questions? He moved to her side to fend off any more queries.

Emily lay awake long after everyone else was in deep slumber. Only the usual night sounds of crickets and tree toads broke the stillness of the camp as the moments crept past. Gazing up from the pallet she and the children occupied in the wagon, she watched the moon crawl across the sky.

She remembered doing this very same thing the night before Robby MacKinnon had come into her life. She had been stargazing and ruing the fact that God had made her a mere girl, thus delegating her to a life of drudgery, while men sailed off to their high adventures. She had bemoaned her unlucky fate to the Almighty. And, oh, how he'd heard her! And answered. The very next night she had been on the run from a redcoat patrol, aiding and abetting a perfect stranger.

She thought back on what a charming and handsome young Scotsman Robby MacKinnon was then. From the very beginning he had bestowed upon her a gallant respect the rest of her family had never deigned to show "their baby." Her untried heart had quickly become captivated. It was with the utmost joy, after having successfully eluded their captors, that she and Robby agreed to have her brother Dan unite them in marriage. They'd known immeasurable happiness during their life together, and Emily hadn't experienced a day's regret since.

Until now.

She swallowed and took a deep breath for strength. Tomorrow evening she would be at the Lyons' Den Coaching Inn. Just imagining the raft of questions, the motherly concern Mrs. Lyons would heap upon her, made Emily's eyes smart. How would she ever get through telling that sweet old woman of this immeasurable loss? Fresh tears blurred the sight of the starry sky, making the pinpoints of light run together.

Next to her, Rusty mumbled in his sleep.

Emily rolled to her side and tenderly adjusted the blanket covering him. So like Robby, he was, her little man. Mrs. Lyons would love him and his little button nose, his boyish strut. She would be amazed to see how much he had grown. He and Katie both. The old couple had doted on their "little princess" during the time Emily and Robby had made their home in Princeton.

Esther Lyons, childless herself, had agonized with her during the births of both children, crying and struggling and grunting right along with Emily. And Esther's gruff old husband, Jasper, had been as relieved as anyone when it was all over. Why couldn't she be happy at the thought of returning to them now? *Why couldn't she go to sleep!*

Easing onto her back once more, she made out the three stars that made up Orion's belt, just above the horizon. It must have been past midnight.

Robby had taught her a lot about the stars. He had picked up most of it during the months when he was cabin boy on the *Gaspee. Oh, Robby . . . why did you have to leave me all alone like this? You were such a good husband and father, so loving and kind. Why did you go away?* When the intense aching inside threatened to unleash a whole new ocean of tears, Emily threw off her cover and climbed out of the wagon. A quiet walk in the moonlight would get her through this lonely night.

She slipped into the moccasins she had left beside the wheel and quietly left the camp. Glancing back only once, she saw Robert Chandler's sleeping form near the smoldering embers of the campfire. Robby had told her that Chan always shied away from responsibility, yet he had been a rock to her. A listening ear when she needed to talk, a silent tongue when she couldn't bear chatter. She would be grateful to him forever.

And how many times on this journey he had endured being called her husband, without a qualm! The thought would have made her smile, except for the constant pain in her heart. Yes, Robby had sent her a treasured friend. Robby . . . and God.

Reaching the far side of the meadow, Emily passed the outer trees of the woods. The earth smelled damp and piney with the scent of evergreens. The air, though cooler, seemed somehow thicker. She continued on into the forest, becoming aware of the soft scurry of woodland creatures, the fluttering wings of a bird she'd disturbed. Familiar sounds.

But then the remembrance of her first nights in the woods with Robby came back with crashing clarity. That time together had been so innocent, yet so intimate. During those nights her heart had awakened to love.

"Whooo, whooo, whoo," an owl hooted.

The swift flapping of its wings startled Emily, and her night shift snagged on something. She struggled to free it, pricking her finger on a sharp thorn in the darkness. Tears, ever near the surface these days, quickly sprang to her eyes.

"Whooo, whoo," came the call again. Questioning.

She faced so many questions now, so many uncertainties. She had no answers anymore. She dropped helplessly onto a bed of pine needles and moss. Beyond her endurance, she relinquished her struggle and buried her head in her arms, giving in to the sorrow she had tried so hard to fight. There, alone and far from camp, she moaned and sobbed and wept out her anguish. When at last the wrenching cries died down to only whimpers, she sat up and drew her knees to her chest, rocking herself for solace. But she found none.

"Emily?"

She felt a hand on her shoulder, and Chandler dropped

down beside her. Without thinking, she leaned against him, needing to feel close to someone . . . it had been so long. When her trembling and sobs began to subside, Emily raised her head, trying to make out his shadowy face. "If God knows . . . how much it hurts," she struggled to say, but was unable to finish.

"Shh." He took her hand and enclosed it in both of his. The warmth of his nearness was oddly comforting.

Neither spoke for several minutes.

"The closer we get to Princeton," he finally said, his low voice resonating in the darkness, "the more the memories of my days there come back. Not just the cursed reminders of Julia's death, but memories of good times I shared with her and my fellow students, of teachers and some of their lessons. I didn't usually pay much attention to the Bible classes, as I think back. But this morning in church, the pastor said something in regard to one of Jesus' great losses. I remember studying it in one of my classes."

"Wasn't the sermon about the feeding of the five thousand?"

"Yes. But that day was very long, and so much more happened than one miraculous meal. The disciples had just informed the Lord of the death of his cousin John, who had so faithfully heralded his coming. Jesus felt deeply burdened over it. His first thought was to get away from the throng, so he went across the lake and up a hill, taking only his closest friends, the disciples, those who might understand the depth of his grief. But finding solitude was not to be."

Emily marveled at hearing Chandler say so much at once—especially when it concerned the Lord. According to Robby, Chan blamed God for taking his wife . . . yet she had no doubt that the Lord was speaking to her through Chan right now.

"Despite the weight of his burdens, Jesus still had to deal with people by the thousands who clamored after him, crowded around him, begging him to ease their suffering. From his Father, Jesus found strength enough to do just that, until the day was far spent. Then he provided the meal for the crowd."

Emily did not respond but waited to see what Chandler was trying to say.

"But still his day was not finished. After witnessing that incredible miracle of the food, the people turned into a riotous mob, wanting to make Jesus their king. He barely managed to send the disciples off in a boat and spirit himself away. And it wasn't until then that he was finally able to find comfort, in the one true source, his Father."

Mulling over the story, Emily began to grasp Chan's point. For all people's good intentions, truest comfort could be found in God alone. "I've never pieced the whole story together before. It's as sad as it is beautiful. Thank you for this gift."

The moment she said the words, an indescribable peace flowed through her, one even more profound than the first wave of peace she had felt soon after Robby was killed. Somehow in the following days she had let it slip away, and now the Lord restored that which had been lost, and even more. "How perfectly wonderful that almighty God absorbed Jesus' pain and lightened his heavy heart."

"I don't recall the gospel saying that, exactly."

"Oh, but it does, if you read between the lines. If Jesus had remained weighted down with a heavy burden, he never could have walked across the water to join the disciples, could he?"

Chandler regarded her steadily for a long moment, then reached and brushed away a damp lock that clung to her cheek. "I'd hesitate to argue that point with Dr. Witherspoon at the college. . . ."

"No matter." Taking a deep cleansing breath, Emily got to her feet. "It's just something I needed this night. I'll be better from now on. The Lord has eased my awful pain and sorrow by placing them on his own shoulders to help me bear. From now on I'll do my best not to take them back."

With an incredulous shake of his head, Chandler looked

straight at her. "You mean, just like that? You can go on now and live as if the one you loved most in this world were not taken from you?"

Emily heard the doubt in that question, and she knew that though Robert Chandler had given this gift of God's Word to her, even now he didn't understand, because he had never accepted the gift for himself. He had spent years shutting himself away from God's peace. But she also knew it was never too late for him to find his own new beginning and then to go on from there. She mustered all the conviction she possessed. "I know Robby will never come back to me, and of course I shall always miss him. But one day I will see him again. And until that day, in spite of the sorrow I'll feel, I know that God will never let me go."

19

As the houses on the outskirts of Princeton became more and more frequent, Chandler found his dread of coming into the town increasing as well. Until now, the children and their incessant questions had provided some distraction from the prospect of the grievous pain that would inevitably assail him here. But observing Emily's patience with them today, he couldn't help but wonder what sort of mother his beloved English wife might have been.

Who could have known how very fragile life was, back then? He and Julia had known such happiness during their months together . . . so sublime, yet so breathtakingly short. Misty fragments of her tinkling laughter still echoed in his mind, as did haunting visions of her red-gold curls, wild and gloriously beautiful.

But those happy memories seemed inconsequential compared with the unspeakable agony of witnessing her futile struggle to live and her tortured descent into the valley of death along with their premature son. The mental pictures slashed ruthlessly across his consciousness again, making him regret his promise to Robby all the more.

The bell tower of Nassau Hall would be visible above the trees any minute now. Chandler's hands began to sweat, and with a constriction in his chest, he labored to breathe.

"Look, Katie," Emily said, pointing out an upcoming home

to her daughter, who sat between her and Chandler. "That's where your friend Cora Beth lives. Remember?"

"I . . . I think so," the child said with some hesitation.

"I 'member," Rusty announced, puffing out his chest.

"Well," Emily went on, "your daddy worked for her daddy when we lived here in Princeton. You and Cora played together almost every day. Oh, and there's the Smiths' place, and the Harrises', and . . ."

Chan tried to concentrate on her chatter. Emily was returning to a happy past, to old friendships. This venture into yesterday was the opposite for him.

Just beyond the college building where he had attended classes would be the turnoff to Holmby House and the simple little room where he and Julia had spent their sweetest moments together. Since students were required to live in the school dormitory, and Chan did not want to risk expulsion by confessing his untimely marriage, the newlyweds thought it a lark to keep their haven a secret.

Everything had been a lark then. Julia, from an aristocratic British family, would have found instant approval from his parents, he was sure of that. But her folks would have been hesitant to accept the union, since it meant leaving her home and country behind and sailing across the wide ocean to the New World.

They met by accident and became completely enamored with one another while Chandler was touring Britain with his friends. The two threw caution to the wind and followed their hearts. Chandler spirited her aboard his returning ship, and once at sea, they implored the captain to marry them.

In their naïveté, they imagined that by keeping their marriage a secret, they could live on Chandler's allowance for years and be free of both sets of parents. A smile curved his mouth at the way some of his classmates, party to their scheme, helped him outwit the professors, just so he and Julia might enjoy some time together. Thinking back on it now, it was hard to believe he had ever been that young and carefree. And that foolish.

Emily's voice once more interrupted his musings. "Yes, Mr. Chandler did go to that big schoolhouse. Didn't you?"

Robert cast a cursory glance toward the immense structure of native stone that housed the College of New Jersey. "Yes," he managed. But seeing the familiar cutoff coming up, he did not elaborate further.

"And so did your uncle Dan," Emily went on, hugging Rusty close. "Now he's the minister of a church. Perhaps someday, when you're a very big boy, you shall go there, too."

"What about me, Mama?" Katie asked.

She smiled. "Girls don't attend that college, I'm afraid."

"Why not?" the little girl demanded indignantly.

Emily smiled. "We learn other sorts of things. But from the look of the place, I hardly think anyone is learning anything there now. It appears vacant."

"Most likely it is," Chan admitted. "Probably in recess until after the war, just as Harvard is, back in Cambridge."

"The war has altered so much more than I would have expected," Emily remarked sadly, then drew both children tighter. "But I'll wager it hasn't changed Grandma and Grandpa Lyons," she added on a much brighter note. "Won't they be surprised at how much you both have grown! We're almost there now. It's just up the road."

"Hurry, horsies," Rusty pleaded as he bounced up and down in excitement.

Approaching the dreaded street Robert had tried so hard to put out of his mind, he snapped the traces over the animals' backs and did his best to keep his eyes fixed straight ahead. Just a few seconds more . . .

It was God's judgment, that's what, came the hateful, railing voice of the landlady in his mind. His gaze swung on its own down the elm-lined street as the wagon passed, taking in the two-story brick house with white sashes. He could not keep from looking up at the second-floor window of the room, where Julia had breathed her last, having their child. *God's judgment on you for trying to make fools out of your family and that good Doctor Witherspoon over at the college. God's judgment.*

God's judgment.

❦ ❦

At last they turned onto the gravel drive fronting the Lyons' Den Coaching Inn. Emily let her gaze freely absorb the welcome familiarity of the huge fieldstone building—three stories, with wide chimneys, neat shrubbery, and a carved, wooden lion's-head sign suspended by chains above the entrance.

Suddenly the doors flew open. *"Emily?"* a young man asked in wonder as he came outside.

She had seen him so seldom once he'd enrolled at the college, it took her several seconds to recognize the now-grown youth who, along with his sister Mary Clare, had been a ward of Jasper and Esther Lyons. He had shot up like a weed, his skinny body had filled out, and his once blond hair had darkened to a sandy shade. "Chip!"

He tucked his chin and grinned, leaping aboard to give her a hug. "I don't go by that nickname anymore. I prefer Christopher. Or even Drummer, sometimes. Some of my friends call me that."

"Well, I like Christopher," Emily said, hugging him back.

Rusty squirmed. "Help! I'm squished!"

"Whoa," Christopher said, rearing back. "What have we here? Your mommy left here with two tiny kids, and came back with a little princess and a big boy. I'm sure glad Robby finally talked you into coming back where it's safe. Ma Lyons will be in her glory with two babies to look after again." He hopped to the ground.

"I am *not* a baby!" Katie announced as she and her brother got to their feet.

Rusty gave an emphatic nod. "Me either."

"Oh. Too bad. I suppose you wouldn't want a piggyback ride, then, would you?" Turning, Christopher took a step away.

Emily gasped as her son flung himself at the young man's back, but she let out a breath of relief when Christopher's arms curved around and held the child secure.

Katie giggled and clambered off the wagon to prance happily alongside. "I know you," she singsonged. "You're my Chip."

"*Uncle* Chip to you, peanut," he teased, giving her nose a tap with one finger.

"Uncle Chip, Uncle Chip," they chorused.

Smiling after them, Emily rose and began to climb down from the wagon. Chandler remained fixed to his seat. "Come on in and greet everyone, won't you? We can see to the horses later."

"No, you go on. I'll tend to the animals first."

From his closed expression, Emily sensed that arguing would serve no purpose, and she let out a quiet sigh. She could understand Chan's grief over the loss of his wife, but she had been praying he would at last begin to accept it. No doubt returning to Princeton, where Julia had died, was bringing up many long-buried memories. She looked at his pain-racked expression, and her heart wrenched with compassion. "Well, please don't be long, all right?" With a thin smile, she stepped down and followed after Christopher and the children.

"Pa Lyons! Look who's here," she heard the lad call as he went inside.

Entering the familiar establishment a few steps after the others, Emily saw scraggly old Jasper Lyons look up from the ledgers he had been studying. "It can't be! Esther!" he bellowed. "Come out here right quick!" His booming voice startled the white cockatoo on a perch in the corner. Methuselah ruffled his feathers and blinked translucent blue eyes, then settled down again.

As Mr. Lyons clomped over and smothered Emily in a huge hug, a pair of chairs screeched back on the plank floor of the common room. Two townsmen who were almost fixtures of the place got up and made a beeline for her, too.

The second the innkeeper released her, she found herself grabbed by barrel-chested Asa Appleton. "Welcome home, Missy," he said, all but suffocating her in his exuberance. "We missed havin' you around."

"That goes double for me," Hiram Brown, next in line, said. Light from candles in the wall sconces glinted off his noticeably balder pate as he beamed from ear to ear.

From behind them, Emily heard a soft cry. She turned right into stout little Mrs. Lyons's cushiony embrace. "My sweet Emmy. Oh, but it's pure heaven to set eyes on you again. Now, where are those 'wee bairns' your Robby's so proud of?"

"Right here, Ma." Christopher, a few feet away, urged the youngsters forward.

"Ohh . . . just look at how my precious babies have grown." Overcome at the sight of the children, the older woman pressed her gnarled fingers to her lips.

"Grandma?" Katie whispered, her eyes shining.

Mrs. Lyons bent over and tenderly wrapped her arms around the child, stroking her long black hair. A tear sparkled in her small eyes when Katie clung back.

"What about this little squirrel?" Christopher asked.

Rusty beamed. "I'm big, too, Gramma."

"You surely are, young man," she returned, tousling his hair before hauling him close.

It truly was like coming home again, Emily decided, relishing the way the old childless couple made them all feel like family. It had been like that from the very first day she and Robby had come to Princeton to live.

"Robby's not with you?" Mrs. Lyons asked.

"No. He's . . ."

"Course he couldn't come, old woman," Jasper said in his usual gruff manner. "There's a war goin' on, remember?"

"Well, at least he sent his dear ones back to us, and that's all that matters now." She gazed lovingly at the children again. "You must be tired after that long trip. But first things first. I want all of you to sit yourselves down, and I'll fetch you some hot stew. Won't be but a minute. Then we'll have time for a nice long chat before the stage wagons get here."

"I'll help," Emily offered, trailing after Esther, while Mr. Lyons began herding the children to one of the long tables in the middle of the ordinary. Since it was Monday, stage wagons would arrive from New York and Philadelphia . . . but not for a few hours, at least. Time enough to relate the sad news to her dear friends.

Mrs. Lyons bustled about the big workroom in her efficient way, seizing a tray and putting it on the table, then plunking bowls from the sideboard on it. She turned to gather utensils.

Emily, on the fringe, whispered a hasty prayer for strength, then stepped in front of the older woman and took hold of her hands. "Would you please sit down first? There's something I must tell you."

A slight frown emphasized the maze of lines on her forehead, but she complied. She drew Emily down beside her, all the while searching her face.

"It-it's Robby," Emily said, struggling to make her voice stop wavering. "He's . . . he's been . . ." She had to take a breath to say the word. It emerged in a whisper. "Killed."

Esther drew an audible gasp, and her hand flew to her heart. Tears glistened at once in her hazel eyes, and for several seconds she appeared unable to respond. "Oh, my poor, poor child," she finally said, tugging Emily to her. "How?"

Being crushed in the older woman's fierce embrace made Emily's throat ache. She struggled to speak. "On the battlefield. Robert Chandler was with him when it happened. He told me Robby didn't suffer."

It took another few moments for Mrs. Lyons to digest the details. "This is such a sad, sad time," she said woefully, gently releasing her hold. "There's a few from the college who can never come back to us . . . and now to hear we've lost our little motherless lad from Scotland, yet. Jasper and I loved him like our own."

"I know," Emily whispered. "I know. And he loved you both

so very much." Her throat clogged completely now. She blinked hard at the tears cresting behind her eyes and tried to keep hold of her composure.

The older woman blotted her own face on the hem of her long apron and sniffed, then drew Emily against her ample self once more. "I'm sorry, child. Truly sorry."

Emily nodded, still in the embrace. "But the Lord has been good. He's helping me through it."

"Sometimes it's hard to understand suffering, though. This will be a tough one for all of us . . . especially Jasper. He set such store by the boy." She wagged her head slowly back and forth, concern evident in her demeanor. "Maybe it would be best to save tellin' Jasper until later, after the babies are in bed."

With such a fragile hold on her own ragged emotions, Emily could only nod.

Mrs. Lyons dried her moist eyes on her apron again, then took a deep breath and rose. "Well, in the meantime, let's see about gettin' the food dished up and served."

When they returned to the common room, Emily found the men all fussing over the children. Katie was snuggled on old Jasper's lap, all smiles, and Rusty was in the middle of the table on his knees, giggling as he tried to catch hold of the timepiece Asa Appleton dangled by its chain inches above the boy's reach.

There had always been an abundance of love here. Even now, with Christopher's hearty laugh and animated face, it was hard to remember his humble beginnings, when the Lyonses had taken him and his sister in. Castoffs of the town drunkard, Christopher and Mary Clare had been worse off than strays. Now the stuttering problem brought on by his father's abuse was only a distant memory, and the young man was studying to become an engineer. Or had been, until the college closed for the war.

Emily and Mrs. Lyons set down their trays, then arranged the sufficient number of place settings.

"Where's Mr. Chandler gonna sit?" Katie asked.

A twinge of conscience reminded Emily that in the excitement she had all but forgotten about Robert. He should have finished tending the horses ages ago.

"I'll see what's keeping him," Christopher offered.

She stayed him with a hand. "No. I'd better go." She turned to her hosts. "It was Robert Chandler who brought us. I'm sure you remember him. He attended the college here for a while."

"Aye," Jasper said, recognition dawning. "That spirited little English gal's husband. There's none of us can forget that sad affair, rest her soul. They took supper here most nights while he was at school, until the day of her passin', and then he up and left for good. After that, his other college friends moped around here for weeks."

"It was real hard on the lads," Esther added. "There wasn't anybody didn't love that Julia. Course, she never lifted a finger to so much as clear a table all her pampered years, I'm sure, but so full of life she was. Always laughing. A room lit up whenever she walked into it."

Emily nodded. "I've heard she was very special. Robert has yet to lay her memory to rest, though. I thought I'd better prepare you before he comes in."

Mrs. Lyons moved near enough to give Emily's shoulder a squeeze. "You're a very special girl yourself, love. Always thinkin' about the feelings of others, no matter what."

The brisk air that greeted Emily when she stepped outside hinted of the coming change of seasons. Soon the leaves would begin to turn all the brilliant hues of autumn. Would cooler weather bring an end to the conflict with Great Britain? Emily could not imagine the militia tramping through cold and snow, facing the enemy across icy rivers. Surely things would be settled by then, husbands and fathers would return to their homes and to everyday life again. Most of them, anyway. She did not allow her train of thought to drift further along that line.

The team, she noticed upon entering the stable, remained hitched to the wagon, though Robby's horse was now settled in a stall with fresh hay and water.

Chandler looked up as he unhooked a feedbag from one of the animals. "I need to get back to New York as soon as possible. With this empty wagon, I could be halfway to Elizabeth Town by midnight."

You're leaving us? she wanted to cry out, but she immediately squelched the thought. She was the cause for his leaving his post without permission for nigh unto a fortnight, as it was. She could not ask any more of him. She had simply come to rely on his steady calm, that was all. She stepped to him, her hand outstretched. "I'll miss you, Robert."

He took her fingers and gently squeezed them. "You'll be fine here, you and the children. The Lyonses will take good care of you."

"As you have. I'll be ever grateful." Unbidden tears gathered, and she blinked quickly and took a deep breath. "And don't ever forget, you'll always be welcome at my hearth. But please won't you come inside and eat before you go? I'll pack food enough to see you back to your battalion."

He shook his head. "I'd best not take the time. I'll be on my way now."

"Without even a good-bye to Katie and Rusty?"

She saw a flicker of remorse in his expression, and she realized that he was probably reluctant to face Jasper and Esther Lyons. But the time had come for him to begin dealing with his feelings, so she pressed on. "Please don't disappoint the children. Not so soon after . . ."

Chandler straightened, visibly fortifying himself. "Very well, I'll bid them farewell, but then I must be off."

"Thank you." Emily grasped his hand. "Come along, then. Perhaps you can eat a few bites before you go. Everyone's waiting."

"Everyone?" The tension was apparent even in his touch.

"And me," she said softly. "I'll be there, too."

20

As he accompanied Emily back to the Lyons' Den, Chandler's feet felt weighted with lead. He berated himself for having dawdled with the horses—he could easily have been miles from here by now. This town had already dredged up far too many gloomy reminders of the past, and the last thing he needed was to call up even more of them. Nevertheless, for Emily and the children he gritted his teeth and trudged after her.

Nothing about the inn had changed. The same carved lion's head filled the wall behind the bar, the same crisp white cloths covered the bare wood tables, the same welcoming fire blazed in the huge hearth at the far end. And as always, happy chatter filled the room.

He felt everyone's eyes on him as he and Emily approached the table where the others were already helping themselves to buttered cornbread and digging in to their stew.

"Mr. Chandler," Katie cried, patting the bench beside her. "Sit by me. See my other grandma and grandpa."

He plastered a smile on his face and moved to take the proffered seat, reaching to shake Jasper's beefy hand on his way. "Good to see you again, lad," the old man said, his shaggy brows winging upward in jovial welcome. On the walk from the stable, Emily had told him that only Esther, so far, knew of Robby's death. He managed a polite nod at Mrs. Lyons and the two other gentlemen he vaguely recalled as regulars.

"You all remember Robert Chandler," Emily said, taking the spot next to him. "He attended the college in '69."

Knowing it was more likely he would be remembered for the scandal his and Julia's secret union had caused than for being a student, Robert cringed inwardly. He was beginning to think that Emily was one of the bravest women he had ever met, with her ability to confront things head-on and get them over with.

"Not only do we remember Robert," Esther replied, a smile rounding out her apple-dumpling cheeks, "but I will always be grateful to him. He's largely responsible for bringing our dear Susannah to us, and then, of course, Daniel. And they, in turn, sent us you," she added, bestowing a look of empathy to Emily. "Yes, Robert, I have a big place in my old heart for you, for all the wonderful people who've become a part of our lives because of you. And certainly we'll never forget your lively Julia."

Robert heard Emily's intake of breath. But somehow, the way the innkeeper's wife had mentioned Julia had not caused the customary jab of pain, only a flurry of happy memories. He could envision her breezing in the front door on a lilt of laughter, her unruly curls bouncing, her eyes sparkling with mischief. He almost smiled. "She did enjoy coming here of an evening."

"Well, have some of this good cornbread, lad," Jasper urged, handing the plate to Christopher to pass. "You look like you could use a few decent meals. Isn't anybody gonna get him a bowl of stew?"

"Oh, my, yes," Esther said in a fluster, getting up and hurrying off. "I'll be back directly."

"Things around here are a sight quieter now that the school shut down," Jasper went on. "Time was, we'd see two or three tables of black-robed students every evening, laughing and carrying on. Now we only see travelers on the stages three times a week, tryin' to leave all the trouble with Britain behind."

Robert heard the last of Jasper's remark as if from a distance. His gaze wandered to the table in the far corner, where he, Julia, and some friends had always sat. Those had been the happiest days of his life. Strange, how that memory did not hurt now, the way he had expected. Maybe it was because everyone here had loved her, too, and felt sorrow themselves that she'd been taken. They had all experienced his loss. Unlike his own family, these people had known her, and loved her.

An unexpected sense of comfort and peace began to flow into him. He leaned to Emily. "Thank you for making me come inside."

Esther returned with a steaming bowl of stew, and as Robert dug in, Christopher grinned at him from across the table. "In one of Robby's letters, he wrote that you and he are assigned to Morgan Thomas, and all you do is haul food and ammunition out to the fighting units. That right?"

Chandler wished the lad hadn't changed the subject so soon after the first truly poignant memories of his and Julia's life together had surfaced. He exhaled a slow breath. "Morgan was sent on special assignment by George Washington. He's no longer at New York. And, well, when the British surprised us by landing on Nassau Island instead of Manhattan, Robby and I happened to be delivering to the only battalion of regular army stationed there. They had urgent need of us and the wagon, so we ended up being attached to the First Pennsylvania Rifle Battalion. I must report to them as soon as I can." He resumed eating.

Now impressed, the young man brightened all the more. "I've got a Pennsylvania rifle myself. Got it two years ago, for my sixteenth birthday. Outshot every single student at the school last winter, right, Pa Lyons?"

"Aye, that's a fact." Jasper bit into a chunk of cornbread and talked around it. "Lad's got a real good eye. Taught him the particulars myself, I did."

"With considerable help from me," the larger of the two townsmen harrumphed.

Not to be outdone, the balding one jutted out his chin. "He shot his first buck with me, I'll have you know."

With his easy smile, Christopher leaned forward. "Any idea when you'll be heading back to New York, Mr. Chandler?"

"First thing in the morning."

Emily met Robert's eyes with a gentle smile of approval. He suddenly realized that he was going to miss her far more than he had a right to.

"You're going away?" Katie puckered her childish features in disappointment.

"'Fraid so, little one." He could tell from her expression that she would feel forsaken, especially since she'd been without her daddy for months before he died. "But first chance I get, I'll come back and see how you're doing. Besides, I need you to teach me a few more songs." He winked at Jasper. "I'll wager your grandpa knows some pretty good ones he could teach you."

The old man chuckled. "Aye, me little Katydid. I've a couple tunes that'll perk up those tender ears of yours right quick."

"*Jasper.*" Amusement twinkled in Esther's small eyes as she shook a finger at him.

"You know, Mr. Chandler," Christopher said tentatively, "I'm thinking about going back with you."

"Chip! You'll do no such thing," Mrs. Lyons shot back, her face white.

The lad's Adam's apple quivered when he swallowed. "But, Ma Lyons, with the college closed, business isn't half what it used to be. And now with Emily around, you won't need me so much."

"That's not the point. I'll not risk losing—" She closed her mouth just in time.

Christopher's face darkened. "I'm eighteen years old. I can take care of myself. It's only right I go."

The old woman jumped up, coffeepot in hand. "Would anyone like more coffee?" she asked, as if the last few remarks had never been made.

Determination became all the more evident in the set of the boy's jaw. "I have to go, Ma. I *have to.*"

"The lad's right, Esther," Jasper said, his own resignation taking the edge off the gruffness of his voice. "We can't be keepin' him here when all the boys in the whole country-side—some even younger than him—went off to do their duty months ago."

Esther's bosom rose and fell rapidly with her breathing, and her plump face became flushed. "And how many will be comin' back, can you tell me that?" she asked, near tears. "I—" with a futile glance at her husband and then Emily, she slammed down the pot and rushed to the kitchen.

A strained silence fell for several seconds.

"That's not like her," Jasper mumbled, a frown knitting his scraggly brows. "Not like her a'tall. Excuse me." He threw a leg back over the bench and got up.

Robert knew exactly what was bothering Esther, and knew that Mr. Lyons would soon understand also. He glanced at Emily, whose eyes were wide and fixed on the innkeeper's retreating form.

"I don't care if she does get mad," Christopher announced defiantly. "I'm going. A man's gotta stand by his convictions."

A man? How young he looked, with that smattering of freckles across his nose, how innocent of the horrors that would soon face him. But Robert knew the boy would not be dissuaded. To a youth, the ideals of going forth to fight injustice ranked on the same plane as saving a fair maiden from threat of harm and then romancing her. The thrill was the same, and as old as time. Not even learning of Robby's death would stop the lad—any more than the possibility of dying prevented a young woman from wanting to bear a child.

Nevertheless, Robert felt it only right to tell him about the Scotsman, to try to change his mind. He stood to his feet. "How about coming out and showing me where to put my team for the night, Christopher?"

Emily caught his hand, obviously reading his mind again, as she had a surprising number of times during the journey.

"Thank you for doing this for me. And, Robert, I'm sure Chip will be going with you to New York. It'll be a comfort to Esther to know you'll be looking after him."

Me? He railed silently. *Responsible for Christopher? Delegated to keep him alive?*

But he could not deny the heartfelt trust, however misplaced, that shone from the depths of Emily's green eyes as she looked up at him. "Just as you looked after us."

※ ※

On the way back to the military camp, Chandler had expected a delay at the Hudson River ferry, since he, Emily, and the children had spent several long hours waiting there a few days ago. It was the only flatboat within thirty miles that had not been commandeered by the Continental army, and with British warships roving the waters near New York, the ferry had to operate many miles upstream from its normal position. But now he and Christopher faced an added delay at the East River, trapped in a long, slow line to cross King's Bridge at the top of Manhattan Island.

"It's been almost two and a half weeks since I left my battalion," Chandler commented. "I'm real glad I made it back before the British invaded New York. Now I'll be here to lend a hand when they do." *Maybe,* his mind added. *Depending on what punishment Colonel Hand will mete out.* He could almost see a line of men, their rifles trained on him, awaiting only the order to fire. No, they'd hang him—powder was too precious.

Christopher didn't respond. The lad was obviously fascinated by the carts and wagons passing by, piled high with household goods, as families left the city to escape the impending battle.

Finally the stone bridge loomed ahead.

"You know, kid," Chandler began, "it might not be to your advantage to stay too close to me right now. More than likely I'll face arrest the moment I set foot in camp. You should give some thought to signing on with the quartermaster instead. He's always in need of a young man with a sharp mind."

Christopher slanted a glance at him. "I'm not a kid. And what the deuce do you mean, you might be arrested?"

"Well, the pure fact is, I didn't bother to wait around for permission to take MacKinnon's body home. I just left."

Christopher's jaw sagged, adding length to his youthful face. "You deserted? You could be hung."

"Maybe. I don't reckon Colonel Hand's quite that ruthless, but that remains to be seen."

"Then why'd you come back here?"

What difference does it make? Robert almost blurted out. But without voicing the futile question, he suddenly knew it made a profound difference. If he died, he wouldn't be able to keep his promise to little Katie . . . or see Emily's winsome beauty ever again. He immediately chastised himself for that traitorous thought, a betrayal of his own dead comrade's memory as much as Julia's. Maybe hanging would be more fitting than dying a martyred hero in the fight for America's freedom.

He inhaled a steadying breath. "I signed on to fight the redcoats, so that's what I'll do until I'm relieved of that duty. Now, surely you can see the wisdom of putting some space between the two of us. When I drop off the wagon at the supply camp, you stay and enlist there."

"No." Christopher shook his head with slow deliberation. "I've wasted enough of my life loading and unloading supplies back at the inn. When all the talk started up about the colonies going to war, I began practicing to become an expert marksman. Not you or anybody else is gonna talk me out of going straight with you to the riflemen's battalion to enlist."

A short while later, after delivering the supply wagon and obtaining directions to Colonel Hand's command, the two of them walked into the clearing about halfway down the island, where the rifle battalion was camped in a pasture. "I sure hope you know what you're doing," Robert muttered.

"I do." Christopher straightened to his full height. "And I'm staying with you. I'll speak on your behalf."

"Don't be stupid, kid. See that big tent over there where the flag is posted? Go in there and ask to enlist. After you've finished and left, I'll report in. But first—" He latched onto Christopher's sleeve, stopping him. "Think about Mrs. Lyons. From what I hear, she's been the next thing to a real Ma to you since you were a tadpole. And one of her other 'adopted sons' has already been snatched from this earth. Are you sure you want to put her through another loss like Robby's?"

"Don't worry about me," Christopher scoffed. "I'm not gonna get myself killed." He wrenched out of Robert's grip and puffed out his chest, walking briskly to the canvas structure.

Robert, following at a slower pace, ducked his head low, leery of premature recognition. He saw Chip approach the sentry, saw the guard raise the tent flaps and admit him. He released a pent-up breath. It wouldn't be much longer.

The guard then began eyeing him. He strode over. "State your business."

"I'm waiting for the young man who just went in to join up."

"Wait somewhere else."

Just then, Colonel Hand parted the tent flaps and walked out into the daylight, tugging on a glove. Recognition registered at once in his shrewd eyes. "Corporal Chandler."

Something about the way his name rolled off the Irishman's tongue made Robert feel that his head would soon be rolling, as well.

21

"Private, disarm this man! Arrest him."

The sentry ripped Chan's rifle from him and leveled his own on him. "Where do you want him, sir?"

Colonel Hand branded Robert with an intimidating stare. "Lock him in the shed with the gunpowder. If it happens to blow, so much the better."

"Yes, sir!" The young soldier jabbed his rifle at Robert's spine. "Move out!"

"Wait!" Christopher bolted from the tent, the haversack on his back catching on the flap. "You can't arrest a man for just doing what's right."

"Stay out of this, Drummond," Robert commanded. He turned back to the colonel. "Sir, the lad doesn't know yet what's expected of a soldier. But once he knows the rules, he should do fine. He's an expert marksman."

"You brought a recruit back with you?" Hand asked incredulously.

"He insisted on coming, sir. He was adamant about it."

"I see." The colonel regarded the lad evenly. "What sort of battalion do you think I would have, son, if it was made up of men who thought nothing of deserting?"

"He didn't desert, sir. He had business that couldn't wait, and he's back now."

Colonel Hand directed a cold glance to Robert. "I hardly think his fellow soldiers would have considered his absence acceptable had the British attacked Manhattan Island while he was off *conducting business elsewhere.*" He spat out the final phrase.

"Drummond," Robert began, "with the colonel's permission, I'd like you to go back inside and finish signing up. *This does not concern you.*"

A glower twisted the fiery youth's face, and he snorted in defeat. "Very well." But he swung back to the colonel instead. "Sir, Chandler had to leave to bury Robby MacKinnon, one of your own brave soldiers, then get his widow and children resettled."

Hand's eyelids closed momentarily in weary frustration. When they reopened, his attention settled once more on the new recruit. "As justifiable as all of that may seem to you right now, lad, no army can succeed if men take it upon themselves to leave at will in order to take care of personal matters. Now, as your friend has told you, this is not your concern. Go inside. Now!"

Christopher's eyes widened. He glanced at Robert.

"Go!" Robert glared until the lad relented and reentered the tent. "Please don't hold this against him, sir. He's a fine young man."

"I'd say loyal to a fault. But since you returned on your own, I've decided not to have you hanged."

Robert felt some of his tension begin to evaporate.

"Tomorrow morning," the colonel went on, "directly after Sabbath services, you shall be brought before the assembly. The charge against you will be announced, and you will be flogged."

Flogged! Robert felt his blood turn to ice in his veins. As the son of a southern plantation owner, he had firsthand knowledge of floggings.

"Fifty lashes."

Dear Lord, no, he pleaded desperately. A sudden light-headedness almost made his knees buckle. During his childhood he had twice witnessed their overseer administering that number to a runaway field slave. Scarcely a strip of flesh would remain on a man's back after that many lashes. If Chan survived, he'd be laid up for at least a week. And if the wounds became infected, his life would be doubly endangered.

"Until tomorrow," the colonel said quietly. Then he turned to the sentry. "Take him away!"

"Sir," Robert implored. "I know I don't deserve it, but I seek your mercy in one small thing."

With unbending sternness, the officer cocked his head sharply to the side. "What?"

"Don't make the new lad, Christopher Drummond, watch, sir. It would be too hard on the boy."

Colonel Hand's gaze wavered, giving Robert a measure of hope. Then abruptly, the man swung to the guard. "You have your order. Lock him up."

❧ ❧

The following morning, the fifteenth of September, dawned with a definite hint of autumn. The air held a crispness, and the brittle brightness of a clear autumn sky peeked through the roughly hewn boards of the shed where the powder kegs were stored. But the chill Robert felt came from the apprehension and sickening dread he felt inside. Loathing the rising of the sun, he sat with his back against a wall, already feeling the sting of the cat-o'-nine-tails laid across his naked skin. The whip was splayed into nine knotted rawhide strips that could slice the flesh with ease.

He had slept little during the night, weighing life against death, cowardice against valor. For hours he had struggled with the thought of requesting to be hanged rather than flogged. A month ago, that would have been an easy decision. Hanging would easily have won out. But every time he so much as considered it now, two pairs of shimmering green eyes—Emily's and Katie's—cut into his very soul, pleading with him not to give up his life. He had given the little girl his promise that he would return. So soon after her own daddy departed this world, could he intentionally abandon his own life—never to smile again over Rusty's little-boy imitation of his father's swagger or hear his childish delight over something as inconsequential as a twig?

But—fifty lashes! How would he bear them?

He had to do it, somehow . . . for them. For Emily, the children. He had to.

A rattle came from just outside, then a scrape of metal at the door.

So soon? The colonel had said after church services. In a sudden grip of fear, Robert rose to his feet.

The door opened to admit a soldier with a tray of food. Another directed a rifle at Chan. Neither one quite met his eyes, but their expressions, to some extent, mirrored his feelings. They departed quickly without a word, locking the shed behind them.

Robert studied the gruel, the coffee, the chunk of bread. A thin column of steam wafted upward from the mug into the chilly air. Nothing except the coffee held any appeal whatsoever. In fact, his stomach churned at the sight of the mush in the bowl. He picked up the steaming mug, cupping it in his icy hands, wondering how many more cups it would take to warm the chill of fear running through him.

He had taken only a few sips when a knock sounded on the door.

"Chandler? Chan?" Christopher Drummond called softly.

Robert had hoped that the things the lad had witnessed yesterday would have sent him packing. But no such luck.

"Chandler!" His voice held more urgency this time. "You in there?"

"Yeah. And I told you to stay away from me. You shouldn't start off here by keeping bad company."

"You're not bad company. I . . . prayed most of the night for you. And I think the Lord heard me."

Just what I need. Another religious zealot. But then, would Emily know any other kind of people? Robert shook his head in resignation.

"When I told some of the men about you and what you'd done, they suggested you throw yourself on Colonel Hand's mercy. They said he's not gonna want any of his men laid up for weeks with the lobsterbacks ready to attack any day. They said that he's had some time to think on it. He'll cut the sentence by half. At the very least." He paused. "Chandler?"

Beg for mercy? The slaves had begged for mercy. Even Robert's own mother had run out in tears, trying to intercede for the field hand. But that never stopped Father or the overseer. They had to make an example of their poor "runner."

Make an example. Could Colonel Hand feel any less strongly, with a far superior enemy force poised to strike?

"Did you hear me, Chan?"

"Yeah. Look, kid, I want you to stop worrying about me. This is all my doing. I just want you to stay away from the flogging, will you do that, at least? You don't need to watch. I don't want you to. Promise."

He heard the lad exhale. "Can't. We've all been ordered to attend. My sergeant says he was given specific orders to stand me right there, up front."

Robert closed his eyes in defeat. So much for mercy *of any kind.*

Chandler was astounded that such a large crowd could be so quiet, so still. He could feel every last eye trained on him as the men before him moved aside, making a pathway to the center of the parade ground. Two sentries walked behind him and prodded him with their rifle barrels if he slowed even a fraction, and it was hard to march fast when his legs wouldn't hold him.

The whipping post came into view.

Colonel Hand stood next to it, grim faced and stiffly erect, with all his subordinate officers beside him like so many tin soldiers. And on his other side, Sergeant Landers . . . coiled whip in hand. His ruddy face appeared all the more red from fury—or betrayal. Obviously this was not a duty he looked forward to carrying out.

Robert's heart pounded so fiercely it seemed it would burst out of his chest. *Dear God in heaven,* he begged silently, *help me to suffer this punishment in silence. Please don't let me cry out like a coward. No matter what.*

His gaze stumbled upon Christopher Drummond in the very front of the assembly, just as the colonel had ordered. It was almost enough to rob Chan of his last shred of courage. The lad was sure to write Emily about this, tell her of this shame. And she had been through enough already. Too much. From somewhere deep inside himself, Robert dredged up a wink at the stony-faced youth, hoping to lighten the moment a little for him.

"Strip off his shirt," Sergeant Landers ordered.

The guards both snatched at the cloth, ripping it off, buttons flying.

"Tie him to the post."

The rough wood, when they shoved him against it, scratched his bare chest; the rope binding his wrists burned. *Dear Lord,* he found himself praying once more, but no words would come to him.

From off to the side, he heard Colonel Hand issue the order to read the charge and the sentence.

Another voice took up immediately, monotonous and flat.

Unable to hear the words above the rushing of his pulse in his ears, Robert suddenly became aware that after so many years of forsaking God and hating him, now God was his only hope. He had blamed the Lord all along for his terrible loss—and, in fact, still blamed him. So why should God answer any of his frantic prayers, show him any mercy whatsoever, give him the strength he so desperately needed?

In utter despair, Chan tilted his head upward and searched the heavens. *Lord God, there is no hope for me. I don't know how not to blame you.*

A heavy silence followed the end of the reading, ominous in its weight.

Someone's footsteps crunched close to the post. "You were

one of my best men," Landers groused. "I don't like it in the least, what you've caused me to have to do."

Not having even considered what this would do to the man wielding the whip, Chandler blanched. "Sorry. I'll try to make up for it, later."

The man muttered a curse as he wheeled away.

Robert closed his eyes and held his breath, steeling himself against the cruel, knotted rawhide strips at the end of the lash.

Without warning the first stroke tore into him, and he could barely draw breath. The taste of blood filled his mouth.

"One!" the sergeant yelled.

Another slash, and a poker-hot wave of pain seared through his entire body. Chandler clenched his teeth harder, digging his nails into the splintery post. Already, warm blood trickled down his back from the multiple cuts the whip had inflicted. How would he find strength to endure one more lash, let alone forty-eight?

"Two!"

Father, I beg you! He braced himself.

Suddenly, the silence around him ended. Murmurings spread in all directions, from scores of voices. Low at first, becoming louder, talking all at once.

Then above the tumult came a shout. "Attention! Men, form your platoons. Report to your company commanders for further orders."

From the corner of his eye, Robert saw men disperse. It could mean only one thing—the British were crossing over from Nassau Island!

"Cut him free," he heard Colonel Hand order.

Robert turned his head toward his commander and met his gaze.

Hand was the first to break eye contact. "Have the surgeon bind his wounds; then have him report back to your company. *For now.*" Then he walked away.

The distant sound of a cannon boom confirmed what Chandler already knew.

"This must be your lucky day, son," Sergeant Landers said, sawing the ropes that secured Chan to the whipping post.

Saved! He could scarcely believe it. Unbidden moisture stung Robert's eyes. But was it merely luck, as the sergeant said?

Or . . . against all odds . . . had God heard his prayers?

22

Robert sagged momentarily against the pole and gathered what strength he had left, fortifying himself. He straightened and turned gingerly around, forcing himself to ignore the pain that even the slightest movement caused in every muscle and nerve along his spine.

"Are-are you all right?" Christopher had moved to his side, holding out the discarded shirt. "Can you make it on your own?"

"Boy!" Sergeant Landers barked. "You were given an order. Report to your squad leader."

"Wait." Robert inhaled slowly. "Please, sir. It's only his second day in the army. Assign him to me . . . at least for today. I promised to watch out for him."

The sergeant looked askance. "Quite a rash promise, don't you think? Considering what was in store for you here."

"Yes, but you know how persuasive mothers can be."

With a disbelieving shake of his head, the man peered from Chandler to Christopher and then back. "Leave it to you to be giving me a hard time about another one of your charges! Expecting to keep the lad out of the fray just as you did that Scotsman . . . for all the good it did him."

"Robert MacKinnon," Chandler said. "His name was Robert MacKinnon. And, no, that was not my intent. This young man has no wife or children to leave behind, and he's accomplished with the Pennsylvania rifle. But this is still his first day in the army. He needs someone to show him the ropes. I want it to be me."

"Very well," the sergeant finally relented. "Who was to be your superior?" he asked the lad.

"Sergeant O'Hara, sir."

Before the man could respond, Robert cut in. "Any reason why Private Drummond couldn't be assigned to my squad permanently, Sergeant?"

"For a fellow who won't even open his mouth to plead for himself, Corporal, you sure are persistent when it comes to others!" He then turned to Drummond. "Take Chandler to the tent over there—" He indicated a large canvas structure flying a surgeon's banner. "Have his wounds dressed. And be quick about it! From the sounds of the bombardment, the battle's two or three miles away, and we've got fieldpieces to move into position."

The unkempt surgeon's ministrations, however, turned out to be anything but swift. Between applying Tincture of Myrrh and bandaging the open cuts, the slovenly man spent an inordinate amount of time drinking from a flask. At last the doctor nodded toward the exit. "You can join your battalion."

"Finally," Christopher grated as he and Robert stepped outside into the deserted camp. "I put your gear with mine." While cannon reports boomed constantly in the distance, the two of them went to Chip's campsite. "If anyone could use a good flogging, it's that so-called surgeon. I pity anybody who has to go to him for anything as serious as a bullet wound."

Robert nodded. At least the bandages would keep his heavy linen shirt from chafing—or worse, sticking to the blood as it dried in all the cuts. "Well, I don't approve of drinking to excess," he added, "but that's the way some men have of coping with their fears."

Christopher tossed his sandy head with a bitter grimace. "What's *he* got to be scared of? We're the ones who have to confront those lobsterbacks."

Robert didn't respond. The young man would find out soon enough about the gruesome effects a bullet or a load of grapeshot from a cannon blast could have on a man's body. The doctor faced his own type of battle every day.

He decided against aggravating his tender back with the weight of a food-filled haversack. Besides, being hungry would be the least of his problems. He hooked his ammunition pouch and water flask to his belt. "Come on. We need to catch up to the others." Even as he spoke, the bombardment ceased. "Especially now." He reached for his rifle.

"The cannons have stopped. Is the battle over already?" The lad sounded disappointed.

"No. The quiet means the redcoats have landed. And General Howe always comes with great force." Clenching his teeth against the stinging of his wounds, Robert struck out across the open ground, toward the woods that lay between them and the eastern shore.

But even after an hour of tramping through the forest, there were still no further sounds of battle. Chandler frowned, checking the multitude of tracks on the ground. He and Christopher had to be going in the right direction. As soon as they broke out of the woods, he would know for certain if it had been a false alarm.

Then another sound captured his attention. He put a hand on the lad's arm, stopping him.

The tramp of men's feet carried from the other side of a rise directly ahead.

Robert motioned for Christopher to follow him into a stand of high, thick ferns. There, bracing himself with his rifle, he managed to ease himself down into them. He couldn't stifle the groan, but inhaled deeply as the wave of pain subsided. He saw the fear in the kid's wide blue eyes and gestured for him to crouch down as well. "Probably some of our boys," he whispered. "We'd best check our loads, though, just in case." Holding his breath, Chandler maneuvered himself onto his belly, then propped his weapon on a chunk of log. His pulse throbbed with apprehension.

The sound of the steps grew louder.

Between the leaves, they could see the tops of heads emerging over the crest. All of them in tricorns.

"Patriots!" Robert released a pent-up breath. "Wave your rifle above your head so you don't surprise them, then get up," he instructed. Wincing and grunting, he cautiously did the same.

By the time he regained his feet, what appeared to be a full company of riflemen reached them.

"Well, well. Our very own deserter," one of them chided.

Christopher stiffened. "Chan did not desert. He just took his friend's body back to his wife and got her resettled . . . and I'll fight anybody who says any different."

"Whoa, boy," the soldier said with a chuckle. "I was only joshin' ya. If you wanted to see some real turncoats, you should've been with us! By the time we reached the crest of the hill overlookin' Kip's Bay, the Connecticut militia that was supposed to be guarding it looked more like a swarm of ants. They was spillin' out of their trenches, runnin' for all they was worth!"

"Which isn't much, that's for sure," another scoffed.

"They deserted their posts in the earthenworks?" Chandler asked, incredulous.

"Aye. Before the lobsters even landed, yet! General Washington come chargin' down there on his horse, fit to be tied. Tried to turn 'em back, but they kept on going. Never saw a man so mad."

"'Twas shameful to see," the other elaborated. "Them redjackets will be hootin' and hollerin' about that flock of scared chickens for weeks."

Robert eyed them both. "Well, why didn't you go down and take their places?"

"'Cause we couldn't make it down there in time. Them English devils was already beaching their landin' craft. They'd have beat us to the trenches. Besides, they outnumbered us three to one."

His pal nodded. "We been ordered to go to the west side of the island to cover the retreat from the port up to Harlem

Heights. Kip's Bay ain't the only place catchin' it. Men-of-war have been firin' on New York all morning long."

"One good thing come from this, though," the first said. "Colonel Hand got a good look at what a real deserter looks like. I don't think he'll give that little leave-takin' of yours much mind now, not after what we all seen today."

"So you're just gonna let them land, then?" Christopher asked, his voice cracking. "We're not gonna do anything to stop them?"

One of the returning soldiers gave his shoulder a squeeze. "Don't you worry none about that, lad. You'll get your chance at 'em. Probably before this day's out."

An aborted flogging, and Christopher had been spared the horrors of battle—at least for now. Two blessings in one morning! Sweet Emily must have been down on her knees in prayer.

❦ ❦

Clay Raleigh stepped out of the carriage, then offered a hand to Prudence. She accepted it with a polite nod. "Thank you, Mr. Raleigh. It was ever so kind of you to escort Evelyn and me to her sister's for tea. Such a delightful afternoon. Melinda does make even a New Englander feel welcome—despite my colony's reputation, of late."

"*Of late?*" he countered good-naturedly. "When during the past century hasn't that Bay Colony been up to something decidedly rebellious, I ask?"

"When, indeed," Evie quipped with the air of an empty-headed twit. She allowed him to lift her down in a swirl of ruffles and lace. He was slow in letting her go.

"Evie, dear," Prudence said, coming to her aid. "We'll be late to supper if we don't hurry inside and change. You know how your mother detests tardiness."

"Doesn't she, though?" Artfully, Evelyn extracted herself from Raleigh's arms and started up the walk. "It's best not to get on her bad side if one expects to have one's desires granted later." Reaching the stoop, she turned. "And, dearest

Clayborne, I'm sure you don't need to be told how disadvantageous it would be to upset the apple cart over the trivial things." She made it sound as if the "apple cart" might yet get dumped, but over something much more scintillating. "We'll see you, of course, tomorrow eve at the theater."

He could do little more than give a reluctant nod of agreement before his little sparrow flew inside.

Prudence was careful to hide her amusement. "Yes, good day, Mr. Raleigh. And thank you again." She raised her hand in a wave as he got back into the carriage and drove off.

Pausing just outside the door, she contemplated Evie's remark about her domineering mother. The truth of the comment cut across the grain. Only out of patriotic necessity had she allowed Morgan's mother to *manage* her from the moment she'd walked into the Thomas household.

It was becoming more difficult by the day to display only good humor when the woman prattled on endlessly about "those dreadful rebels" while trying to remold Prudence into her own image. There was never any middle ground with the woman. . . . It was either prepare for battle, or submit. Steeling herself against the next encounter, Prudence stepped inside.

"But you can't!" she heard Evelyn wail. "Not without me."

Glancing toward the staircase, Prudence saw her sister-in-law halfway up. She expected to see Mother Thomas, but instead Evie faced Morgan a few steps above her.

"Tell him, Prudence," Evie said. "Tell him he can't go without us."

"Go?" she echoed. "Go where, pray tell?" She directed her gaze to her husband, noticing now that he carried a valise in each hand . . . and wore a markedly guilty expression besides.

"New York!" Evie cried.

The door to Mr. Thomas's study opened, and he emerged. "Evelyn, I'll not have you making a spectacle of yourself. Go to your room this instant."

"But, Papa—"

"This instant! And Morgan, you and Prudence come into

the study. Business—particularly of a marital nature—should never be conducted in open hallways."

How like a merchant, she thought bitterly, to think of marriage as just one more business deal. Well, she was one item of business that would not be handled so easily. *Not this time.* She crossed her arms and strode into the room. When Morgan came in a few steps after her, she fought a strong urge to pummel him with her fists.

"It's not how it looks, sweetheart," Morgan offered, his expression appearing as lame as the excuse. "While you were at tea, word came that the British have taken control of New York City."

She blanched at the dire news. "And you were going to run off without me?"

"They occupy New York, but not yet the north end of the island. Washington will quite likely regroup and field a counterattack."

"I think not, Son," his father said. "From what I heard at the merchants' club, rebels have been deserting in droves since the Crown took Nassau Island. And when the army landed on Manhattan, they abandoned the beach, running for their lives. I'd say the rebellion is all but over. I'm sorry, Prudence."

Sorry? All her hopes for her country, for freedom, their noble dreams, were being dashed—and all he could say was, I'm sorry?

Morgan's arm slid around her waist, and he pulled her close. "Don't be so quick to give up. This is just one battle, and you know how each side always exaggerates. All I'm certain of is that I must go there at once. If ever General Washington needed accurate information, it's now."

"I agree," she finally answered. "I'll pack only the barest of necessities and arrange for the rest to be shipped."

He shook his head. "No, you won't. You heard Father. Both armies are still on that one little island. It's far too dangerous."

Wrenching free, Prudence opened her mouth to protest, but Morgan placed a finger to her lips.

"Please, love. Leaving you is difficult enough already. Don't make it any worse. I can't deliberately take you into a battle-field. . . . You know that."

"But—"

"No. We've discussed this matter many times." His intractable expression gradually softened. "Please, don't make me leave like this. Send me off with your blessing, wish me Godspeed, . . . and give me a kiss I'll not soon forget. Will you do that for me?"

Prudence had no other alternative but to do as he asked.

At least for now.

23

"No! I will not hush!" Evelyn stood at the foot of Prudence's bed, only her white night shift and flashing eyes visible in the faint light from the windows. "I held my tongue all evening, but no more. No more." She shook her head violently in declaration.

Prudence, propped on her pillows in the lonely bed, stared up at the ceiling and folded her arms. She was really not up to this confrontation. The entire evening had been simply dreadful as it was. Missing Morgan was bad enough without having to endure Mother Thomas's endless gossip about one nonsensical tidbit after another all through supper. And Evelyn, clearly in the foulest of tempers the whole time, had sat sullen and pouting until Prudence finally finished the meal and sought refuge in her bedchamber. But even that melancholy quiet was short-lived when her sister-in-law burst into her room, ranting like a madwoman.

Prudence swung her feet off the high bed and went to Evelyn. "You really don't want to wake your mother, now, do you?"

Evie glared and averted her face. "I don't care if I wake the whole blessed household. Morgan knew how urgently I wanted to go to New York. *And I will go. Do you hear me?*" Her tirade all but shook the windowpanes.

Prudence sighed. "Well, we can't even discuss the matter

unless you calm yourself. In the morning we'll take a drive out in the country, where no one will overhear us."

"Fine." Arms crossed over her chest, the younger girl tapped a foot in defiant impatience. "But I have no intention of *discussing* anything." She whirled and tramped to the door, flinging it wide. Halfway across the threshold, however, she swung back, lowering her voice a notch. "Jamie hasn't written me even once. He has to be either hurt or dead. I'm going to find Jamie . . . with or without you."

From the middle of the hallway, the rustle of satin night-clothes could easily be heard as Mother Thomas appeared just behind Evie, her salt-and-pepper hair in a long braid over her shoulder. "What on earth is going on here? And exactly *who*, Evelyn, is this Jamie?"

Her daughter's mouth gaped. She glanced at Prudence with an expression of helplessness.

Someone needed to say something. Prudence crossed the room to stand at Evie's side. "Jamie is her . . . new kitten," she blurted out, immediately regretting the silly lie.

Mother elevated one eyebrow and peered over her patrician nose. "Evelyn has never been able to abide cats. They set her eyes and nose to running."

"Oh, yes, I know," Prudence said, trying for the most off-handed tone she could. "It's just dreadful, is it not? That's why we've been keeping the dear little thing out in the carriage house." She pinned Evie with a conspiratorial glare.

"Yes. And now he's gone, Mother," Evie finally contributed. "Our little stray has disappeared. I'm afraid if we don't find him soon he'll die. But Prudence simply refuses to go out with me and look for him."

The older woman eyed them each in turn, then settled her attention on Prudence. "Well, I'm quite pleased to hear that, at least. Perhaps there's a sensible side to you after all." With a curt nod, she turned and swept back to her room.

Mother Thomas at her best, Prudence concluded. No compliment was complete without an insult tacked on for good measure. "I bid you both good night, then," she called politely after Mother Thomas, while giving Evelyn a firm nudge out the door. "Tomorrow morning, Evie. We'll go looking in the morning."

❦ ❦

Prudence settled back against the plush leather seat, relieved that Evie had taken it upon herself to drive the summer carriage rather than have a groom to worry about. The day was mild, with a gentle breeze stirring the leaves. Letting her gaze rest on the heavily wooded hillsides beyond the city, Prudence knew that soon autumn's palette would stain the countryside, turning all the trees to breathtaking shades of yellow, red, and burgundy. It was always a sight to behold, one that made it possible to forget the strife in the colonies . . . at least for a little while.

Absorbed in her thoughts, Prudence suddenly noticed that Evelyn had turned toward the river instead of heading away from town. "I thought what we had to talk about would best be discussed out in the open countryside."

Evie gave a nonchalant shrug. "There are a few things I must find out first." No amiable smile accompanied the statement, only tight-lipped determination as the horse's hooves clopped over the cobbles.

Her answer made Prudence uneasy. "What kind of things? Where are we going?"

"To see Jamie's older brother. Micah Dodd runs a ship's bakery down near the docks. Morgan told me Jamie left to enlist with a Colonel Hand. Surely by now his brother has had word of some sort. Mr. Dodd must at least know where he is, if he's been wounded or . . ."

"Very well, then. We'll go talk to him, if that will make you feel any better. Nevertheless, if we do end up going to New York, it will be to join Morgan. *Not* to scour the picket lines in search of your young man. You might as well accept that."

Evelyn, obviously in no better humor than she had been the previous evening, cast Prudence an indignant glare. "A fine one you are to talk. Seems I recall a merry tale of you riding all the way from Boston to New York *alone* to be with *your* young man."

"Yes, I must admit it's true. But that was different, I assure you. Your brother was stationed behind the army lines at a supply camp."

With a purposeful sniff, Evie pressed onward. "Who is to say Jamie isn't safely at the rear of things himself?"

Prudence inhaled a steadying breath. It was useless to reason with the willful girl until they'd had a chance to speak to Micah Dodd. Why had she never realized what a handful Morgan's younger sister could be?

Seeking a more pleasant diversion, Prudence switched her attention to the lovely brick homes lining the street. Tall, stately trees with thick crowns of green and yellow contrasted strikingly against the red brick. Once the leaves turned color and fell in droves to the ground, this verdant early autumn hue would be just a memory.

The nearer the carriage got to the warehouses and docks, the more of a curiosity she and Evie became, or so it seemed to Prudence. Workers, tradesmen, and shipbuilders alike paused in their work and gawked at them. One even whistled. Another had the audacity to give a bawdy wink.

Evelyn neither slowed nor indicated her awareness as she guided the horse to the bakery and reined to a stop.

Prudence was struck by the absence of the normal tantalizing smell of baking bread. In fact, the place seemed deserted. Had she and her sister-in-law chanced being accosted by uncouth men for naught?

Evie, nonplussed, stepped down and walked to the front door. It opened to her touch, and she went right in without a moment's pause. "Mr. Dodd," she called. "Are you here?"

By the time Prudence reached the entrance, a stocky man of medium height was coming toward them, weaving between rows of long tables. "Aye? May I help you, miss?"

"Mr. Dodd?" she asked, and at his nod, continued. "My name is Evelyn Thomas. I'm sure you're acquainted with my older brother, Morgan." She extended a gloved hand to him.

"Aye." He wiped his on his apron, then took hers. "I see the resemblance," he said astutely, then looked at Prudence. "And you must be his new bride. I sure hope the message you two young ladies have brought me is worth the risk you took gettin' here." Thick triangular eyebrows dipped into a frown in his round face, darkening his amiable blue eyes.

"Message?" Evie shook her head. "We have no message. I've come to question you."

"Did you now?" Concerned creases furrowed his brow.

"Perhaps while we're here, you might appreciate knowing that Morgan left for New York yesterday," Prudence remarked.

"I would indeed. Thank you, mistress. Thank you very much." He turned back to Evie. "What is it you need to know, missy? And be quick about it. There's no sensible reason I can think of that you two would visit a ship's bakery—one that's not even firing its ovens at the moment. Not a ship has been given permission to sail for days."

His brusqueness had no effect on Evelyn. She took a step closer. "It's about Jamie. Have you heard from him since he left? Is he well?"

The man nodded with a knowing grin. "Ah. I should've guessed. But I'm sorry. Me brother's not much of a hand at writin' home. His colonel, though, would have notified me if he'd been—if there'd been a problem of one sort or another."

"Perhaps we could write to him," Prudence suggested hopefully. "Express our concern at the lack of news."

"Sure thing," Micah Dodd replied, still grinning. "There are pouches leaving here for Washington's army near every day, what with the Congress wantin' to keep in close touch. I'll see the letter gets there, *if* you promise not to bring it here yourselves."

"That's very kind of you," Evelyn said. Then her tone switched to a syrupy coo. "But to which militia should I address it?"

"Not any militia at all. To the First Pennsylvania Rifle Battalion. Can you remember that?"

"I'll try ever so hard to. Good day, Mr. Dodd." With a grateful smile, Evelyn swept gracefully toward the door.

Prudence, observing the younger girl's departure, exchanged a dubious glance with Jamie's brother. It was apparent that Evie was up to something, and Prudence wouldn't rest until she found out precisely what it was.

Leaving the wharves behind, she took charge of the reins this time, planning to do the same with her sister-in-law as well. With a harsh glare at Evie, she clucked the horse into a faster trot.

Evelyn, however, didn't seem disconcerted.

The moment they were on a relatively empty stretch of the street, Prudence let loose. "I know that mind of yours is working like a waterwheel in a spring thaw, Evie, but you might as well tie it down. We are not doing anything or going anywhere until we hear from Morgan. Do you understand?"

The girl huffed and looked away.

"I said, do you understand?"

The lift of one shoulder was the nearest thing to an answer she offered.

"And agree."

Evie narrowed her eyes. "That could take weeks!"

"No, it won't. Morgan gave me his word he'd write as soon as he is settled."

"And what does that mean, exactly—*settled?*"

"We'll receive a letter from him within a week, I'm sure. A fortnight at most. Please, agree to bide your time until then."

Evelyn stared hard for several seconds. Finally her shoulders sagged. "Oh, very well. But not a day longer. You can't count on a man to write. The last time my brother left home, there wasn't a single word from him for more than a year."

❧ ❧

Heavy smoke billowed over the bay from New York. Morgan's horse, Prince, began to whinny and prance nervously.

Standing beside the Thoroughbred, Morgan tightened his grip on the bridle. The flat deck of a ferry was no place to try to calm a frightened stallion. He could kick himself for attempting the trip from Staten Island in the first place. From what the British dragoons at the landing had said, General Howe had given the order that his men *not* fight the fire.

"*Serves them Yankee-Doodles right,*" the dragoon sergeant had sneered. "*Let their saboteurs burn the whole blasted town, for all we care.*" It had taken all of Morgan's restraint not to ram a fist down the bloke's throat.

Stroking the horse's muzzle, he talked softly to the animal. But every few minutes, the wide nostrils would flare, and the stallion would try to jerk free.

As the ferry neared the New York side, the wind shifted, carrying the smoke away from the flames so that they were clearly visible. The Thoroughbred became all the more agitated. Morgan hoped he'd reach land with his arm still attached to his shoulder.

A large crowd of civilians, luggage in hand, waited ashore to be evacuated. Morgan considered remaining aboard the craft and returning, particularly with ash drifting down like snow over the area.

The ferry bumped the dock, and the front man jumped down. "How close is the fire?" he asked the waiting passengers. "Think it'll reach the wharf?"

"Hmph!" railed a hefty woman. She planted a fist on one wide hip. "Now that my house—along with the rest of the whole block—has burned down, our champion, the good General Howe, has deigned to order his men to put out the fire!"

"Aye," another man yelled as he tied off the stern. "It suddenly came to the fool that *he* might not have a place to sleep tonight!"

Well, Morgan decided, that sounded somewhat promising—despite the fact that it looked as if the entire town was ablaze. He could at least go ashore to investigate. He pulled a shirt from his valise, wrapped it over Prince's eyes, and walked him onto the landing.

"A pity about your home, madam," he said, passing the

large-boned woman as she boarded. "I only hope the place where I planned to stay is still standing."

A deafening explosion ripped the air just then, and a blinding light illuminated the sky.

The Thoroughbred wrenched free and bolted, still blinded by Morgan's shirt as it clattered crazily away.

"Must've been a powder magazine," Morgan heard someone holler.

The stallion crashed through the waiting crowd and headlong into a stack of barrels, where it stumbled to its knees with large kegs bouncing and rolling around him.

Morgan finally caught up. He snagged Prince's bridle before the animal regained its feet and sent up a swift prayer of thanks that no one had been trampled. Then, coughing as a drift of smoke wafted by, he did his best to calm the Thoroughbred with soothing words.

"You'd best keep that nag under control," a soldier warned, lifting his musket, "or I'll put a bullet between his eyes." From the man's expression, the deed would clearly have given him pleasure.

Morgan placed himself between the soldier and the horse as he guided the stallion away from the landing, through the dense smoke and fallen ash. Why had he ever volunteered to come here? He was beginning to think the ferry had caught the wrong current and docked in Hades.

And unless things improved drastically, one thing was certain. He would definitely not allow Prudence to come to this place.

Exhaling in resignation, he strode into the hysteria and chaos of a town on fire.

24

"Eighteen . . . nineteen . . ." Robert counted off as Christopher jabbed a ramrod up the long barrel of his rifle. "Twenty . . . twenty-one . . ."

"Done!" The young man said in triumph. "Beat my last time by two seconds!" With his short load, he shot a small branch off a tree a few yards away.

Chandler gave him a noncommittal smile. "Let's see if you can do as well lying on the ground."

"On the ground?"

"Down."

The lad obeyed, and with concentrated fervor, set to the awkward task of reloading.

Chan was more than pleased with Christopher's marksmanship. But that skill needed to be paired with quick, adept loading if there was any hope at all of keeping the kid alive. He might have been unsuccessful with Robby MacKinnon, but he wasn't going to lose this one.

As the lad poured a trickle of powder in the flash pan, Chan moved up behind him and bent down. *"Boom!"*

Christopher started, spilling powder. "Now look what you made me do," he cried indignantly.

"Get used to it." Chan straightened, wincing as his movements pulled at the wounds on his back. "The battlefield is full of surprises. Keep loading. You're wasting time. The enemy could be on you by now."

Hearing approaching footsteps, Robert looked up to see Sergeant Landers coming with a couple of other new privates. "Thought you might as well drill a few more while you're at it," his superior said with an amused quirk of his mouth. "How's the back?"

"Coming along, sir."

"The bandages been changed yet today?"

Preferring not to be reminded of the flogging—or that the sergeant had administered the lashes—Robert shrugged.

"It's been three days, sir," Christopher answered.

The older man grimaced. "Can't afford to have one of our best men laid up, now, can we? The surgeons have set up shop about half a mile down the road. Look for a white farmhouse trimmed with blue. And," he added with an unmistakable grin, "march these boys smartly up there with you. They need the practice." His levity faded. "Wouldn't hurt them to see where they'll end up if they're not quick enough to follow orders."

As Landers left, one of the new recruits turned. "The sarge is just tryin' to scare us into obeying everything he says."

"Because he prefers his men alive," Robert added pointedly. "You heard him. Line up."

Hastily the men fell into step. They kept the cadence as they marched past fields with the remains of buckwheat and corn. Low wooded hills spotted with jumbles of rocks and outcroppings lay on the outer edges.

The farmhouse the sergeant had indicated was situated in a ragged field of moldering wheat that should have been harvested a month ago. Robert couldn't help thinking of his North Carolina home and wondering how the plantation was faring in the war. It had been weeks since he had written to his mother. . . . This evening he would set that to rights.

As they approached the building, Robert saw soldiers with a variety of injuries occupying the narrow porch, seated on chairs and steps, lounging listlessly on the railings.

"You three stay outside," Robert told his men, "and keep these fellows company while I see the doctor." He knew they were apprehensive, but it would do them no harm to observe firsthand some of the consequences of battle. He went on inside the somewhat cramped dwelling.

"What can I do for you?" a soldier asked, peering up from a desk near the door.

"I'm supposed to have some bandages changed," Chan responded.

The soldier flicked a cursory glance over him, then gestured down the hall. "First room on the right."

In what was probably the dining room before the war, three long tables occupied most of the center area. Chandler noted with relief that they appeared clean—and empty, at the moment, which was also comforting. He spotted two men drinking coffee at a small square table in one corner, and he went to them. "Corporal Chandler, First Pennsylvania Rifle Battalion, reporting, sir."

The two eyed him. "What's the problem?" one of them asked, stroking a thick growth of whiskers.

"I need some new dressings on my back."

"Guess you can look after this one," the other surgeon told his companion, "while I go check on our new patients." He nodded in dismissal, and light from the window gleamed over his bald pate as he strode away.

The whiskered man indicated one of the long tables with a wave of his hand. "Take off your shirt, lad."

Robert complied, then eased himself onto the table, turning so that the man could observe his wounds.

"You must be that deserter who didn't know when he was well enough off," the physician said wryly, slowly peeling away the old strips of cloth.

"I didn't desert," Robert grated through his teeth. "I had urgent business that couldn't wait."

"I see. Well, they must've believed you. Never saw a man with so few lash marks after a flogging. And I see you weren't busted to a private, either."

"No, that's a fact. They've been making a sport of threatening to make me a sergeant."

The surgeon laughed. "Hard to say which is worse, considering the precarious state of our army." He applied some ointment and fresh bandages. "I think I heard you mention Colonel Hand's battalion, that right?"

"Yes, sir."

"Well, there's a patient here that you can take back with you. I was fairly sure he was malingering, since his wound isn't severe. Then this morning, when the father of a young gal from the next farm came in threatening to put a bullet in him, I decided the lad's plenty fit to return to his company. There," he said, finishing. "You can put your shirt back on. The cuts are healing quite well. In fact, three more days and you can take the bandages off for good."

"Thanks." Robert slipped into the shirt and tucked it into his trousers.

Christopher and the other two recruits glanced at Robert as he and the doctor stepped onto the porch.

"I'll go round up our faker," the surgeon remarked. "We've taken to calling him the Manhattan Lover."

Robert stopped by his men. "We'll be taking another fellow back to camp with us," he explained as the surgeon strode to a lad lounging beneath a maple tree.

Christopher sidled up to Robert. "What did the doc mean by that?" he whispered.

"No doubt we'll find out soon enough."

"Well, here he is," the older man said, returning with the skinny, copper-haired soldier. "I'll trust you to see that Private Dodd is returned to his superiors."

"Will do. Fall in, Private."

As the surgeon strode back inside, Robert and his small group began the trek back to camp.

"My friends call me Jamie," the lad said with an infectious grin as he marched along with the others.

"What's this we overheard the sawbones sayin', about you bein' called the 'Manhattan Lover'?"

Jamie colored slightly. "Not what it sounds like. I was just keeping company with a kind lass who brings cookies to the wounded soldiers here."

"And," Christopher injected, "who just happens to be as pretty as she is kind, I'll wager."

"Or as pretty as he is brave," another chortled, and the rest hooted with laughter.

Anger set Jamie's jaw in a hard line. "Not that she's any concern of yours." His voice cracked.

"Aw, I was just kinda hankerin' after some cookies," the lad next to him said. "Thought maybe I'd take me a stroll over there of an evening."

"Won't do you any good," Jamie returned. "She's spoken for."

Robert cast him a dubious look. More than likely the young man was merely staking out his territory. "Let's pick up the pace," he ordered, hoping the increased tempo might put an end to the conversation.

When they came within sight of the camp, Robert raised a hand and slowed the lads down to a normal march. "Who's your sergeant, Dodd? I'm supposed to deliver you personally."

"Sergeant Little."

Robert nodded. Sergeant Landers's tent was directly ahead, and the noncommissioned officer sat just outside on a stump, cleaning his rifle as he talked to another officer. "Excuse me, Sergeant," Chan cut in at a break in the conversation. "I'm returning a Private Dodd to Sergeant Little. Can you point out his tent?"

Landers and the other sergeant exchanged glances. "Little and his men were manning the picket line last night. He got shot in the head."

"Sorry to hear that. Who replaced him, sir?"

"That's just what Sergeant Fields and me were talking about. The lieutenant asked us to recommend somebody."

Robert sensed what was coming. He regretted having hurried back from the surgeon.

"All of Fields's men," Landers went on, "are too green. Till we come up with somebody else, Chandler, move your gear over to their camp and keep an eye on them."

"What about me, sir?" Christopher asked. "May I go with Corporal Chandler, too?"

"Yeah, sure, kid. If that's what it takes."

What it takes, Robert thought dolefully. "Sir, I'd rather not—"

"You have no say in the matter, Corporal. Little's platoon is camped on the other side of those boulders." He pointed toward a jumble of rocks on a rise several yards away.

Clenching his teeth, Robert left the other recruits he'd brought back and went to his own tent, where he and Christopher retrieved their belongings. Then they started for the other camp with Jamie Dodd tagging along.

"Meaning no disrespect," Christopher said, turning to Jamie, "but is she pretty? Your girl, I mean."

The fact that this very topic seemed uppermost in most of the lads' minds was singularly irritating to Robert.

"Aye, she sure is. Hair like corn silk, eyes same color as the moss growing down at the creek. . . ."

Like Emily's. A lonely ache gripped Chan's heart. What pure pleasure it would be to find her beyond the boulders ahead, instead of dirty smelly soldiers. For the flicker of a moment, he allowed himself to picture her sitting near a campfire, the flames making a halo of her golden hair as she favored him with a beckoning smile.

A distant gunshot was no less a jolt than the forbidden thoughts. He must have taken leave of his senses. Frowning, he cut a sidelong glance at Christopher and Jamie. "Step lively, you two. We're not out on a Sunday stroll."

25

The tick of the mantle clock echoed in the quiet sitting room, the only sound besides the stab of the embroidery needle in the taut fabric as Prudence labored over her design. Why did this tiresome chore seem to be the only gentle endeavor acceptable for society's elite to pass an afternoon performing?

Across the room on the settee, Mother Thomas held her own project at arm's length while she assessed her handiwork, then resumed stitching. Prudence sighed and glanced at Evelyn, a few yards away in another silk damask chair. The younger girl's oval hoop lay idle on her lap, and she appeared lost in thought.

The front door opened and closed.

"Father!" Evie sprang to her feet, her embroidery falling unnoticed as she rushed to the foyer.

"I often wonder," Mother Thomas commented, eyebrows elevated, "if that child ever recalls a single lesson on the rudiments of proper etiquette."

Not certain exactly how to respond, Prudence smiled.

The older woman returned the smile. "It does please me, however, that my daughter has been inordinately eager to receive word from our Mr. Raleigh since the very day he left for New York. I suppose I should be thankful for that."

"Well, give it to me!" Evie cried, her whine carrying easily from the hall.

Prudence doubted that a letter from Clay Raleigh would even begin to appease her sister-in-law's unrest. The girl wanted to hear from Jamie Dodd . . . almost as desperately as Prudence sought word from Morgan.

"Don't be so hasty," Father reprimanded, coming toward the sitting room. "This happens to be addressed to Prudence."

Praise be! Prudence's heart swelled. Laying aside her stitchery, she rose to meet Morgan's father as he approached with the letter outstretched. From his taciturn expression, she wondered if the missive was from her stepmother in Boston, rather than from Morgan. She quickly checked the handwriting.

"Well?" Mother said in her imperious voice. "Is it from Morgan?"

"Yes."

"Then *read* it!" Evie demanded.

Father Thomas gave her a sharp glare. "It's addressed to Prudence. It is for her to decide if she wishes to share it."

Prudence, hoping Morgan had foresight enough to know that any word he sent her might not be exactly private, barely had time to exchange a thankful glance with her father-in-law before his wife cut in.

"Nonsense. If it's from our son, of course he would want all of us to hear what he has to say."

"So hurry," Evelyn pleaded, coming to Prudence's side.

Prudence pried open the wax seal, then unfolded the two pages, wishing she had time to peruse them alone first.

"Do sit down, dear, while you read," Mother said impatiently.

There was nothing left for Prudence to do but breathe a silent prayer as she returned to her chair and began reading aloud:

> *"My dearest wife,*
> *I am thankful to report that my journey to New York was without mishap. However, as I am sure you must have heard by now, the city was ablaze when I arrived. The entire town has*

been in chaos ever since. Hundreds of families have lost their homes and are now camped on the Common. Fortunately for me, the home of Father's friend, Horace Dillard, was untouched; thus, I have a roof over my head. But alas, I must share it with three junior officers of the king's army.

Please inform Father that Dillard will be of no assistance whatsoever in dealing with the British. He and his family departed for England two days after the fire, leaving me to look after their home."

"Oh," Mother declared, "our poor Hortense. How utterly dreadful this must have been. First having her city overrun by rebellious rabble rousers, then the horror of a great fire. And to make matters absolutely intolerable, she had to suffer having her home occupied by total strangers. A season in London was certainly called for."

"Please, Mother, let her finish," Evelyn begged. "Go on, Pru."

The slight interruption, however, provided Prudence a chance to scan the next paragraph, which concerned the conflict. If Morgan inadvertently revealed his true position regarding the matter, Prudence knew she would have to think fast when she came upon anything compromising. She began reading once more:

"As to the war news, there is not much to tell. Once General Howe secured the city, he made no further effort to take the remainder of Manhattan. He merely set up a picket line about midway up the island, and the rebels have done the same."

Prudence felt herself relax at Morgan's reference to the *rebels.* If the letter had been strictly for her benefit alone, he would never have called the Continental forces by that name. She inhaled with confidence and continued:

"General Howe's primary concern seems to be to establish a comfortable command center for the winter. Most military effort

has been expended on moving supplies from Staten Island and off their huge fleet of ships.

I am sad to report, dear, that Micah's friend was killed while fighting the fire. You might send him our condolences."

Morgan's contact . . . killed? Quickly, Prudence read on, hoping that no one noticed her surprise:

"My darling wife, I know you are waiting impatiently for permission to join me in New York. But until order has been completely restored in the aftermath of this horrendous fire, and until the rebels have been driven from the island, coming here would be most unwise. As much as I desire your presence, I cannot allow it just now."

Evelyn gave a huff of rage. "He cannot allow it? *He cannot allow it?* Who does he think he is? King George?"

Her mother turned a reproachful glare on the girl. *"Evelyn.* That will do. Your brother is only looking out for everyone's best interests."

Evie clenched her fists and appeared ready to explode. She flung a withering glare at all of them and bolted out of the room and up the stairs.

"Our daughter has become completely unmanageable, Waldon," Mother remarked with a wag of her head. "You must do something about it." She paused, then continued. "I don't know what the child expected. She merely toyed with Mr. Raleigh for months on end, never giving him an affirmative response to his proposals. But now that he's gone to New York, she can't wait to follow him. I'll never understand her. Never."

Father shifted uncomfortably. "Is there more to the letter, Prudence?"

"Not much. He misses all of us and asked me to relate his love to the family. Other than that . . ." She felt herself coloring. "There are some private words to me." Which she would read again and again once she was alone. *Oh, pray, let it be soon.*

Mother gave an emphatic nod. "Then, Husband, I expect you to go see to that daughter of yours."

"Oh, let me," Prudence blurted. No telling what Evie might divulge in her present state of mind. "She was so counting on some word from Clay Raleigh, you know. She's terribly disappointed—especially since she's talked of nothing but going there to be a part of the victory celebration."

"Silly girl," her mother scoffed. "Surely even she must know there must first *be* a victory."

Gathering her letter and her stitchery together, Prudence avoided meeting her father-in-law's eyes as she left the room. The man had not the slightest idea of his daughter's secret life, and having to lie outright to him was quite disconcerting. But if her father knew his youngest child had involved herself in a deadly game, he could quite easily side with the Loyalists . . . particularly since his son had also been less than honest in keeping Evie's duplicity from him.

Upstairs, Prudence rapped softly on her sister-in-law's closed door. When she received no reply, she walked in, startling the girl. But Evie was no less shocked than Prudence herself was when she saw the girl throwing things into a large valise on the bed. "What are you doing?" she asked.

With a toss of her dark curls, Evie resumed her task. "Exactly what it looks like."

"I think not," Prudence challenged. "Even if I must resort to tying you to the bedpost, you'll not escape into the dark of night, young lady."

She turned with a huff. "I doubt someone as small as you can stop me."

"You're right," Prudence answered, undaunted. "Your father, however, would find it measurably easier."

"Is that right?" Evie hurled back, eyes flashing. "And I suppose you intend to tell him about me. Well, do what you must. But let's not overlook Mother. I'm sure she would be interested in hearing a few things, too. Shall I call her now?"

Prudence needed no one to tell her that in Evie's present state of hysteria, she would not hesitate to do that very thing.

She inhaled a strengthening breath and forced herself to speak calmly. "Evie, dear. Please, sit down. You know I'm on your side." When the girl refused to move, Prudence took her hand and tugged her down on the bed beside her. "I want to go to New York every bit as badly as you do. Truly I do."

Evelyn pursed her lips, her gaze downcast, but gradually she began to crumble. "It-it's been two months since Jamie left. Two long months! He *promised* me he'd write. I just know he has to be dead, or lying somewhere mortally wounded. It's all I can think about. I have to go. I just have to. Now!"

"But Morgan said—"

"A pox on Morgan!" Jumping to her feet, Evelyn seized her valise and dashed for the door.

Prudence picked up her skirts and gave chase, lunging for her just before Evie gained the back stairs. They landed unceremoniously in a sprawl, and Prudence was more than aware of the racket they were making. She heard herself capitulate. "Very well. We'll go. But there are a few things we must do first."

Evie stopped struggling. She turned, brushing a wayward curl from her eyes. "You'd better not be trying to trick me."

"I—"

"What in the world is going on up there?" Mother Thomas railed, her footsteps echoing from the front stairwell. "It sounds like a herd of wild horses!"

Prudence and Evie scrambled to their feet, smoothing their skirts. Evie deftly positioned hers over the bag at her feet. "Nothing, Mother," she called. "We were just chasing a . . . a mouse."

"A mouse!" her mother gasped. The footsteps stopped.

"Yes." A mischievous smile spread across her lips. "But everything's all right now. We stomped it to death."

A sound of smothered horror came from the older woman.

"Never fear, I'll dispose of it out back."

"Yes . . . well . . . I'd better get back to your father." Her hasty retreat faded from the stairwell.

"She abhors mice," Evie giggled.

Prudence, torn between guilt and relief, was very glad that, if nothing else, at least Evelyn's mood was lighter. "Let's go back to your room. You have a letter to compose."

The younger girl frowned but complied.

Once inside the chamber, Prudence closed the door. "You must pen a convincing letter to your parents, or they'll send agents after us."

"What should I write?"

Prudence thought for a minute. "Tell them that just before Clay left Philadelphia you said some horrid things to him. Say that you won't have any peace until you go to him and make things right. Hopefully, that will take care of your mother."

Evie nodded. Turning to her desk, she sat down and took out a sheet of paper, then dipped a quill into the inkwell.

"Now for your father," Prudence went on. "Write that when you threatened to sneak away at the very first opportunity, I agreed with great reluctance to accompany you as chaperon. And don't forget to say *with great reluctance*. Tell him I will take every precaution, that sort of thing."

As Evelyn nodded and began to write, Prudence stepped to the door. "I'll go and pack a few necessities. For safety's sake we should wear men's clothes. I'll bring some of Morgan's back for you. Oh, and Evie . . . be sure to request that your mother have our clothes shipped to us as soon as possible."

"My, you do think of everything," the younger girl said in amazement.

"That's not all. Before we leave town, we must find Micah Dodd and relay Morgan's message."

"And find out if he's heard from Jamie," Evie added with renewed emotion.

"Yes, dear, that, too. Now, do you know where your father keeps the key to his weapons cabinet?"

"Weapons?" Evie whispered.

"I'm hoping he has a pair of pistols."

Her light blue eyes flared. "But I don't know the first thing about guns."

"Then it's time you learned, don't you think?"

26

A knock rattled the door of Morgan's bedchamber. Assuming that it was either one of the king's men in need of some service or a servant with yet another complaint regarding the same, he reluctantly set down the volume on the history of the Roman Empire that he had obtained from the library downstairs. He did not appreciate being left in charge of the Dillard household. Were it not for Prudence's tendency to snoop herself right into a noose, she could be here now to run the place—not to mention warming his heart and his bed, since winter was not far off. But Morgan knew he could not trust his beautiful wife to remain out of danger. Irritated by the tangle of thoughts, he answered the summons.

Captain Gorton, the highest ranking of the three officers lodging at the house, stood stiffly at the door in full dress, military hat cocked under one arm. "Good evening, Mr. Thomas. I hope I'm not disturbing you. I was unable to return home in time for the supper hour, having accepted a rather last-minute invitation. You mentioned wanting to meet some of the quartermaster officers, did you not?"

"Why, yes. Absolutely." The offer piqued Morgan's interest. "As you know, I've come representing a number of Philadelphia merchants."

"Then throw on your coat, and let's be off. General Howe is hosting an impromptu gathering this eve. I've a feeling he intends to make an announcement of some import. Even the governor himself is expected."

"Splendid. One would not want to miss such a fortuitous occasion. I appreciate this immensely, Captain. I shall have to think up a worthy reward for you."

The man's eyes sparkled with anticipation. "My pleasure, to be sure."

A pity the remainder of the world's problems couldn't be handled as simply, Morgan mused. "Give me five minutes, will you? I must change into something more appropriate."

"As you wish. I shall wait for you downstairs."

A short time later, in his best satin and lace finery, Morgan accompanied Captain Gorton to one of the grandest homes in all of the city. Made of pink brick with white columns, it occupied a broad expanse along one side of a tree-shaded street. But no amount of wealth could dispel the lingering odor of burnt ash that still permeated the air.

Morgan noted a number of fine carriages of the New York elite already lining the horseshoe drive. Apparently, not everyone had been fortunate enough to escape the chaos of the city as the Dillards had. But then, not all had wished to take leave. Wise Loyalist businessmen knew that the opportunities for profit were prime at this time, with lucrative contracts—if not outright monopolies—to be gained.

As Morgan walked up the drive to the entrance, an unexplained feeling of disquiet went through him. Although he had heard nothing to substantiate his strongest fear, it was entirely possible that some of Boston's exiled Tory merchants might have come with the army from Halifax—merchants who might now suspect that he was responsible for the loss of a number of their cargoes last year.

The captain tapped the brass knocker, and a butler ushered them inside to a huge and already crowded room. On the far end of the elegant expanse, a string quartet was making a feeble attempt at being heard above the drone of conversation.

Morgan scanned the face of every man he could see who

was not in uniform, and then he relaxed. Not a familiar Bostonian among them. The evening could be spent quite fruitfully, putting together deals for his father and associates while keeping his ears perked for any valuable military information.

Beside him, the captain groaned. "Not a female here under fifty . . . and precious few even of them."

"Shipped off to the safety of London, no doubt," Morgan said, chuckling, "as were the Dillard daughters."

The officer gave a sly smile. "I don't understand. I volunteered personally to see to the safety of the oldest girl."

"Quite. But don't despair. If ever you happen to be in Philadelphia, I'll introduce you to some of our loveliest." As he casually spoke the words, Morgan realized another reason he could not allow Prudence—and more important, Evie—to come here. With three British officers having the run of the house, he would be forced to keep a constant eye on his wife and young sister.

"I shall hold you to that," Gorton remarked. "I've no doubt we'll be dropping in on that city the moment we tire of New York hospitality . . . which, from the look of things, won't be long."

"The look of things?" Morgan returned. He hadn't thought the man was privy to command decisions, much less that he would have knowledge of a possible movement to Philadelphia.

The officer smirked. "One cannot deny a substantial loss of charm in a town that's been half burned down. And it's said that the farther south one goes, the prettier the belles."

Morgan dismissed the comment as no more than wishful thinking on the captain's part. He gazed around the room again and spotted the commander, William Howe, and his admiral brother, Richard, at one side of the room. A number of high-ranking officers surrounded the pair. "An incentive like that should inspire your soldiers to finish business here quickly so they can move on," Morgan said to Gorton. He began gravitating toward the commander, a large, slow, sleepy-looking man with a dark complexion.

"Morgan Thomas!" The voice came from behind.

Morgan cringed. He only hoped it belonged to friend, rather than foe.

"Morgan," Clay Raleigh said, making his way over to him. "I'm glad I found you here tonight."

"I didn't realize you had already come to New York."

The Englishman drew up his snobbish mouth. "My father, I'm afraid, insisted that I accompany him. Alas, I was obliged to tear myself away from your sister's charm and beauty. And as you can see, those particular qualities are sorely missed here." He took a sip from his goblet. "Have you, perchance, sent for her yet? She said that she would anxiously count the days until her arrival."

"Actually, I thought it might be wiser to wait until things are more settled here."

Clay's expression fell. "When do you think that might be?"

"I've no idea. Perhaps the good captain might be able to tell us. Oh, forgive my rudeness. Captain Gorton, may I present Mr. Clayborne Raleigh."

"Of the tobacco-buying Raleighs?" the officer asked, his eyes widening in undisguised interest.

"Yes. One and the same," Clay said with pride. "And we would be most grateful if you would hurry and make the city a safe place into which our gentle ladies might be brought."

The man looked from him to Morgan and back. "This lovely damsel you spoke of . . . would she be residing with her brother?"

Clay nodded. "Of course."

"Hmm. A lovely young flower at the Dillards' once again. You've come to the right person. I'm captain of the city guard. I should be happy to assume full responsibility for her comfort and safety, once she arrives."

No doubt, Morgan thought wryly. Time to extract himself from yet another womanizer who would care not a whit that the girl was barely sixteen. "Your father," he said, turning to Raleigh. "Is he here this eve?"

"Yes. Busy conducting business, as usual. He's over yonder, talking with the quartermaster of a regiment of light infantry." He motioned with his glass.

"Splendid. I'd like to meet him."

Excusing themselves from Gorton, Morgan and Clay joined the elder Raleigh. Somewhat taller than his impeccably groomed son, the man was far more reserved in demeanor—and more attractive as well, with thick brown hair and clear hazel eyes. Morgan knew him to be a true trader, with his attention squarely on the margin of profit—and he respected the man for not assuming airs as his son did.

Morgan immediately set upon immersing himself into the intricacies of price haggling with the quartermaster, and within moments managed to secure a good price for his proffered cargo of beans and molasses.

"If you don't mind," Clay muttered, obviously bored, "I think I'll mingle a bit."

"I'll join you," Morgan offered. Having concluded a piece of business for his father, it was high time to take care of a few matters for General Washington.

They turned to move on toward the Howes.

Morgan, struck by a sickeningly familiar face directly in his path, stopped dead. "Captain Long," he said with forced enthusiasm. "How delightful." He offered a hand, hoping his initial shock had not been noticed. "I've been in town for nearly a month. How is it we just now meet?"

The man's shrewd, hooded eyes narrowed as he took Morgan's hand. "Mr. Thomas. I've been kept quite busy, preparing for the mass of prisoners we'll soon be incarcerating, questioning those already in my confines . . . executing spies. I trust you heard about the young fellow we sent to the gallows a few weeks back. Nathan Hale, as I recall. A spy posing as a tutor." Though his tone was cordial enough, Morgan knew the comment was little more than a veiled threat.

"Ah, yes. Well, I'm glad I bumped into you," Morgan lied,

hoping to ease the officer's distrust, if not his dislike. "I'm afraid when I left Boston to return to Philadelphia, I lost track of Andy Sewell. Do you know, perchance, if he stayed in Halifax or went all the way to England?" Morgan instantly regretted having this conversation in Clay Raleigh's presence. The young man might mention that Morgan arrived in Philadelphia but a short time ago, rather than the two years he wanted Long to believe.

The captain's expression remained unreadable. "While you were enjoying yourself in the 'City of Brotherly Love,'— and I was enduring endless dull months in Boston, then Halifax—the Sewells sailed to England."

Morgan realized that the man would never forgive him for not wrangling a transfer for him to the detachment in Philadelphia, as he had once offered to do as an attempted bribe . . . only to have one of the man's subordinates inadvertently witness the exchange. "Well, Captain, you have the good fortune to be precisely where all the excitement happens to be. Compared to New York at the moment, Philadelphia is rather tiresome, indeed. In fact, I intend to find the highest vantage point from which to sit and view the unfolding of the great drama when your commander decides to field his attack. I'm sure he'll deploy the most brilliant of strategies."

"Yes," Raleigh added. "And when *is* the big day?"

Only now did Long's gaze withdraw from studying Morgan to fasten instead on Clay.

"Oh, forgive me, Captain Long," Morgan said. "I'd like to introduce Clayborne Raleigh, a tobacco buyer from London."

As the two shook hands, Morgan seized the chance to depart. "If you'll excuse us, sir, there are some other officers I'd like my friend Clay to meet." Then, with no little relief at having wrested himself from Long's presence, he led the way across the room toward the other two lieutenants who were lodging at the Dillard home.

A drumroll interrupted their passage.

General Howe stepped onto the stage, and the instruments lapsed into silence. Quiet immediately descended upon the rest of the room. "Ladies and gentlemen," he began, "I do hope you are enjoying our hospitality. But that's only one of the reasons I invited you here this evening. I am pleased to inform you that within the next few days, the rebel army will be no more."

A great roar of cheers followed the words.

Howe raised his hand. "On a very near day and hour—which, unfortunately, I am not at liberty to divulge—our brave men shall go forth and march down on the enemy like the Roman soldiers of old . . . *and crush them beneath our heels!*"

Another cheer exploded.

"Then," he went on, "all you merchants and tradesmen will be pleased to hear that we shall settle here for the winter. We will await Parliament's further orders concerning the punitive action to be taken against any remaining pockets of rebellion in every colony—and particularly, their leaders holding that Yankee-Doodle Congress in Philadelphia."

I must get this news to Washington at once, Morgan thought as the commander stepped down and derisive laughter and happy chatter broke out. But without a contact, he would have to take it himself.

Clay Raleigh, at his shoulder, grabbed him in an exuberant hug. Morgan could only pray he would make it past the pickets alive, for Prudence's sake . . . and his own. The thought of never seeing her or holding her again was almost too much to bear.

Feeling the fine hairs on the back of his neck begin to prickle, Morgan glanced up to find Captain Long's intense gaze on him, as if daring him to pass on the information just related. But then logic took over. If the man even remotely suspected him of spying, he would be only too glad to make the arrest personally. It was merely the thwarting of Long's desired transfer and the accompanying hefty bribe that caused the ill feelings between them. *Merely that.*

Nevertheless, Morgan knew he had to leave. Now. Perhaps if he invited Clay Raleigh to go with him, it would appear less suspicious. As he turned to do just that, he bumped into a middle-aged woman servant.

Wine sloshed over the lip of a decanter she was carrying and spilled down his front. "Oh, I beg your pardon!" she gasped, obviously flustered as she took the corner of her apron and began mopping at Morgan's waistcoat. After a few futile seconds, she grabbed onto his sleeve. "I can do a much better job of this in the kitchen. Come with me, before the stain sets."

There was nothing for him to do but comply. While she labored feverishly over the satin waistcoat, he stood in the flurried workroom in his shirtsleeves, hoping there wouldn't be a water stain. He had brought very few clothes on the journey.

Finally the maid returned and held the garment up for him to slip into. The evidence of the spill was next to invisible, and she had blotted the spot almost dry. "Oh, yes," she said quite cheerfully. "I almost forgot. The baker said your order is ready. You're to pick it up at the Dog's Head Tavern, down at the docks."

Much relieved at not having to sneak through the pickets himself now that there was a new contact, Morgan spun around and planted a kiss on her forehead. "I do thank you for the fine job you did on my waistcoat." With a spritely wink, he exited the kitchen.

His good spirits were swiftly doused, however, upon seeing Clay Raleigh and his father conversing with Captain Long. Hoping fervently that no damage had yet been done, he hurried over to them.

"Yes," the older Raleigh was saying as he approached, "we've had excellent success marketing that particular variety of tobacco. Excellent success, indeed."

Morgan really preferred to meet his contact without the complication of Captain Long's presence in town, but since that was not possible now, he pulled Clay aside. "Some party, is it not, with such a dreadful lack of fetching damsels to liven it up. You must be as weary of it as I. What say we visit a few of the local taprooms?"

Clay perked up at once. "I say, that's a capital idea. If what General Howe says is true, you'll be able to send for your lovely bride and my darling Evie very soon. There might not be many opportunities for an evening free of their genteel restraints then."

"Thomas," Captain Long said, stepping closer. "You didn't mention you'd wed."

"Oh, yes," Clay answered. "To one of Boston's loveliest belles."

"Is that a fact." The more than interested gleam in Long's eyes intensified. "Which one would that be?"

Morgan knew he had to change the subject. Prudence may have been from Boston Bay, but she was far from being one of the Loyalist belles. And with such a limited number, the man would surely have been acquainted with them all. Worse, if he ever saw Prudence, he just might recall a remarkably fetching, remarkably nosy serving girl. "Clayborne, I'm afraid, is much too taken with my youngest sister to give my wife a second glance." He snagged Clay's arm and pulled him away before his loose mouth could get them in any deeper. "Time is of the utmost, old chap."

27

Clay Raleigh peered nervously over his shoulder through the gathering fog. "I should have insisted that we take the carriage."

"The place came highly recommended," Morgan said lamely, feeling no less anxious as the two of them walked to the Dog's Head Tavern. The drunken laughter and occasional woman's cry echoing through the night was enough to set anyone's teeth on edge. "It shouldn't be much farther."

"I should hope not. Next time, I'll do the choosing *and* provide transport."

In the misty dark recesses behind them, a door slammed shut, and Morgan heard someone running. He listened intently, wishing he carried a weapon, but the footfalls receded in the opposite direction.

Morgan shook his head in disgust. Here he was, searching through the dark, deserted streets to find an unknown contact—while accompanied by a British boor whose company he had to pretend to enjoy. How had he gotten himself into this mess?

But even as the question arose, he knew the answer. He had lied. Less than a year ago he'd made a solemn vow to God not to lie again, and he had not been faithful to his promise. No amount of rationalizing that his deceptions were for a higher purpose made his feelings of self-reproach lessen . . . especially with Clay believing that the two of them were even now going to the tavern to get drunk and carouse with fallen women!

Past the corner of one warehouse, they reached the boardwalk fronting the piers. Morgan could make out a lantern glowing through the mist, and as they neared, he recognized the sign with a large carving of a dog's head hanging directly beneath it. Having only casually noticed the tavern a few days before when he'd been in the area discussing sailing permits, Morgan was glad they had found it so swiftly. He breathed easier.

"At last!" Clay said, lengthening his strides.

"Before we go in," Morgan said, matching his pace to Raleigh's, "I feel it only right to confess that I only overheard a few men talking about the place. It might behoove us not to mention where our sympathies lie, until we're sure it's not a rebel den."

"Quite right."

They entered and found themselves in a rather large dim room. Low ceilings confined the tobacco smoke and stench of liquor in a suffocating haze. Raleigh, seeing more redcoats and Royal Navy men than dockworkers and merchant seamen, immediately appeared at ease.

Morgan, however, remained guarded. With the city overflowing with Crown forces, he should have expected them to frequent every mug house in existence. He even spied a group of green-uniformed Hessians in one corner involved in a loud discourse in their native German. And, as was typical for this manner of establishment, a few women in gaudy, revealing dress sat among the patrons, as well.

Raleigh nudged him in the ribs. "Ah, there's a comely wench, old boy." He nodded his head toward a serving girl fetching drinks from the bar.

Morgan, gladder than ever that Evie was merely pretending interest in the rake, barely concealed his disgust. "Get us a table, would you? I'll fetch some drinks."

"Simply order them," Clay said. "Let the girl bring them to us."

"It would appear she's busy enough." Morgan motioned toward a vacant table, and Raleigh strutted over to it. Glad to be rid of the bloke for even a few minutes, he approached the bar. "Two tankards of flip, please, sir. And," he added, with no change in tone or manner, "I was told my bakery order is ready."

The burly barkeeper gave him a blank stare.

Morgan wondered how he would explain away such a nonsensical statement if this was not his contact. He envisioned himself walking about the room uttering the inane inquiry to every civilian present.

"This is a taproom, not a bakery," the man said gruffly, filling the tankards from a spigoted keg. Then he turned with a lazy smile. "You'll find your bread out back."

Morgan breathed a quiet sigh of relief, then suddenly remembered Clay Raleigh. "I'd appreciate it if your serving girl would bring our drinks over. I wouldn't want my companion to become bored and come looking for me while I pick up my order."

"Glad to." The barkeeper pulled a hot poker from a brazier and plunged it, sizzling, into the first tankard while Morgan rejoined the Englishman.

"I can see why this place was so highly recommended," Clay remarked. "Take a gander at the lass entertaining the dragoons."

Morgan slid a glance toward the table of soldiers and noted a comely woman flirting with them.

The flaxen-haired serving girl delivered the flip just then, along with a very inviting smile for Clay Raleigh.

He paid for the drinks with a flourish of coin, adding a hefty tip.

Her smile became much more accommodating.

Raleigh caught her hand when she turned to leave, and he rose to his feet, tugging her close as he held his tankard aloft. "Gentlemen, ladies, I wish to propose a toast. To our gallant fighting men."

A raft of cheers rang out as almost everyone got up to join in the tribute.

Morgan, among those who stood, counted only one table of men who remained seated. Observing their stony faces, he figured they were patriot sympathizers who refused to relinquish their hangout to the enemy.

"And another toast," Clay announced, raising his drink again. "To our commander, General Howe, whom I heard announce this very evening that you brave soldiers will soon be marching forth to mete out swift, decisive, and final punishment to the rebellious colonial rabble."

"Hear! Hear!" The banging of dozens of tankards on the wooden tables accompanied the resounding cheer.

"Refills, lass," someone shouted, and the server slipped away from Clay to tend them.

He took his seat, lounging back with a smug smile. "I rather like this place."

Knowing that Clay had managed to convey in an instant that he was a free-spending Englishman with very influential friends, Morgan felt that it would be only a matter of time before the patrons reciprocated in a most friendly and generous manner. He was not far off the mark.

Before they'd had time to warm their chairs, a handful of lobsterbacks appeared at the table. "Mind if we join you?"

"Certainly, certainly." Clay beamed. "The more the merrier, I always say."

A small crowd quickly congregated, complete with garishly dressed women. A spontaneous celebration began.

"You say you were with the general this eve," one of the soldiers commented.

"Ah, yes." Clay puffed out his chest. "'Twas a grand party, to be sure."

Morgan watched the young man take center stage and grin as he looped one arm over a pair of creamy shoulders. "Pity he's been so lax. I'd have had these colonies whipped into proper submission long ago."

With everyone at the table absorbed in the conversation,

Morgan bowed politely. "If you'll excuse me a moment, I'm afraid I must answer nature's call."

Clay, wallowing in newfound popularity, waved him off.

Outside, a lone lantern burned to dispel the misty darkness. Morgan inhaled deeply, finding the salty tang especially refreshing after the heavy atmosphere in the tavern.

A redcoat emerged from the outhouse and returned to the taproom.

Morgan waited until the soldier was inside again before checking the area. The rear yard was closed in on one side by a long warehouse, and on the other by a ship's outfitter. He wondered when and where he'd meet his contact. Deciding to try behind the store, he started toward the inky darkness beyond the circle of lantern light.

The tavern door opened and closed.

Morgan peered back to the lighted area, recognizing the three men who hadn't cheered with the soldiers. One must surely be his contact, he decided. "Good evening," he called pleasantly, retracing his steps. "I always forget how delicious baking bread smells down on the quay by night. I—"

Without warning, the threesome hurled themselves at him and dragged him to the ground. Before he could land a single blow, his arms and legs were pinned. One slapped a hand over his mouth. "Quick! Look inside his coat."

Morgan struggled to breathe, to wrench free as his frock coat was yanked open.

"Check for a money belt."

He bucked harder, but to no avail. And all his money was on him.

"Aye. There's a coin pouch, and a heavy one it is, too." The bloke lying across his chest sat up and hefted his purse.

"What in blue blazes is going on here?"

Recognizing the bartender's stern voice, Morgan strained to turn his head. The burly man loomed over the lot of them. "Get off him, you idiots. He's one of us!" He yanked the nearest one away.

Morgan managed to shove the other pair aside and regain his feet.

"You sure?" the one with the money pouch asked.

The tavern keeper snatched the bag and handed it back to Morgan, still glowering at the attackers. "Sorry, lad. In times like these, things aren't always as they seem."

One of the threesome shifted his weight and sniffed. "Guess we made a mistake, mister. But you're askin' for trouble, ya know, hobnobbin' with the king's generals and all." He made a futile attempt to brush off the back and shoulders of Morgan's coat. "Tell ya what. To make up for roughin' ya up tonight, if ya find yourself in trouble and in need of something—anything—I'm workin' down here at the docks every day. Just ask anybody for Percy Maxwell. They'll tell ya where I am."

"Thank you, Mr. Maxwell. I appreciate that." Morgan stretched out his hand. "There *is* something. Have any of you heard of a sailor friend of mine? a redheaded joker by the name of Yancy Curtis?"

"No! You're a pal of Yancy's?" another asked, thumping him on the back. "Well, any friend of that barnacled sea rat is a friend of ours."

"Aye," the third piped in. "Only we've been blockaded since the British tubs sailed in . . . 'cept for the odd ship His Highness has allowed to pass."

"I know." Morgan released a long breath. "But knowing Yancy, he's probably hanging from the topsail of some privateer, looking for a man-of-war to blow out of the water."

"We're wasting time," the barkeeper said. "You fellows run on home to your good wives. My friend and me need a couple minutes alone."

❦ ❦

When Morgan returned inside, he had the names of contacts residing in three different sections of New York. And it wasn't hard to see that Clay Raleigh hadn't missed him in the slightest. The rake now had a wench draped across his lap as if she belonged there.

"Sorry to break up the party, Clay," he said, rejoining the group at the table. "But I'm afraid I must have eaten something that didn't agree with me." He rubbed his midsection with a wince.

"So that's why you were gone so long," one of the other women remarked.

"Hmph," another snorted. "Looks to me like he's been down groveling in the dirt."

Morgan realized a bit late that he hadn't bothered to check his clothing before coming back inside. "I was a bit dizzy outside," he returned, rubbing his temples for good measure. "Perhaps we'd better leave."

Clay Raleigh eyed him with a hint of disdain. "Actually, old man, I'm rather enjoying myself at the moment. And the corporal, here, has promised to show me a few souvenirs he acquired in India. Isn't that right, Tupman?"

"Huh?" The soldier frowned. "Oh. Of course. Whatever you say, your lordship."

Morgan fought the urge to laugh aloud at Clay's sudden elevation in station . . . a lord, no less. And all in the time Morgan was occupied out back. "Well then, I'll be off." He took a step away, then turned back. "Do drop by in a day or so, and we'll go to dinner or something."

But Raleigh was otherwise occupied.

Outside once again, Morgan strode along the wharf boardwalk. Did Clayborne Raleigh have a single redeeming quality? Even as he pondered that, an old saying crossed his mind— one his mother had mouthed whenever he'd run into the house covered with dirt, much the same as he was this very night. *Cleanliness is next to godliness.* Morgan chuckled. Well, if nothing else, Clay Raleigh's appearance was always immaculate.

Morgan turned up the street between the warehouses. He conjured up a comical picture of an indignant Raleigh standing before the judgment seat of God, appalled at the audacity of having his sins read off to him when everyone knew he'd always been so very tidy.

A shuffling sound echoed softly behind Morgan.

He had already been set upon once this night. Without slowing, Morgan glanced over his shoulder. He could see nothing. Must be rats, he told himself. But the four-legged kind weren't the only ones that might be lurking in the dark.

28

Prudence roused in her sleep and turned over, her hand brushing the other side of the empty bed. Where was Morgan? It took a moment to remember she was not at home but at a travelers' inn outside Elizabeth Town, New Jersey. And her husband was not with her; his sister was. And she should have been occupying the rest of the bed! Quietly sitting up, Prudence scanned the darkened room.

Prudence exhaled in frustration. Evelyn was nowhere to be seen. The younger girl had been nothing but trouble since the two of them had left Princeton that morning. Looking back, Prudence could see that stopping there had not been one of her more brilliant ideas. Morgan and Chandler and Robby—poor, departed Robby—had spoken so highly of the place. But once Evie had discovered that Robert Chandler and the Lyonses' ward, Christopher Drummond, had been transferred to the very battalion that Jamie Dodd had joined, there was no putting her off. She had questioned Emily and the Lyonses relentlessly regarding rumors of heated battles, and they fed Evie's fear that Jamie was one of the casualties.

The instant Mr. Lyons relayed that Christopher's battalion was camped four miles west of King's Bridge on the Worcester causeway, the girl's stubborn streak took over.

Prudence rose silently from the bed, plucked her wrapper from the foot of the bed, and slipped into it as she padded to the door. Her sister-in-law might have gotten hungry and felt in need of a late-night snack. But a sixth sense told Prudence that that was just wishful thinking. The inn lay at a crossroads. One lane led to British-held Perth Amboy with its ferry to New York, and the other led westward up the Hudson River to a ferry that could transport the girls to within twenty miles of the colonial force. Prudence and Evie had gone to bed in bitter disagreement over which fork they would take in the morning.

Stepping out into the hallway, Prudence glanced in both directions.

The clatter of erratic hoofbeats out back broke into a gallop. Prudence sprang to the end window and peered out. In the moonless night it was impossible to discern anything more than a vague slender outline, but she had little doubt of who it was. The rider was heading west.

Prudence rushed back to the room and lit a candle. Quickly she pulled her breeches and Morgan's shirt on over her night shift, then shoved her stockingless feet into her riding boots. Throwing the rest of her belongings into her satchel, she refrained from thinking about the explanations she would have to give Morgan if she were to actually lose his sister. She would catch that willful brat even if she had to ride all the way to Canada to do it!

Much later that day, Prudence's bottom felt as if she might have covered at least half that distance. The sun's rays had been slanting at her through the trees for nearly an hour now, and still she'd seen neither hide nor hair of the wretched girl. But at least traveling at such a swift pace had prevented anyone from taking notice of her. She hoped it was the same for Evie.

Coming up on a settlement she recognized from when she'd traveled from New York with Morgan, Prudence knew she would soon reach the ferry crossing. Relief filled her as she started down the grade leading to the quay and noted the long line of people waiting to cross—for once, a blessed sight, because Evelyn would have had no choice but to wait her turn. When the young girl was caught, Prudence would give her a talking to she would not soon forget . . . right after she finished strangling her.

She peered along the line as she rode slowly past the waiting carriages, carts, wagons, riders, and quite a number of young men on foot—who, Prudence fervently hoped, were reinforcements for an army whose soldiers were fleeing in droves, according to the letter Mr. Lyons had read them.

No sign of Evie. None at all. Prudence wondered if the girl had seen her coming and hidden. It would be just like her to do such a featherbrained thing. Working her way past the people and down the steep hill, she considered going back up to the top of the palisade and checking some of the buildings.

Absently she glanced out over the water at the crossing flatboat of passengers and animals.

Evie! On the ferry, out in the middle of the water!

In a line as long as this one, how had she managed to get so far ahead? And despite Prudence's lectures about maintaining her disguise and staying inconspicuous, Evie's hat was off. Shining brunette curls were in glorious display for all the world to see.

Prudence bypassed everyone and rode to the front, stopping at a broad-shouldered, whiskered man who was threading the ferry rope, which mules on the far shore were reeling in on a giant wheel. "I beg your pardon, sir."

The scruffy face turned to her, and the stubby cigar he'd been chewing on shifted to the other side of his mouth. "Aye?" His loose glance wandered up and down her.

Prudence ignored it. "I've been trying to catch up with my sister—" Removing her tricorn, she pointed out to the water. "She's wearing men's clothes, too. I can't imagine how she caught such a quick ride. She was only a little way ahead of me."

The man gawked at her like a dumb ox, saying nothing.

Was he deaf? Prudence started to repeat herself more slowly, but a woman with her husband on the seat of the first wagon gave a derisive sniff. "You'll not get a straight answer from the likes of him, dearie. The lass sweet-talked him into lettin' her get in front of all of us who've been sittin' here this whole livelong day."

The fellow spat the cigar stump into the water. "Now that's not exactly how it was. Told me she'd got word her husband had been wounded and was near to dyin'. She needed to get to him before he passed on. Seemed only right, for someone layin' his very life down for his country."

Prudence shook her head. "She has always been good at spinning tales. The truth of the matter is, she's running off to be with her young man. And there's been no word of anything befalling him at all."

"Didn't I tell ya, Phineas?" the woman groused. "Just like an old man to turn to mush when a pretty young miss favors him with a smile."

Prudence looked from her to the ferry tender. "Oh, please, sir. I must catch my sister. She's sure to get into trouble without me to look after her. Please, I beg of you, let me on the next boat."

"What's one more, old man?" the woman challenged. "It's obvious the silly goose needs her big sister with her, before she's ruined for good. That one will be in need of a good dressin' down, too," she added to Prudence.

The boatman peered indecisively up the long line snaking up the hill behind him, and creases deepened in his sun-burned forehead. "Just hope I don't end up with a riot on me hands."

"Oh, thank you. Thank you!" Prudence sank gratefully into her saddle. It had been a long, long day. But the end was finally in sight.

❧ ❧

It was near dusk by the time the flatboat delivered Prudence to the other side of the river. Lamps glowed in the windows of the farmsteads sprinkled along the Hudson. And by that time, her ears were fairly ringing with advice from the woman in the wagon, who had also boarded on the same load. Truly glad to be leaving the talkative Mrs. Downy behind, Prudence turned her horse east and started downriver toward the colonial army.

Her fears for Evelyn had grown steadily with the passing of time. With a heartfelt prayer that she'd catch up to her reckless sister-in-law before it was too late, she tried to calm her disquiet. Deep inside, she had to admit that the younger girl was no less willful than she. It had been her own secret desire to have Evie persuade her into going to Morgan.

The arrival of darkness swiftly brought nippy fall air. Slowing her pace, Prudence took care that she didn't stray from the rutted trace alongside the river. About every half mile she spotted the lights from another farmhouse, and it came to her that Evie might have turned in for the night at one of them. But rather than lose time by checking each out, Prudence continued on. Far better to reach the Pennsylvania Riflemen ahead of Evelyn than after her. Her one consolation was that she had passed no one on the road since it had grown dark. The more deserted the road was, the less Evie's safety would be threatened.

The air along the river grew steadily colder and more damp. Without stopping, Prudence reached behind her saddle for the rolled up blanket and wrapped it around her shoulders. It might very well be another extremely long night.

Morgan finished the last of his meal alone. None of the other officers had come to join him in the Dillards' formal dining room this eve . . . an ominous sign. Three nights had passed since General Howe proclaimed his announcement of an imminent attack. It could conceivably happen this night—or tomorrow morning at the latest. He rose and went to the foyer to retrieve his greatcoat.

Tossing it about his shoulders, he headed out the door to see what he could ascertain. But before he reached the street, he saw Clay Raleigh stepping out of a carriage. *Not tonight,* Morgan groaned inwardly.

"Ah. Morgan. What a fortuitous coincidence to catch you on your way out. You must come celebrate with me."

Leave it to the useless fop to keep abreast of all the latest happenings, Morgan conceded. He feigned enthusiasm. "Do tell. What's the good news?"

Raleigh looped an arm around him and turned with him toward the carriage. "Let's adjourn to the Dog's Head, and I'll tell you as we go."

Morgan could think of no way out. But once they were aboard the conveyance, he could keep silent no longer. "I insist you tell me what's happened."

In the low lamplight inside the carriage, Raleigh arched his brows. "My, my. I had no idea you were such an impatient sort. When Captain Long inquired after you last eve, I told him you were quite the relaxed fellow."

Morgan's marrow froze. "You spoke with the captain regarding me?"

"Oh, just in passing," Clay said with a flutter of his hand. "He was pretending a rather intense interest in Philadelphia society . . . but I could tell his attention lay more in my father's selection of fine cigars. The man invited himself over to our table at the Provincial House and managed to smoke two while we chatted."

"Two, you say." Plenty of time for Long to find out everything he wanted to know about Morgan. He quickly assessed the situation. As long as the captain didn't meet Prudence, Morgan was confident he could handle the rest. He could come up with a plausible reason why he hadn't gone to Halifax with his wife as Raleigh thought, and why he had just returned to Philadelphia—a good solid alibi. It certainly wouldn't do for the redcoat to discover that he had actually been exchanging musket fire along the Concord road and at Bunker Hill.

Morgan relaxed into the plush cushion. Yes, it was best to face this Captain Long problem head-on, get it behind him, rather than put it off and end up looking over his shoulder as he had while walking home the other night. "Well, Clay, I'm waiting. What's the big news?"

Raleigh smiled smugly. "All soldiers have been ordered to report to their regiments. They'll move out first thing in the morning."

"You don't say. Why, that *is* splendid news. We've been waiting a long time for this." And even more splendid, good fellow that Raleigh was, he was delivering Morgan right to the very doorstep of one of his contacts. He returned a broad smile.

But soon the dire reality of the news struck him. He had heard rumors that so many in Washington's army had deserted, it was down to half-strength. They were bound to be cut to pieces.

Thankfully, Prudence wasn't here to witness it.

Prudence had been riding for the better part of twenty-four hours. She was cold and miserable, her teeth had taken to chattering, and now as a thick fog began rolling off the river, she had to dismount and continue on foot to be sure she didn't stray from the road. But there was one consolation . . . if Evelyn was still traveling, too, the fog would provide some safety from any evildoer who might be lurking in the night. Anyone with any sense would stay home and keep warm.

Lady's breathing had grown labored and more intense. The poor animal had been cruelly overworked. Prudence stopped walking and ran a hand over the soft muzzle. "You've been such a good girl for me on this trip," she murmured for the dozenth time.

The good-natured mare gave a low rumbly whinny.

Another horse answered out of the darkness.

Prudence felt gooseflesh rise. But then, realizing that it could be Evie's horse, she gave Lady her head, allowing the animal to lead her into the trees and brush. After all, the two had been stabled together for some months now and were quite companionable to one another.

After stumbling through the undergrowth for several minutes, she and Lady came upon a horse that had been picketed
for the night. In the heavy mist, Prudence had to come within
inches of the animal to confirm from the blaze on its face that
it was, indeed, Evie's. But the girl was nowhere in sight.

There was no light from a farmhouse anywhere, either.
Prudence knew Evelyn couldn't have gotten far without her
horse. She had to be hiding. "Evie," she called out.

No answer.

Prudence cupped her mouth with her hands. "Evie!" she
demanded.

Still no answer. Not even a nightingale broke the silence of
the fog-enshrouded darkness.

The girl was being unacceptably stubborn. Hands on her
hips, Prudence figured Evie would wait for her to fall asleep,
then steal away again, as she had last night. But that simply
would not do. Prudence knew she needed to deliver Morgan's sister safely to him and in the same unsullied condition
she'd been in when the two of them had left home.

"Evelyn. I promise to go with you to the army camp."
Prudence strained her ears but heard only silence. "I *promise,*
Evie. We'll search for your Jamie until we find him—even if it
takes all year."

No response.

Prudence huffed. "Have I ever once broken a solemn
promise to you?"

Nothing.

The dreadful thought struck her that perhaps Evie's horse
had gone lame, and she'd gone on without it. Prudence
peered fleetingly back toward the road.

"No, you haven't." The voice came, small but clear. A slight
figure stepped out from behind a tree. "First light. We'll go
find Jamie at first light."

"Yes." Prudence nodded, overcome with relief. "Absolutely."

Then, like a whirlwind, the younger girl threw off her

blanket and rushed into Prudence's arms. "I'm so glad to see you! It's scary out here."

Prudence hugged her hard, then held her at arm's length. "Yes. It's very dangerous for lone women in the dark. That's why as soon as we find your friend, we're going on to Morgan. Is that understood?"

"Yes! Yes!" Evie hugged her again. "Whatever you say. But won't Jamie be surprised to see me!"

29

Fields of unharvested corn and buckwheat had been trampled almost flat by hordes of Continental soldiers camped along the road. The misty morning lent a ghostlike appearance to the scene as Prudence and Evie rode their horses toward the encampment of the First Pennsylvania Rifle Battalion.

"Slouch, Evie," Prudence muttered in exasperation as soldiers glanced up at them. "Try to look more like a lad."

The atmosphere here was quite warlike, much different from that of the soldiers they had passed farther inland. Those men had been occupied with varied mundane chores or aimlessly milling about. A few had even been helpful, providing the two of them with directions to the rifle battalion. But here, near the fog-obliterated shoreline facing both Nassau and Manhattan Islands, the soldiers were unusually still, their muskets positioned in readiness. They glanced at Prudence and Evie, then quickly returned their attention to the faint marshy coastline below them.

Robert Chandler and Jamie Dodd were obviously at the forefront of an expected invasion, Prudence concluded. But aside from that danger, what would Morgan say and do when he found out she and his sister had come here?

The queasiness she had been experiencing for the past few mornings added another niggling fear. She tried to dismiss the thought, but it returned. There was every possibility that she might be with child—and perhaps even endangering their firstborn.

Evie guided her mount closer to Lady. "Can't you just feel the excitement? the danger?" Her eyes sparkled as she placed her hand over the big pistol jammed inside her belt. "I just wish you would've had time to teach me more than how to load and aim. I only got to fire two shots."

Prudence swung her a withering glance. "And when, pray tell, was I supposed to teach you? Yesterday, when you were trying your hardest to lose me?"

"Well, if I hadn't, I'll wager we wouldn't be here now."

"Don't remind me. Now hush. An officer is walking out into the road."

The uniformed man faced them and raised a hand. "Halt. This road is closed to all civilians."

"But we're not civilians," Evie said, effecting the lowest voice possible. "We're on our way to join up with the First Pennsylvania."

"A couple of baby faces like you two?" His tone was rife with disdain. "Colonel Hand won't take you on."

"I heard it said he welcomes a lad who can shoot the eye out of a squirrel at a hundred paces," Evie bragged convincingly.

The officer remained skeptical, but relented. "All right, you can pass. You'll find his headquarters a few rods down the road, just before you come to the mill pond. But if I know the colonel, you'll be back this way in short order. See if you aren't."

"Much obliged," Prudence said in her best imitation of a male voice, and they rode on.

"Just a few more rods," Evie whispered.

The younger girl could barely contain her excitement, but when they were safely out of range, Prudence exhaled a sigh of relief. She was anxious to leave the area as quickly as possible. "When we get to headquarters, let me do the talking. I don't want to hear one more outlandish remark from that mouth of yours."

Flattening her lips indignantly, Evie lapsed into silence.

As they rode into a sprawling military encampment, Prudence sought the banner that marked the largest tent. She veered her mount in that direction and noted that a number of men were converging on the very same place. It appeared that she and Evie were riding in just as some kind of gathering of officers and sergeants was taking place.

One of the sergeants noticed them. "Come forward, lads."

There was nothing to do but comply. She and Evie wove their mounts through them toward the tent.

"I'm Colonel Hand," a tall, granite-faced man said, his voice carrying the hint of an Irish brogue. "Have you brought me a message?"

"Sorry, sir, no." Prudence fought the heat rising in her face. "We've come to inquire after a young man we haven't heard from since August."

He stared blankly, incredulously, for a full five seconds. Then his gaze narrowed in barely suppressed anger. "If the lad had been slain, I'd have notified his family. Now, get yourselves out of here and back up the road." He turned away.

"No! Wait!" Evie yanked off her hat, letting her mass of dark tresses tumble around her shoulders and back. "I've come too far to give up now."

Prudence, in irritated defeat, removed her own tricorn as well. No sense trying to pretend any longer.

"Prudence?" a voice called out in shock. "Is that you?"

She swung around in the saddle and saw Robert Chandler striding toward her.

"You know these women, Sergeant Chandler?" Hand inquired.

He came to attention. "Just one, sir. The wife of Lieutenant Thomas, one of Washington's special aides."

The colonel eyed Prudence with scorn. "Then she should surely know better than to come here. Take them aside and deal with this *missing person* problem with the utmost dispatch. I don't have time for such foolishness—the British are landing out on Throg's Neck this very minute."

Prudence wasn't the only one shocked. From the murmurings running through the crowd, she concluded that the soldiers were just now hearing the news.

"Yes, sir!" Robert saluted, then grabbed Lady's bridle and began leading them away from the others and toward a tree on the outskirts of the grounds. Evelyn prepared to dismount when Robert came to a stop.

"Stay put," he ordered. But his expression appeared a bit softer when he all but smiled at Prudence. "I'd like to say how good it is to see you, Prudence, but what in the world are you doing here?" He wagged his head. "I swear, when it comes to danger, you're like a fly to honey."

Evie gave her no chance to answer. "She's not the adventurer. I've had to practically drag her every step of the way."

Robert switched his attention to the younger girl and looked at her quizzically. "And you, I assume, must be some relation of Morgan's."

"His sister," she said.

"His *baby* sister," Prudence amended.

"I'm plenty old enough," Evie huffed.

Robert swung a fleeting glance toward the dispersement taking place behind him. "There's hardly time for pleasantries. Why have you come?"

"It's my friend," Evie answered. "Jamie Dodd. He promised he'd write, but it's been two months. I just know something dreadful has happened to him."

"Dodd? James Dodd?" Chan's brows rose. "I'm sorry, but he's no longer with us."

Evelyn went white. "Oh, no."

"It's not what you think," he added hastily. "He's missing. For three days now."

"Missing?" Prudence echoed. "Have the British captured him?"

"No, I wouldn't say that." Robert appeared hesitant to give more details.

"Then what?" Evie demanded. "We've ridden all the way from Philadelphia. Please tell us."

Robert exhaled heavily. "I'm sorry. You're not going to like this. Private Dodd . . . ran away. With the daughter of a farmer from Manhattan Island."

Evelyn stiffened. "I don't believe it! He would never—he's too patriotic to desert. You must be speaking of someone else."

"Afraid not, Miss Thomas. You have to remember, the lad is young, inexperienced. And the girl's father had declared his own personal war on Dodd."

Evie's eyes shimmered with unshed tears as she sat rigidly in place.

Prudence reached over and touched her shoulder. "I'm so sorry, Evie. Truly I am."

"So am I," Robert said quietly. "I wish you hadn't come so far only to be given such unhappy news. But now our immediate concern is to get the two of you safely out of here."

He looked back at headquarters even as a young sandy-haired soldier started running toward him. "Chan. I just heard. What do you want us to do?" He stopped short upon seeing Prudence and Evelyn. "What are *girls* doing here?"

"Christopher," Robert said, "tell Corporal Meeks to take charge of the men. Have them stay put until they receive further orders. Then you hightail it right back here."

"Yes, sir." Backing up with an uncertain expression, he turned and ran.

"I'd best go speak to the colonel myself," Robert muttered, his lips determined.

Prudence followed on horseback as he struck out for the big tent but held back when he approached the commander and saluted.

"Sir," she heard him say, "Special Aide Thomas's wife and sister are ready to leave now. With your permission, I'd like to take along another man and escort them to safety a mile or so inland."

"The last time you went to help a lady, Chandler, you were gone two weeks."

"One hour, sir," he said evenly. "I give you my word. No more than one hour."

The leader cocked a brow and smirked. "I made you a sergeant last time you were tardy. Any longer and I'll commission you an officer."

❦ ❦

Robert could not believe this was happening. Riding double behind Prudence, and Christopher riding with Morgan's young sister, they trotted out of camp—with a battle about to break out at any instant. "I hardly know whether to hug you or throttle you," he finally confessed.

"I'd prefer the hug," Prudence said. "No doubt Morgan will personally see to the other."

"And where is he?"

"New York. He's been dispatched there to spy now. Evie and I were on our way to join him . . . but the willful baggage took it upon herself to take this little detour. She's amazingly stubborn."

"And Morgan actually agreed to allow the two of you to go to New York?" Robert asked in disbelief. "Spying in Philadelphia was bad enough. New York will be quite virtually the lions' den."

Prudence nodded. "Speaking of that, Evie and I spent a night with the Lyonses in Princeton on our way here. I was very surprised to find Emily there. Oh, Chan. What a heartbreak to hear about her dear, kind Robby. Such a loss. Morgan will take the news especially hard, I know it."

"Yes. As we all have." Robert did not trust himself to say more.

"But it seems Emily is faring amazingly well," Prudence went on. "Always a smile for her little ones. She seemed rather cheerful, actually . . . or nearly so. I know from what Morgan has told me that she and Robby shared an exceptionally strong faith. That must be what has helped her through this sad time."

"I'm sure."

"That reminds me. She said that if by some happenstance

our paths should cross—little did she know Evelyn would take off for here without me, giving me a merry chase—"

"What did she say?" Chan interrupted. He was astounded at how very deeply he wanted to know what Emily had said.

Prudence swiveled and turned a look of mild surprise on him. "Emily said to give you her warmest regards, and she renewed her thanks for your services. She told me how you took time off to take her and the little ones to safety. I must say, I would most certainly want a friend like you if I ever were called upon to suffer such a loss."

"Don't even think such a thing." Suddenly Robert thought of the British invasion that was happening even now—and very close by. "Let's not take the road, Christopher," he called over his shoulder. "It's too open. Head for the woods."

As the lad complied, Robert couldn't help but notice the tears streaming down Morgan's sister's face. Christopher gave him a helpless shrug.

"I take it your sister-in-law was quite smitten with Private Dodd," Robert commented.

"Yes," Prudence sighed. "They had been friends for a few years. But I think she was as infatuated with the idea of his going off to fight the good fight as anything else. His desertion was probably as much a disappointment to her as knowing he left with another girl."

Robert mulled over Evelyn's sad plight only briefly. His thoughts insisted on drifting back to Princeton, to Emily. Prudence had seen her mere days ago. "You say Emily seems to be settling in at the Lyons' Den all right? And the children . . . how are they?"

Prudence smiled at him, then turned forward again. "Oh, those little ones are really a pair, aren't they? Already they've got everyone wrapped around their little fingers, doting on them, chasing after them. How it brought back memories of my own little half brothers and half sister. And Emily, well, she has scarcely a thought for herself. She's worried about her parents and the horse farm. Oh, and did I mention? She told me to remind you that the children miss you terribly and that you'll always be welcome at their hearth."

Robert was immensely glad that Prudence had turned to the front and couldn't see the smile that had broken out on his face. After all, there was no sense in having someone read anything untoward in it.

They rode in silence for a few minutes. Then Prudence squeezed his arm. "I'm dreadfully sorry for always being such a bother."

"Well," he said good-naturedly, "at least you're a very dear bother. Now, when Christopher and I leave to turn back, stay off the roads for a few miles. Take advantage of whatever cover you can find. Then head straight for the ferry. If you're wise, you'll go back to Philadelphia, where they're throwing parties rather than cannonballs."

She nodded rather unconvincingly.

"You know," he added, "I don't believe Morgan has the slightest idea you're on your way to him. He would never have permitted you and his sister to travel the roads alone, especially with things in such a volatile state."

"Well, we did leave a little earlier than he expected," she admitted. She slumped against him with a sigh of resignation. "Please understand, Robert. I just can't turn back. Especially not now. I need to be with my husband. I . . . I'm beginning to suspect I'm . . . with child."

"*What?*"

"Shh. I haven't mentioned it to Evie just yet."

"And you've been out riding across the country for days on end?" he whispered angrily. "Not to mention being exposed to all sorts of danger lurking about. . . ."

"Chan!" Christopher called intensely, bringing his mount alongside. "Redcoats! Riding this way! Fast!"

30

"Quick! Dismount!" Robert commanded. "All of you!"

The urgency in his voice chilled Prudence, and before she had time to act, he snatched her from the saddle and dropped her to the ground.

"Down, into the bracken."

She threw herself headlong beneath a canopy of broadleaf ferns and clawed as fast as she could through the under-growth as the others did the same. Their mounts had tramped a telltale path through the greenery, one which could all too easily be followed by mounted redcoats. They needed to get as far from the trail as possible.

When the horses lurched into a rapid gallop, she knew even without looking that their only transportation was gone. But inching up between the fronds, she saw that they weren't running away on their own. Robert had remained in Lady's saddle and was stringing Evie's horse behind as he charged away from the hiding place and out into a small clearing.

"Halt!"

A musket discharged.

Her heart in her throat, Prudence saw Robert speeding onward, apparently unhit. He gained the other side of the clearing and crashed into the dense woods beyond.

The mounted patrol of eight king's men clattered past the stand of ferns in chase.

Prudence's mouth went dry. Cautiously she rose to her

knees to watch, her pulse throbbing in her ears, her breathing hard and shallow.

One of the British soldiers raised his musket as the scouting party crossed the small meadow. Another shot exploded. Then he and the rest of the redcoats vanished from sight into the woods.

"Oh, please, dear Father in heaven," she pleaded with all that was in her. "Please, don't let them catch Robert."

"Amen to that."

Prudence saw Christopher Drummond rise in the midst of the bracken. Evie clung to him, her expression frantic in comparison to his grim but more composed one.

The lanky young man clutched her to him with one hand and pointed his long-barreled rifle with the other. "Let's move into that thicket over there. And try not to disturb these ferns any more than necessary."

Following his lead, Prudence and Evie moved carefully and quickly until they were ensconced within a growth of young trees too close for a horse to pass through without difficulty.

"Might as well get comfortable," Christopher muttered. "We'll have to stay here till Chan comes back for us."

"What if he doesn't?" Evie's voice sounded unnaturally high. She took a firmer grip on the lad's neck.

"Oh, don't worry about him," he said confidently, giving her a reassuring grin. "He can take care of himself."

But Prudence noticed the way the youth's blue eyes remained riveted to the forest in the distance. He didn't appear nearly as strong as Chandler, yet he didn't seem to have a problem calming Evie as he took control of the situation. She suddenly realized that Evelyn no longer had her tricorn covering her hair. "Evie, where's your hat?"

The younger girl's eyes widened. Relinquishing her death grip on poor Christopher, she reached up to feel her head. "I-I don't know."

The lad released a *whoosh* of breath. "You two stay here. I'll go find it."

"Keep low," Evie whispered, her words conveying her fright.

Prudence hoped Evelyn had at last acquired some understanding of the danger of their present situation. When Robert returned—*if he returned*—she and the younger girl would ride out of here as fast and as hard as their horses could go. She felt her sister-in-law reach over and latch onto her hand as the two of them watched Christopher searching through the bracken.

Eternal minutes later, he poked his rifle into the greenery and retrieved the three-cornered hat from where it had fallen. He waved it at them with a triumphant grin.

Evie, her face still devoid of color, answered with a mute but urgent wave of her hand.

Finally she realizes we are not on a child's backyard adventure, Prudence told herself, *however belated her newfound understanding may be.*

Once Christopher got back and the three of them settled into a bed of dry pine needles for the wait, Evelyn's terror began to subside. "I thought the British were supposed to be landing on Throg's peninsula. Someone said they'd have a real fight to get from it to the mainland."

"That's right," Christopher conceded. "They're still there, or we'd have heard sounds of battle."

The words were barely out of his mouth before a series of cannon booms thundered one after another from the direction of the mill dam . . . not much more than a mile away.

Evie's eyes flared in horror. "But—but how can that be? They just rode by us."

Christopher, with an earnest smile, wrapped an arm around her. "Pretty scary day, huh? Riding all this way just to learn your trust had been sadly misplaced in someone less than honorable, then being beset by lobsterbacks. But have no fear. On my honor as a gentleman, I'll die before I let any harm come to you."

Evelyn relaxed noticeably, leaned her head against his shoulder, and raised her eyes to his face. Though not the dark cobalt of Morgan's, her eyes were equally deadly in their soft, feminine way. "But where did the soldiers come from?"

"Most likely the scouting party landed many miles to the north and rode through the night to check us out from behind. But don't worry about them," Christopher added valiantly. "They're behind our lines. They'll have to ride fast and keep going if they don't want to be caught."

"If that's true," Prudence mused, "perhaps they've already broken off the chase after Robert."

"If they haven't already shot him," Evie said morbidly.

They fell silent. Evelyn huddled against Christopher, and Prudence positioned herself where she could get a fairly clear view of the bracken and the meadow beyond. For some time there was no movement other than a few squirrels scurrying about, busily gathering nuts and acorns for winter.

After what seemed the longest half hour in history, Prudence spied a lone rider coming toward them. Lady's white forelegs were unmistakable. *Oh, thank you, Lord,* she breathed. "Robert's alive!" She jumped up and ran to him.

Chandler grinned one of the fullest grins she had ever seen displayed on his normally serious face, and he reined toward her.

"Where's my horse?" Evie asked in dismay as she and Christopher joined them.

He shook his head. "Sorry, miss. I had to sacrifice him."

"Dead?" she cried in a high voice. "My horse is dead?"

"No, no. I had to send him off on his own to divert the scouts. I hid until they passed, then I took off in the opposite direction. I'm just glad I was able to find my own way back to this spot."

"But this is terrible," Evelyn moaned. "All my things. My brush, my soap, my clothes. They're all on that horse."

"Never mind, dear," Prudence said, moving near to comfort her. "We'll buy new things when we reach New York City. Until then, we'll share mine. And, of course, we'll ride double on Lady until we can find you another mount."

"In the meantime," Robert added, "Christopher and I will walk awhile longer with you to make sure you don't run into any more redcoats. Then you're to hightail it for the ferry."

He looked straight at Evie. "And there'd better not be any more of your tricks, young miss. You listen to your sister-in-law and ride straight to Perth Amboy and across the bay to Morgan. If I hear one thing to the contrary, you'll get the tanning of your life, I promise. Even if you're not *my* little sister."

His stern look softened when he turned to Prudence and handed her the reins. He put a hand on each of her shoulders and leaned close. "And you take care. You hear? Take very good care of yourself."

For a little while, Prudence had forgotten about the new life she suspected was growing within her, one she'd yearned for since her marriage to Morgan last spring. But Robert hadn't. And, she vowed, neither would she again.

❦ ❦

Robert could see and hear the battle taking place by the time he and Christopher jogged to the top of a rise on their way to rejoin the First Pennsylvania Rifle Battalion. They stopped to catch their breath after the long run and assessed the situation.

High tide had made the peninsula an island, filling in the marshy crossing, which existed only during low tide. Colonel Hand had positioned his men where they could best answer the British field artillery, and the flashes and reports from their rifles carried easily to Robert. But he could see that General Howe was trying to outflank the patriots on all sides. Scores of landing craft were still debarking enemy and equipment onto the neck from New York, and he knew their men-of-war also patrolled the Hudson on the other side of Manhattan.

"Looks like a pretty fierce battle over that way," Christopher remarked, pointing toward the near side of the neck. Causeways and a connecting bridge had been constructed between the peninsula and the mainland to create a milldam—a passage the British appeared determined to take. But twenty or thirty riflemen, high on the back side of a huge pile of cordwood from the sawmill, were doing an admirable job of standing them off. Not even the British cannonballs were making much of a dent in the woodpile.

"Of all the places Howe could've landed his men," Robert mused aloud. "Our battalion has managed to be positioned precisely where the British decide to land . . . two times out of the first three assaults."

"Then it must be more than luck," Christopher remarked. "From what everyone said, the First Pennsylvania did a masterful job of slowing down the British on Nassau . . . unlike those Connecticut boys who took off running at the first sight of redcoats when they landed on Manhattan. Washington must've had a fairly good idea that the lobsterbacks would pick this spot. And this time he wanted men he knew he could count on to stay and fight. That's us, Sarge." He started running again. "Come on," he tossed back. "I don't want to miss a thing."

Robert set off after him. He knew the lad couldn't miss much, considering the size of the landing force. He only hoped General Prescott didn't forget to send up the reinforcements he had promised.

With their line of troops strung out for more than a mile, Robert had no idea where the lieutenant might be. But he spotted Colonel Hand on horseback, riding along his line of defense. Though Robert knew he and Christopher had been gone for more than an hour, he headed toward the commander.

Hand caught sight of them and cut his horse in their direction. He came to an abrupt stop. "Looks like you're bucking for that commission real hard, Sergeant."

Robert gave a sharp salute. "Begging your pardon, sir. We had to outwit a British scouting party."

"*Where?*"

"About a mile into those woods, sir." He indicated the direction.

"I'd better let General Prescott know," Hand said, eyeing the west. "I trust the ladies are a good distance away from here by now." At Chandler's nod, he continued. "I've placed your platoon with Sergeant Morrison. Go out to the woodpile and help those men hold that bridge. Take fixings for at least two hundred rounds."

"Yes, sir!" *Two hundred rounds?* Robert thought incredulously. The colonel certainly was optimistic that they'd be able to hold the British at bay for quite some time.

"Oh, and Private," Hand said to Christopher. "Didn't you say you were a sharpshooter?"

"*Yes, sir!*" the lad cried, snapping to attention in youthful eagerness.

"Go with your sergeant," he said, jutting his chin in Robert's direction.

"But, sir . . . ," Robert argued. "He's never been under heavy fire before."

The colonel studied Christopher, then wheeled his horse. "Do me proud, son."

31

"Oh, I *do* hope this is the Dillard house," Prudence told Evie wearily as she slid off Lady's rump. "Being turned away at a wrong door once would have been bad enough. But three times? That exceeds mere humiliation!" Shaking her head ruefully, she held the horse's bridle while Evelyn dismounted, then looped the reins around a hitching ring in front of a large stone house.

Evie shoved a loose shirttail beneath the cinched belt of her oversized breeches and started up the wide steps. "Well, the directions the butcher's delivery boy gave me were so vague. Anyone might have misinterpreted them." Lifting the brass knocker, she rapped on the door, then rubbed at horsehair on her trouser leg in disgust. "I declare, I've never smelled so terrible in my whole life. The minute I get these filthy rags off, I'm having them burned."

"Yes, well, we'd best ask Morgan first." Eight days of travel had done little to dull Prudence's apprehension of facing her husband with an explanation for her uninvited presence. *Again.* And destroying his clothing would not earn points in her favor, either.

The door opened, and an impeccable manservant stared for an instant, then stepped back and withdrew a kerchief. He covered his long nose in distaste. "Those seeking work should go around back," he said, starting to close the door in their faces.

Evelyn propped her foot on the threshold. "Wait! We haven't stated our business."

He maintained his insolent glare. "Very well, then. State it and be gone."

"Is this the Dillard residence?" she asked, a defiant spark in her eyes.

"Yes, it is, young man."

"Oh, good!" Whisking her hat from her head, she shook out her thick curls. "Then you may run inside and inform Mr. Morgan Thomas that his sister and his wife have arrived." Elevating her chin, she pushed audaciously past the pompous servant. "But first, show us to the sitting room."

Regaining his dignity, the butler admitted Prudence also, then closed the door. "This way, if you please."

Prudence and Evelyn followed him across the wide entry to the first door on the left, which opened into a rather somber but quietly elegant open-beamed room.

"I believe you'll be comfortable in here," he said, turning to leave.

"Before you go," Evie said, "inform the housekeeper that I'll be wanting a bath. I'll perish if I don't get one soon. Tell her to heat plenty of water. For both of us."

Graying eyebrows rose high on his narrow forehead. "As you wish."

"How could you order the man about like that?" Prudence asked softly after he had exited the room.

"Like what?" the younger girl asked in mock innocence. "He is a servant, is he not?" She turned and casually began taking stock of the well-turned mahogany furnishings.

Despite Prudence's own anxious state, she couldn't help seeing humor and irony in Evie's conduct. The girl might consider herself in rebellion against everything her parents stood for, but what she didn't realize was how much she took the comfort of their position for granted. Not wanting to soil the lovely upholstery by sitting down, Prudence moved to stand by the cold fireplace.

Evelyn, however, plopped down on a wing chair. She

straightened almost immediately. "Wouldn't it be marvelous if our clothing has arrived already?"

"Ahead of us? I certainly hope not. Morgan would be sick with worry. We're four days overdue." Her hands turned clammy at the very thought.

"Oh, I wouldn't fret overmuch about my brother," Evie said with a sigh. "From the butler's surprise at our arrival, no one could have known we were coming." She caught her breath. "You don't suppose Mother is in such a temper she's refused to send our trunks! Whatever would we do?"

Prudence smiled to herself. The girl had certainly rallied from her disappointment over Jamie Dodd. A bit too quickly, perhaps. "We'd manage. In an emergency there are always the sellers of used clothing."

"*Used!*" Evelyn's big eyes widened in horror, and she gave a shudder. "They could be crawling with lice."

"When you fly out from under your mother's generous wing, dear, you can't always have—"

Running feet pounded down the stairs. Prudence felt her chest tightening with each footfall, and she gripped the mantel for support. Out of the corner of her eye, she saw Evie kick her tricorn under her chair. The younger girl was nervous, too, whether or not she would admit it.

The harried steps echoed across the parquet floor of the entry. Morgan burst into the room, his eyes latching instantly on Prudence's. "It's true! I can't leave you alone for one minute!"

"Two weeks," his sister corrected pointedly. She planted her hands on the arms of her chair. "You didn't write for more than two whole weeks. Then when you finally did, you had the audacity to tell us not to come. Well, *I* refuse to be ordered about by my brother."

After her tirade, Morgan refocused on Prudence, his face completely unreadable.

Prudence's mind went utterly blank. She knew she must look a terrible sight, her hair unkempt, clothing rumpled—she even smelled bad.

"You needn't blame Pru," Evie said in her defense. "She had the choice of either coming with me or explaining to Mother why I'd gone off alone. And, of course, with her being such a devoted 'big sister,' and all, what else could she do?"

"I see. And since you're masquerading about in men's clothing, I can also deduce that my permission was not the only one you lacked. Mother and Father must be quite livid. Traveling alone, no escort . . ." He narrowed his eyes. "And that waistcoat looks very familiar."

"That's not the half of it," Evie almost bragged, baiting him. "I left Prudence behind along the way and rode off by myself to find Jamie Dodd. I am a thoroughly willful and disobedient girl." Abruptly, she stood. "And now that we're all in agreement on the matter, I would really appreciate a hot bath and a soft, bug-free bed. Which room will be mine?"

Morgan's guarded expression turned to astonishment. He opened his mouth to speak.

"Oh, it sounds like that uppity butler is in the hall," she interrupted, starting for the doorway. "When can I expect my bath?" she called to him.

Prudence remained rooted to the same spot as Morgan followed his sister out of the room; then she bolted after them.

"Mr. Chester," Morgan said. "Please put my sister in the Dillard girls' room for now, since the other guest rooms are all occupied."

The servant's face registered the same disapproval it had earlier, but he escorted Evelyn upstairs.

Obviously the man thought it inappropriate to house a stranger in the Dillard family's private chambers, Prudence realized. Everything about her and Evie's arrival had been dreadfully wrong from start to finish. And there was yet more wrath to come. Sensing her husband's tightly harnessed fury, she could only follow him meekly back into the sitting room. She didn't want to look into his eyes and see the depth of his dismay and disappointment, but bravely she forced herself to meet his gaze.

To her surprise, his countenance softened, and he stepped close, cupping her cheek in his palm. "Sweetheart, you look frayed to threads."

She had expected anything but tenderness. Completely unprepared for it, her vision blurred with tears, and she reached out blindly for him.

He drew her close, rocking her in his arms. "It's much harder, is it not, when you have someone else to worry after?"

A chill tore through her. How could he possibly know about the child she was carrying? Easing back, she searched his face.

"From the look of you, my sister must have led you on quite the merry chase."

Immense relief surged through Prudence. "Yes. Quite."

"Well, dearest wife of mine," he said, scooping her up into his arms. "I want to hear every last detail. Even if—" His lips found her neck. "Even if it takes hours and hours. In fact," he breathed huskily against her ear, "I'd best have our supper sent to our room. It may take all night."

"And don't let them forget my bath," she whispered.

One part of Morgan was delighted at having Prudence here with him, but that part warred with the rest. While she soaked off the layers of travel dust, she had related many alarming bits of news. Robby MacKinnon, dead! Chandler escorting Emily to Princeton. Young Chip Drummond now with Chan at the forefront of the colonial defense. The pieces tumbled over one another in Morgan's mind. But more often than not, anger at Evelyn surfaced to top them all. How dare that brat pull Prudence into danger, not once, but over and over?

Prudence rose from the tub and wrapped her shining, lithe body in a thick towel. After drying herself, she slipped into one of his long nightshirts, then took the seat opposite him at the small bedroom table.

Morgan noted the deep circles under her eyes. How much sleep had she lost chasing after Evie? As she ate with relish, he also wondered how many meals she had missed. Yet, his beautiful and beloved wife was here . . . not merely in the city of the enemy, but in the very house where three of them lodged!

"You're not eating," she said. "Aren't you hungry?"

Only now realizing that he hadn't touched his meal, Morgan picked up his fork and sampled the first bite. "Perhaps," he said after swallowing, "it's a good thing you stopped off at the Lyons' Den and met the good people who run it. Should anything ever happen to separate us here, I want you to go there at once."

Her light gray eyes clouded with alarm. "Not back to your family?"

He shook his head. "Nor to yours. Those are the first places the British would look. And make it a point to tell Evie not to mention a word about Princeton to anyone—especially Clay Raleigh. He's here, or didn't you know that?"

She smiled. "You don't think he would have left Evie without voicing loud objections to his father, do you?"

"I can well imagine," Morgan said scornfully. "He already puts on airs as if he's married into the family. I've been obliged to take several meals with the bloke."

"My, that is persistent of him, considering you can't abide the man."

"He hasn't seemed to notice," Morgan said with chagrin. "His presence, however, has created somewhat of a complication. Did I ever mention a Captain Long to you?"

Prudence frowned.

"An officer I first met in Boston. He had a very suspicious nature then, and has even more of one now . . . particularly when it comes to me. He's been prodding Raleigh for information about me. And there's this large gap of time, you see, between my departure from Boston and my arrival in Philadelphia."

Still frowning, Prudence tipped her head. "Does it matter?"

"It might to him. I've decided to tell him you and I took an extended—if unapproved—honeymoon to the Caribbean. One I'd just as soon my parents did not learn about."

"And you feel that will suffice."

Morgan shrugged. "Actually, now that you're here in the flesh, it'll be a miracle if he doesn't remember you from the night you were serving refreshments at that Christmas party instead of partaking of them as any pampered daughter of a Tory merchant should."

"He was there?" she asked in shock. "At the Clarkes' house?" Her fork hung suspended in the air. With a grimace, she filled it again. "I'm sure he wouldn't remember one serving girl from nearly two years past."

"I never forgot you," Morgan said softly. "Despite your plain attire, you were by far the most beautiful woman at the affair."

"And you, my dear husband," she said, covering his hand with hers, "are biased."

"Quite right." Standing, he pulled her up and slid his arms around her, relishing her fragrance, her touch, her essence. "And I'm madly in love. Have I told you, of late, how much I adore you?"

She circled his neck with her arms and smiled up at him. "You told me you loved my hair, when you were washing it, but the rest of me you left sorely in want."

"I did, did I? Well, we shall have to remedy that." He leaned forward for a kiss, but a knock on the door interrupted him.

"Morgan? Pru? Are you in there?"

"Go away," Morgan groaned.

Evie barged in anyway. "Sulk all you want. I have marvelous news for Prudence. See?" She whirled in place, billowing the skirt of an elegant gown.

Prudence moved out of his embrace and stepped toward her. "Where did you get that?"

She grinned from ear to ear. "There are three whole closets full. Come see."

Grabbing Prudence before she could follow, Morgan scowled. "What's going on here?"

"Clothes! Evie has found us some clothes." Pulling him along, she traipsed after the younger girl.

Entering the spacious, feminine chamber with three frilly

beds, Morgan saw an equal number of wardrobes . . . and each was full to bursting.

"I can't believe anyone would sail to England without taking everything they owned," Prudence uttered as she surveyed the closets.

Morgan nodded. "Seems I recall the young ladies bemoaning the fact that everything smelled of smoke. Their mother told them they could have all new if they'd be ready to sail before eventide. They departed the very day after the fire, sure the rebels were bent on the utter destruction of the city."

Prudence pulled a green frock from the closet and held it up.

"A tuck here and there," Evie cried, coming to fit it to her waist, "and it will do perfectly. Now we can go out in public at will . . . and this time I'm going to dance the night away. I've wasted so much time mooning over that worthless Jamie. I'm going to flirt with each and every dashing officer I see, while charming all their most important secrets right out of them."

Morgan remembered Prudence's explanation of Jamie Dodd's less than honorable departure from the army, and he also remembered that Evie had been utterly smitten. The lad had hurt her deeply, and now she was in a dangerous mood. He would have to keep a close watch on her.

"Speaking of information," Prudence said seriously, "we heard so many conflicting reports on our way here. How is the battle going? Do you know, sweetheart?"

"Actually, not too much has happened as yet. Washington was able to remove all his men from Manhattan without a hitch, except for the men he left at Fort Washington, overlooking the Hudson. Howe landed the bulk of his army on a neck across the East River, planning to cut off the patriot retreat. It was a perfect scheme. The British picket line already in place would hold the colonial troops to the upper half of the island, and the warships would stop them from crossing the Hudson. Howe's main force was to surround and capture them as they tried to flee across King's Bridge to

Westchester on the mainland. Simple. Deadly. But God intervened in his miraculous way once again."

"Well, sit down," Prudence pleaded, lowering herself to one of the beds. "Tell us the rest."

He complied with a broad grin. "Wait till you hear this. Howe's army is still on Throg's Neck, the peninsula where they landed two days ago. A mere handful of Pennsylvania Riflemen withstood an entire division of lobsterbacks for more than four hours, giving reinforcements time to move into position. The sharpshooters were hiding in a big pile of wood and couldn't be blown out, no matter what the British threw at them."

"That's right," Evie announced. "It was a huge pile. I saw it."

Morgan's mouth gaped. *"You saw it?"* He swung to Prudence. "Just how close to the shooting did the two of you get, may I ask?"

One look at his wife's guilty expression, and he concluded that she had left more than a few pertinent details out of her story.

32

"That appears to be everything." Emily dried her hands and hung up the dish towel. "The kitchen's finished for another day." She brushed a strand of damp hair behind her ear.

Mrs. Lyons sank to a chair. "And none too soon, either. These old feet of mine are killing me."

The twin girls Jasper had hired the previous week rushed to her and bobbed in a curtsy. "May we go, then, mum?" they asked almost in unison.

The innkeeper's wife raised an eyebrow as if doubting their enthusiasm. "I suppose."

"Oh, thank you!" The freckle-nosed redheads ran for the common-room door, wedging themselves through it together.

Emily smiled after them. "You're aware that the Branson boys are waiting outside for the girls, aren't you?"

Mrs. Lyons stretched out a slippered foot and wiggled her toes with a groan. "Not till now. Oh, to be that age again and have so much energy. And happy feet."

"Sounds like you could use a spot of tea. I'll fix us some." Emily poured the last of the hot water into the teapot, then refilled the kettle and suspended it over the fire again. "A pity for Sarah and Selina that the college is in recess for the war. Such fetching lasses should have more lads circling around them than they could shake a stick at."

"Well, it's only because classes are in recess that their pa decided to leave them here with us. When the fightin's over and he comes home, he expects his curlyheads to be returned to him as pure as when he went off."

"I'm sure Mr. Lyons and that squawky cockatoo of his will keep a sharp eye on them," Emily said, measuring aromatic leaves into a teaball and lowering it into the pot.

"Won't they, though," she said with a chuckle. "Not much gets by that pair. I'm purely glad the girls are such cheerful workers, though, and sweet, like you." With a gnarled hand, she patted the seat beside her. "Sit yourself down, love. It's time I told you what a good girl *you've* been."

"With those poor feet of yours needing attention, I think we can dispense with the flattery," Emily chided, too weary herself to be entirely serious. She got the tea fixings together and brought them to the table.

"It's not exactly flattery I had in mind a'tall. Just wanted to tell you how proud I've been of you these past four weeks. A good many women spend months, sometimes years, carryin' on when they lose their man. But you haven't been like that. Nobody knows better than I how much you loved your bonny Scotsman. And though your loss is no less than anybody else's, you've managed to let him go without fallin' all to pieces. I know you still have hurtin' times when you're by yourself . . . but you've been a real blessing to your wee ones. The rest of us, too."

"Well, don't put my name in for sainthood just yet," Emily teased. "I may have mouthed a lot of very brave things when I first came back, but every single day I have to remind myself that Robby's gone. I often find myself . . . resenting, if I might admit it . . . that he's with God instead of with me. Then comes the light of day, and I must spend half my time repenting of my sorry thoughts." With a melancholy smile, she poured some of the amber liquid into a cup for Mrs. Lyons, then filled another for herself.

"Well," the older woman said, her careworn face soft with understanding, "don't you fret overmuch about that. The

Good Lord gave us the capacity to love to the fullest and to ache with the loss. In his compassion for us, he understands."

They sipped in momentary silence, with Emily relishing the first rest they'd taken all day. Now that the mornings and evenings had grown chilly, hot tea was especially welcome and soothing whenever they had a chance to relax.

"Speaking of loved ones," Mrs. Lyons said, "I wish the stage wagons were still comin' in from New York and Philadelphia. Chip hasn't sent word home for ages . . . and the bits of news we hear aren't encouraging. I hope it's not true that our army's losing battle after battle, retreating deeper into the New York countryside."

"Christopher is with Robert," Emily reminded her. "He couldn't be in better hands."

The older woman frowned, wrinkling the skin beside her narrow hazel eyes. "Wasn't too long ago your Robby wrote to tell me he didn't think Robert Chandler cared a whit about livin' or dyin'."

Emily sighed. "I pray that isn't true anymore. But even if it is, I know he cares very deeply about his friends staying alive. He's a wonderful and thoughtful man." Catching Mrs. Lyons's odd look, Emily wondered if her words had been misread. But she had only expressed her honest feelings. Robert truly had been very thoughtful to her and the children. He *was* a wonderful person. Anyone who knew him had to admit it. If only he would return to the peace of the Lord, he could consider finding another nice Christian wife, one who'd bring out the best in him. He had been alone much too long. She took another drink, then heard the faint crunching of horseshoes on the gravel drive.

"Not another customer who'll be wantin' to be fed," Mrs. Lyons moaned.

Emily set down her cup. "I'll go see."

"No need, child. Jasper will let us know if a body wants something. We deserve a few quiet minutes to ourselves."

"Which don't come very often," Emily said with a light laugh, "since I arrived with my two children."

"Never you mind about them, love. Those babies are keepin' us old fogies young. Why, old Jasper's middle has trimmed down considerably from chasin' those kids around outside."

The door to the ordinary opened, and to Emily's joy, there stood her brother Ben. It had been months since he had delivered the silver bracelet from Robby.

"Ben!" She sprang up and ran to him.

"Hi, Sis. How've you been?"

"Best not ask her," Mrs. Lyons said, coming to her feet. "She's mostly too hard on herself. Anyway, these tired old bones need a good hug."

After he laughingly complied, she sat him down and dished up a plate of food. "Now I must see to that husband of mine. You two youngsters have a nice visit . . . and don't even think of leavin' tomorrow morning without a decent good-bye. Hear?"

"Wouldn't dream of it," Ben said with a wink.

Emily, so full of questions she couldn't think where to begin, eased down opposite him, waiting impatiently while he wolfed down a few bites.

"Sorry," he said, wiping his mouth. "I was starved. I haven't eaten since leaving Philadelphia. I wanted to catch you before you turned in."

"Philadelphia? You went down there without stopping here on your way?"

"Wasn't much point in it, not in the middle of the night. I was in too much of a hurry anyway. I had an important message to deliver to the Congress . . . and they dispatched me back to New York with the same urgency."

Emily gave a helpless shrug. "Riding back and forth that often, I can't believe you didn't stop to see me at least once during the month I've been here."

Swallowing the bite he had just taken, Ben shook his head. "That's what you thought? Sorry, but this is my first trip through New Jersey. I was sent north, to Fort Ticonderoga. The war up there is going about as bad as everywhere else.

The British have regained control of Lake Champlain, but not the fort . . . yet."

"What about Jane and Ted and the baby? Did you see them? Are they in danger?"

He shrugged. "So far the Crown seems happy just to have control of the waterway south from Canada. They don't have much of a force, and," he added with a chuckle, "I doubt they're too eager to take on those grizzly Green Mountain Boys. Speaking of danger, though, that's why I'm here. We'll be riding out of here at first light. Pack only four satchels. I'll take one of the youngsters with me on my horse, and you can take the other on yours."

"What?"

"I know Robby thought you'd be safer here than in Rhode Island. But as it turns out, you've ended up right in the path of the conflict. Washington has crossed the Hudson into New Jersey, and the British are hot on his heels. Rumor has it Howe wants to take Philadelphia before the first snow. Our forces will try to slow them up, make them turn back to New York for the winter. Whatever transpires though, baby sister, you are sitting smack in the middle between those two cities."

Emily blanched at the disturbing news. It wasn't at all what she had expected. "The war is going that badly?"

"That bad and worse. It seems Rhode Island was the safer place for you and your babes after all. When we reach Washington's army, I'll request a few days' leave and get you back home where you belong."

"Home . . . I'd like that." Leaving her family behind after Robby's death had been one of the hardest things she had ever done. She missed them so much but had not allowed herself to dwell on it. Now, with the prospect of returning to them, the ache she had managed to suppress came forth all the stronger. "Well, when we do reach the army, I must find Christopher and Robert, see how they are. It's only right I let Robert know that we're returning to the farm, and why. I owe him that . . . and so much more."

❦ ❧

Morgan stood beside Prudence at the entrance of the Dillard home as they greeted an arriving couple—a quartermaster at the division level and the man's sumptuously dressed, but rather homely, wife. "It's splendid that you were able to come this eve, Colonel Farrell, Mistress Farrell. It's such a pleasure to meet you both at last. May I introduce my lovely wife, Prudence?" He turned to her. "These are the Farrells, sweetheart."

"I'm so pleased to make your acquaintance," she said.

At her radiant smile, the tall, portly man lingered overlong above her hand after the perfunctory kiss, his expression revealing without words how taken he was by her exotic beauty.

Morgan swelled with pride. In bronze satin with ecru lace, her olive skin absolutely glowed. Prudence was always a joy to have nearby, but she was proving to be quite an asset, as well. For their first dinner party, he had chosen who would be included on the guest list with great care. The event was sure to be fruitful. Quartermasters and New York merchants. A perfect business gathering . . . and a perfect occasion for information gathering, as well.

From experience, Morgan knew that the high command made no move without conferring with their quartermasters. The merchants, of course, would be trying their zealous best to anticipate and provide the military's every need and desire.

Ah, yes, he said to himself as he greeted the next arrivals, a merchant and his wife. *A businessman would have so many questions to ask, so many answers to obtain.*

The tinkling sound of laughter—a little too cheerful— drifted from the staircase. As the New York couple moved on, Morgan was afforded an unbroken view of Evelyn coming down the steps, dressed to the nines and on the arm of Lieutenant Johnson, the one officer out of the three lodging at this residence who was not presently in pursuit of the Continental army with General Howe. Morgan was hard-pressed to concentrate on the next guests—one of General Clinton's quartermasters and his companion. Evie had managed to dazzle not only Johnson, but no less than a dozen other officers who had come to call within the past three weeks.

As Evie swept toward Morgan, her curls cascading from a ribbon in the same sage green as her velvet gown, he had to admit that she looked especially grown-up. If it weren't for the fact that she was his baby sister, and a contrary imp at that, he might even admit she was becoming a true beauty.

Stealing a swift glance at Prudence put Evie's appearance in proper perspective. He took a mental note of how uncommonly docile and agreeable his wife had been since her untimely arrival. He hoped it wasn't merely her way of smoothing over her most recent disobedience. After all, the harrowing experience had taught her a much-needed lesson. With his mind otherwise occupied, Morgan mouthed polite pleasantries to the quartermaster at hand.

Evelyn fluttered her lace handkerchief in a flippant wave at him as she and Lieutenant Johnson strolled to the music room, where refreshments were being lavished upon the guests. With the butler ill, Morgan found himself forced to remain at the door, which was especially harrowing this evening. Evelyn was becoming more and more impetuous, and he could not afford to leave her to her own devices.

As he was about to give in to the temptation to follow after her, he heard another carriage enter the drive. He grimaced and turned to Prudence. "Tonight we won't merely take turns overseeing Evie. We'll both make it a priority."

"But then you wouldn't be free to mingle," she replied. "Trust me, I won't let anything distract me from looking out for her."

He scowled. "Did you see that lowcut gown she chose for the evening? I'll take care of business and still watch her. Men are not above spiriting young misses off into hidden corners."

"And might I assume you speak from experience?" she asked, arching her slender brows high.

Morgan chose to ignore the question. "It's hard to believe my parents are so blind when it comes to Evelyn. In Mother's letter, instead of ordering the girl home, as any responsible parent would, she only encouraged Evie to be *devastatingly charming* to any *good prospects*. It's ridiculous. Completely ridiculous."

With a light laugh Prudence gazed up at him. "Your mother is every bit as astute at marriage prospects as your father is at the business ones."

For a few seconds Morgan lost himself in his wife's captivating smile. Dismissing his sister from his thoughts, he stole a quick kiss. When was the last time he had told Prudence how luscious and tantalizing her lips were? At the sound of footsteps outside, he reluctantly forced himself to release her. He opened the door.

"At last I get to meet the elusive Mistress Thomas."

Morgan felt the hairs on the back of his neck bristle. What in blazes was Captain Long doing here?

33

"I knew you wouldn't mind if I brought Captain Long with me," Prudence heard the other British officer say. So this was Captain Long, the very man Morgan had not wanted her to have any contact with whatsoever . . . and who now stared at her with such intensity. "My wife took to her bed with a chill this morning," the quartermaster went on.

"So sorry to hear that," Morgan said, and Prudence knew how seriously he meant it. He extended his hand to the interloper. "Marvelous that you could come in Mistress Buchanan's stead, Captain Long. As you said, you've yet to meet my beautiful wife."

The man's sly eyes roved up and down Prudence. "Ah, yes. Delighted, Mistress Thomas. And now that I've seen you, I'm convinced we've never met. You, my dear, couldn't possibly have been in Boston during my stay there. You'd have been the lone blossom among the weeds in that dreary town."

"Oh, aren't you the naughty one!" Prudence did her best to smile coyly even as she suppressed her anger at his pointed insult of her people. "Now, if you'll allow me to show you to the music room, Captain Long, I'll put your curiosity to rest."

She couldn't help but notice the color drain from Morgan's face as she reached for the officer's arm and accompanied him away. So courageous regarding himself, her husband seemed the complete opposite when it came to her. But after having rehearsed at least half a dozen times the story they had concocted, he must rely upon her ability to tell it convincingly. "I'll see that our latest arrivals get settled, sweetheart," she told him over her shoulder, "and then return directly."

"Yes, well, just don't linger," he said, his eyes speaking volumes. "There remain a few more guests I still wish to present to you."

Prudence walked slowly down the wide hall with the two officers. "I'm dreadfully sorry not to have been in Boston a sufficient time to relieve your boredom, Captain Long. But I'm afraid I, too, endure that same affliction whenever I visit my cousin's family there. Perhaps it's just as well they've all departed from the city now."

"And what family might that be?" he asked with barely veiled interest.

She was prepared for the question. "I presume you knew the Hutchinsons?" Casually, she eyed the exquisite Oriental vases on pedestals along the paneled hall.

"The governor?" His tone revealed mild surprise. "No, I didn't have the pleasure. Governor Hutchinson left the colony some time before I arrived."

"Oh, yes. He did depart rather suddenly, didn't he?" she said smoothly. "But he's once removed from the cousin I visited. There are quite a number of us, actually. But then, of course you've heard." She gave an artful titter. "One of the reasons the Bay Colony rabble wanted Cousin Thomas ousted was because he leaned so toward giving his family the best appointments and contracts."

"Yes. So I heard."

"The captain says that as if it's a crime," she said, turning with an elaborate show of dismay to the other officer. "If one may not express loyalty to one's own family, pray tell, what else might a person do?"

The quartermaster chuckled.

"Wars have been started for less cause," Captain Long returned. "But you say you're not from Boston. I assume, then, that you're from Philadelphia?"

"Oh, no. Baltimore." Morgan had already assured Prudence that with Clay Raleigh around, a close connection to Philadelphia could too easily be investigated.

Reaching the music-room door, the captain stopped and turned to Buchanan. "Why don't you go on in, Frederick? I'd like to chat with Mistress Thomas a moment more before joining you." When the man nodded and left, Long turned back to her, his pretense of mere curiosity a very thin veneer. "This is all quite confusing. Clayborne Raleigh informed me that you hailed from Boston."

"Clay said that?" Prudence elevated her brows innocently. "Well, that shouldn't surprise me. He's so smitten with my little sister-in-law, I do believe it's impaired his hearing—save for that desperately hoped-for word *yes*. The truth is, my husband was considered quite the catch in both Philadelphia and Baltimore circles. When I learned he'd gone to those cold and dull climes of the north, I knew—as you said yourself, Captain—a southern blossom is so much more noticeable among so many . . . weeds." She tittered again.

Enjoying her own embellishment of the story she and Morgan had fabricated, Prudence tilted her chin fetchingly and continued. "So, as one might term it, I set my cap for Morgan *and* very quickly succeeded where so many others before me had tried and failed." Having studied the way Evie unfolded her fan and peeked demurely from behind it, Prudence spread hers and gave a slow, ingenuous blink. "Of course, if you dare let word of this reach my handsome husband, I shall deny it to my very dying breath."

"Indeed." Amusement lightened the ruddiness of his face, and he patted her hand where it rested in the crook of his arm. "It was rumored he had returned home to his ill father, yet Mr. Raleigh said you'd only recently arrived."

Prudence knew he was baiting her, but she refused to stray from her fable. "Oh, yes. That. I do hope you didn't mention it to Clayborne. We led Morgan's family to believe he was still in Boston, caught in the trouble and unable to return home, while we went off on such a romantic adventure," she sighed.

"Married aboard ship, a glorious year strolling the isles of the Caribbean and on to his friend's plantation in North Carolina. But, alas, funds do not last forever. When they grew sparse, we could do naught but return to Philadelphia." She rolled her eyes the way she'd also seen Evelyn do. "Thus far, Captain, no one is the wiser."

He did not answer immediately. "I must confess, I find it rather strange that you would tell me, a veritable stranger."

"Yes, but you, my naughty man, have an unfortunate memory. I do hope you didn't leave Clayborne any the wiser." With a small smile, Prudence leaned closer. "Oh, well. Even so, this is not Philadelphia or Baltimore, now, is it? What possible harm could be done here?"

"Ah, my pretty. One never knows how soon you and I might find ourselves in either place." He picked a nonexistent piece of lint from his immaculate red sleeve. "And secrets can be such fun, don't you think?" Weasel eyes cut directly to her.

Morgan was right. The man was a scoundrel. The sooner she rid herself of him, the better. "That would, of course, depend," she allowed, preceding the captain into the music room.

"Upon what, my dear?" His smug expression all but turned her stomach.

"Upon whether one is the cat . . . or the mouse."

"Indeed." A low laugh rumbled from his chest. "Along that same line, I can't help feeling a great measure of gratification knowing that some of the most *vexing* mice in these colonies are about to be dealt with, and quite severely. General Howe is amassing a fleet even as we speak."

"Why, that is good news. And surely no more than the upstarts deserve."

"Quite. How I wish I could go along to watch them squeak and scurry for their holes. But, alas, duty forbids it."

"You're referring to Philadelphia, are you not?" Realizing that all pretense of small talk had fled her voice, Prudence quickly amended the question. "I do hope your loyal friends there will be given warning first. Morgan's mother, for one, is ever so terrified that, given the slightest excuse, the rebels will run amok and burn us out, as happened here in New York."

"Well, put your mind at rest, mistress." He took two drinks from a passing servant and handed one to her. "The 'City of Brotherly Love' is not our destination. *Yet.* We've chosen a far more prickly rebel camp. The Rhode Islanders have thumbed their noses at us for the last time. And in a matter of days, they'll rue their every lawless deed."

Rhode Island! A colony that considered smuggling an honorable profession, whose honest citizens had set fire to one of His Majesty's policing vessels, whose troops had taken the fort at the entrance of their bay from the British even *before* the battles at Lexington and Concord. Rhode Island—where the Haynes family lived. They must be warned!

It took supreme effort to remain calm and continue her game with the vile man. "Oh, who wants to discuss such tiresome matters at a party?" she asked, touching the tip of her fan to his chest. "Now that you know everything there is to know about me, I think it's only fair to tell me something about yourself. Where are you from? And in what capacity do you serve in our glorious military?"

As he opened his mouth and began rattling off inane nonsense about having a fleet of his own, Prudence only pretended interest while her mind wandered to Rhode Island's jeopardy.

". . . so I've been outfitting several empty vessels in the harbor to house the prisoners General Howe will soon be bringing me."

Prudence almost choked on a sip of punch as she swallowed too quickly. "You're expecting more prisoners?"

He sneered. "If the general will cease being so cautious."

Prudence latched onto her own opportunity to taunt. "From what I heard of the great slaughter at Boston's Bunker Hill, it would seem he's afraid to risk that sort of loss a second time—particularly against an army as ill-equipped as the rebels are reported to be."

The muscles in his jaw tensed. "And next, I suppose children in the street will also be talking about his cowardice," he snapped.

Prudence parted her lips in false shock. "Surely, sir, you didn't think I meant that."

Captain Long, with deliberate effort, managed to regain his composure. "You, dear lady, merely speak the truth. Four times within the past two months our commander has allowed the insurgents to slip from his very grasp . . . when he had only to close his hand!" He demonstrated the act with forceful ardor. "When the Crown learns of his ineptitude, I doubt he'll be in command much longer."

"Oh, dear, speaking of commanding generals," Prudence said, grasping at the chance to leave, "I'd better hurry back to mine. As much as I've enjoyed our little chat, Captain, I'm afraid I must excuse myself." With her brightest smile, she dipped her head and stepped out into the hall.

Word had to be sent to General Washington about Rhode Island's peril at once.

The high midday sun warmed Emily's shoulders as she, Ben, and the children rode on horseback alongside the Hudson River Road, about twenty miles north of Manhattan Island. "That's probably Colonel Hand's camp," she told Ben at the sight of a huge assortment of makeshift canvas lean-tos and dugouts sprawling back into the trees along the high bank. "I told you it wouldn't take long to get here."

Ben, with Rusty nestled in front of him on Rebel's back, branded her with a brotherly scowl. "Half a day to Peekskill, *and* half a day back downriver. You know I can't be wasting entire days just to take you visiting."

"Oh, stop complaining. You were right beside me when I promised Mr. and Mrs. Lyons I'd find Christopher and tell him to write home. They need to know he's all right. If he's still . . ." Hesitant to suggest the alternative since Katie was riding with her, she just let the sentence dangle. "I should just be grateful you didn't have to obtain leave. Now, my patriot among patriots, you won't have to miss out on being in the middle of things for a single moment."

"Excuse me, but I'd call an entire day a little more than *a moment*. This pouch I picked up from Washington's headquarters was supposed to go directly to Rhode Island. Without delay, I might add."

Emily averted her eyes and shook her head. "I swear. I don't know how Abigail puts up with you."

"She manages quite nicely, thank you. Abby doesn't drag me forty miles out of my way on a whim."

As they reached the first clusters of tents, Ben nudged his mount ahead. Several unkempt and unshaven men stood around the various campfires, some warming their hands while others cooked the noon meal. The aroma from the boiling cauldrons was unidentifiable.

Emily's heart went out to the ragtag soldiers. Everyone they passed as they rode deeper into camp appeared equally beaten down, and she knew the nights could get quite cold this time of year. She couldn't help noticing that their little party was drawing considerable interest, as well. It was probably a rare event to have a woman with children casually drop in.

"We'll head for the banner sticking up over there," Ben announced, and reined his horse toward it. "Someone at the command tent should be able to tell us where Robert's group is positioned."

"We're here?" Katie asked in her high voice. "Hurry, Uncle Ben. I want to show Mr. Chandler my new shoes."

"And I'm hungry!" Rusty added, bouncing up and down in the saddle. "Hurry."

"Emily!" a familiar voice called. "Ben!"

Quickly scanning the area, Emily wasn't able to pick out a recognizable face.

"Over here."

Emily stared, puzzled, at the bearded fellow coming toward them. If he hadn't smiled, she never would have known him.

The whiskers made him appear much older than eighteen. "Christopher!"

"Uncle Chip!" Katie cried in delight.

The lad reached them, and Emily handed her daughter down to him. Then she quickly swung down herself and grabbed him in a hug. Her happiness made it hard to effect a look of reprimand. "A whole month has gone by, and not a word to the Lyonses. They're sick with worry, dear boy."

Slack jawed, the young man had the grace to look guilty.

"Mama," Katie asked. "Where's Mr. Chandler? You said he was with Uncle Chip."

Emily glanced around at the dozen or so men standing around the nearest fire. Robert was not among them. A fluttering in her chest surprised her as she whipped her gaze back to Christopher. "Where *is* Robert?"

34

"Don't fret, ma'am," one of the soldiers told Emily as he stepped from the campfire to join her and Ben. "The sergeant is around here somewheres. Probably just down the river washing up. He pays more attention to that sort of thing than some of the rest of us." He grinned sheepishly.

Christopher nodded. "We've been digging trenches near the bluff most of the morning. The sarge will be back any minute."

"Oh," she said with a nervous laugh. "You frightened me, Christopher."

"So," Ben remarked with a glance around. "You boys are spending your time here fortifying. That's good. But I don't think you'll have to worry about General Howe for some time. Being an express rider for Washington and Hancock, I get around. From the placement of Howe's men, he'll be going after Fort Washington on Manhattan Island next, and probably Fort Constitution across the river from it. No doubt he hopes to have the island completely out of our hands when he settles in for the winter. I'm sure if he had time, though, he'd love to blow our Continental Congress right out of Philadelphia. I'd say you're quite safe here, for now."

"Maybe," Christopher said thoughtfully. "But if the Canadian general takes Lake Champlain and Fort Ticonderoga before winter, he could sail down from the north quick enough. That's why we're here. To stop him."

"Whatever you say. But I just got back from the north, and believe me, Colonel Arnold put up one good fight, and against tremendous odds. He did lose the run of most of the lake, but not before doing plenty of damage to Carlton's fleet in the bargain. And I don't think Carlton will take Fort Ti, which guards the south end, any easier. Like I said, you're safe for the winter."

"Well, now," another soldier cut in. "Our officers at headquarters might be interested in hearin' that. Soon as we eat, I'll walk ya over."

Rusty squirmed in Ben's arms. "Eat. Goody."

"Come on, kid," Christopher said as the others laughed. "I'll dish up some for you."

"Me, too?" Katie asked, and latching onto Chip's hand, tagged happily along to the campfire.

Emily, hesitating, gazed toward the river. Robert still hadn't arrived. "Where's the trail down to the water?" she asked. "I'd like to wash some of this travel dust off."

"Right next to that split tree yonder, ma'am," another soldier answered with a knowing smile. "Just follow it, and you're bound to run into your sergeant."

A flush warmed her cheeks. Robert was not "her sergeant." Only a dear friend. People shouldn't be so quick to jump to the wrong conclusion. Turning quickly away, she started for the trail, then worked her way down the narrow pathway etched out of the bluff overlooking the river. Trees clung to the uneven ground with gnarled roots, stretching like old fingers across the trail, waiting to trip her. Jutting stones presented an equal hazard, but she continued on.

The swift-running river below looked like a black ribbon under the slate sky and dull November trees. She wondered if it might have been more prudent to have remained above with the men. There was no sight or sound of any wildlife or birds, nothing but the constant drone of the big river.

About halfway down, she could make out a man. Stripped to the waist, he was on his haunches, washing his upper body. Just imagining how icy the water must feel in such a chilly temperature gave her goosebumps. She couldn't deny that the fellow must be a stalwart sort. A few steps farther, and she realized it was Robert.

He'd given no sign that he had heard her coming. But then, considering how loud the current sounded, she wasn't surprised.

A tangle of vines and boulders blocked the path, and she had to climb over tumbled rocks to reach the bottom. She was only a few feet away now. He was still turned away from her as he picked up a piece of toweling and rose.

And then she saw them . . . angry red scars lacing his back. "Robert!" she gasped. "What happened to you?"

He spun around and stared. "Emily? How on earth did you get here?"

"Never mind me. Your back. What have they done to you?" When he did not reply, she drew her own conclusions, and her eyes burned with tears. She blinked them away. "It was because of us, wasn't it?" she whispered. "You were whipped for bringing Robby home. For taking me to Princeton." Aching inside, she tried to step around him for another look.

"Don't." He caught her arm. "Nothing I decide to do is ever your fault. Don't even think it."

"But—"

"No buts, Emily." As if suddenly remembering he was only half clothed, he grabbed his shirt from a nearby bush and shrugged into it, but he did not take his eyes from her. "You look . . . fine. Are you?"

"I'm managing. Everyone I know has been praying for the children and me, and that does a lot to get one through a sad time. It's . . . getting easier. And you?" she said with a thin smile. "How have you been? We haven't heard a word from you or Chip since that first week after you left. We've been worried."

"Sorry, I'll tell him to write more often."

"And will you, too? The children and I worry about your welfare every bit as much as we do his, you know."

At first it appeared as if Chan was about to say something.

But not a word passed his lips as his gaze remained fixed on her face. He reached for her hand and squeezed it lightly, encouragingly. "I think a lot about . . . Katie and Rusty, too. One of these days, perhaps . . ."

There was something in his expression she couldn't quite read, but new lines of care were already etching themselves into his forehead. She knew that he, too, must still be trying to get over Robby's death. They had been best friends. Or was it something else? The weight of more responsibility—he had been made a sergeant—or perhaps his obsession with Julia. "How about coming to see Katie and Rusty right now?" she asked brightly. "They're up above with Ben and Christopher. Probably eating your share of the food, too. They were quite hungry."

"They're here with you?" He broke into a smile, but it faded almost at once. "Tell me, why *are* you here?"

"Ben. He came by the inn and informed us that we were in the path the war is taking, so he felt the children and I should return to the farm for a while."

Robert shook his head gravely. "Being on the coast, Rhode Island is as vulnerable as it ever was, Emily. Promise me, if there's any hint of trouble—no matter how slight—you'll ride away from there at once." He placed his hands on her shoulders. "Promise. Don't take chances . . . with the children."

"Surely you know I wouldn't do that."

"Forgive me." Dropping his hands, he frowned and ran his fingers through his hair. "Of course you'll do your best for them. It's just that—I worry."

"Well, so do I," she said evenly, lowering her gaze. "Promise me you'll write me every week at my folks'. I need to know you're alive and well."

His lips narrowed, then relaxed. "I will, if you promise. We'll both keep our promises to each other, won't we." It was more a statement than a question.

Emily had to smile. "Yes, dear friend. Both of us. Well, come on, Katie and Rusty have been saving up hugs and kisses for you."

❧ ❧

The balmy Indian-summer day seemed a special treat to Prudence as she and Morgan, along with Evie and Clay and another pair of military officers the girl had charmed, took an afternoon horseback ride on Nassau Island.

"I'm ever so pleased you could get away from your business today, sweetheart," Prudence remarked. "Evie is certainly enjoying her new mare."

Even as she spoke, Evelyn raced up a rise with Clay Raleigh and Lieutenants Johnson and Kildare in close pursuit. A gust of wind caught the ends of her silk neck scarf, billowing out the long, emerald green strands like fronds of a fern against the clear blue sky.

Morgan grinned. "It was a capital idea of Lieutenant Johnson's, taking a ride here. With the unrest on Manhattan and the mainland so volatile right now, this is undoubtedly the safest place for my little sister to try out her new hunter."

The sound of Evie's merry laugh reached back to them as she disappeared from view over the hill, the others giving merry chase.

"I sometimes think she's wilder than I ever was," Morgan mused, shaking his head in wonder.

Prudence smiled. "Nevertheless, that matter with Jamie Dodd hurt her more than she will admit. I think she's bent on proving to herself that she's still desirable—even if it is with the enemy."

"I talked to her about it this morning over breakfast. Johnson hadn't come down yet, so it seemed the perfect time. I warned her again about the risk of holding too many tigers by the tail."

"How did she respond?"

"She didn't, actually."

Prudence had asked the question more out of relief than anything. She was thankful that he hadn't made an issue of her not joining them regularly at the early meal. Hesitant to confess the matter of her morning sickness, she had given the excuse of wanting to lose a few pounds . . . but from his reaction, she could tell he didn't quite accept it.

She really should tell him about the baby . . . but he would send her back to his domineering mother posthaste, no doubt about it, and Prudence couldn't bear the thought. What could it hurt for her to wait until after Christmas? Yet it was a subject she couldn't even pray about. The Lord would undoubtedly side with her husband. But she was being extremely cautious these days, doing absolutely nothing that would bring suspicion upon her or harm the baby. Even Morgan had praised her for finally finding her *good sense,* as he'd put it. Yes. Christmas. She would tell him at Christmas.

". . . I suppose she's right," Morgan was saying as they passed an abandoned farm. Having lost track of the conversation, Prudence hadn't the slightest idea whom or what he'd been talking about. "Evie says the competition only makes the men boast more, have looser tongues."

They came to the crown of the small hill and saw Evie and her admirers in a mad race across the stubbled wheat field below. Prudence had to smile at the sight of Clay Raleigh, whose bright peacock blue stood out in stark relief against the red of the officers' uniforms. "Poor Clayborne," she said, breaking into a giggle. "He must feel at such a disadvantage, not being in uniform. He gave Evie a very expensive brooch earlier this morning. I suppose he's hoping to buy her favor."

Morgan chuckled. "Ah, yes. The competition has become rather fierce. I'll wager Raleigh never dreamed he'd find himself vying for the affections of some mere colonial commoner."

"Of considerable wealth, my dear," Prudence finished.

"So be it. Did I tell you the idiot is even considering applying for a commission himself just so he, too, can strut around in a uniform? Not that anyone could parade more than Johnson or Kildare, since their army has taken the forts on the Hudson."

Prudence shook her head sadly. "And so many prisoners from Fort Washington. My heart goes out to them."

From the top of a distant hill, Evelyn waved.

The two returned the gesture as they watched her turn and disappear on the other side once more.

"I suppose there's one small thing that may come out of all of this in our favor," Morgan said. "Captain Long may be too busy with the prisoners to attend many of the social functions for some time. The cur's still making inquiries about me, like a bulldog chewing on a favorite bone."

"I really thought he had accepted my story." Prudence grimaced as their mounts plodded steadily onward. "And it's just dreadful, the thought of all those men cooped up on his ships. I'm just glad that Robert Chandler's battalion was not among them." Then another thought occurred to her. "Morgan, General Howe wouldn't ship our soldiers to England, would he? And leave them to rot in those horrid prisons?"

"I seriously doubt it. At least, not for a while. They're of much more value here—as bargaining chips for the return of any redcoats we acquire along the way."

"Then we must pray for a big victory. And soon." She urged gentle Lady to a faster gait.

"I'm afraid that won't happen unless our army can replace its losses," he answered, catching up. "I've hesitated to tell you this, but I've heard that Washington is down to about three thousand men. Too few to make any sort of stand. And Howe has a large force chasing after them across the New Jersey countryside. For now, all they can do is try their best to stay out of Howe's way until General Lee and his men from Fort Constitution can catch up. And Philadelphia has promised to send a couple of their militias."

Taken aback, Prudence glanced at him. "Where have all our thousands of men gone?"

He shrugged. "As their yearly enlistments are up, many are not renewing them. I know this is painful to accept, but short of a miracle, this war may well be over before the first snow."

"You don't mean that. Tell me you don't. How can so many simply walk away from our cause? our righteous cause?"

Morgan's helpless look was his only answer.

But it wasn't enough to quench Prudence's fervor. "If a miracle is what it will take, then that's what God will provide. He'll not forsake us." Spurring her horse into a gallop, she took the lead. "Race you to the top!"

His long-legged Thoroughbred easily caught up with her and beat her shorter Narragansett Pacer to the crest of the hill—just as she had known it would. But no matter. The challenge had put a grin on Morgan's handsome face, and it grew broader as he watched her drawing up to him. That in itself was more than worth the loss.

Abruptly his smile vanished.

Prudence followed his gaze. From this vantage point they could see the open sea, where upwards of thirty men-of-war were even now heading in a northerly course. The fleet Captain Long had spoken of was on its way to Rhode Island.

"Oh, Morgan. It's happening. It's truly happening."

He reached over and touched her cheek with his fingertips. "Washington may have lacked men to send to the aid of their militia, but because of you, my love, the people of Narragansett Bay won't be caught completely unaware."

35

Emily, astride a nineteen-month-old filly in the corral, breathed deeply of the crisp fall air as she put the animal through its paces. For several days the weather had been quite mild, but it was hinting at a chillier turn. She knew winter would be upon them soon, but she hoped it would be some time yet before the biting north wind made outdoor work miserable.

"Looking pretty good," her father commented from the next pen. He returned his attention to the foal he was teaching to walk on a lead.

Emily glanced over at him. It felt wonderful to be with her parents again, and even more, to be working outside with her father. Since their aged hired Negro, Elijah Moore, had taken to his bed with a bad case of rheumatism a few months ago, training of the foals and colts had fallen behind. With Mama, Abigail, and Elijah's wife, Tillie, occupied in readying the house and food stores for the season of bitter cold, neither Mama nor Papa had objected when Emily suggested taking on some of what were considered men's chores. In times such as these, rules had to be set aside. At least, that's what Mama planned to tell any neighborhood ladies who raised their eyebrows.

Emily pulled in on the reins and nudged the filly's flanks. "Back. Back."

For a few seconds Rosebud pranced nervously, then obeyed the command. "Did you see that, Papa?"

"I sure did. She's catching on quickly."

"She should be ready to sell in another week or so, don't you think?"

"Could be." He tugged his stubborn foal toward the fence that separated the corrals. "That'll make four. When you finish with her, I'll take her to Boston with the rest. One of the livery stables placed an order for two, and I shouldn't have a problem selling the others on market day. So many of the city's horses were slaughtered for food during the siege."

Emily sighed as he shook his head, the lines in his face deepening as his brow furrowed. The starvation that had taken place in the barricaded port would take years to forget. "The war's turning out to be longer and harder than anyone expected, isn't it?"

His brown eyes met hers. "I imagine they usually do, honey-girl. Let's just pray we've got what it takes to see it through."

Emily dismounted and pulled out a carrot to reward the young filly. "And let's pray this little one doesn't meet the same fate as Dan's poor horse. He told me taking dear old Flame to the butcher was the hardest thing he'd ever done." She watched her father's face cloud with sadness. He had also felt the loss of the faithful pacer, who had seen Dan through his days as postrider and courier. "I don't think I could have done it," she added softly.

"Well," Papa returned thoughtfully, "if they hadn't, they and many of their friends might have starved to death. One does what must be done for the good of all."

"I suppose you're right." Emily brushed a forelock from Rosebud's face. "But to look into those big velvet eyes and—"

A clatter of approaching hoofbeats interrupted her words.

Emily started for the fence. Papa unhooked the lead from the foal and went out the gate as Emily climbed the corral rails. Grady Lee, a cranberry farmer from down in the bogs near the bay, was coming down the lane.

"What's the big hurry, Lee?" Papa asked, coiling the rope. "Something afire?"

The craggy-faced man nodded. "The Brits are bombardin' the battery out on the island. A whole fleet of 'em." He paused to catch his breath. "Come to see if any of your young menfolk are at home."

"No." Papa moved closer. "But I've a musket and a brace of pistols. I'll fetch them and be right with you."

He held up a bony hand. "No, I gotta keep spreadin' the word. Folks are s'posed to meet down at the wharf in Providence." He wheeled his mount and galloped away.

Papa started for the house with long, fast strides, and Emily had to run to catch up. "Don't go. Please," she begged.

He slowed for barely a second. "I have to, Em. They're here. At the entrance to our bay."

"But-but what difference could one man make?" she asked, chasing after him again.

His steps did not slow, nor did he respond. When he reached the front steps, he turned. "I'll leave a pistol here. If the British make it into Providence harbor with a large enough force to take it while I'm gone, I want you to shoot the horses."

Emily stopped dead, stunned.

"Did you hear me?" he asked, his voice sounding hollow to her ears. "I'll not have my animals fall into English hands to be turned on our own people." Without further comment or delay, he slammed into the house.

Staring after him, Emily was unable to even consider obeying her father's order. She swung to gaze out over the serene pastures and the treasured herd of strawberry roans grazing placidly on the dry grasses. She could never do as he had asked. And the children . . . how would she ever explain such slaughter to her little ones, or to Abby's? No. The very idea was absurd.

She went inside, lingering beside the door to pull off her gloves. Her children and Abigail's were on a quilt on the floor before the parlor hearth, sharing a picnic lunch. The little girls chattered happily to one another. The boys were stuffing chunks of bread into cheeks already puffed. Emily smiled at the typical scene. Everything was as it should be. Until she knew more, she would concentrate on keeping things this way, concentrate on the children and the farm. Nothing else.

❦ ❦

In the dark of night, footsteps in the hall and hurried whispers roused Emily. Four tense days had passed since her father had left, and sleep had been hard to come by. He'd sent word to them just yesterday that it was unlikely that Newport, at the mouth of the bay, would be able to stand off the Crown forces much longer. Was it indeed lost? Had he come back?

Rising quickly, she threw on a wrapper and rushed out of the bedchamber. The hall was still dark. No one had lit a candle, but a strange light glowed from the window of Abigail's room across from hers, outlining her mother and sister-in-law huddled together. Papa was nowhere to be seen. "Is that the sun coming up?" Emily asked as she became aware of a drumming sound, distant and deep.

Mama turned. "It's Providence, Emily. It's under attack."

Newport had fallen. And now the British were within five miles of the farm!

Abigail turned slightly, the glow from the night sky glistening against her tearstained cheeks. "Ben told me to go to Worcester, to Caroline's, if the British came. I should have listened to him. I was such a fool. What if the redcoats have already landed troops?" She swallowed, and her voice rose in panic. "Emily, help me. Go saddle two horses while I wake my children."

"No, wait." Mother placed a hand on Abby's shoulder. "Cassie and Corbin will catch their death if you drag them out in this damp night air." She looked at Emily. "Ride to the hill and see if you can tell how bad it truly is. But be careful."

"But Mother Haynes," Abby cried. "Look. The whole sky is ablaze. I can't wait."

Emily, fighting her own fears, forced herself to speak calmly. "Listen, Abby. You and Mother get all the children up and dressed in good warm clothing. I'll go see what there is to see. If it looks really bad I can have horses saddled for you in no time at all." Then she hurried to her own room to change.

"What about you?" Abigail asked, following her.

"I can't know until I see what's happening. I'll decide then what has to be done."

Moments later, Emily galloped bareback out onto the road and up to the knoll. She couldn't even let herself consider the horror of destroying the herd. The concept had been so unthinkable that she hadn't mentioned it to her mother or Abby. They had been anxious enough in Papa's absence.

I cannot do it, she assured herself. *I could never do it.*

When she reached the rise, she could see beyond the hamlet of Pawtucket to Providence-Town. Her heart stopped. The constant glow of a burning city and flashes of cannon fire could no longer be denied.

Oh, Father in heaven, why is this happening? Only three months have passed since I laid my dear Robby to rest. I cannot bear it. No, she could not do as her father asked. Better to let the British have the animals.

But the picture of an enemy cavalry blazed across her mind, soldiers mounted on sorrel horses, riding deep into the countryside, pillaging, burning, murdering. . . . How would she justify that to her neighbors?

Her heart throbbed as she rode to the highest swell where her worst fears were realized. The bay was a bright orange reflection of the fires as smoke rose straight up into the night sky. Beyond, nearly thirty ships were strung out in Narragansett Bay, sailing onward toward Providence Bay. Longboats were already making for the shore on the south side, landing troops. Burning buildings blocked any view of the nearest warships, the ones even now bombarding the city. Providence was doomed.

A profound ache filled Emily. Where was the Continental

army? Surely such a huge fleet of English vessels couldn't have left New York unnoticed.

She had to drag her horrified gaze from the panorama below. *Dear Father, what am I to do? My children are in peril, and Abby's children. Mother. All of us. Everything.* Just before she turned away in hopelessness, another glow appeared on the horizon southeast of the carnage. The gathering dawn.

Straightening her shoulders, Emily turned her horse and raced for home.

When she reached the lane, she could make out a strange wagon and team parked in front of the house. The growing light revealed a haphazard load of household goods piled in the wagon bed. On the porch, a coarse-featured woman with children clinging to her skirts was talking to Mother.

Emily skidded the horse to a stop and dismounted, then ran up the steps. "What is it? What's happened?"

Her mother's bleak expression answered before she spoke the words. "Your father's been shot."

"Papa? He's—"

Mama rushed over, arms open, and hugged her. "No, dear. He's not dead. It's a leg wound. Mistress Lippet says he was taken to her house on the road to Providence."

"You're Emily?" the woman asked. "Your Pa says you know what to do. He's sorry he can't take care of things himself, but he's counting on you."

With each word, Emily felt herself sinking deeper into a chasm of hopelessness. Her blood was turning to ice.

"You young'uns get back up on the wagon," Mistress Lippet ordered. "We need to be getting along. The post road to Boston is already clogged with folks trying to escape, so I'm taking the Worcester road. I got kin in Brookfield. God be with you, Mistress Haynes."

"And with you, Maggie," Mama responded, embracing her.

"Wait," Emily said suddenly. "Please. Two minutes. Mother, hurry Abby and the children downstairs while I saddle their horses." She sought the stranger's face. "Mistress Lippet, my brother wants his wife and their little ones to go to Worcester, and I can't leave just yet. Would you be so kind as to allow her to travel with you?"

"Why, of course." Her smile was genuine. "Wouldn't mind the company a'tall. We womenfolk can look after each other."

Time did not allow for more than brief hugs and kisses those few moments later. Emily's sadness at the tearful good-bye was tinged with a measure of relief as she and her mother, arm in arm, dabbed at their eyes and waved after their precious threesome. Now at least Abby and her children were taken care of.

"Bye, Cassie," Katie called long after they were out of earshot. "Bye, Corbin."

Mother sighed. "I don't understand why you didn't go with them. I'm sure you could still catch up, if you hurry."

Emily turned to her children. "Katie, you and Rusty run upstairs and bring me all the blankets off your beds. Hear? And hurry."

Her daughter's eyes rounded, but without a word she grabbed her brother's hand and tugged him into the house. The two had been unnaturally quiet. Emily knew they must sense that something was very wrong.

She made herself look straight at her mother. "Papa wants me to shoot the horses."

"What?" Mama's hand flew to the neck of her night shift. "He couldn't."

"He doesn't want the British to get them." Emily swallowed a lump in her throat. "But I can't do it, Mama. I just can't."

"No, of course not. And neither could I." She frowned, her gaze flicking toward the barn and corrals. "We'll open the gates, turn them out. Then you can catch up to Abby."

Emily shook her head. "No. It wouldn't do any good. They'd only come back . . . unless . . . ."

Her mother took her by the shoulders. "Emmy. Listen to me. Those horses have been our livelihood, but a hundred herds could never take the place of you or those dear little ones. Please, dear, do as I ask. I must go to your father now, this minute, so promise me."

"I-I will." Even as she uttered the oath, the echo of the vow she'd made to Robert Chandler not three weeks ago flew into her thoughts. "Help the children get their blankets and clothes downstairs, would you, Mama? I'll hitch a horse to the cart. That way you'll be able to move Papa to some safer place, if need be. Remember, the two of you are as precious to us as we are to you."

Her mother took Emily's chin with trembling hands and bent to kiss her forehead. Emily knew her mother's heart had to be pounding with the same intensity as her own. "If he can travel, I'll try to convince him to go to Caroline's, too." She made an attempt to smile. "I doubt he'll agree to abandon the farm he's worked so hard for, but I'll do my best."

For a moment Emily debated whether or not to voice her thoughts aloud. "Mama, what if I could get people along the road to help me drive the horses to Worcester?"

Already halfway inside, her mother stopped. "I don't even have the time to consider something so insane. Remember your first responsibility—the children. That's all I can say." She went into the house, and the door closed behind her.

"The horses are far more than our livelihood," Emily whispered. "They're our responsibility, too."

Working quickly, she hitched the cart for her mother, then saddled two of the horses. Two others she rigged for packing. As she led them to the house, her mother came out, one arm loaded with her own blankets, the other curled around Emily's valise.

She dropped the case and hurried to the cart parked at the end of the walkway. "Whatever happens, I'll contact you at Caroline's. The Lord will see us through." She threw the blankets inside, hugged Emily once again, then climbed aboard and snapped the reins. "God be with you." The horse took off at a fast pace.

Emily, knowing that her mother was even now headed straight toward the enemy, wanted with all her heart to call her back. But it wouldn't have stopped her, and there was no time to dwell on her own mounting fears. *I'll have to trust both of my parents to your care, dear God. Please surround them with your angels. Keep them safe. And help me do what I must.*

As quickly as she could, she got Katie and Rusty situated atop Papa's gentlest gelding. Then, with the pistol tucked into her saddlebag, she mounted their most valuable stallion. "Wait right here," she told the children with a firm look. Then, with another desperate prayer, she steeled herself to accomplish the impossible. She unhooked the first pasture gate and rode in to drive the horses out onto the lane, then did the same in the remaining corrals until all were empty.

The quarter-mile fenced lane to the road now held sixty horses and provided a central corral. But at the sight of the rambunctious animals, she wavered. The grand dream of rescuing the herd revealed itself for the staggering impossibility it truly was. There was no way on earth she would be able to see it through.

I can't do this, Lord. Not by myself. But neither can I shoot them all or leave them here to be confiscated by the British. You're going to have to be our shepherd. Take us to your green pastures and still waters.

36

"Yee-hah!" Emily yelled.

Many of the horses flicked their ears in her direction, but they continued to mill about.

She snatched her whip from around her pommel, let it uncoil as she nudged her mount forward, then cracked the lash overhead. "Yee-hah!"

Those at the rear bolted for the others. Most of the herd was now on the move.

With a surge of optimism, Emily turned and smiled reassuringly at Katie and Rusty on the gelding behind her mount, then gave the whip another sharp snap.

This time the horses at the front started to move, too.

"Turn right!" Emily shouted to those running out onto the road—as if they could understand her. "Turn right! *Right,* I said!"

But they barreled straight ahead. Crossing the road, they galloped into an open field, one that Emily knew ended at a tangle of brush and trees bordering the Blackstone River. Blast. Trapped at the rear, she could hardly get to them.

But this was no time to be disheartened. Once she was out in the open, she would be able to turn them. She had to.

Too soon she discovered how wrong that notion was. Most of the pacers headed right into the thicket. And try as she might for the next two hours, she had yet to make any progress with the unruly creatures. No sooner would she flush one group out of the brambles than another would move in to take their places—lured by a number of volunteer apple trees among the native vegetation. She blew a wisp of hair from her eyes in disgust. It was useless. This job required more than one person.

Emily glanced toward the children, playing contentedly a safe distance away beneath an oak where she had tied their gelding. The packhorses munched serenely on the surrounding weeds. But the smoky sky and the dropping ash were constant reminders that she couldn't delay much longer. With a last utterly frustrated glare at the wandering sorrels, she rode over to her son and daughter. "Grandma was right. I can't do this by myself."

"I can help, Mama," Katie said bravely, standing as tall as her three-and-a-half-year-old frame could stretch. "Let me help."

"Me, too," Rusty chimed in.

Emily attempted a tender expression. "That's very sweet of my two angels. I know you would really like to help, but I've been given very strict orders not to take any chances with you." Maneuvering her mount next to one of the packhorses, she unhooked a long coil of rope. "I'm going to string three or four brood mares together. With those we already have, we'll have six. That will have to do. And I'm already on the best stallion." Suddenly aware of the silence, she looked in the direction of Providence. The cannonade had stopped. A bad sign. "Stay here now, and be good. That's the most help I could ask. I'll try not to be long."

Perusing the scattered herd, she tried to recall which brood mares were the youngest. She spied one of them, some yards off, craning its neck to reach a shriveled apple still dangling from a leafless tree. Slowly she reined her mount toward it at a nonthreatening gait, fashioning a lasso from one end of the rope as she went. But when she neared the mare, it shied away and crashed into the thicket, still chomping on the apple.

Emily knew that that particular mare had birthed two sets of twins in the past four years, and she was not about to give up. She rode doggedly after it into a patch of briers. The woolen divided skirt Mother had fashioned for her, to be more "ladylike" than men's trousers, snagged on a sharp branch and made one more tear to go along with those she'd already acquired during the past couple of hours. Shrugging off the damage, Emily saw that the horse she was following now seemed more cooperative, especially with most of its interest centered on a bounty of fallen apples under another tree. Moving stealthily up on it, Emily managed to snag the valuable mare.

One down. Cutting off a length of the rope, she tied the animal to the tree, then headed out of the brush in search of another. Emerging from the thicket, she glanced toward her children to be certain they were still safe.

The spot where she'd left them was empty!

Her heart froze. Soldiers? She slapped the reins across her pacer's neck and charged toward the road, searching both directions as she went.

A piercing whistle came from behind her. Almost unable to breathe for the constriction in her chest, Emily swung in the saddle.

About a hundred yards away were two riders. Neither, thankfully, wore a red uniform. She could also make out Katie's royal blue coat and Rusty's brown one. Men on horseback must have found them wandering. *Thank you, Father. Oh, thank you!* And now if the Good Samaritans would help her get all the horses on the road and headed in the right direction, she might still be able to manage.

About halfway to the approaching riders, they began to look amazingly familiar—like Robert Chandler and Christopher Drummond. It had to be her imagination. But—how could it be?

It didn't matter. With a squeal of delight, she heeled her stallion into a gallop and raced toward Robert, who at the same time urged his horse to canter toward her. They came to an abrupt halt beside each other. She seized his outstretched hand—the only thing she could reach from the saddle. "I don't believe it. You're here. The army has come to save us after all!"

Robert's mouth curved into a smile. "You and the kids look really fine," he said, not releasing her hand. "Katie says you're on your way to Worcester?"

Laughter bubbled out of Emily. "Yes. That's right." She took in the children's beaming faces, then glanced down the road once more. "Where are the rest of the riflemen?"

Christopher, too, arrived and brought his horse into the little circle. "Well, Em," he said jokingly, "it would appear you're not quite the horse expert you led us all to believe."

Emily hiked her chin. "Say anything you like. But if the two of you—and any more of your men you can spare—would help me round up Papa's horses . . ." She frowned, searching the distance. "Where is everyone, anyway?"

Robert shrugged with chagrin. "I'm afraid, dear girl, we're all there is."

"Oh, of course," she said, apologetic. "They've gone on to Providence. I'm lucky they could part with you. Do you think they'll be able to stop the British?"

Robert and Christopher exchanged a glance, then Robert's eyes locked on hers. "The army isn't here, Emily. Only us."

"But-but how can that be?" she asked.

"A couple days ago," Christopher answered, "I overheard some lieutenants mention the fleet that had sailed for Rhode Island. There we were, in some backwash of the war, doing nothing, yet no one could be spared to aid the Rhode Islanders. They'd heard that the militia guarding the bay had been put only on special alert, nothing more. Headquarters didn't want the Rhode Islanders to panic."

"Panic?" Emily echoed in angry disbelief. "We're not given to panic, I can assure you."

"And neither are the Pennsylvania Riflemen," Chip returned. "We held the English at Throg's Neck for four days. If they'd have let our battalion come, I'll wager those lobsters wouldn't have sailed into Providence with such ease. Right, Chan?"

Robert nodded. "But four hundred men can do only so much, lad. All we would've done was exact a higher toll from the redcoats. Nonetheless, our Colonel Hand felt so bad about the matter, he gave us permission to come help you. I have to admit, though, I did exaggerate a mite, telling him that you, a woman, had been left to run an entire horse farm by yourself."

With a droll smile, Emily made a sweeping gesture with her arm. "Well, as you can see, it was no exaggeration. The minute Papa heard about the invasion, he left and hasn't returned. In fact, he's been shot in the leg. Mother has gone to him."

Robert's smile quickly faded. "I am so sorry, Emily. And I'm doubly glad your father was no more eager than you are to hand over your horses to the enemy."

Christopher's face had taken on a look of amusement as Robert talked. His smile broadened. "There's more to it than that. Chan made a deal with Colonel Hand. Promised that if he'd give us leave to come move the herd, Chan would accept a commission as an officer when we return."

"You did?" Emily asked in amazement. Was this the Robert Chandler who, according to Robby and Morgan, had shunned all responsibility from the day he left his family plantation to come north? And perhaps, she suspected, for even longer than that? She shook her head in amazement. "I'll be forever in your debt."

Robert's gaze slid away as if he was embarrassed to be the recipient of her undying gratitude, but he quickly recovered. The edge of his mouth twitched into a partial smile. "I wouldn't be so free with your indebtedness just yet. We've still got to flush these nags out of who knows how many acres of brush. Oh, and which way do we point them?"

"That way." Emily pointed north.

"Wait a minute. Isn't Worcester between Albany and Boston?"

"Yes."

"Surely you have somewhere else you can go. If the British do succeed in pushing south from Canada before the freeze, they just might send a force across to take Boston from the rear. You might be no better off there."

Emily's shoulders sagged.

"I know a good place to take them," Christopher interjected. "To Dan and Susannah. The war will never reach that far into the Pennsylvania mountains. The Wyoming Valley is too remote for the British to bother with."

"But that's hundreds of miles from here," Emily said, her hope dwindling further.

"Well, last time I visited my sister and her husband there," Christopher replied, "I dropped by Dan's, too. He figured it's only about 350 miles away. That's not so far. Wouldn't take more than a couple weeks at most. And then the herd would be safe, wouldn't it?"

The more Emily thought about the idea, the better it sounded. "He *is* the oldest son," she said. "They belong with him far more than they do in Worcester with our sister's husband."

Robert held up a hand. "Hold on, you two. Aside from the major undertaking this venture would be, considering there are only three of us—and two small children besides—every last head of these horses will have to be ferried across the Hudson."

No one spoke for a few seconds until Christopher broke the silence. "We could drive them farther upriver—to Peekskill, where our battalion is. We could get them across on some of those flatboats our men have been building. If we offer the colonel a few head, I bet he'd get us ferried over quick enough."

Robert glanced around at the scattered pacers, a thoughtful expression pinching his straight brows. "You could be right." He turned to Emily. "But it's already December and getting colder all the time. How will your little ones fare out in the open for who knows how long?"

She slowly exhaled. "If I keep them dressed warm during the daytime, we should be able to find folks along the way who'll put us up at night. They'll be fine. I only wish Papa were here to make the decision."

"Mama?" Katie said, her voice unnaturally high. "I heard you tell Grandma that Grandpa wants you to shoot all our horsies."

"I'm so sorry you heard me talking, angel. Grandpa was very sad when he told me to do that. He wasn't being mean. He just didn't want the king's army to take them away, and he knew I couldn't move them all by myself. You saw the mess I made when I tried."

She giggled.

"But come to think of it," Emily went on, "I know Grandpa would be very happy if they were all safe with Uncle Dan." She took another breath and smiled at Robert. "If you're willing, let's do it."

37

With an aggravated sigh, Prudence went to answer the door. Again. Entertaining every afternoon was becoming a tedious ritual. Evelyn had given half a dozen soldiers and some merchants' daughters a standing invitation for tea . . . and of course there was always Clayborne Raleigh forever underfoot.

Her hand on the latch, Prudence assumed a bright smile and opened the door, recognizing the beaming officer immediately. "Oh, good afternoon, Lieutenant Crider. Do come in. Evie is in the music room with a few friends."

"Thank you." The muscular young man with a pronounced underbite bowed politely over her hand, but it was not hard to see that his attention was on the merry chatter coming from the far end of the hall. No doubt his thoughts were already on the lovely Evelyn, who was fast becoming adept at using those extraordinary Thomas eyes to their very best advantage.

Ushering him to the small gathering, Prudence took note that there were now three officers, Raleigh, and the two Deerfield sisters present. She would inform the cook. With the household understaffed since so many of the servants had sailed to Britain with the Dillards, Prudence found herself doing whatever she could to help out.

"Mistress O'Malley," she said, entering the cluttered kitchen. "We'll need refreshments for seven."

"Aye, seven it is this time, is it?" the frazzled Irishwoman said, blotting her forehead with the long sleeve of her work dress. "I'll see what's in the pantry."

After watching the cook bustle away, Prudence took two silver trays from one of the shelves. She gathered the tea service and set it out on the first, then continued with the tea preparations.

"Ah, here we are, lass," Mistress O'Malley said, returning. "There were still currant scones left. They should do nicely." She covered the remaining tray with a crisp linen square and arranged the baked treats in a circular design. "I think that's adequate. And I dearly appreciate the extra pair of hands."

Prudence returned her grateful smile, and the two took the refreshments to the music room, where Evelyn was playing the pianoforte for a duet sung by Melanie and Priscilla Deerfield. Around the room in ornate French chairs, the young men sat in rapt attention. The scene brought back the memory of Prudence's own musical debut. It was with no small relief that she had now put considerable distance between herself and Mother Thomas's unyielding demands.

Prudence set the tray on one of the smaller tables, then began to serve the tea.

"How about this one, Melanie?" Evie asked, flipping through some song sheets. 'Tender Rose, Flower of Love' is all the rage back in Philadelphia."

As the girls tittered among themselves and then attempted the number, which was obviously new to them, Prudence served Clay his tea. He flicked a glance up at her, and she offered a sympathetic smile. Accepting his drink, he winked, as if the two of them shared a secret. Prudence wondered why the young man still bothered to visit, with Evie neglecting him more and more. But, then, the competition of other eligible bachelors increased the value of the prize.

Returning for the next cup and saucer, Prudence did her best to maintain proper posture. Her bouts of morning sickness had ceased now that she was three months along, but her dresses were starting to feel tight around her waist. Odd that Morgan hadn't mentioned the subtle changes in her figure as yet. Dared she hope she'd make it past Christmas before telling him about her condition?

She shook off the troubling thought and stirred sugar into the next cup.

Melanie Deerfield fluttered over to her and helped herself. "Dear Mistress Thomas, you are such a godsend. I'm about to perish from thirst." She fanned herself for effect with her free hand as she returned to the pianoforte carrying her tea.

Judging Melanie's age as hardly a year less than her own, Prudence stifled an inward grimace at being referred to as Mistress Thomas. It made her feel as old as Morgan's mother. But then, her function here was more to chaperon than to enter into the gathering.

Evelyn snatched a cup of plain tea and added her own sugar with a sly smile while the Deerfield girls took seats among the men. Then Evie sashayed back to the instrument and leaned artfully against it, sipping her drink. Prudence knew it was a bold command for attention.

"Where is your brother this afternoon?" Clay asked Evie.

She toyed innocently with one of the shiny brown ringlets dangling beside her ear and deferred to Prudence. "Sister?"

"He should be home shortly," she answered. "He went to see the harbor master, hoping to expedite a sailing permit for a vessel belonging to a Philadelphia merchant." *One of the prime reasons that the colonists revolted in the first place,* she restrained herself from adding.

"Oh, the business of shipping is so tiresome," Evie sighed with a wave of dismissal. "So many rules and regulations, endless forms one must fill out. . . ." She sauntered up to the nearest pair of soldiers. "Particularly when we could be celebrating our latest victories. Do tell us, Lieutenant Crider, is there any more news? Has our good General Howe crushed those nasty insurgents yet?"

Don't be so obvious, Evie, Prudence thought, watching her cozy up to the military man.

But Crider merely straightened his spine, densely unaware that he was being used. He even appeared honored at having been singled out. "I do have some news regarding the cow-ardly rebels that you might find interesting."

As he continued, Prudence's mind drifted to Captain Long. If Morgan had not managed to arrange their social functions to avoid the scrutiny of that overbearingly distrust-ful man, save for that one tense evening, she and Evie wouldn't be able to probe so freely.

"And that's another matter," another of the officers was saying as Prudence's thoughts returned to the present. "The blasted rebels refuse to stand and fight like men. They're naught but a crafty lot of cowards."

"Aye," Lieutenant Crider affirmed, not to be upstaged. "Snipers sneak close at night, picking off our lads. In the light of day, however, they manage to stay at least a day's march ahead of our troops. General Howe's force is chasing them all over New Jersey. I just wish I could be there when we catch the blokes, rather than being stuck here in New York."

"Oh, but, Lieutenant," Melanie cooed coyly. "We would be deprived of your most charming company." She fluttered her pale lashes.

As if he hadn't heard the smitten young woman's thinly veiled hint, Crider turned to Evelyn, but she was casting an interested glance at the slightly less outspoken Lieutenant White.

"I'm sure the general has a plan," White assured her, his smile little more than a slash in his painfully thin face. "He has not failed us thus far."

"Well, I do so hope it's a clever one," Evie gushed, drifting back to the pianoforte. As she took the stool and brushed her fingers lightly over the smooth, yellowing keys, Lieutenant Crider rose and followed, spewing forth his calculated guess regarding Howe's plans. The other girls and Lieutenant White weren't far behind him.

Prudence found it quite amazing the way Evie managed to draw them all to her at will. All except Clay Raleigh, that is, who came to join Prudence on the other side of the room. "I wouldn't concern myself about those young officers," she reassured him. "Evie is merely flattered by all their attention, nothing more."

He turned a disinterested glance at the group, then shrugged a shoulder. "Yes, she's still quite young. Rather impressionable, as well. When these buffoons leave, I'll simply show them for the fools they are by telling her what General Howe's actual plans happen to be."

Trying not to reveal her own interest in his statement, Prudence wondered if the Englishman truly did know something of value. Morgan had told her Clay socialized with the higher ranking officers fairly often—far more than the two of them were able to do, since they had to avoid Captain Long as much as possible. "Now you have intrigued me, Mr. Raleigh," she said, her voice casual.

He gave her a calculating smile. "You shall have to promise not to breathe a word. Those fools—" he indicated the military guests with a jut of his chin— "would undoubtedly blab it all over the city."

"My lips are sealed," Prudence murmured, placing her hand over her heart as if in oath. "And whom, pray tell, would I pass it on to anyway?"

Apparently satisfied by her sincerity, Raleigh bent closer. "The general is merely pretending to play the rebels' game of cat and mouse. Once they're all ensconced deep in New Jersey, he'll abandon the chase and march his men to Philadelphia before Washington can so much as get wind of it and set up a defense. And in the bargain, Howe will capture most of the Continental Congress." Thus said, he leaned back again with a conceited expression.

"Why, that's . . . brilliant," Prudence managed, stunned. "I only hope, for the sake of my in-laws, it will be a peaceful takeover."

"General Howe is a most civilized man. You needn't trouble yourself. And then the general will control the two major ports before the first snow. After all, your Boston is all but finished as a port already."

Prudence flashed a disarming smile and touched his arm.

"I can see why you've been sitting here with such confidence this afternoon. Evie will surely be impressed by the amount of trust the leaders place in you—a trust, it would seem, far beyond what they bestow upon their own junior officers."

With a tip of his head, Raleigh demurred slightly. "A trust enhanced by their appreciation of a good cigar."

At the sound of someone in the entry hall, Prudence hoped it was Morgan and not another guest. "If you'll excuse me, I believe someone's at the door."

Walking quickly out, she raised a hand to prevent Morgan from proceeding farther and placed a finger to her lips. Then, with a glance over her shoulder to make certain no one else had ventured out of the music room, she took his hand and led him upstairs.

This information was much too important to delay.

Morgan didn't bother with the pretense of amenities as he eyed the barkeeper of the Dog's Head Tavern, on his way through the common room and out the back door. The information Prudence had related to him was crucial to Philadelphia and the Continental Congress. Everything was at stake. Messages had to be dispatched by land and by sea. No chances could be taken.

Behind the tavern, he paced impatiently, waiting in the chill December dusk. Tonight. The messages had to be sent tonight, even if he had to ride to Philadelphia himself.

What was keeping that bartender? Turning, Morgan tried to will the door to open. But to no avail.

If he did take upon himself the role of courier, Prudence and Evelyn would be left alone in New York. Perhaps the barkeep knew a trusted man who might be sent to look after them. One who could pretend to be an uncle from out of town or something.

Show your face, man!

Morgan hoped fervently that Prudence had followed his instructions, made whatever excuses it took to rid the house of all guests. He didn't want *anyone* to linger, not even for supper. She had to know the importance of—

The back door squeaked open, and the barkeeper emerged.

Morgan expelled a breath and gestured for the burly man to follow him behind the storage shed. With relief, he heard him comply.

"What's up?" the barkeep muttered.

"Washington is playing right into Howe's hand. General Howe will chase after our army only until they're deep enough into New Jersey, then he'll break away and make a beeline for Philadelphia. And, I'll wager, the fleet Howe sent to Rhode Island is on its way south as we speak."

"Why would you think that? Won't the Brits want to hold on to the city?"

"No doubt Howe will leave a policing force there, but his reason for going to Providence was more punitive than strategic."

"Yes. A great plan, that." The words came from out of the darkness!

Morgan wheeled. *Long!* The captain stood no more than a rod away in the fading light, a pistol in his hand.

The barkeep broke and bolted down the alley.

"After him, men!" Long shouted. His single-shot weapon remained fixed on Morgan.

At the sudden sound of more running feet, Morgan searched the growing darkness. "Tell Pru!" he yelled, hoping against hope that the barkeeper heard him. As he looked back at his captor's gloating sneer, Morgan prayed with everything in him that the barkeep would somehow elude his pursuers and reach Prudence—and that she would do exactly as she had been instructed in the event that they were exposed.

"So," Long said, the word taking on the menace in his hooded weasel eyes. "I see our Mr. Raleigh was kind enough to deliver my message. He's such a prattling fool. But then, I shouldn't have to tell you that, should I?" A vile grin of triumph spread across his swarthy face as he stepped closer. "And my war plan—quite ingenious, is it not? Ah, such a waste, a man as masterful as I, relegated to the lowly task of prison warden. Don't you agree?"

Had it been any other man, Morgan might have attempted to talk his way out, but with Long that would be futile. Staring at the cold barrel of the pistol, Morgan's duplicitous life unrolled like a scroll in his mind. He had utterly failed as a Christian. Reneged on a sacred vow. Corrupted his own wife and sister. Lied. Betrayed his parents. No amount of smooth talking would justify any of that tomorrow when he stood face-to-face with an altogether holy and righteous God. Acute guilt sent blood surging to his head as he stalled, collecting his thoughts. "No one ever suspected me. Not even my own family. Only you . . . from the first moment we met."

Long gazed into the distance, the action revealing his concern over whether or not his subordinates had caught the barkeeper. He slowly turned back. "Surely you didn't believe you could visit a known rebel in my Boston stockade, then show up as a houseguest of a prominent Loyalist without arousing my curiosity. And how quickly you disappeared once your attempt to bribe me into releasing that traitorous friend of yours failed. Any fool could see right through you."

The reality of imminent death settled on Morgan. He struggled to breathe, attempting an offhanded tone. "But regarding the prisoner Dan Haynes, the things I said and did concerning him were quite straightforward. No scheme, no plot." Even as Morgan spoke, the cruel irony of it all struck him. He almost laughed. "I've spied and plotted for the patriots for years and never once was suspected. But the one time I try to do an honest favor, that's when I'm foiled."

"Yes," Long said, "and you just foiled yourself again when you yelled for the tavern keeper to warn your wife. I wasn't sure she was involved . . . until that very second. I must thank you. And dare I say, your lovely bride will look extremely fetching . . . in a hangman's noose. It's sure to be a novel occasion. A double hanging."

38

Prudence heard a horse gallop up the drive. She laid aside her embroidery and went to the parlor window, but she saw no sign of Morgan.

"That brother of mine can never get home to you fast enough," Evie teased. "He must have gone around back, and in such a hurry."

The girl took nothing seriously, not even the impending attack on Philadelphia. An unexplained feeling of dread filled Prudence, and she cast an anxious look at Evelyn. The younger girl sprang to her feet, and together they hastened to the kitchen.

The servants were in the midst of evening meal preparations when the two entered the busy workroom. "There'll be only our family and our lodger for supper this eve," Prudence told the cook in passing.

"Very good, mistress," the Irishwoman replied with relief. Undoubtedly she'd never had so many extra mouths to feed before Evelyn began her daily invitations.

Prudence and Evie raced out the door, but it was not Morgan they saw when they reached the stable. An unfamiliar horseman, burly and grim faced, waited atop his mount in front of the stalls. "Mistress Thomas?"

"Yes." An icy dread raced through her at his expression.

"I'll help you saddle up." He swung down as he spoke. "Run

back inside, get whatever funds you can find, and grab your cloak."

Prudence frowned in confusion. "Who are you? What is this?"

"No time to gab, mistress. You must leave the island at once. There's five, maybe ten, minutes at most. I commandeered a horse on the way, or you wouldn't have that much time."

"Morgan!" she cried, panic gripping her. "Where's my husband?"

"He's been taken. It was a trap. Get a move on, will you?"

"But-but what do you mean, *taken?* Where is he?"

"He's been arrested. There's nothing you can do for him now but give him peace of mind." He turned and gave her a firm nudge toward the house. "Move! You must make it to King's Bridge before the sentries are alerted to watch for you."

"But *you* escaped. How can you be certain my husband didn't?"

"I'm *not* sure. What I do know is you'll be caught if you don't get outta here now!"

Prudence, trembling, felt as if she were being torn apart. "How can I go anywhere without knowing what's happened to Morgan?"

"You have to go. You must." He paused, and a look of understanding warmed his beefy features. "Look. As soon as I'm able to find anything out, anything at all, I'll get word to you. Now, is there someplace you can go? someplace safe?"

She couldn't think. Kneading her temples, she finally remembered where she was supposed to go. "Well, it's—it's quite far. But yes—Princeton." Hardly able to bear the thought of leaving so suddenly, and with Morgan in peril, Prudence had to consider, above all else, the tiny child who even now was growing within her. She raced to the house. "Evie," she called urgently, when the younger girl did not follow. "Come! Now!"

Evelyn shot forward like a flushed rabbit.

"You mean, you'll need *two* horses?" the rider called after them.

"Yes," Evie answered. "Two."

❦ ❦

A wisp of steam curled up from Robert's cocoa, the second cup kind Mrs. Cogswell had poured him just before she and Emily started washing the supper dishes. Still seated at the worn table, he glanced around the homey farmhouse where they had been offered lodging for the night. When his gaze reached the sideboard, Chan allowed it to linger, to wander over Emily's slender form as she worked with her back to him. All her movements, whether seeing to horses or tending her children or taking care of housework, were graceful. And he found more than a small measure of enjoyment in watching her. Robby must have, as well. . . . And *he* should have been here now, admiring his "bonny Emily."

She chatted pleasantly with their tiny hostess as she worked, but she kept her voice low in deference to Christopher and the little ones sound asleep near the hearth.

Not paying any mind to what was being said, Robert let her soothing tones flow over him. Such a part of her, that airy voice with its utter sincerity. Added with the other homey sounds here, it awakened memories of the years in North Carolina that he had taken for granted . . . and only now made him realize how very much of life he had lost by shutting people out. He had missed so many joys.

But he needed to corral his wayward thoughts. The winsome lass he was permitting his gaze to linger over was his best friend's widow—and her husband's death was partly Robert's own fault. It wasn't proper to entertain even the tiniest fantasies about her. It wasn't chivalrous. His responsibility toward her was to see her safely to her brother's place. Better to leave that part of him that had been dead and buried for the last six years as it was—sealed up, with a great wall around it built from the petrified ashes of his dreams.

He gulped some of his hot drink and looked at Emily again.

Flickering candlelight danced among the honeyed strands of her long, golden hair and glowed from those incredible green eyes whenever she turned to make a comment to the hostess. Her skin, so creamy and flawless, looked like satin. She was so beautiful. So gentle and kind, yet strong. The epitome of the faithful, loving wife. A woman of priceless worth. *And much too good for the likes of you,* he reminded himself. Downing the last of the cocoa, he rose and carried the empty cup to the women.

Emily took it with a smile, then placed a hand on the older woman's shoulder. "Mistress Cogswell, we're all but done here. We've imposed on your kindness enough for one night. Pasturing our herd, putting us up for the night. You've been so wonderfully generous. Please, go to bed, won't you? I'll finish up what little is left."

The mobcapped hostess looked from her to Robert and back, then nodded, drying work-reddened hands on her apron. "Truth is, I'd purely appreciate that. If you're sure you don't mind?"

"Of course not."

"Then I bid you both good night." Padding across the cozy main room of the house, she retreated into her bedroom just beyond it.

Robert remained near Emily while she washed his cup and set it on the drainboard. She picked up the dishpan and started for the door.

"Here, let me," he offered, taking it from her. His fingers brushed her damp, slightly soapy hands, sending a jolt of electricity through him.

She didn't seem to notice. "Thank you. At least let me unlatch the door."

He followed as he silently reminded himself of his commitment merely to look after her. Nothing more.

The icy breeze that rushed past them caught his breath. "Shut the door behind me," he said as he ventured outside in his shirtsleeves.

He gave the water a quick toss over the split-rail fence, then walked back toward the house. Overhead, the millions of stars blinking against the indigo darkness appeared almost close enough to touch. *God is sure in his glory tonight.*

Chan stopped short. When had he begun thinking of God so matter-of-factly again? Since the flogging, perhaps? Or since the battle at Throg's Neck, when he and Christopher had come away unscathed, despite impossible odds? Whenever it had started, this new truce with the Almighty had been a long time coming.

He gave the pan a last shake, then returned to the back door and entered quietly, in deference to the mostly sleeping household.

"Hang it on the nail above the drainboard," Emily said softly. Seated at the table, she was drinking the remains from her own cup.

This time as he crossed the room, Robert felt her eyes on him. He turned to face her.

"Join me for a moment?" she asked.

Robert knew it was absolutely the last thing he *should* do, but he ignored his conscience. Everyone was asleep, the two of them as good as alone.

"I think we've done quite well this past week," Emily said when he sat down. "And now that we've gotten the herd across the Hudson without some man-of-war sailing upstream and firing at us, we should make it the rest of the way just fine. Don't you think?"

Much as he hated to shatter her illusions, Chan could only be honest. "Emily, we know that Washington's forces have retreated as far as the Delaware while they wait for General Light-Horse Lee and his command to join them. And since the British routed Lee's men out of Fort Constitution, they've been on the run across New Jersey."

"Yes, but we can cut west from Princeton and avoid all that."

Her eyes searched his face, and Robert steeled himself against their guileless beauty. "First we must cross most of New Jersey. And like I said, who knows where Lee is—or the British troops chasing him, for that matter?"

"God will see us through," she said with a confident smile.

Robert stared at her for a long moment. "Yes, he probably will . . . for you."

"Oh, not just for me," she said airily, her friendly tone still casual. "Chip told me God has been taking care of the two of you, as well. Exceptional care, if I may say so."

"That, I'm sure, is for Christopher's sake, not mine."

Emily frowned and shook her head. "You remind me so much of Robby when we first met. It's strange." A wistful smile touched her lips. "Maybe it's a curiosity that goes along with the name Robert. Like you, there was a time when Robby was angry with the Lord. Did he ever tell you about it?"

"Robby?" Chan seriously doubted that.

She nodded. "I suppose he told you some of his past, how he and his father scrimped, did without for years just to send him to the New World. His poor father, rest his soul, knew it was the one legacy he could give his son . . . that and a firm belief in God."

Chandler, enjoying the sound of her voice, didn't interrupt.

"Robby was kidnapped right off the Bristol docks before he had a chance to book passage. Impressed into service aboard a royal ship, forced to labor on it for months while it plied our coastal waters, he felt as if God had not only betrayed him but was taunting him besides. He was so close to his dream, you see. So close. It was almost always within sight, yet he was never allowed to set foot on it. Of course, you know he eventually managed to jump ship—and in the nick of time."

The tale was almost as fascinating as her voice, Chan noted. He wanted to hear the rest. "And?"

"That's how we met. I helped him escape the redcoats. It wasn't until afterward, when he could look back on it all, that he realized God had neither betrayed nor forsaken him. Robby had forsaken the Lord, had forgotten to keep the faith. As the book of Hebrews says: 'Faith is the substance of things hoped for, the evidence of things not seen.'"

Mulling over those words, Chandler smiled. "Scriptures are a whole lot easier to quote than to live."

Emily smiled. "I know," she said cheerfully. "So isn't it marvelous that the Good Lord blessed us with his mercy for those times when we fail?"

Robert could see in Emily's eyes her sincerity and the abiding friendship he knew she held for him. It was more than he deserved.

Abruptly, she looked away. She picked up her cup, took another sip, then smiled rather tentatively at him again.

Her expressions were usually quite readable, but this one puzzled Chan.

With a glance across the room at the sleeping forms, she leaned closer. "There's something I've been wanting to ask you in private. Do you remember when Prudence and Morgan's younger sister, Evelyn, stopped to see you a month or so ago?"

Vastly disappointed at the shift of topic, but not about to dwell on the reason, Robert brought his reaction to her back into line as she continued.

"Well, Christopher has been asking me untold questions regarding Evie. How old she is, are there many beaus . . . that sort of thing. Am I to assume the lad is taken with her?"

Robert's amusement took over. "Odd that you would notice. He scarcely mentions the girl to me more than twenty or thirty times a day."

A lighthearted smile softened Emily's features. "I thought so. When Evelyn was younger, she was always as cute as a button-nosed doll. I wasn't the least surprised she turned out to be such a beauty."

Chandler grinned. "She couldn't have been half as cute as our little Katydid is."

Tilting her head to one side, Emily's eyes took on a lively shine. "As cute as *your* Katydid. My Katherine's head has been swelled to twice its size since you told her she was the cutest little girl in any church."

"You mean, she's not?" Robert challenged, entering into

the good-natured banter. He was immeasurably relieved he hadn't ruined it all. He had come frighteningly close, with his comment about *our* Katydid. It wouldn't happen again.

The door to the bedroom opened, and Mr. Cogswell hurried out, tucking his nightshirt into his breeches with one hand. His work boots were clutched in the other. "A rider's comin' fast."

Jumping up, Chan snatched a lantern, and he and Emily dashed out the front just as the horseman reined his mount to a sudden halt.

"That you, Clem?" Cogswell asked from the porch, tugging on his second boot.

"Aye. Thought I'd ride over and let your company know I had some of me own this eve. A patrol of British officers stopped by to water their mounts. Asked about all them horse tracks on the road. I said they were from a herd bein' driven to Staten Island. But just to be on the safe side, I'd be outta here before sunup, if I was you. And stay off the roads."

Robert stepped to shake the gloved hand. "You're a good man for coming. I thank you."

"Well, best I get back home now. Don't want the wife to worry." Wheeling his mount, Clem galloped back the way he'd come.

Emily was so near, Robert could feel her trembling as she hugged herself. It took all the strength he possessed not to wrap her in his arms and pull her close. "I think it might be best for you and the children to stay here," he told her. "Christopher and I can handle the herd by ourselves. Then I'll come back and get—"

"*No,*" Emily said emphatically. "If it's too risky for us, it's too risky for you. Besides, what's the worst thing that could happen? They'd just confiscate the horses."

He could see by the look in her eye that there was no reasoning with her. He had been down this road before since he had been caring for her. But he wasn't her husband. . . . He couldn't resort to forbidding her. Not that Emily would take kindly to such actions even if he *were* her husband.

Chan figured he might as well give in now and get it over with, save valuable time. "Very well. But whenever there's a stretch of open ground tomorrow, we're going to run the horses. We're getting across New Jersey as fast as humanly possible."

"Right after we stop by at the Lyons' Den," she said in all seriousness, placing her fingers on his arm. "We can't leave the colony without going there first."

Mr. Cogswell, standing slack-jawed to the side, stepped closer. "You'd do better to cut across the northern end to Easton, not get anywheres near the road to Philadelphia."

"Thanks for the advice, sir. I'm afraid Emily can be quite stubborn at times."

"Can't they all." Chuckling, he returned inside.

"That may very well be," Emily said, her tone flat. "But Princeton is a good ten miles this side of Trenton. Surely both armies will be well beyond by the time we get there. It would be such a shame to deprive the Lyonses of a short time with Christopher. It would mean so much to them . . . and to me. Who knows when I'll see them again? Please, Robert, couldn't we at least head in that direction?"

With her looking up at him so pleadingly, it was impossible to refuse—even though Chan knew he was right.

"Please, Robert, pray about it. If afterward you still feel we can't go that way, I'll abide by your wishes. I promise."

When she released his arm and walked toward the farmhouse, the warmth of her touch went with her. Yet Chandler remained rooted to that spot.

She wanted him to talk to God, to listen to him. To forgive. To plant again that small mustard seed of faith . . . and find embers of hope among the ashes of his life.

For Emily, he had to try. He lifted his gaze to the moon peeking through the branches of a leafless tree. For her.

And for himself.

39

"Emily."

A hand gently stroked her hair, its touch as soft as her whispered name. She opened her eyes.

Robert knelt beside her, his face gilded by the flickering fire glow. "Time to go," he said quietly.

It took a few seconds for her to recall in which farmhouse they had stayed overnight. She yawned and sat up, still dressed in yesterday's clothes, and tried to gather her wits. Robert set her shoes beside her. Noting how helpful and solicitous he was being, Emily suddenly realized she must look a sight. She smoothed her rumpled dress and finger-combed her hair the best she could.

Chandler began rolling his and Christopher's pallets. The lad was also up and dressed—and she had heard neither of them stir. Emily stifled another yawn and quickly slipped on her shoes. The little ones were still fast asleep, and their kind hosts, the Cogswells, remained in their bedroom.

Emily rose to her knees and rolled up her own blankets, then turned to the children.

Robert stopped her with his hand. "Let's wait for Chip to bring our mounts around. It's well below freezing out. I thought we'd just pick up the kids wrapped in their blankets and keep them with us till after sunup."

Emily nodded, even though she knew it would complicate herding the horses through the darkness with a sleeping bundle in her arms. But the children had been such troopers, she really didn't want to disturb their sleep. She would manage somehow.

She handed Chan her bedroll, and he helped her to her feet. There was something especially comforting about having a very capable man looking after her and the children. Emily found herself enjoying the attention . . . but this arrangement was only temporary at best, and a man like Robert Chandler would be considerate to anyone.

She retrieved her cloak and started for the door when she heard the clop of the horses.

"Just stay by the fire till I've tied the bedding to the saddles," Robert said, striding past her. "No sense going out in the cold any sooner than you have to."

"Thank you." As she watched him go, Emily realized that she had always considered herself a rather independent and capable person. She and Robby had been so young when they married. They had both had to do some fast growing up. And they had not only been husband and wife but best friends and comrades, as well. It was odd to feel safe and secure in these dangerous times, especially now that she was a widow with two small children and sixty horses to move across hostile territory. But Robert's concern had brought back some of that old security, and she appreciated it more than she could voice.

Spreading her fingers before the warmth of the banked fire, Emily wondered if Chan had actually discussed the situation with God last night. As much as she wanted to ask him, she knew she could not. Better to wait patiently and hope. But it would be a terrible loss if he wasn't able to find peace with God again.

The door opened, and both men came in. Christopher swept Katie into his arms while Robert picked up Rusty. "When you mount," Chan told her, "I'll hand Rusty up to you; then Christopher can give Katie to me on my horse."

Biting cold assaulted her as soon as she stepped out the door, and her breath rose in clouds of mist. The skies had been dreary for days, but so far the clouds had done nothing but threaten. Positioning herself on her stallion, Emily admired Robert's sureness of purpose, the trust he instilled in those around him. She could see why Colonel Hand wanted to make him an officer.

An entirely new curiosity surfaced within her. Had Chan's family been disappointed when he abandoned that natural bent toward leadership after Julia died? What were his parents like? She couldn't recall his ever having mentioned them. Had they been praying for his restoration to faith?

Once everyone was situated, they headed for the fenced pasture to round up the herd, and Emily realized that she still didn't know which direction they'd be traveling. Surely he wouldn't mind her asking just that. Nudging her pacer ahead, she rode to his side. "Which way are we going, Robert?"

In the murky darkness, she could not discern his face. "Both, actually."

"Both?"

"You cost me a good deal of sleep, you know," he added wryly, then softened with a small smile. "But I don't mind. It was way past time for me to straighten out a lot of things. I had forgotten how much easier life can be when we trust the Lord rather than ourselves. Last night, although I still didn't have the answer I sought regarding our route, I finally decided to trust God to direct us today."

"I'm so very, very pleased to hear that. But . . . why would the Lord tell you to go both ways? That I do not understand."

He chuckled. "To make a long story short, I mentioned our dilemma to Chip this morning. He just shrugged and told me there was no problem. He has a cousin with a farm a few miles north of the Raritan River on the way to Easton. Since we're starting so early, he thinks we can leave the pacers at his cousin's, then take fresh horses for the ride to Princeton. There should be time for at least a late visit this evening. Of course, should the British get close, the plan might very well change."

"Oh, I don't know," Emily said, smiling. "I think I'll just

trust God for this plan, if you don't mind. And thank you, Robert. Thank you."

"For what?"

She shrugged. What could she say? For listening . . . to her and to God? For being so thoughtful and kind? For being exactly what she needed? She merely smiled. "I guess for simply being you."

It had been a long, hard day, with intermittent sprinkles of rain throughout, yet Emily felt good. They had made Christopher's cousin's farm well before dark and left the herd under Mr. White's care. On fresh, borrowed mounts, they were sure to reach the Lyons' Den not long after dark. Yes, it had been a wonderful day.

And added to all its other blessings was one more . . . there was something very right about knowing her dear friend was now taking his direction from the Lord.

Hugging Katie to her, Emily glanced across at Robert and Rusty, little more than silhouettes in the deepening dusk. She wished she could see Chan's face clearly. He had been wearing a smile every time she had looked at him today, more often in one day than in all the time she had known him. She was beginning to understand that Robert's being sent to care for her had been as much a part of God's plan for him as it was for her. He had made his peace with God. Perhaps now, at last, he could put Julia to rest.

It was amazing the difference a smile made in his countenance. It took away from his long chin, adding a bracket of laugh lines beside his mouth, and displayed teeth that were white and even. The spark in his dark blue eyes diminished the years that grief had added to his age . . . and along with that incredible smile, it was more than appealing.

Perhaps, in time, Robert would find someone to love again. He had much to give, and he deserved to be loved, especially after so much wasted time.

She, on the other hand, would never seek the same for

herself. Robby's love had been a once-in-a-lifetime blessing, and the special bond they had shared she could never imagine replacing. Her heart constricted as memories assailed her. Anyway, it was Robert she was concerned about. She slid a sidelong glance at him, trying to conjure up the sort of woman he might find appealing—a woman who would be incredibly wonderful, breathtakingly beautiful, adept at all domestic duties. . . .

Christopher's shout cut into her fancies. "This way! Through the trees." He veered his horse to the right and led them through a dormant field into a stand of trees.

Emily could discern some shadowy buildings in the drizzle ahead, and a few dots of light. They must truly be close now. The trees were likely the woods behind the Lyons' Den.

Within moments her hopes were confirmed. They broke from the grove near the barn at the rear of the inn.

Jasper charged out of the back door with lantern in hand as they came to a halt. With a scowl on his craggy face and his hair bushing about, he looked like the very devil himself.

"It's only us, Pa Lyons," Christopher called. He dismounted and went to help Katie down from Emily's horse.

"Chip?" He raised the lantern higher, and his fiery expression transformed to one of joy. "And Emily! Praise the Lord! You're here. Safe. But what are ya doing ridin' through New Jersey?"

"We're taking Emily's herd of horses up to the Wyoming Valley, to Dan and Susannah," Christopher explained.

Jasper looked incredulous. "Don't you know our countryside is teemin' with redcoats? A patrol stopped off here not more'n an hour ago."

"When?" Robert rode into the circle of light. "Which way did they go?"

"They rode off toward Trenton." Jasper lifted Rusty down from Chandler's saddle. "Never thought I'd see the day when I'd be forced to serve the enemy."

Robert swung to the ground. "Do you happen to know where the armies are? If they've engaged yet?"

The innkeeper grimaced. "Not from what the redcoats were saying. But they sure were braggin' on the capture of General Light-Horse Harry Lee. Never heard the likes of it."

"*Lee?*" Chan asked in dismay. "Aside from Washington, he's the best general we've got. His command—did they capture his command, too?"

"Nay. Him and his staff were stayin' in the comfort of Morristown with a guard of only about fifty. Oh, enough war talk. We need to get these kids in outta the rain."

The fireplace in the huge common room gave off a heavenly warmth, and the children ran to it, discarding coats and scarves and hats as they went. Emily followed at a more sedate pace, picking things up after them. She couldn't help noticing that the ordinary was empty of customers—unusual for the supper hour. Obviously the invasion of New Jersey was playing havoc with business.

Mr. Lyons regarded Robert. "I'm assumin' the army gave ya leave to help Emily this time." From his demeanor, Emily knew he was concerned for Christopher's sake.

"That's right," Chan answered good-naturedly. "This time we have permission."

The older man nodded in affirmation, then turned toward the kitchen. "Esther! Come out here! It's Chip and Emily."

One thing Emily could always count on was the lively sparkle in old Mrs. Lyons's eyes. She fairly burst into the room and rushed to give everyone a hug.

Then Emily noticed others coming to join them. Morgan's wife! And his sister! Even as her mouth gaped open, she saw Prudence fly into Robert's arms.

For a split second he looked stunned; then he enveloped her in a hug. "Well, this is a surprise," he said with a smile.

Emily felt an unaccountable stab of resentment. She averted her gaze from the embrace to see Christopher go to Evelyn, eyeing her in wonder. The girl allowed him to take her hands, then moved closer, her own expression as openly pleased as his.

Looking from him to Robert, Emily could not deny that

Robert seemed no less pleased to see raven-haired Prudence. A vague memory surfaced of one of Robby's letters mentioning how fond he *and Chan* were of Morgan's Puritan wife. Surely a man like Robert Chandler would not allow himself to entertain feelings for his friend's wife, she protested inwardly. Yet clearly Chan did care for Prudence—perhaps even he wasn't aware just how deeply his own feelings went.

"What are you doing, traveling through New Jersey at a time like this?" he asked her.

Prudence's luminous gray eyes swam with tears, which spilled over and ran down her cheeks. She opened her mouth, but not a word came out.

Jasper stepped up to rescue her. "Morgan has been taken by the British."

Emily was speechless. She had known Morgan most of her life. Her mother's family and his were friends of old standing.

"We don't know that for certain," Evelyn declared with an angry pout.

"Is this true?" Robert asked Prudence, cupping her chin.

She nodded, and her tears trickled over his hand as she swallowed hard. "The man who came to warn us said they'd captured him. And it's been days. *Days.*" Her breath caught on a sob. "If he had managed to escape, he would have come for us by now. Or at least sent word." She sniffed in misery.

Robert's eyes met Emily's, and she could see how worried he was. Spies were sent to the gallows almost immediately— made an example of. Chan drew the crying young woman close again.

"Prudence may be married to my brother," Evelyn announced in defiance, "but she obviously doesn't know him as well as I do. No two or three soldiers would be able to hold Morgan. There could be any number of reasons for him to be detained getting here." Then she, too, started to crumble. "All kinds." The last words came out garbled as she began to cry.

Christopher pulled her into a comforting hug, pressing her head against his shoulder. "She's right," he said, looking at

Prudence. "No mealymouthed lobsterback could outsmart Morgan Thomas."

A shuddering sigh came from Prudence as she remained in Robert's arms. "I only pray that's true."

Emily found the news of Morgan's capture unbelievable. He had always been so clever. But then, she wouldn't have believed that Robby would be shot, either.

Prudence rose on tiptoe and whispered something to Robert.

He stiffened. Taking her by the shoulders, he held her at arm's length. *"You never told him?"*

"Told whom?" Evelyn asked. "What?"

"I, um . . ." Prudence's face drained of color as she met her sister-in-law's gaze. "I'm . . . with child."

"Pru!" Evie gasped.

Jasper whacked a nearby table. "Well, that settles it. I'm not takin' any more chances with these lasses. We've been hiding them from lobstercoats every day for the past week. Day before yesterday, the leader of a patrol asked for 'em by name. Described 'em perfectly." He turned to Robert. "I'm sendin' these two on with you. I know you'll look after them, just as you have our Emmy."

Emily regarded Robert and Prudence, the two still clinging to one another as though they belonged together, and her spirits sank. Despite Prudence's suffering and her jeopardy, despite the fact that Emily knew inside that she had no designs on Robert herself, she still regretted having insisted upon coming here.

40

"No!" Prudence wrenched out of Chandler's grasp, tears streaming unchecked down her face. "I can't go anywhere." Warding off Robert and Jasper with her hands, she backed away. "Morgan told me to come to the Lyons' Den. No place else. I must wait here. I have to. Unless . . ." She rushed back to Robert and seized the front of his coat. "Please, take me back to New York. I can't bear the uncertainty, not knowing. *Please.*"

Emily witnessed the return of the old pain to Robert's eyes as he stared at the willowy, black-haired girl. It caught at her heart. Earlier today, for the first time since she'd known him, Chandler had seemed unburdened, happy. And now this. Why, oh, why, had she compelled him to come here?

He looked from Prudence to her and then back and slowly shook his head. "You'd be putting your unborn child at risk. You know that."

"I know." In anguish she flung herself against his chest. "I know."

"Jasper?" Robert asked. "Do you know anyone who might be willing to ride to New York? We would pay well for any information on Morgan."

"Yes!" Evie cried with renewed hope. "That's a wonderful idea. *Please.*"

The innkeeper scratched his head, causing further disorder to the straggly white strands. "I might be able to find somebody."

Chandler gave a grateful nod. "If so, the message will have to be carried on up to Dan Haynes. As you said earlier, it's too dangerous for Prudence and Evelyn to remain here."

"But—" Prudence's light gray eyes flared. "If Morgan should come—"

"Jasper knows where Dan and Susannah live. I'm sure he'd waste no time at all sending him on to the Wyoming Valley. In the meantime, come on to bed. You'd best get whatever sleep you can. We'll be leaving Princeton before dawn."

In misery, Emily watched them go . . . Chandler holding Prudence close as they climbed the stairs together. This was the woman Chan and Robby had taken under their wing, looking after her in Morgan's absence last year when the men were at Cambridge. Robby had mentioned her in so many of his letters, proclaiming to no end all her marvelous attributes. At times Emily had wondered if he had merely found her fascinating . . . or was there more to it? Had he grown to love her a little? And might Chandler have felt the same?

Her feelings made no sense, and Emily tried to rid herself of them, but still the unanswered questions gnawed at her. She clenched her teeth together as she cast another look toward the stairs. If Prudence was supposed to have such *strength of character,* as Robby had put it, such *unfailing trust in God,* what had become of those noble virtues?

Even as the scornful thoughts crept into her mind, Emily knew they were not only uncharitable but also unfair—and more than a little unchristian. Prudence was living in a very precarious state right now, her future completely unsettled. The poor woman had been left to wonder if her husband had been imprisoned or, more likely, already sent to the gallows. And she was with child.

A tug on her skirt drew Emily's attention downward. Katie and Rusty, each with a hand clutched on a fold of the navy wool, gazed up at her, their little faces filled with confusion and fear. She bent down and drew them into her embrace.

"Ah, now, methinks some cheerin' up is in order." Mrs. Lyons stepped forward and scooped Rusty into her arms. "I've got a special treat in the kitchen for my two favorite young'uns in this whole world. And now's the perfect time for it, too. Comin', Katie?" she asked, turning to go.

"Uh-huh!" A big smile broke forth as the child latched onto the older woman's hand and skipped along.

"Thank you," Emily murmured. "They haven't had anything hot to eat this whole long day."

"Now that you mention it," Christopher said, looking longingly toward the kitchen himself, "neither have I. I'm starved. How about you, Evie? Come sit with me while I eat?"

Evelyn cast a fleeting glance toward the stairwell, then shrugged, and the two of them left the room.

"Have the twins heat up some extra bricks to warm the beds," Jasper called after Esther as he started for the entrance. "I best get to findin' somebody who'll brave traveling the roads to New York. Can't imagine that little gal bein' willing to leave here unless she knows someone's already been dispatched." He plucked his greatcoat from a peg by the door on his way out.

Emily looked around and found herself utterly alone, with nothing breaking the silence but the occasional crackle of burning wood in the great hearth. Even Methuselah's cage had been covered. This empty room, this solitude, were not at all what she had anticipated when she'd had the brilliant idea of coming here. She exhaled a ragged sigh.

A few huge, fluffy snowflakes drifted tentatively down from the leaden sky, promising the first real winter storm. Emily, riding at the rear of the herd not far from her children, found the dreary afternoon a perfect match for her mood. After leaving Princeton three days ago and crossing the Delaware, they had spent a good part of the last two days traveling up a river road that wound through mountainous country. When the trail finally meandered away from the river, they climbed toward a cut in a pine-covered ridge. The temperature was dropping as they went higher, and icy winds buffeted them mercilessly.

According to Christopher, they would reach the Wyoming Valley by evening, but Emily wasn't so certain. Robert was being extremely careful of Prudence, traveling in her delicate condition, and insisted that they all stop to rest every hour or so. He had yet to stray more than a few yards from the girl, Emily noted, as she watched them riding side by side. She tried to check her bitterness. After all, having lost his own wife late in her confinement, Robert would naturally take special care of a woman with child.

If this horrid uncertainty turned out to be a confirmed fact, and Morgan truly had been put to death, what then? She could not imagine Robert forsaking Prudence, leaving her completely on her own. If the rider dispatched by Mr. Lyons came to impart the dreaded news at Dan's, Prudence would have nowhere else to turn. Only to Robert.

Emily let all her breath out at once. Her sole consolation was that sometime tonight they would finally get to Dan and Susannah's. She and her children would be safe there at her brother's, and so would the horses. She would have to be contented with that.

Emily rebuked herself. This was pure self-pity, and it was time to stop wallowing in it. She had no reason to resent Robert Chandler's concern for Prudence and her child, and she had a great deal to be thankful for, after all. There had been no sight of any redcoats on this entire journey. And her children, despite being so very young, had been amazingly good along the way, riding double for hours with scarcely a complaint. Katie, especially, had thought of the whole thing as a grand adventure. For a little girl not even four, she had become quite adept at handling the gentle mare and could actually be of help riding at the rear of the herd.

The snow was beginning to increase now, coming down steadily. And so was the wind. Cold and sharp, it managed to cut through their layers of clothing and rub raw any exposed inch of skin. As Emily neared the youngsters, she saw with alarm that their cheeks were red and chapped. Rusty was shivering profusely but gave a proud grin as she came alongside. They needed to get out of the storm, to someplace warm. "Come to Mama, Rusty," she said, reaching for her son. She wrapped the blanket from behind her saddle around him and tucked him close, then smiled at Katie. "Think you can do Mama a favor, *Miss* Kate?"

Her daughter straightened in childish pride. "Uh-huh. What?"

"Stay right here and make sure the stragglers keep moving while I go ask Uncle Chip where the closest house is. Can you do that?"

"Yes, Mama."

"Good girl. I'll only be a few minutes." With a nod of confidence at her daughter, Emily smiled and urged her own mount to a gallop.

As Emily approached Evelyn and Christopher, she noticed that Evelyn was also shivering and windburned, her curls whipped by the wind beneath her heavy scarf. Emily doubted that this city-bred girl had ever been at the mercy of the elements before. With a sympathetic smile, she switched her attention to Chip. "We haven't passed a farmhouse lately. . . ."

"Because there aren't any," he answered flatly. Then at her obvious alarm, he elaborated further. "Now that we're out of the Lehigh River Valley, we won't see a home until we cross these ridges and come down into the Wyoming Valley."

Emily glanced at Evie for a sign of panic, but there was none. Obviously she had more grit and determination than Emily had given her credit for.

"We have to keep going, Em," Chip said. "Do our best to get across the last ridge before dark."

She stared at him for a long moment. "Well then, keep Rusty warm for me, will you? I need to talk to Robert." She handed him her little boy. "Try to make sure his hands and feet stay inside the blanket."

"I'll look after him, too," Evelyn offered, moving her horse closer to Chip's.

"Thanks. And keep your eyes open for any kind of shelter. Anything. A hunter's shack, a shed, anything that can keep out this wind." Emily wheeled her mount, smiling at the realization that Rusty provided the young couple with a legitimate reason to ride even closer to each other.

By the time she got back through the steadily falling snow to Katie, Robert was with her already, lifting the child onto his horse. It made Emily feel a few degrees warmer to think his obsession with Prudence hadn't completely negated the concern he had for her children. *I'm surprised,* she thought cynically, *that he didn't put Prudence on his lap instead.* Emily pushed aside her wayward thoughts and smiled gratefully at him as she approached. Tugging the other blanket from behind her saddle, she handed it to him to wrap around Katie.

"See, Mama," her daughter said, pointing a mittened hand. "I kept the horses moving."

"Yes, and you did a good job, too, Miss Kate. I'm proud of you."

"Did Chip tell you where the nearest home is?" Robert asked.

Emily sighed. "He says there aren't any until we cross the mountains. There'll be farmsteads on the other side."

"We can't risk it," Robert answered, looking down at Katie with an ominous shake of his head. "I'm going to ride over into that grove of trees yonder, see if I can find a place to build a shelter. Tell Chip to bunch the herd here on the road. I don't reckon they'll stray in the storm. I'll tell Prudence on my way."

The snow was coming down fast and hard, swirling about on the wind and beginning to stick to the ground. "Don't go far. You might not be able to find your way back."

He smiled, hugging Katie close to him. "We won't, will we, Katydid?" Then he took off into the pines.

Emily breathed a prayer for their safe return as the packhorses were cut from the herd and the rest bunched up. When the chore was almost finished, she looked across the sorrel rumps of the huddled animals and saw Chandler and Katie emerge from the woods. "They're coming back," she called, then, trailing a packhorse behind her, went to meet them.

Robert's face was glowing from the cold, but he flashed a confident grin as Emily and the others rode up to him. "I've found a stone outcropping that will protect us from the north wind."

Half expecting Prudence to whine and play on his sympathy, Emily was again humbled when the hollow-eyed young woman sat in stoic silence on her mount.

The biting wind whipped at the treetops, whistling through the pine branches on the outer fringe of the woods, slapping icy snow against their skin. But within the forest growth, the storm was considerably less vicious. Chandler led the little troop into a cut that turned into a gully, beyond which a wall of stone reached up nearly as high as the tops of the pines. He dismounted with Katie, carried her to the wall, and set her down in the shelter.

"Take the saddles and packs off the horses," he said above the howling wind. "Stack them around the children. Prudence, you stay with the little ones and keep them warm while the rest of us build a shelter."

Emily felt her blood rush to her head. Was Prudence now even usurping care of her own children? Then, just as quickly, she recalled the dark-haired girl's condition, and she prayed silently for forgiveness. Of course the able-bodied would have to look after those more vulnerable.

"Emily," she heard Robert say firmly. "You and Evelyn look under all the trees for dry wood to build a fire. Find as much deadfall as you can. Chip, start cutting evergreen branches. I'll strip some poles and start making a frame."

Then, quieting, he went to kneel by the children with a gentle smile. "You'll keep much warmer if you share the blankets," he said softly. Tugging them from each, he placed the shivering tots with Prudence and wrapped them all together. "This is gonna be great fun. We're going to play

Indian as we build the lodge and get a good fire going. But we're all going to need Indian names. All of us. Can you think of good names for us?"

The children nodded in unison.

Emily's heart melted as she watched this tender interplay. Robert was so good for her little ones. Better than many fathers she had seen. And in many ways he was good for her, too. Unexpected tears threatened, and she had to fight hard to keep them from spilling over.

"Hey, what's everybody standing around for?" Robert asked, swinging around. "Get going. We've got to get a warm place for these kids."

41

While the storm raged outside, the temperature felt quite moderate within the rough, pine-bough shelter—or Indian lodge, as Chandler had termed it for the children's sake. Emily, taking her turn at watching the fire, huddled before the crackling flames, feeding a steady supply of kindling to keep it going. Robert had left a small hole at the top, and the interior of the makeshift haven was amazingly smoke-free. She couldn't help smiling at yet another example of his ingenuity. Of course, Chandler gave the credit to his experiences the previous winter, during the time he had been camped outside Boston. But all Emily knew was that she and the rest of the small group would have frozen, were it not for him.

"Katie," Rusty moaned restlessly in his sleep. "Don't." He rolled over.

Emily glanced at her son, lying between Christopher and Evelyn for warmth, and wondered what mischief was being attributed to his big sister in his dream.

Katie was sound asleep herself, with Prudence on one side of her and Robert on the other. Fleetingly, Emily thought her slumbering babies looked like bundling boards used to separate courting lovers. But she dismissed the idea as quickly as it had come. She had never been one to entertain uncharitable feelings toward others, and why she'd been doing so during the past several days remained a mystery to her. She hardly needed a reminder that Robert's sole reason for being here in this wilderness was to help her and the children. He didn't need to be repaid with bitter, unkind thoughts.

The howl of the wind began to abate, and within moments the sound died away completely. As she silently lifted her thanksgiving to God, she realized with stark clarity that she had been neglecting her prayer time of late. The fifth chapter of Galatians flitted across her mind. If she had been walking in the Spirit, as she should, she wouldn't have been trying to devour Prudence or anyone else. She had no cause to think ill of Morgan's beautiful wife—and it was time to go to the Lord and ask his forgiveness, to reclaim the indescribable peace God had given her since Robby's death.

In the stillness of the night, Emily bowed her head. *Dear heavenly Father, I don't have to tell you I've been wallowing in self-pity and resentment for days and days . . . and this after talking so much to Robert about trusting you. Our country is being torn asunder by the awfulness of war, and every day more men are dying. And here am I, but one of many widows, facing the loneliness of a lost loved one. Prudence, too, has most likely experienced the same kind of loss . . . and I, who should be the first to comfort her and lift her up in prayer, have instead been shunning her, looking for reasons to dislike her. I can't even fathom why I'm so consumed with this lack of charity! I ask you to forgive my sin and cleanse my heart. I must have become too used to the comfort of having this caring man around. But that is no excuse for my thoughtless disregard of another person in need. Please help me make it up to her.*

Emily stole a glance at Chandler, sleeping with his back to her, and traced the outline of his broad-shouldered form in the glow of the firelight. Yes, this very dear friend would make some fortunate young woman a wonderful husband one day. And when that time came, he would do his own choosing. She could only be thankful that she'd had such a mate herself not so long ago. She had loved Robby MacKinnon with every fiber of her being, and that love would never die. She could do no less than wish happiness for her husband's dearest friend . . . her own dearest friend.

She bowed her head once more and continued pouring out her heart to God.

I thank you so much for sending Robert Chandler to us. He's been so very wonderful to me and to the children. They love him deeply. And I . . . I will always treasure the memory of his kindness. Please, keep me conscious of the fact that I need to press more closely to you and seek your will. You are the one who knows the future. I can only ask that you remind me to stay faithful to you, and please show me your will, dear Lord. And, yes, I know . . . help me to be the friend Prudence needs right now. The uncertainties of carrying a first child are more than enough. But to lose her husband as well, how will she bear that? Fill me with the love I should have had for her all along. I ask all these things in the name of your dear Son, Jesus.

Even as she raised her head at the close of her prayer, Emily felt a heavy unchristian ugliness fall from her heart. In its place flowed a new love and tenderness, and a resurgence of that first blessed peace God had given her weeks ago. She gazed through a blur of joyous tears at the sleeping group. *Thank you, dear God. Thank you.*

Emily added a few more twigs to the fire, and the spicy tang of pine pervaded the confines of the shelter, adding a pleasing aroma to the comforting crackle of the flames. Hearing no more gusts of wind outside, she wondered how much snow had accumulated. It wouldn't hurt to go and see.

She gathered up her blanket, wrapped it securely around her shoulders, and rose. She eased quietly out of the opening and stepped out into half a foot of newfallen snow.

The heavy cloud bank had moved on, leaving behind a star-spangled sky, and a half-moon glowed in magnificent splendor over a pristine world of blue white. Long branches of evergreen drooped to touch the ground beneath the weight of their burden. The glorious sight filled Emily with awe. *And thank you for this, too, Father . . . the loveliest gift of all.*

Not too far from the shelter, their mounts and packhorses dozed peacefully, huddled together. Emily hoped the others had fared as well out in the open. She took several steps to check on them, but remembering the fire and the constant attention it required, thought better of leaving. With the clouds all but gone, the temperature would likely drop a bit more.

"Beautiful night."

Robert's low voice startled her. Emily fought to calm her racing pulse as she turned to him. "Yes. Almost makes up for our being caught in the storm."

"Almost." He chuckled, then quickly sobered. "I've been wanting to catch you alone. I need to talk to you about Prudence."

For the first time, Emily felt empathy for the young woman, and she nodded at him to go on.

"She's in a terrible way. Nothing I say seems to ease her suffering. I've tried to avoid asking this of you, so few months after your own loss, but I was wondering if tomorrow you'd spend some time with her. You always know the right thing to say."

"I'm profoundly sorry you had to ask," she said quietly. "I should have gone to her on my own, instead of leaving the entire burden on you."

He smiled and lightly brushed a clump of snow from her shoulder. "I'd say you already have your hands full."

Emily knew Robert was just too chivalrous to let her accept her rightful blame. "Not with you here to help." She paused. "I'll do what I can."

He nodded gratefully. "It's more than only her mourning for Morgan. She's carrying a great weight of guilt over the matter, and nothing I say seems to make any difference. Fact is, she really is guilty."

"Why would you say that?" Emily asked, trying to conceal her surprise at his curious remark. "I probably should know what I'm dealing with."

Glancing into the distance, Robert appeared to be gathering his thoughts. Then he lifted the blanket flap of the shelter and checked inside before replacing it and meeting Emily's eyes. "Prudence's entire life and upbringing centered upon what was righteous and what was not. Honesty was one of her most rigid standards . . . so much so that she even rejected Morgan at one time for having taken money from his father for false purposes during his earlier spying days."

"I already know all of this," Emily said evenly. "Robby told me the whole story."

"Well, all that she ever condemned Morgan for doing, she's done herself, and worse. She encouraged him to renege on a vow of truthfulness he had made to the Lord, just to go back into spying again, even though she knew he did not feel peace about it. Her reasoning was that it served the greater good of our freedom; therefore, it wasn't actually *sin*. But now, not only does she question that conviction, but she bears the burden of having committed a far worse sin against him. She never told him about their child."

Emily's lips parted in shock. *"But, why?"*

"She feared he would send her back to Philadelphia. As it was, she and Evie went to New York without his permission."

"Oh, my. I can understand why she's inconsolable."

"There's more. She was the one who relayed the false information to Morgan. She sent him into the trap. She is positive it is all her fault and that his capture was God's retribution for her sins."

Emily exhaled in a rush, her breath vaporizing in the wintry air. This was what poor Robert was having to deal with just when he was beginning to find his own peace with the Lord. And she had left him to cope with all of it alone. Had his fragile new faith been crushed before it had a chance to take root? She needed to know. "And what do you think, Robert? Do you believe our heavenly Father is heaping vengeance on his daughter?"

He pondered the question for a moment. "What I think," he finally said, "is that *she* is reaping what *she* sowed."

"And what about Morgan?"

"According to Prudence, he accepted Washington's request to spy again before thinking it through, much less praying about it first."

Recalling her own prayerful struggle mere moments ago,

Emily had to smile. "That is something perhaps all of us are guilty of, one time or another."

"Except you."

"Especially me. But isn't it wonderful that we only need to repent in order to receive forgiveness? I think perhaps Prudence has forgotten that."

A slow smile widened Chandler's lips as he took Emily's hand in both of his. "I knew you'd know just what to say to her. I do thank you."

"For what?" she asked, refusing to acknowledge a strange fluttering in her heart. Surely it was only a friendly gesture on his part to warm her fingers in the freezing weather. She only hoped her voice would come out normal. "Don't thank me yet. I haven't even talked to her."

He continued to smile. "As you said to me a few nights past, I'm thanking you just for being you."

❦ ❦

Travel the next day was a little slower as they trekked through snowdrifts and icy creeks, but Emily felt warmer and lighter. She knew there was absolutely no reason to make more of Robert's words than he had intended, yet they were immensely fortifying. She rode, as always, at the rear with Katie and Rusty nearby, while the pacers made steady progress, eating up the distance between them and Dan's place. Emily could hardly wait to see her oldest brother and his wife again, to say nothing of her nephew and niece.

Ahead and off to the left, she glimpsed Robert as he rode away from Prudence and fell back toward her at the end of the herd. Emily knew this would be her cue to go and have her talk with Prudence. She glanced at Christopher and Evelyn to ensure that they were keeping watch over the horses nearest them; then she nudged her mount into a canter.

Robert, riding toward Emily on his way to the children, graced her with a smile. "How!" he called with an upraised hand as he switched his attention to Katie and Rusty. "Eagle

Eyes comes bearing greetings from Black-Haired Woman for Running Bear and Little Fawn."

The children giggled. "How, Eagle Eyes."

"Time for a powwow," Robert went on.

"Powwow?" Katie asked. "What's that?"

"That's what we Indians say when we want to get together and talk."

"Well," Emily returned with a hopeful smile, "I shall go have a powwow of my own."

He gave a nod. "For her sake and the baby's."

On her way, Emily prayed for wisdom and for the proper words. As she neared Morgan's wife, she felt much greater shame for her lack of compassion on the previous days. And how had she missed the dark circles shadowing Prudence's light gray eyes? Small wonder Robert had felt so concerned. She reined her stallion alongside Prudence's mare. "Robert is back visiting with the children," she began tentatively. "Thought I'd come ride with you for a while."

The dark-haired girl glanced behind them with a thin smile. "He does relish their every word. He's forever relating one antic or another to me."

Emily found the news oddly gratifying but had no inkling why she should. But now she debated whether to start right in or wait for an opening. A few moments of silence lapsed. She drew a calming breath. "Being with Katie and Rusty is only part of the reason Robert went back there, Prudence. He wanted you and me to have an opportunity to talk. He's quite worried about you."

Prudence met Emily's gaze, then looked away. "I know. He doesn't want anything bad to befall Morgan's unborn child . . . no matter who the baby's mother is."

"Surely you know Robert is genuinely concerned about you, as well as your baby."

A pink flush rose on Prudence's high cheekbones. "Yes." She urged her mount to a quicker pace.

Following behind her for several minutes, Emily used the

time to pray again for wisdom, then heeled her pacer to catch up. "Prudence?" she asked gently.

Silver eyes turned toward her for a fleeting second.

"I know something of what you're suffering. Truly, I do."

Prudence's expression turned bleak, and she emitted a sigh. "Forgive me, but you couldn't."

"Yes, I could." Emily reached to touch the other girl's arm. "Robert told me . . . everything."

With a sharp intake of breath, Prudence sought a glimpse of Robert, then turned forward, her demeanor haunted.

Emily pressed on. "I know a little of the guilt you're feeling . . . and so does the Lord. He's always there waiting to extend mercy and forgiveness. That's one of our most precious promises."

With a slanted look at Emily, Prudence grimaced. "I know most of his promises by heart, Emily. I attended church my whole life. I know I have God's forgiveness for the asking. It's my own I cannot give or accept. Thanks to me, our unborn child may never know his own father. How can I forgive that?"

"You have to find a way. The baby will need a healthy mother to care for it. No matter how much punishment you feel you deserve, you must forget your past mistakes and forgive. You must go on for your baby. Live today for today's sake, and try to make each tomorrow a little better. You can do that with God's help."

Prudence didn't respond. A tear traced a glistening path down her olive skin.

"With winter setting in, we're going to be together for some time to come. I'd like to be your friend. If you ever need to talk, I'll be there for you. And so will my brother Dan."

"Once they know the truth, they'll hate me. Morgan was one of their closest friends."

Emily smiled gently. "Dan and Susannah are very understanding people. Nonetheless, I'll speak to Robert. Neither of us will tell them anything. We'll leave that to you."

Nearing the next crest, Emily hoped it would be the last before they could start the downward trek into the Wyoming

Valley. "Just a little farther," she murmured, "and we can all rest and begin to heal."

"That does sound good," Prudence admitted quietly, looking ahead with a hopeful expression. But when she settled back into her saddle, the look vanished. "You know, I was always a very rigid person in my younger days. Very judgmental. But now I doubt I'll ever view another's imperfections—any failing—with disdain again."

Emily gave her a small smile. "This trip has been one of much soul-searching. I've had to face some of my own ugly secrets. But look." They had reached the summit, and she pointed at the vast expanse of the shimmering, snow-covered valley as it came into view far below. "It's all downhill from here."

Prudence didn't appear overly comforted at the quip. "I don't see how. We've lost so much, and if we lose the war, it will all have been for nothing."

Emily reached for her hand and gave it an encouraging squeeze. "It's time for us to let go, Prudence. Let go of everything. Even the war. God will see us through somehow. I just know he will."

"It all seems so hopeless," she answered miserably.

Emily nodded. "But when times are darkest, that's when we need God most."

42

"We're getting close," Christopher yelled to Emily, and excitement coursed through her. As they drove the herd by the quiet settlement of Wilkes-Barre, along the Susquehanna River, folks they passed waved and shouted greetings.

"We're taking the horses to Dan Haynes," Christopher answered, veering closer to the nearest settlers. "All the way from Rhode Island."

Emily could tell from the expressions of amazement that it was highly unlikely anyone had ever driven a herd this size into the area before. In her concern over evading the British, she had almost lost track of the arduous undertaking herself. She lifted her arm in a joyous wave to the plainly dressed townsfolk, wondering how many of them might be part of Dan's congregation.

"Howdy," Katie called, sitting tall and proud on her docile mount. She and Rusty waved, grins on their bright faces.

Emily's attention drifted across to Robert and Prudence. He was grinning, also. He turned in his saddle and waved— but not to the strangers. His wave was directed at her!

Her heart leaped, and she returned the gesture. This beautiful day marked the end of a long, incredible journey. But a rush of sadness dampened her enthusiasm. Tomorrow, or the next day at the latest, Robert would leave to go back to his battalion. Emily knew she would more than miss him. And he would once more be part of the desperate attempt to drive the

British from the continent. She had spent so much time needlessly feeling jealous of Prudence that she had lost sight of that very present danger.

After about a mile, Christopher motioned to turn the herd eastward, and they drove the animals across cleared fields. The afternoon sun glistened over the melting snow, lending a breathtaking beauty to the long, wide valley.

When they came upon a rude log cabin, a column of gray smoke churned upward against the stark blueness of the sky in a welcoming spiral.

"Halloo the house!" Chip hollered.

The door flew open, and out came the smiling family of four. Though Dan had always tended toward leanness, Emily observed that neither he nor Susannah had regained much of the weight they had lost during the months of deprivation they had endured inside the closed port of Boston. Yet to her, they had never looked better. Her brother was growing more and more to resemble their father, and a twinge of homesickness overtook her for a moment.

Dan, however, fairly beamed as he administered enthusiastic handshakes and stout hugs. Four-year-old Miles, with hair the same shade as his mother's, stood straight and tall, his dark eyes alight as he got in line for all the handshakes.

Emily remained in her saddle for a moment to look upon two-year-old Julia Rose, the niece whose name now took on an entirely new meaning. No longer would Emily think of her merely as the namesake of Susannah's best friend but as that of Robert's great love. The fair-haired child clung to her mama's skirts, peering shyly around them with huge blue eyes.

When one of the pacers milling about meandered a little too close, Dan snatched the child up into his arms. "I don't believe it! What is all this, Em?" He came to her side, a smile of incredulity lighting his dark brown eyes.

Emily laughed lightly and slid to the ground, only to be grabbed into a crushing embrace by her brother along with his little Julia. "I decided I have much better things to do than nurse this scrawny herd," she said after finally catching her breath. "You've been footloose quite long enough, big brother. Time you took on some responsibility."

"Well, not that I mind, you understand," he returned, "but as you can see, I don't even have a fenced pasture."

Robert, still on horseback, threaded his way through the pacers to join them. "That grand stack of logs yonder from when you cleared your land would make a fine split-rail fence."

"Robert Chandler?" Dan exclaimed in surprise. "And Prudence Thomas, too? I'm thoroughly confused now. But you can explain later." He turned to Christopher. "Chip, ride back to town and round up as many men as you can, even Connecticut lads and our friend Jon. Together we'll have a corral built before the sun sets."

❦ ❦

At Robert's insistence, Prudence had immediately been ushered to the bedroom normally used by Felicia Curtis, Yancy's wife, who had gone to visit her father for the Christmas holiday. Hesitant to take chances, he carried a tray of food to her instead of having her rise for supper. The children, exhausted from the trip, had been put to bed in the loft with their cousins right after the meal. And the men, weary and sore from the hasty fence building, stretched their aching muscles and retired early in Dan and Susannah's room, leaving Emily and Susannah alone to linger over cups of hot spiced cider.

Taking a soothing sip, Emily reflected upon the reunion, a curious mixture of joy and sadness. Her brother and sister-in-law had received word of Robby's death some months ago, but news of the invasion of Rhode Island and Morgan's capture were hard blows, particularly coupled with learning that the British had overrun New Jersey.

Susannah replenished their beverages as they relaxed at the dark pine kitchen table. "You've been on our hearts and minds so much, of late," she said, her pleasant British accent

❦ 367 ❦

soft and familiar. "Now I know why Dan and I have felt burdened to pray for you." The concern in her blue gray eyes was mirrored on her face as she retucked a tendril of tawny hair into a ribbon at the nape of her neck.

Emily willed herself not to cry while she relived her grief one more time, answering all the hard questions for Susannah's sympathetic ear. It was so much easier to be strong when, moments later, they finally got beyond that subject. "And all I could think of," she confessed, "was Papa's dream, his herd. Knowing that his lovely farm might soon be destroyed, and that he and Mama were in danger, it suddenly became imperative to save the horses—or, at the very least, to keep the redcoats from confiscating them. Perhaps one day soon we'll be able to return them."

"Yes, well, we can only hope and pray that's so. In the meantime, I know Dan will take wonderful care of them. It astounds me that you were able to get them across all the rivers and over those mountains. God's miracles seem more wonderful by the day."

The front door opened, and Christopher and Evelyn walked in from the cold. They didn't appear to notice the two women as they crossed the room to the door of the room where Evie would be spending the night. Their doleful expressions as they bid one another good night would have been comical had Emily not been aware that Chip would be going with Robert, leaving Evelyn with the uncertainty of ever seeing him again. With a soft sob, Evie sniffed and entered the bedchamber, then closed the door.

"Oh, the bittersweet pangs of young love," Susannah said softly. Then her smile faded. "Speaking of that, is it my imagination, or is Robert's concern for Morgan's wife somewhat deeper than that of one friend for another?"

Emily almost choked on her cider. Recovering, she set down the empty cup. "Well, they've known each other quite a long time. And she's with child, you know. . . . It brings back memories of Julia."

"Oh, of course. I hadn't thought of that." She peered into

her empty mug, then reached for the warming pot at her elbow. "Would you care for more?" Without waiting for an answer, she refilled both their mugs one more time. "I'm sure it must be good for him. When he visited us in Boston, I doubt I saw him smile more than once or twice all the time he was there. It's quite refreshing to see such big grins on that handsome face of his. Several times today I even heard him laugh out loud."

Emily smiled as she pictured Chan's amiable face with its strong, chiseled features, the compelling blue eyes that sparkled with laughter or caring. "Those smiles started before we picked up Prudence and Evelyn in Princeton. Robert has finally accepted his loss after years of blaming God. He's repented and returned to his faith."

"That *is* marvelous—another of my daily prayers answered. God has been so good."

"Robby and I always prayed for him, too," Emily murmured.

"You are positive you're all right?" Susannah asked, giving Emily's hand an empathetic squeeze. "You've been faring well?"

Emily could not hold back a sigh. "I miss Robby, of course. I always will. But I know he's with the Lord, and with his father. Robby was quite heartbroken when he heard his father had died alone in far-off Scotland. I try to think of the wonderful reunion they must have had. It helps quite a bit."

"A reunion somewhat like ours today."

"Yes, I'm sure it was."

Susannah lightly tapped the tiny cleft in her chin as her fine brows furrowed in thought. "But there's something else troubling you, isn't there? There's a sadness in your eyes that isn't about Robby."

Emily swallowed hard. It was true; there was a strange unrest in her spirit. But she wasn't completely sure it could be expressed . . . even if she could confide in Susannah. "Oh, I suppose it's the war," she said, hedging. "It's all but lost."

Susannah's intent gaze remained fixed on her. "And?"

She raised her chin. "There's nothing else. Really. Well, only something too petty to discuss, to actually put into words."

"Nothing that makes you sad is unimportant, Emmy."

"I . . . don't know where to begin." A new wave of tears threatened, and it was all Emily could do to quell them. She averted her attention to the confines of the cozy room, with its finely crafted furniture and the homey touches Susannah had fashioned for their little home.

"It pains me to see you like this, Emily," Susannah coaxed. "Please know that you can always talk to me."

"It's-it's Robert Chandler," she finally blurted, the confession astounding even her. "I hate to think of him going back to battle." Suddenly aware of how deeply she meant those words, Emily felt that she had to justify them, lest her sister-in-law get the wrong impression. "When Robby died and Chan came to take the children and me to Princeton, he was so good to us. I can't tell you what a comfort he was, what a mountain of understanding and strength. He . . . was punished quite severely for leaving his post to bring my husband home to me, but he had made Robby a promise, and nothing could stop him." Emily flicked a nervous glance to Susannah, but seeing only compassion, she continued.

"Then when the British invaded Rhode Island and Papa sent word back to me to shoot the horses, Chandler was there again, taking charge. If it weren't for him, you know, I never would have made it all this way. He was a godsend." Her mouth twitched with a smile, and words came much more easily. "He has a remarkable sense of humor, did you know that? And he's so good with the children—" Realizing that she was no longer whispering, but talking far more loudly than she had intended, Emily stopped short.

"And now," Susannah finished for her, "all that attention he gave you he's now giving to Prudence. And you're a bit jealous."

Jealous! Emily felt the warmth of a flush. "Well . . . I suppose so. But it doesn't make sense. He's never so much as hinted that there might be anything between us. Not that there is . . . or-or should be. Oh, I don't even know what I'm trying to say. He's always been a perfect gentleman. I want you to know that. But . . . I can't help it. I've prayed, truly I have, but it hurts. You must think I'm a disloyal, selfish—"

"I beg your pardon, I didn't mean to eavesdrop."

Swinging toward the sound of the voice, Emily saw to her dismay that Robert stood in the doorway. Her face burst into flame. Never mind Susannah . . . what must *he* think of her!

"I heard voices," he went on. "I thought something might be amiss with Prudence."

Complete humiliation engulfed Emily like a wave. She fixed her eyes on the table, unable—and unwilling—to meet his gaze. No one spoke for several seconds.

Then Robert broke the silence. "Susannah, would you mind leaving the two of us alone for just a few moments? We need to talk."

No! Emily wanted to shout. *Stay here! Please!*

"Of course." With a troubled glance at Emily, Susannah quietly withdrew to the bedchamber.

Mortified, Emily hunkered slightly into herself.

Robert came to her side and took her hands, drawing her gently to her feet. He did not let go.

Unable to meet his eyes, she glued her gaze to the middle button on his shirt. What must he think of her? What had he heard? For that matter, what had she actually *said*?

"Tell me you meant it," he said, his voice low but firm. "What you told Susannah."

Emily turned her head aside. To her recollection, she'd been babbling like a lovesick—

"These . . . feelings . . . you have for me, they go beyond those of a mere friend?"

"I—" Did that mean he *wanted* her to have them—or *didn't*? And *did* she? *Could* she, so soon after Robby? Was that possible? Her heart pounded almost painfully in her breast. "But-but what about Prudence . . . if Morgan doesn't return?" she asked lamely.

"What about Prudence? If the worst happens, we'll see her through the rough times, be there for her, of course. But that isn't what I asked."

Hesitantly, she looked up at him. From the intensity of his stare, Emily suspected he could see into her very soul, read what was there even if she didn't say the words. She could not look away. Nor could she deny feelings which only now she began to recognize. "It's . . . true."

He expelled a rush of breath. The beginnings of a smile touched the corners of his lips, and his fingers tightened around her upper arms. "Does that mean you'd allow me to court you?"

She searched his gaze, still unsure. "If . . . you would have me."

"*Have you?* Oh, Emily, Emily." He crushed her against his chest, and she realized the thundering of her own heart was no match for his.

Too soon he broke away, but he stroked her face as he talked. . . . "I can't believe someone so good, so perfect as you . . . would want someone like me."

"Robert." Emily eased back warily. "I am not perfect. You must never think that."

He tilted his head, studying her, then bent and kissed her nose. "For now, this moment, I choose to consider you perfect, my angel. After this war is over, God willing, we'll have a lifetime to discover one another's flaws."

"Only if you stay alive," she whispered, a mist of sudden tears blurring his face before her eyes. "Promise me you'll come back."

"How could I not? I love you, Emily Haynes MacKinnon. You brought me back to life. And I promise you, nothing in this world will keep me from coming back to you." He tugged her close again, into the security of his strong arms. "And I know you need time . . . more time to grieve, to heal. But I'll come back, and I'll wait—as long as it takes."

Emily's heart was near to bursting with joy, with fear. Robert loved her. And she knew he couldn't really promise to stay alive. She could only put him in God's hands, but she knew somehow she could trust him there. And right now, tonight, she felt loved again. "I'll be here waiting . . . when you return."

43

All was quiet in the big room. Assuming that everyone had gone outside at last, Prudence threw off the blankets and quilts and got out of bed. The smell of baking bread was too hard to resist.

Emily's and Evie's sleeping pallets had been straightened, she noticed as she padded across to the birch commode, and someone had brought fresh water in the china pitcher. Wanting to be alone rather than face questions regarding Morgan, Prudence had feigned sleep most of the morning, and she hadn't seen who had been so kind. Soon she hoped to have the luxury of a full bath, but for now washing up would have to do.

The cool water was both stimulating and refreshing, and when she finished she turned to retrieve her clothing. The costly gown she had worn on the journey, soiled by days of travel, was not where she had left it. In its place was a much simpler frock Prudence decided must be Susannah's. Mere months ago, in Boston, she herself had worn plain things, and Morgan had fallen in love with her—the simple, straightforward Puritan girl. So much had happened since those days. What had become of that girl?

She let out a soft sigh as she shrugged off her night dress and slipped into the indigo linen frock. Perhaps the devious side of her had always existed somewhere deep within, just waiting for the right excuse to allow it to surface. *Righteous excuse,* she amended with disdain. She didn't deserve this sort of kindness now. She should wear her own soiled clothing as penance for her willful stupidity. Morgan had tried to warn her about rushing into the foolhardy life of spying, but ever out to prove how equally capable she was in the art, she'd been too stubborn to listen. Too *proud.* And as it said in the Scriptures, *Pride goeth before destruction, and an haughty spirit before a fall.*

Sharp thuds echoed outside the house as she laced the bodice of the gown. Prudence moved to the window, where she saw Christopher hard at work splitting logs. Off to one side, Evie watched with adoring eyes as her hero's youthful muscles rippled with each swing. Prudence observed the touching scene for several minutes, noting the vast change that had come over Morgan's sister. Gone was the brittle gaiety she had displayed during her weeks in New York, and in its place was a wide-eyed innocence Prudence had barely glimpsed when they had first met. Still, for one who had known nothing save the comforts wealth could provide, was it possible to find true happiness in a life of hardship with a man of the people?

Prudence shrugged. She supposed they would just have to find out on their own, with time.

Beyond the two young people, a movement within the herd of Narragansett Pacers drew her attention. Dan, Robert, and Emily walked among them, running their hands down flanks and forelegs, checking hooves. Everything seemed so pastoral, so peaceful. It was hard to believe that just across the range of mountains the world was "turned upside down," as the British marching tune proclaimed. Her thoughts drifting, Prudence started to turn away from the window, but something caught her eye. Robert came up behind Emily and placed his hand on her waist . . . and Emily leaned back against his chest with a smile!

How could they? Prudence was appalled. Robby had been gone but a few short months. How could his own wife—and his best friend, no less—have forgotten him so quickly? She would *never* forget Morgan. *Never!*

She swung away, tears smarting her eyes as she made haste for the main room. A tantalizing cloud of baking aromas enveloped her when she opened the door. Golden loaves of bread and several varieties of scones and cookies lined the side counter. Susannah, swathed in an oversized work apron, was even now putting a large plucked bird into a Dutch oven, obviously preparing a feast.

After placing the lidded iron kettle on the glowing coals, Susannah turned and looked up. "Oh, good. Do come and sit down, dear, and I'll pour you some coffee."

Prudence waved her off. "No, finish what you're doing. I can wait on myself." She fetched a cup and filled it, while Susannah hefted a bulky sack to the table and took several good-sized turnips from it.

Susannah smiled pleasantly as she began peeling. "You're looking quite a bit better this morning. But then, you come from good, solid New England stock. I'm sure you'll be blessed with a fine healthy babe soon to carry on the—" Stopping abruptly, she blushed and stood up. "Let me cut you a slice of bread to go with that coffee."

Prudence needed no one to finish Susannah's sentence. *To carry on the Thomas name.* She touched her rounding abdomen. Morgan had been his father's only son. And this baby he had known nothing about would be the only tangible proof that he had ever lived. Everything depended on her safeguarding this priceless child of their love.

Susannah returned and placed a plate of bread before her. "Try to think more on the happy times, if you can," she said gently.

Prudence, knowing that Susannah meant well, tried to lighten her expression. "But there's so much that was left unresolved. How will I ever explain all of this to his parents—about Morgan, about Evie being a fugitive . . . the baby." Even if it had been safe for her to do so, she couldn't have returned to them.

Susannah gave Prudence's hand a comforting pat. "Dan will help you write a letter to Morgan's family. I'm sure he won't mind. And, Prudence, I know it's very difficult, but just take things one day at a time. We're celebrating Christmas today."

"Christmas? It can't be."

"Quite right. It's not actually December twenty-fifth. But Christopher and Robert have agreed to delay leaving for their battalion until tomorrow, so Chip and Evie rode over to his sister's early this morning. Mary Clare and Jonathan and their children will be coming soon with some pies and cider. We shall have our Christmas feast while we're all together. I truly believe, dear heart, we need to dwell on our blessings for a little while. So many sorrows have befallen us in the past few months. We must not allow them to overwhelm us."

Prudence had heard scarcely a word after the mention of Chip and Robert's departure. "They're leaving tomorrow? We have to talk them out of it. I couldn't help seeing Robert and Emily outside awhile ago. If she cares anything about him, how can she let him go back there?"

The front door opened just then, and Emily breezed in with a smile. "Is there anything I can do before Mary Clare and Jonathan arrive?"

"Yes," Prudence announced. "Convince Chan not to go back. The war is lost. We've sacrificed enough."

A look of compassion warmed Emily's rosy cheeks. "That's tomorrow, Prudence. Let tomorrow take care of itself. All of us want to set today aside simply to love and rejoice with one another." Emily stepped behind Prudence and began unplaiting her long black hair. "Today I just want to love you and your baby. Let me start with this, fixing your hair. After all, I'll be showing you off to Mary Clare and Jon. He and Morgan were best friends in college."

"I know," she said wistfully. "'The Lords of Dunce,' as I recall. Or so Mrs. Lyons dubbed them when they had to remain at school during spring recess. They had been so busy being pranksters they hadn't taken time to prepare for their orals." She paused. "Oh, Emily, they're going to hate me."

"Not today they're not." Emily gave a playful yank on the braid.

Miles and Katie burst inside, their faces glowing from the cold. "Mama," Miles cried. "They're here! Esther and Bethy!"

"Those are the children," Susannah said. She wiped her hands on her apron. "I must go greet everyone."

By the time Emily finished tying off Prudence's plait, the front room was bursting at the seams with smiling faces and running, laughing children. Prudence saw a ruddy-faced young man she assumed was Jonathan walk into the house with his arm around Robert, both men grinning broadly. She didn't really feel up to all this. Perhaps she could slip quietly away to the bedroom without being noticed.

Emily, with another slim blonde in tow, cut off her escape. "Prudence, I'd like you to meet Chip's older sister, Mary Clare. Mary, this is Prudence, Morgan's wife from Boston."

"I'm pleased to meet you," Prudence said politely.

Mary Clare ducked her head slightly and didn't quite meet her gaze as she bobbed into a curtsy. "And you, Mistress Thomas."

Prudence took the shy girl's hand with a reassuring smile. "Please, call me Prudence. Morgan has spoken so fondly of you and your husband."

"He has?" Her look of surprise was overtaken by a pleased one. "I knew he would choose someone like you. Pretty and sure of yourself. Someone who could stand right up to him."

What an odd thing to say, Prudence thought.

"Evelyn told us all about you this morning," Mary went on, "how smart you are and how brave. And . . ." Her gaze faltered briefly, then settled once more on Prudence. "I know Morgan will come out of his predicament just fine. He could always talk his way out of any mischief he got into, couldn't he, Emily?"

Robert stepped up behind Emily and put his hands on her

shoulders. "That's right. We're not about to give up now, are we?"

Emily turned and gazed lovingly up at him, and the look made Prudence want to cry from loneliness.

Jonathan then came to join his timid wife, casually draping an arm over her shoulders. He extended his other hand to Prudence. "I'm Jon. It's a real pleasure to meet you. Welcome to our valley."

His eyes, oddly mismatched, with one green and the other blue, provided just the distraction she needed to keep her from drowning in her emotions. "Thank you," she managed, then glanced around for a plausible excuse to extricate herself from the group before falling apart. Seeing Evie and Christopher at the fireplace, their heads close together in conversation, only made matters worse. The love in the room was enough to suffocate a person. "We . . . need water," she blurted, and seized the bucket.

❦ ❦

Robert watched Prudence flee, and his heart went out to her. He knew her excuse was only a pretense. "Think I'd better go talk to her," he murmured to Emily, reluctant to part from her for even a few minutes on this, their last day together.

"I'll miss you," she whispered back.

The look in her green eyes made it all the harder to go, but he knew he needed to do what he could to calm Prudence's spirit.

Outside, he found Prudence leaning against a tree with her back to him, the pail dangling aimlessly from her fingers. He approached as quietly as possible on the snow-covered ground and placed a hand on her shoulder. "We all love you, Prudence . . . enough to talk straight to you and not beat around the bush."

Her head drooped, but she said nothing.

He knew she was crying. "I've learned some very hard lessons of my own, dear friend, since this war started. One of them is that dying is easy. It's living that takes all a person's

effort. Love Morgan's memory; miss him. . . . But whatever
you do, don't shroud yourself in guilt and remorse the way I
did. Don't waste the gift of life God gives you each and every
day. Make the most of today and every tomorrow as it comes.
Forgive yourself . . . or you'll end up a useless shell of a
person, as I was for far too long. Your baby needs—*deserves*—
more than that."

Prudence turned and raised her eyes to his, her face awash
with tears. "Is this really you talking? You've changed so;
you've come alive. I . . . saw you with Emily."

He smiled with chagrin. "I admit, I've finally crawled out of
that black pit I dug for myself. What a waste of years. But
thanks to her . . . and God . . ." His throat tightened. "Just
don't turn your back on God's healing power, as I did. Trust
him."

She reached to touch his cheek with a thin smile, but she
didn't quite look at him. "Careful . . . you're beginning to
sound like Robby MacKinnon."

"Wouldn't that be something!"

"But . . . how can Emily forget him so quickly?"

"She hasn't forgotten him. Nor have I. He'll always hold a
very special part of both our hearts. But war has a way of
compressing time, of making things happen more quickly
than they might under ordinary circumstances. The Lord has
taken Emily beyond the sadness, the mourning, and now
she's able to go on. We're all different, Prudence, and we all
handle grief in our own ways. But God knows what we need.
Trust him to help you, Prudence. Lean on him . . . and on us."
Robert took her hand. "Come back inside."

"Not just yet. But, thank you. The others have said practically the same thing to me. From you, though, who suffered
for so long, it has far more meaning. I need to think for a
while, to be by myself."

He stepped back to study her, noting the tenuous courage
in the lift of her chin, the flicker of hope in her gray eyes.
"Then, you're going to be all right?"

She nodded and favored him with a small smile. "Now go back to Emily. Your day is fast slipping away."

Robert lingered another moment, just to be sure she was being truthful, then took the bucket from her and returned to the house.

※ ※

Prudence watched after him, unable to mistake the new spring in his step, the new straightness in his stance. She was happy for Robert, that he had finally been able to come to terms with his loss. Only now could she understand the depth of such pain, how it would cause a person to want to give up. How tempting it would be to wrap her own sorrow around her like a burial shroud and close herself off from the world. But then she thought of Emily and how the Lord had taken her through the death of her husband in a matter of months. Prudence knew it was her choice—to turn from God and the love and strength with which he would sustain her in the lonely years ahead, or to place her hand in his and allow him to be all that she needed.

Not far away, a half-grown colt suckled its mother, its head ducked low. Prudence strolled toward the large pen the neighbors had come together to build despite their recent territorial disputes. Either the war or Dan and Susannah's ministry had brought a new unity to the Pennsylvania and Connecticut settlers. Boston had taken a toll on the Haynses, especially Dan's gently bred English wife, and this rustic way of living could prove even harder. But Susannah possessed a peaceful spirit that always shone through. Perhaps Morgan's pampered little sister would also adjust to the added rigors.

The countryside surrounding this small town was incredibly beautiful. There was much to be said for moving to virgin territory, carving out one's own place in the world. The Haynes land was rich and flat, with hills rising behind it, a small creek running off to one side, the river below. No doubt, with the herd and his ministerial work, they'd do very well here. It was a fine place for new beginnings.

The stock moved about in the corral. None of them looked particularly the worse for the hasty and difficult trip.

It still amazed Prudence to think of the horsewoman Emily had turned out to be. She was as capable as any man, yet she possessed such a sweet spirit. Emily . . . and Robert. The thought no longer brought disquiet. Now that she thought about it, that loving calm that seemed so much a part of Emily was probably exactly what Robert needed after so many years of spiritual unrest. The union would be good for Emily and her children, too. Robert would see that they had every advantage. He was the only male heir of a prosperous family . . . like Morgan.

She rested her hands on her blossoming belly. Had her duplicity cost her child his birthright?

That thought was discarded almost as soon as it came. Morgan's father and mother would welcome this grandchild with all the love they had, despite everything. Prudence knew she had judged her mother-in-law far more harshly than the woman had deserved. True, Mother Thomas was domineering, but she herself admitted as much . . . and everything she had insisted upon had been because she wanted the best for those she loved.

With a regretful sigh, Prudence propped her arms on the corral fence. The memory of her singing lessons surfaced in her mind . . . and her debut. A little smile broke free. Who would've thought Morgan could sing like that? Ah, what a champion he'd been that day! Despite herself, she laughed.

"What's so funny?"

Prudence's heart stopped. *Morgan?*

She whirled around. He truly was there, alive, and in the flesh. She flung herself at him, kissing him and crying and touching him to make sure she wasn't dreaming. "I thought you were . . . I thought they'd hanged you."

"I'm sure you did," he said gently, his lopsided grin sobering as he stroked tears from her cheek. His strong arms wrapped around her in a crushing embrace that stole her very breath. "When Jasper and Esther Lyons told me how upset you were, I rode straight through."

She reached to touch his unshaven cheek, taking in his mud-splattered clothing. "But—how did you manage to get away?" Prudence searched his cobalt eyes, still trying to convince herself it was not a dream. She lost herself in their rich depths.

"I was able to wrest the pistol from Captain Long. Shot him in the leg in the process, I'm afraid. Needless to say, he was less than pleased. He yelled all manner of unkind references to me *and* my mother as I ran off toward town. Then I doubled back and sneaked aboard the ship I had acquired the sailing permit for earlier that afternoon, and it sailed with the tide. The only problem was, when we reached open water there was no wind. Just a dead calm. It took six days to reach port. I can't tell you how sorry I am at being delayed."

Prudence, loving the sound of his deep voice, struggled to assimilate everything he was saying. "I was afraid even to hope you were still alive. I only knew I didn't deserve to ask God to keep you safe, not after all the horrid things I've done. I felt it would have been my just punishment if you were taken from me." Fresh tears trembled on her lashes.

"Shh." He drew her into his arms once more, rocking her gently until her shaking stopped.

Prudence relaxed into his comfort, and she never wanted to draw away. "When you reached Philadelphia, did you stop in to see your parents?"

He stiffened a bit. "By the time I reached them, soldiers had already been to the house. They were beside themselves with worry . . . and disillusionment. My spying days are through, Prudence. No cause can be so noble if it creates such grief. I can hardly bear to think about all my lies, the bad influence I've been for Evie."

"The blame is much more mine than yours. If I had been the kind of wife I should be . . . the kind of Christian I should be . . . none of this would ever have happened." She hesitated. "How was your mother when you left her?"

An odd expression clouded Morgan's rugged features, erasing most of the cockiness that normally resided there. "You know, I've only lately discovered how fragile she really is. She's always lived protected from the harsher realities. And Father actually does love her very much, despite his complaints to me about her overbearing ways. He was trying very tenderly to comfort her when I departed."

"I could use a little of that myself," she whispered.

A slow smile spread across his mouth, and he lowered his head, their breath intermingling for a sweet eternity before he covered her lips with his. She slipped her arms around his neck and pressed closer, deepening the kiss until it left them both breathless. Neither spoke as they stood in each other's embrace, their hearts beating as one.

Prudence eased back and looked up at him. "Someday we must make amends. I only pray the damage we've wrought can be undone."

"I quite agree. And to make matters worse, the whole city is in chaos with both armies heading there. As it turned out, Captain Long hadn't been that far off with his fabricated information. The Congress left and relocated in Baltimore. Anyway, when I reached Princeton, I sent a note to my parents letting them know that you and Evie were safely tucked away for the moment."

Prudence smiled. "Yes, we are. All three of us."

His thick brows drew together in a slight frown. "Oh, you mean Emily, too?"

She shook her head. "Not exactly. I mean Evie, me, and our baby."

"*Baby?* We're going to have a child? You and me, the two of us?"

Smiling, she nodded.

"Praise be!" He grabbed her exuberantly and swung her around in a circle, then caught his breath and stopped as suddenly. "Oh. Did I hurt you? And that long horseback ride—"

"I'm fine, truly I am. And more than fine, now that you're here. Just a little tired . . . which is quite normal."

"Well, you must stay put from now on. Here, where it's safe. Promise me you'll do that, Prudence. I won't rest until you do."

"Believe me, sweetheart, I'll never put our baby in jeopardy again. I now understand what it is to be totally responsible for another's life. I shall try never to worry you with my reckless-ness from this day forward."

He breathed a sigh of relief, and a trace of a cocky smile lifted one corner of his mouth. "It's about time you learned your place."

Prudence ignored the spark of mischief in his demeanor. "My *place?*" The very thought rankled her.

Morgan laughed and pulled her cloak more securely around her. "And right now, my love, your place is inside, out of this December cold."

"And yours," she teased, "is right beside me, hugging and kissing me at least once every minute for the rest of this day."

Desire darkened the blue of his eyes. "That's a rather tall order, but I'll give it my best shot. Starting now." He hauled her into his arms and kissed her again, an unspoken promise that made her blush, especially when accompanied by the knowing grin that followed.

Prudence struggled to regain her composure as he ushered her to the house. She nudged Morgan off to the side and put a finger to her lips. Then, opening the door, she paused on the threshold, gazing at the happy gathering, her own heart fairly overflowing with joy.

Emily, slicing carrots at the table, looked up. "Oh. We were getting worried. I was about to go looking for you."

"No need," Prudence answered, scarcely able to maintain a straight face. "I'm sorry for worrying you. But—I've found a Christmas gift that just might make up for it." Stepping aside, she made room for Morgan.

When he entered, a collective shout of joy rang the rafters, and the two of them were swallowed up by a jumble of hugs and laughter.

Dan finally raised a hand for calm. "I didn't think it was possible for one more blessing to fall upon us this day, but apparently the Lord saved the best for last. Let's join hands and thank God for his goodness."

Prudence slipped her hand into Morgan's much larger one and smiled across the ring at Robert and Emily. This truly was a place—and a time—for new beginnings. And she was beginning to like the thought. No matter what lay ahead for the dear folk in this gathering, the Lord would see them all through. She couldn't ask for more.